THREE HILLS HOME

ALFRED SILVER

D0109890

NIMBUS
PUBLISHING

Nimbus Publishing Limited
PO Box 9166
Halifax, NS   B3K 5M8
(902) 455-4286
www.nimbus.ns.ca

Printed and bound in Canada

Design: Margaret Issenman, MGDC

Back cover photo: Rick Janson

National Library of Canada Cataloguing in Publication Data

Silver, Alfred, 1951-
    Three hills home

ISBN 1-55109-401-0
    1. Acadians—Expulsion, 1755—Fiction. I.
Title.

PS8587.I27T52 2002   C813'.54
C2001-904053-9
PR9199.3.S51765T5 2002

Canadä The Canada Council | Le Conseil des Arts
for the Arts | du Canada

We acknowledge the financial support of the Government of Canada through the Book Publishing Industry Development Program (BPIDP) and the Canada Council for our publishing activities.

Contents

Salut à Mary and Warren Perrin and the many others who've worked so hard to keep the spirit of Beausoleil alive.

PART ONE

ACADIE

*The more I consider these people [the Acadians], the more I believe
they are the happiest people in the world.*
– DANIEL D'AUGER DE SUBERCASE,
GOVERNOR OF ACADIA, 1708

*If these people [the Acadians] behave amiss... you should take an eye for
an eye, a tooth for a tooth; and, in short, life for life, from the nearest
neighbour where the mischief should be performed.*
– COLONEL CHARLES LAWRENCE,
GOVERNOR OF NOVA SCOTIA,
SECRET ORDERS TO MAJOR MURRAY, 1755

I

In a South Louisiana town stands a blood-grained granite monument to a man who died two centuries before it was carved and who lived almost all of his life a thousand miles north. The British of his day called him an outlaw, a murderer and a pirate. The French called him a patriot and the founder of New Acadia. But one thing neither his friends nor his enemies called him was his baptized name, which was Joseph Brossard. They called him *Beausoleil.*

n a spring Market Day in 1755, in the village of Piziquid off the Bay of Fundy, a British soldier brushed his hand across the left breast of a dark, young Acadian woman named Eulalie La Tour. She told herself that it might have been an accident—the soldier was obviously drunk enough to see double, and he might just have been reaching for the eggs she was holding out for sale. So she just kept smiling the fixed smile she pasted on for Market Days, and holding up the three eggs cupped in her palm.

The soldier smiled sloppily at her, reached out his hand again and this time grabbed her breast and squeezed. Eulalie crooked her fingertips around the eggs, swivelled her wrist and straightened her elbow, driving her hand forward and upward.

The eggs shattered against the soldier's forehead and the bridge of his nose. He stumbled backward, flapping his hands across his eyes and losing his hat. Eulalie bent down and wiped her hand on the grass. When she stood up again, the soldier had cleared his eyes and was yelling words at her that she didn't have to know English to understand.

He raised his hand and stepped toward her. Two Acadian men nearby jumped up and got between them. A couple of other soldiers came up to see what was going on.

Pretty soon there was a ragged line of red coats facing a line of sun-bleached homespuns, with just over an arm's length of space between them. Some of the men were yelling, some glowering, some standing stiffly and looking like they wished they were somewhere else.

Eulalie got a choking feeling that something terrible was about to happen. It would only take one man stepping across that gap. All because Eulalie La Tour could no more control her impulses than a cat with its tail stepped on. But then, she would've done the same thing if that English soldier had been an Acadian farmer.

A redcoat officer bellowed his way through the line of soldiers and addressed the line of Acadian men in French. It was Parisian French, almost a different language from what Acadians spoke after five generations in North America, but it was possible to get the gist.

One of the Acadian men pointed at Eulalie and explained more or less what had happened. The gold-buttoned officer turned to Eulalie and said: "Is it true, *mademoiselle*, that this oaf masquerading as a soldier of King George the Second did commit a vulgarian physical insult upon your very person?"

Eulalie found the elegant embroideries a little hard to follow exactly, so she just nodded. The officer smirked at her, then in one motion spun around and swept the back of his hand across the cheek of the soldier who still had bits of egg on his face. The soldier was a lot bigger than the officer, but the blow caught him by surprise and knocked him off balance. The officer tripped him up and pushed him down on the ground, then drove the toe of his gleaming boot into the soldier's ribcage three times.

The soldier didn't try to defend himself or get away, just took it like a dog beaten by its master. A few of the other soldiers laughed. Eulalie could see some of the Acadian men glancing at each other sideways, in disbelief that one human being could treat another one that way.

The officer shooed the soldiers about their business—one of them stooping to help his *confrère* to his feet—then gave Eulalie a condescending little bow and sauntered off.

The Acadian men drifted away, murmuring and shrugging. All except a hump-shouldered, gray-bearded one who lumbered toward Eulalie and rasped out: "Time we was starting home anyways."

"I should've said that ten minutes ago, Uncle Benoni. I'll go find my children."

Benoni wasn't really her uncle, but it was only polite to call older people 'uncle' and 'aunt'. And Eulalie could point to the fact that her 'Uncle' Benoni was truly her blood relation, since his mother had been the daughter of Eulalie's grandfather's second cousin.

Eulalie's children weren't actually her children, either, but her cousins. They were the children of her mother's brother Joseph Brossard, who took Eulalie in when her mother and father died of smallpox. But they *were* her children in that she'd been mother to them ever since Joseph Brossard's wife died giving birth to Josette.

By the time Eulalie had sheepdogged the children from the flock hunting shell-fish in the tide mud, Uncle Benoni had hitched up the ox and was waiting to go. Eulalie lifted Josette into the back of the cart, Jean-Marc and Marie scrambled over the rails to join their sister, and Eulalie climbed up beside Benoni. He clucked the ox into motion and they started east on the road away from the bay.

Uncle Benoni sat glumly chewing his gums and didn't say a word until the village of Piziquid dropped behind them. Piziquid Village wouldn't have looked like a village to someone from England or France, or from Quebec or the Boston colonies. They would've seen it as a haphazard scattering of far-flung farms and fishing stations. Acadian families liked to have neighbours within shouting distance, but not so close as to get each others' cattle in each others' gardens.

When Uncle Benoni finally did speak, it was to mutter: "Not good, not good..."

From Benoni, 'not good' could mean anything from a distant stormcloud to a pinch too much salt in his soup. So Eulalie waited for him to tell her what it was this time. She waited until the smell of the air changed from salt water and kelp to pine and moss, then gave in and said: "What's not good, Uncle Benoni?"

"What happened at market—English soldiers and Acadians growling and snapping at each other. It's not good to give them the notion we're their enemies. Because it seems not even the good God can stop the English King and the King of France from going at each others' throats soon."   ·   ·

"Uncle Benoni, as long as I can remember, people have been saying that every spring. And every summer's gone by without a war starting."

"This year is different."

"It is just another year."

Benoni replied to that by grimly pointing his ox goad over his shoulder. Eulalie looked back and saw the last vestige of the village still visible: the blockhouse tower of the recently strengthened Fort Edward, with the Union Jack floating above it.

Sometimes Eulalie found it hard not to laugh out loud at Uncle Benoni's divine gift for finding doom in anything. A fleck of dry-rot on a rafter meant the roof was about to cave in on his children in their beds. She said: "The English are always building forts—it gives their soldiers something to do."

"You think they build a fort in a place like Piziquid for nothing? Or built Halifax on the seacoast for nothing?"

"There, you see? They built the big fort at Halifax five years ago—and there was no war that year and no war any year since."

"They built Halifax to get *ready*. They built Fort Edward to get ready. And they cut this road between them to get ready." Uncle Benoni nodded at his own logic. "Now they are ready."

Eulalie felt a shiver. She reminded herself that the point of the game was for her to convince the old dear that the sky wasn't falling, not for him to convince her it was. She said: "Well, and so what if there *is* a war? It has nothing to do with us. Didn't you sign the loyalty oath the old English governor made us swear?"

Benoni nodded warily, but added: "But now there is a new English governor."

"What difference does that make? Didn't the loyalty oath say no Acadian would ever have to fight in a war between the King of England and the King of France?"

Uncle Benoni grunted and shrugged, but he didn't seem any less dour. Eulalie said: "It seems to me I heard that England and France have fought wars around us before. How many times before I was born did Acadia go from being Acadia to Nova Scotia and back again? Six? Seven...?"

"My grandmother told me five. Let me see..." He tucked his ox goad under his arm and counted on his fingers. "Acadia—Nova Scotia—Acadia—Nova Scotia—Acadia—Nova Scotia. Six. My grandmother was wrong! But no, no she wasn't—because when she told me 'five' we were still Acadia."

"And after all those wars and changing of names, we Acadians are still living our lives here—as we have since my great-great-great grandfather and before."

"There *were* no Acadians before your great-great-great grandfather."

"We all have ancestors who were here before then."

Benoni grunted and shrugged again, since he couldn't argue with that. Like all Acadians, he undoubtedly had some Mi'kmaq or Maliseet blood in him, but few made as much of a point of it as Eulalie did. The point she made of it was that she was Eulalie *La Tour*. That meant that her great-great-great grandfather was Charles La Tour, one of the first governors of Acadia and the very first *courier de bois*—a white man who takes to the woods with *les sauvages* and takes an Indian wife, or two.

The name didn't make Eulalie feel she was any more important than anybody else, but it was something that helped tell her who she was. And it was all she had to prove she knew who her father and mother had been.

The children started tussling in the back of the cart. Eulalie said over her shoulder: "If you turn over Uncle Benoni's cart and break a wheel, you will have to hold up the axle till he gets home." They settled down to just calling each other names. After six years of being their mother, Eulalie knew them well enough to guess when they should be reined back and when let go—although sometimes she still guessed wrong.

The road climbed up the shoulder of a hill that a stranger would think no different than the other hills the road had wound over. Uncle Benoni clucked the ox to a halt beside a spot on the left that looked no different from any other spot along the forest wall: just a red-veined boulder hemmed-in by scrub spruce and sumacs. It had looked that way even back in the days when this stretch of the Halifax Road was still the Old French Road. Acadians didn't trust French governors any more than English ones.

Eulalie climbed down off the cart and reached up to give Josette a hand down while Marie and Jean-Marc fended for themselves. Uncle Benoni said: "No one gets to see you much, Eulalie, stuck off in the backwoods and no river by your door. It's a long ways for young men to come courting. But I bet they come anyways, eh? I think André Melanson's worn a new rut in this road."

Eulalie affected not to hear him and busied herself arranging who would carry what. Not that there was all that much to parcel out. They rarely had much of a load to carry back from market, since everything from the food in their bellies to the clothes on their backs came from their own land and hands. Except for a few foreign necessities, Eulalie's stepfather much preferred that the goslings or maple syrup she took to market got turned into coins to be added into the strongbox he kept hidden in the barn. His branch of the Brossards had always had a fondness for gold, which was why Eulalie's home was where it was.

A twinge of guilt tweaked Eulalie when she remembered that she wouldn't be bringing home even a brass farthing for three of the eggs she took to market. She assured herself that her Uncle Joseph would consider the story worth a lot more than a farthing. But that only made her blush—she could almost hear him laughing now.

Little, golden-haired Josette said: "I can carry something, too."

Eulalie said: "Here, you can carry your papa's tobacco," then slung the sack of squarehead nails and pig-lead over her own shoulder. "Thank you for taking us to market, Uncle Benoni."

"Well, you don't take up much room in the cart. You had better walk quickly if you don't want to get caught in the forest at nightfall. Last full moon my old woman heard a howling that she swears was a *loup-garou*. Get along, Trumper."

Eulalie pushed through the curtain of sumacs and came out onto an overgrown cart-track running north through the woods, with a footpath beaten down its middle. The path was only wide enough for one. Eulalie stepped aside to let Josette take the lead, so Josette could set a pace her short, little legs could manage.

After the bright sunlight on the road, the forest seemed dark and enclosing. Eulalie was relieved to notice that the soles of her feet weren't noticing the surface of the path as much as they had last Market Day. Except for those who lived on marshy farms, Acadians went barefoot in the summer and wore moccasins in the winter. It always took a while of spring for feet to harden up again.

But feet were one thing and legs another. The path was difficult enough on legs that were fresh in the morning: winding up and down ridges, and gnarly with tree roots and rock lips. Soon Jean-Marc and Marie began to complain that Josette was going too slow and they were going to get caught in the forest at night. Josette protested that she couldn't walk any faster, and then began to whimper about *loups-garous* and natural wolves and bears.

Eulalie felt herself growing annoyed. Josette wasn't a whiny girl by nature, but when she got tired she got tired and there wasn't anything she or anybody else could do about it. Eulalie said: "Wait, Josette," and picked her up.

It wasn't easy carrying Josette in her arms while still maintaining a grip on the sack of lead and nails, but Eulalie locked her left hand around her right forearm and held on. As they carried on along the path, she sang Josette a little song she'd made up to sing for herself when she was Josette's age and thought the path would never end:

"Three hills home, my dear,

"Three hills home,

"Three hills home, only

"Three hills home..."

In the years since she'd made up the song, Eulalie had learned that the three "hills" were actually only the elbows of hills, but they still felt like whole hills at the end of the day. Now that she and Jean-Marc and Marie didn't have to hold their pace to Josette's, they covered the ground much more quickly. In not very long at all, the song became "Two hills home, my dear," and then "One hill home."

They crossed a trickle of a stream in a wooded hollow and climbed the other bank into what would seem to a stranger to be just more forest. But once they were through the stand of poplars on the north side of the hollow, the sky fanned open and they were at the base of the hillside farm Joseph Brossard's father had imagined sixty years ago.

Forty-some years before Eulalie was born, young Jacques Brossard had come into this valley alone, looking to see if the old, secret, gold mine on the south hill had truly been scraped dry. Eulalie had never been told whether or not he'd found any gold—although there were still days when Joseph Brossard would ask her to pack him a lunch and disappear up the south hill—but Jacques had found something else. Looking out across the valley, he'd seen that the north slope, where the sun always fell, was scarred with a forest fire burnoff that would save him the trouble of clearing land. He'd christened the valley *Ardoise*, for the wrinkled slate that lined the streambeds and jutted out of the high hill to the east.

Once Eulalie was out of the poplars and into the open, she paused to look up at the place that had been her home since she was younger than Josette. The sunset washed a glow like dying embers into the thatched house and barn, and turned the garden patch green-gold. The apple trees were in bloom. The cattle were lowing goodbye to the sun, and the chickens flapping up to their roosts. The other four children came running down the meadow to see what Eulalie and their brother and sisters had brought back from market. Eulalie's *"beau-père"*, white-haired Joseph Brossard, stepped out of the barn with his hand shading his eyes. He didn't wave or call out; they were home and that was that.

Eulalie's arms had gone so dead she was afraid that if she tried to lower Josette to the ground they'd give way and drop her, so she knelt down before letting her go. She managed to find just enough breath to sing the last line of the song, "Now we're home, my dear, now we're home," then buttoned Josette's nose and said: "See? No matter how long the path seems, we will always get home."

II

❧

In the over-grown garrison town called Halifax, six corporals of His British Majesty's Land Forces stood around a barrel in the back room of Fat Franny's knocking shop. One of them tugged out the tent peg bunged into the barrelhead, sniffed at the hole and said dubiously: "I don't think she be done yet, Cully."

A corporal slightly taller and lanker than the others said: "She has to be," and produced a piece of paper from the cuff of his uniform coat. "We followed the recipe to the letter. 'Take seven pounds of spruce boughs and three gallons of molasses...'" The other five nodded and shrugged and Cully left it at that. He didn't like to flaunt the fact that he could read and write.

"Now all we have to do," Cully assured them, holding up a crude tap he'd whittled together in his off hours, "is stick this in her hole and roll her on her back—just like Fat Franny."

Before the other corporals could laugh appreciatively at his fine-honed barracks wit, the door crashed open and a bass voice bellowed: "Corporal Cully Robin!"

The six corporals automatically fell into a formation masking the barrel from the sergeant in the doorway, uncertain of whether he'd approve of them manufacturing their own version of the 'medicinal' concoction that the quartermaster sold them to augment their daily gill of rum. Cully said: "Yes, Sergeant."

"You're wanted, Corporal Robin. By Captain Namon."

"What for?"

"I didn't ask. Maybe he wants you to tea. He'll have you *for* tea if you don't get your rosy-red back up there double-quick. Up the hill, stone house on the corner of the parade square."

As Cully snatched up his hat and made for the door, the sergeant leaned his halberd against the wall and said: "I'll give you lads a hand with that barrel..."

Cully stepped out of Fat Franny's into the usual mid-day tapestry of Barracks Street: whores showing their wares out the windows, three soldiers persuading an unwise sailor to return to his own haunts on Water Street, two Grenadiers arguing finger-numbers with an Acadian farmer selling cabbages, a laundrywoman herding her children in front of her handcart...As Cully threaded his way, he racked his brains for some reason why this mysterious Captain Namon would summon him. Barracks gossip being what it was, Cully knew that a certain Captain Namon had arrived on the troopship that hove in last week, but he seemed to be attached to no particular regiment. That was all that was known.

At the nearest cross street, Cully turned up the hill toward the parade square. The hillside had changed considerably since he'd peered out a troopship porthole six years ago at a tangled slope of forested rock. Now it was row upon row of barracks buildings, civilian houses, government offices and even two spired churches—all enclosed within a three-sided log palisade, with the fourth side open to the harbour.

As he crossed the parade square, he noticed that the private whose punishment the regiment had been called out to witness that morning was still tied to the tripod, with his heaving, bleeding back pointed toward the sun. After fourteen years of soldiering, Cully paid no more attention to such a sight than to a seagull on the dock. The private's ten lashes for "dumb insolence"—failing to say "Yes, sir" with sufficient enthusiasm—was downright mild. Cully had once taken forty for the same offence— back in the days before he'd accepted the fact that the only legal ways out of the king's service were death, infirm old age, or losing a limb or two, so he'd best learn to make the best of it. The illegal way out would get you hung if you got caught, and most deserters got caught.

The door of the house Captain Namon was reported to be quartered in was opened by a very unmilitary-looking maid. She beckoned Cully toward a closed door down the hall and left him there. He tucked his hat under his arm and knocked. A preoccupied-sounding male voice came from within: "If you propose to enter the room, I would suggest that you manipulate the doorknob."

Cully manipulated the doorknob. A puffy-looking man in puffy shirtsleeves was denned-in behind a desk littered with papers. His peachfuzzed head was uncovered, but a powdered wig stood on a stand behind the desk, with a goldbraided red coat folded meticulously beside it.

Cully said: "Captain Namon, sir?"

The man behind the desk leaned back and raised his eyes, slitting his puffy eyelids as though Cully had asked him to verify a suspicious quantity of information. A voice in Cully's head remarked: "Cully, lad, those are the evilest eyes you've ever seen." Cully assured himself that it was just because they were yellow. He'd never seen yellow eyes before, except on a cat. They would've been disconcerting enough in any human face, much less an officer's.

The yellow-eyed man didn't say whether he was or wasn't Captain Namon, just said: "Who are you?"

"Corporal Robin, sir, reporting as ordered."

"Ah. Yes, I am Captain Namon. *Comment allez-vous,* Corporal Robin?"

Cully dug far back into the corners of his memory and came out with: "*Pas de quoi pleurer, monsieur.*"

"Yes... Yes, I think you just might do. You have unique qualities, Corporal Cully Robin."

Cully had learned a long time ago that when an officer said something cryptic, wise soldiers kept their mouths shut and their faces bland, and waited.

"Your Sergeant Major informs me, Corporal Robin, that you were born and raised on the Channel Islands, so you know the French language. And not the French of *l'Academe,* which any well-bred British officer might be expected to know, but the peasant *patois* of your childhood playfellows."

"That was a very long time ago, sir. I doubt I could recall more than a few words."

"Ah, Corporal Robin, what we learn in our youth stays with us always—for good or ill. It only takes a bit of a jog to bring it back. Speaking of which, I'm also told you were a tinker before you volunteered for the army."

"Before I was *press ganged,* sir."

"Corporal Robin, His British Majesty's Land Forces do not employ press gangs. *All* of the lower ranks have volunteered for life as a soldier."

"Yes, sir, I certainly volunteered. When I was seventeen years old a Recruiting Sergeant offered me a shilling to run 'round the corner and fetch him a twist of tobacco. When he'd put the shilling in my hand, he informed me I'd just taken The King's Shilling and that made me a soldier." Cully decided he'd already been impertinent enough without mentioning the bludgeons and halberd hafts coming down on him before he could drop the shilling and run out of the tavern. "And so I volunteered."

"Just so: you volunteered. I am told you can read and write."

"Passable well, sir."

"Rather an unusual skill for a tinker to pick up during his apprenticeship."

"Not all tinker's apprentices, sir, were born to the trade." Cully didn't like to be reminded that he'd had a childhood. It put him in mind of a trim, white house on the seashore, with gardens behind the back door for a boy to play in, and enough viciousness behind the front door to drive a boy to take to the road with a travelling tinker.

"All those attributes combined, Corporal Robin, make you uniquely suited for a particular duty. I suppose it is no secret that we shall soon be at war with France...?"

"I heard some rumours, sir."

"For once, barracks rumours have some truth to them. When the rumours come to fruition, we shall naturally have to keep a close eye on all French sympathizers residing within British territory. And in this corner of the Empire, that means the Acadians—the so-called Neutral French of Nova Scotia. Most of them live along the coasts and are easy enough to enumerate, but some chose to make their homes in backwoods valleys or hidden estuaries. In point of fact, the Acadians' entire pattern of settlement, even under the French regime, bespeaks a tendency to take up residence as far away from centres of authority as possible. Suggests a certain native intelligence on their part.

"The Acadians are notoriously disinclined to divulge information to representatives of the crown. But a travelling French tinker would naturally, at each place he visited, ask directions to the next farm along his way, and would naturally be given them. If said tinker happened to be of the literate persuasion, he could surreptitiously make a list of the *exact* location of each Acadian home he visited, and *all* the inhabitants thereof. If a certain Corporal Robin would furnish me with such a list, I would furnish him with a promotion and a purse of ten gold guineas.

"Within the week I shall be embarking on a supply ship sailing around the Nova Scotia peninsula to Fort Edward on the Bay of Fundy. If you set off today along the Halifax-to-Piziquid road, you could rendezvous with me at Fort Edward."

Cully hesitated. Ten guineas was more than he would see out of ten years of soldiering—what with the profiteering sutlers, and the colonel finding ingenious new deductions from soldiers' wages to increase his own share of what the king paid him to maintain a regiment. And a promotion would mean one less rank above him who could take a whim to stand him out in the rain in full marching kit. But he was far less confident than Captain Namon that he could remember enough of the French language and the tinker's trade to fool anyone.

An even larger reason to hesitate was the Halifax-to-Piziquid "road"—actually barely a cart track through the forest. The French in the citadel of Louisbourg, up north in what was still French Acadia, paid a healthy bounty for any British scalps brought in—just as the British paid for Mi'kmaq scalps. It wasn't that long ago that the outlaw Beausoleil and his Mi'kmaq friends had killed and scalped a work crew just outside the palisade of Halifax.

Cully said: "I would like to think about it, sir."

"Thinking is not a prerequisite for non-commissioned officers. Or most commissioned ones, for that matter. As I believe I said but a moment ago: you've volunteered.

"Your colonel has already been informed that you have been seconded to duties that are none of his concern. Civilian dress has been laid out for you in the next room, along with a pedlar's pack and everything else you will need. Beyond that room is an exterior door with a horse waiting. You step into that room as Corporal Robin and step out as a tinker, and no one but you and I know they are the same man."

"But, sir..." Cully's hand fluttered up of its own volition to indicate his hair: greased and powdered stiffly and clubbed into a tight roll at the back of his neck.

"I am not a hairdresser. You shall have to manage it yourself. And you shall have to manage it quickly, if you hope to get beyond the palisade before the gates close for the night, and if you hope to not find yourself making your first camp in the dark."

"Yes, sir." Cully turned to get on with it.

"Oh, and Corporal Robin...?"

"Sir...?"

"If you reach Fort Edward before me, or after I have departed that place, they will inform you that I do not exist."

In the next room, Cully found a patched suit of civilian clothes, a pair of boots that fit him better than his marching shoes—given that the boots were actually moulded as left and right—a gunnysack filled with tinker's tools and scraps of tin, two blankets rolled up in an oilcloth, and another sack containing provisions and cooking gear. There was a smooth-bore carbine with a supply of ammunition ranging from musket balls to birdshot. There was a small axe and a very large knife, and a pouch containing a tinder box, a flake of flint and a steel striker.

But the parts of his equipage that Cully was sure Captain Namon would consider the most important were several pencils and a hand-sized notebook in a waterproof wrapping.

Captain Namon had obviously thought of the problem of Corporal Robin's hair before Cully had. In one corner of the room was a washstand with a pitcher of hot water, a saucer of soap, a stiff brush and a mirror. He unknotted the leather band binding his club in place and went to work. For one of the first times in his life, he was thankful he'd been born with thin, straight hair. After a half hour of scrubbing and brushing he'd got most of the powder out but not all the grease and left it at that.

The horse tethered by the side door looked exactly like a tinker's horse: scrawny and scruffy and aged. But she proved livelier than Cully would've preferred, especially with the gunnysacks rattling against her flanks. Horsemanship wasn't one of the sciences footsoldiers were drilled in.

By the time they left the gates of Halifax behind, the horse had learned to tolerate him and the sun was slanting through the leaves. The "road" swung inland from the harbour inlet and the forest closed in. Cully had to think a very long way back to remember the last time he'd been in a forest alone—and that hadn't been a forest where any tree might be masking a Mi'kmaq scalphunter, or even Beausoleil himself.

To keep himself from thinking about the forest, and to practice his French, Cully talked to the mare, whom he'd christened *Maudit*. "What the devil else am I to do, Damned One, but make the best of it...? 'Volunteered'... What kind of captain tells colonels something's none of their concern...? If we come out alive at the end of this road, I'll use a piece of one of my ten guineas to buy you a bushel of oats. And a barrel of beer. Do you like beer? I personally make very good spruce beer, maybe—if I'd ever had the chance to taste the damned stuff..."

When the shadows grew long, he found a place by the side of the road to build a fire and roll out his blankets. After frying up a few strips of salt pork with flour mixed in the fat, he opened up his sack of tinker's gear to see what he could remember. Captain Namon was proven right: the memory was in his fingers. Although it was frustrating that they could remember what to do but couldn't quite do it right.

As he practised soldering tinker's dams and rivetting patches, he found himself cast back into the happiest year of his life, when he'd finally managed to accumulate his own tools and had learned enough from old Giorgio that he didn't have to be his slaveboy anymore. He was Cully the Tinker once again, camped under the stars with an old nag tethered in good grazing and the whole of the wide world to ramble where he would. He began to hum in time to the clinking of his hammer, trying to translate The Tinker's Song into French:

"I am a roving journeyman,

"I roam from town to town,

"And wherever I meet a job of work,

"I'm ready to sit down—"

A tomahawk appeared in front of his face. Cully's body immediately flung itself backwards, sprawling him on the ground. There was laughter from behind him. The tomahawk was dangling from the hand of a lean Indian with the top half of his face painted black. Another Indian was looking into Cully's food sack and sniffing. A third Indian was inspecting the carbine, and a fourth was leading Maudit forward by her cut tether. The one with the half-black face was looking down at Cully and stepping toward him, with the tomahawk slowly weaving from side to side.

Cully sputtered desperately: "*Parle français?*"

The tomahawk stopped weaving and the black eyes within the black paint became less certain of their purpose. The Indian said in halting French: "Some little. You Acadian?"

Cully sat up very slowly, trying to calm his lungs from taking in as many breaths as possible before his throat got cut, reminding himself that more than once he'd proven himself capable of methodically reloading while the men on either side of him fell screaming. He wanted intensely to reply: *Yes, I am one of your Acadian friends!*

But the very fact that the Mi'kmaqs and Acadians were so intertwined made it too chancy a lie. So he said: "No, I am Frenchman from," he made a very small gesture to indicate the east, "...across the water."

The tomahawk bobbed up and down again contemplatively, as though the hand holding it were weighing whether men from France counted as Acadians, or whether the French bounty-payers at Louisbourg could tell the difference between an English scalp and one of their own. Cully blurted: "Beausoleil!"

The tomahawk went rigid and the chortling of the booty-inspectors stopped dead. The Indian who'd taken possession of the carbine stepped forward to stand beside the black-faced one looking down at Cully. Blackface said: "You know Beausoleil?"

Cully lined his finger along his nose and winked: "No one *knows* Beausoleil."

The black forehead wrinkled. The Indian put his finger to his nose in imitation, then looked at it as though maybe it would tell him something. Cully scrambled to remember more French, "War... come against the English any day. I go find Beausoleil, to join him fight the English."

A discussion ensued, the only word of which Cully recognized was the repeated "Beausoleil." Finally, the one with the tomahawk put his free hand on the carbine and tugged. The one holding the carbine tugged back. Blackface held up his tomahawk and the one holding the carbine gave up and let it go.

Blackface handed the carbine to Cully and said: "Because you go Beausoleil, we let you keep you gun. And you scalp. And..." He gestured the tomahawk around the camp to indicate the rest of Cully's equipment. "But we take you horse."

"Thank you."

III

Eulalie was plucking weed sprouts out from among the cabbage sprouts when Rouge and Noir started barking furiously. She looked in the direction their noses were pointed and saw a man coming out of the wooded hollow at the bottom of the meadow where the sheep and cows were grazing between the apple trees. At first she thought it was André Melanson come too early for an appropriate evening visit. Except for Sundays, young men were only allowed to visit the homes of young women on Tuesday or Thursday evenings—otherwise how would anyone get any work done? On Sundays young men could come visiting at any time, but today wasn't a Sunday. When Eulalie came to think of it, it wasn't a Tuesday or a Thursday, either.

Then she saw that the only reason the man's shoulders looked as heavy as André Melanson's was that he had an awkward-looking packsack attached to them. And she saw that he was carrying a gun. She called out toward the barn: "*Beau-père—étranger!*"

Her uncle and stepfather, Joseph Brossard, hobbled wheezing out of the barn. He peered down the slope and whistled for his dogs to come guard him instead of nipping at the stranger's heels. Eulalie dusted her hands on her skirt and went to stand beside him.

Beau-père said out of the corner of his mustache: "Someone you know, *petite mère?*"

"I don't think so."

As the stranger came closer, Eulalie noticed that he was heavily loaded down for a man walking any distance, that he had an odd way of kicking his toes out with each step, and that he made a clanking sound. He wore a wide-brimmed, floppy hat that left everything between his forehead and shoulders in shadow.

The stranger stopped in front of them and took off his hat, disclosing a face that looked as cheerful as iron, and lank, brown hair that gleamed in places—as though it had once been beargreased like a Mi'kmaq's. He said brightly: "Good day to you, *monsieur et madame*, I am a tinker, Cully Robin by name." His French had an odd tang to it. But then, the few people from France or Quebec Eulalie had ever encountered had all sounded odd to her.

Eulalie said: "*Mademoiselle*."

Beau-père said: "I am Joseph Brossard." The tinker's head jerked, which Eulalie knew would please *Beau-père*. He always tried for the same joke on anyone he introduced himself to. *Beau-père* laughed and then coughed and then wheezed out: "No, no—not the Joseph Brossard who is known as Beausoleil. He might be a second or third cousin at most. From Cape Sable to the Gaspé, Brossards are as common as ducks.

"So... how is it that you came to find the path and follow it all the way here to our little valley of Ardoise? There are a lot of paths through the woods that lead nowhere."

"Oh, when I left your neighbour Benoni's I asked him who was west of him that might need a tinker. Do you have any pots that need mending, or hinges that are sagging, or cracked cowbells...?"

Beau-père pursed his mouth and his eyebrows. The tinker shrugged his left eyebrow and the right side of his mouth and said: "No fear of killing me with disappointment—I've come to expect it. When I had the clever idea to go a-tinkering through Acadia, I didn't take account that people who've had to make their own ploughs and rakes and harness-buckles since donkeys' years likely know how to mend their own pots and pans."

Eulalie felt sorry for him. Especially since she knew only too well how long the path was that he'd walked from the road for nothing. She said: "The soup pot needs a new handle. And the candle mould has a crack in its side that's getting bigger. It will only be a few pennies' worth of work, but you can share our supper and spend the night in our hayloft."

As Eulalie escorted the tinker toward the house, she mouthed over her shoulder at Joseph Brossard: "It's only a few pennies..." As for the meal and the bed in the hayloft, they would've been forthcoming to any wanderer who appeared at the door.

The "house" was actually only an over-grown kitchen enclosed by four squared-log walls and a thatched roof—except for a sleeping loft for the younger boys and girls, and four cabinetted beds along two of the walls. Eulalie pointed to a corner and told the tinker he could put his things down there, then watched as he unburdened himself of two bulging sacks, a bedroll, an axe and several pouches. She said: "You don't travel light."

"I had a horse when I started out."

"Did it die from carrying all that weight?"

He laughed. "Something of the sort."

As he leaned his short-barrelled gun against the pile, she said: "Is your gun loaded?"

"Yes."

"The children will be running in and out of here all day. I will tell them not to touch it, but—it would only take an instant while my back was turned. You know children..."

"Not much, but I'll take your word. It's easy-enough remedied." He opened the gun's priming pan, shook the priming powder out into his hand and tossed it on the coals in the hearth. The powder flared and belched black smoke up the chimney. It didn't actually damage anything, but it did make her wonder whether the tinker had ever been housebroken.

She reached down the cracked candle mould and the pot whose handle was coming loose. He opened up one of his sacks, took out some tools and sat down to work at one end of the long table that the family's indoor life revolved around. Eulalie built up the fire, swung the big stewpot in over it and began adding things into the stock. Hélène, Marie, Louise and even little Josette came in to help her put supper together, running down to the root cellar for carrots and turnips and cutting them up on the other end of the table from the tinker.

Eulalie didn't need all four girls to help her, but she listened to them chatter to the tinker while they cut up vegetables. Strangers were a rare commodity in the valley of Ardoise, especially strangers who had been and seen so many places. It seemed he'd been born on the Channel Islands and had spent much of his life tinkering his way around France and England and the German Lowlands before deciding to have a look at North America. He'd even been to the West Indies and eaten a coconut. But he seemed at least as interested in the family of Joseph Brossard as they were in Paris and London.

The tinker had lots of bits of news about their neighbours and relatives east along the Halifax road or south along the Piziquid River. It seemed remarkable to Eulalie that he could remember so many people's names and where they lived. She put it down to his trade: if he passed this way again, he would want to have a memory of which families had given him a bit of work and which had sicced the dogs on him.

He finished his work just as the girls started setting the table. Eulalie nodded at Marie to go clang on the iron bar hanging outside the door, to bring in the boys and their father. As Beau-père came in and headed for his chair, Eulalie stepped in front of him and showed him the mended pot and candle mould. He glanced at them, muttered: "Hm, yes, good," and started to step around her.

She stepped in front of him again and said: "Aren't you forgetting something?" jerking her head at the tinker.

Beau-père said: "Hm? Oh, yes..." He dug into his pocket and came out with three English pennies, which he'd no doubt dug out of his strongbox hoping he'd be able to put them back in again. The tinker thanked her when she handed them to him, but for someone who made his living mending pots he seemed remarkably blasé about if and how much he got paid for it.

The family and the tinker stood at their places while Beau-père said grace, then sat down to empty the platters and bowls. Once Eulalie had filled her plate, she stood up and worked her way around the table with a loaf of bread under her arm and a knife in her hand, cutting off as thick a slice as asked for. As usual, it took two loaves. The tinker ate like he'd been living on dried crusts for most of his life. At one point he pointed at the cold pastry beside his soup bowl and said: "This is delicious. What is it?"

"Thank you. Muskrat pie." He went a little pale. "Haven't you ever eaten muskrat pie?"

"Not as I knew of."

After supper, Beau-père took out his pipe and offered his tobacco pouch to the tinker. The tinker said ruefully that the one thing he'd forgotten to pack among all his weight of travelling gear was a pipe, so Beau-père rummaged up an old one of his and told the tinker he could keep it. Eulalie had long become accustomed that the only thing Joseph Brossard wasn't generous with was cash money. For some reason, he regarded the things that could be traded for coins as an entirely different matter from the coins themselves.

The younger children curled up with the dogs in front of the hearth to listen to their father and the tinker talk of the world outside their valley. As the older children cleaned up the table, Eulalie sat down at the loom Joseph Brossard made for his Marguerite, who lay in the little, fenced-in, family graveyard just up the hill. The clicking of the shuttle and foot-treadle pleasantly punctuated the men's voices and the peaceful murmur of the valley of Ardoise cozying in for the night. But when Beau-père asked the tinker if he'd seen any signs in Halifax that the English were preparing for war, Eulalie had to remind herself of all the reassuring things she'd said to Uncle Benoni. The tinker's reply was that since he'd only ever been in Halifax for the few days after he'd climbed off a ship from England last month, he couldn't say whether there were more soldiers there than usual.

After the children had lined up to kiss their father good-night, Beau-père creaked up off his chair, picked up a candle and wheezed at the tinker: "I should light you to the hayloft."

"No need, *monsieur*—just point me the way and you can sit and rest."

"No, no—a walk to the barn and back will do me good." He took down the cane hanging by the door as the tinker picked up his bedroll and one of his sacks.

The tinker turned to Eulalie from the doorway and said: "Good-night, *mademoiselle*."

"Good-night, *monsieur*."

When Eulalie's stepfather came back from the barn, she was the only one still up and about. He said: "You know, *petite mère*, there is something I like about that man, and something I don't like."

"Which is which?"

"I'm not sure."

IV

ully sat in his bed of hay and blankets, being careful: careful that the candle didn't topple into the hay, and careful that one of the night sounds didn't signify a member of the Brossard family coming to check something in the barn and incidentally catch him recording them in his notebook. He wrote:

> *Ardoise Valley—3 miles west Benoni's, path north off the road, reddish boulder by pathmouth.*
>
> *Joseph Brossard, widower. 50? yrs age. Infirm.*
>
> *Eulalie La Tour, adopt. daughter. 18?*

He crossed out 18 and wrote in 19—no eighteen-year-old could possibly be that calmly in command of seven children and their father. The appearance of the pencilled x's on the white page made him pause to reflect. They put him in mind of the black x's of the lacing on the front of Eulalie La Tour's corselet against the white background of her blouse, and the interesting way those x's widened and then narrowed again as one's eyes travelled from her waist to her throat. There was definitely something noticeable about her, and it wasn't just because she was the dark-haired cuckoo among the paler Brossards.

But Acadian women were notoriously indifferent to the charms of non-Acadian men. There were exceptions, though. He was quite sure he'd detected hopeful signs from that farmwife back on the Piziquid River. Several years of being Tom Soldier billeted in English inns or farms had taught him how to recognize hopeful signs in innkeepers' and farmers' wives and daughters, and how to seize the moment. But the Piziquid farmwife's husband had come home from fishing before he'd had time to press it.

Cully shrugged and put his pencil back to work:

> *Henri Brossard, 14 yrs. Knows how to use a musket + is big enough to carry one.*
>
> *Jacques Brossard, 13 yrs. Ditto use + almost carry...*

By the time Cully'd finished adding the Ardoise Valley Brossards to Captain Namon's list, the candle was guttering dangerously low. He blew it out and rolled himself into a softer bed than any he'd known in a barracks, and a cleaner one than any of his billets.

He woke up to a rainy morning. Judging by the depth his boots sank into the farmyard, it had been pelting down since he blew out the candle. To begin the day there were pancakes with blueberries and maple syrup, with fried eggs and bacon to round them out. As the plates were being cleared away, old Joseph Brossard wheezed: "I think, Monsieur Robin, this is not a good day for travelling."

There was nothing Cully would've liked better than to snugly laze away the day in the Brossards' kitchen, watching Eulalie La Tour bend over the hearth. But Captain Namon might well be at Fort Edward by now. And the cautions of broken-down old men hardly applied to young men accustomed to marching twenty miles a day in all weathers. He said: "I thank you for your hospitableness, Monsieur Brossard, but losing my horse has slowed me down and I have a rendezvous in Piziquid, with a man whose boat might speed me along toward Quebec."

Eulalie La Tour said: "So you won't be passing by this way again...?"

"Not soon. Not unless there's no pots to be mended in Quebec." *Or unless*, he added to himself, *you fancy a roll in the hay with Tom Soldier.* She pressed a loaf of bread on him, which he happily added into his ration sack—regretfully informing himself that the loaf of bread signified nothing more than her inclination to give a crust to any passing beggar. Maybe the next farmwife along the road would have a husband who stayed out fishing longer.

He loaded himself down like a mule again, working the improvised pack straps around his shoulders. When he opened the door, the rain had slowed to a drizzle. He turned back to Joseph Brossard and gestured to show him it was no longer a bad day for travelling. The old man muttered dourly: "It isn't only when it's coming down, but after. The paths you climbed easy yesterday will be slick mud today. And find a stout branch to hang onto crossing streams."

Cully nodded sombrely, although his inclination was to laugh—none of the streams he'd crossed yesterday had been higher than his ankles. He said "*Adieu* to all," the Brossards and Eulalie La Tour called back *adieu*, and he closed their door behind him.

By the time he'd got halfway down the back pasture, even the drizzle had stopped. There was nothing left of the storm but a mist rising out of the hollows. He began to hear a roaring in front of him. When he came to the wooded grotto at the base of the farm, he found that the streamlet he'd stepped over yesterday was now a torrent, boiling through the rock cleft to his left. He'd wondered yesterday why the streambed was a scoured trough of solid slate, instead of pebbles and mud.

Something on the other bank caught his eye, a bright flash whiter than the foam on the cascade. He stopped and squinted across the stream. It was a jutting lump of quartz, with its rain-sheened crystals catching the sun breaking through the clouds. He remembered somebody-or-other saying that where there was quartz there was gold.

He told himself to stop stalling and get on with it. He'd waded swift-flowing streams before, and ones a lot deeper than this. Holding his carbine crosswise as a balance pole, he raised his right foot and thrust it down into the foam. The water was numbingly cold and higher than his knee, and the tug of the current was like a team of horses. Once his right boot was planted firmly, he swung his left leg up and forward quickly and plunged his left boot down.

He crabwalked his way jerkily into the stream, with the water rising gradually up his thighs. When he was almost within reaching distance of a tree limb on the other side, his left boot came down on what seemed like a solid purchase, but it was only a striation in the slate. His boot slipped off it, he lost his balance and the current carried his legs out from under him.

He threw the carbine at the shore as he was swept downstream, trying to grab for overhanging branches while sacks and packstraps tangled his arms. Rocks battered his body, and green water kept closing over his face. His head hit something, then his right leg hit something else and exploded in flame. Then his head hit something even harder and the pain in his leg didn't bother him anymore.

※ ※ ※

He awoke laid out on his back in a dark, enclosed place that smelled of clean linen. He moved his right hand to the right and immediately encountered wooden planking. I Ie moved his left hand to the left and found the same thing. He was lying in a coffin.

He hammered on the sides of the coffin and shouted: "I'm alive!" He heard voices, so they hadn't filled in the grave yet. They opened the coffin and light came in—but not from above, from the side. He was lying in an Acadian-style, cabinetted bed.

The sight of old Joseph Brossard through the opened cupboard door made Cully realize he'd shouted in English. The sight of Eulalie La Tour made him realize he was naked, with bedclothes pulled up to his armpits. He had a bandage wound around his head, and his right leg was bound in splints which didn't stop it hurting like a bastard.

Joseph Brossard shrugged: "I told you it was a bad day for travelling. Lucky for you it was a Tuesday."

"How so?"

"Tuesday evenings young men can come visiting. André Melanson came visiting a little early, saw you washed up against a deadfall downstream and brought you here. We sent André for the joiner who lives down the road to set your leg. The joiner said it is a clean break, but you will have to stay splinted for three weeks at least."

Eulalie La Tour said: "Beau-père wanted to give you his bed, but I told him he's too old for sleeping on the floor. So we put you in my bed."

"Um, thank you."

Joseph Brossard said: "The boys went a ways down the creekbanks trying to find your things. Your gun has a bent cock, but maybe a good tinker can fix it. They found your tool sack, and wiped dry your tools, but everything else is gone. Except what you were wearing."

Joseph Brossard stepped back so Cully could see that his clothes, or what was left of them, were hanging in front of the hearth to dry. Standing in front of the hearthstone, propped open to face the fire, was the notebook containing Captain Namon's list.

Joseph Brossard said offhandedly: "The waterproofing held well, your little book is only damp. Not many tinkers can read and write." Cully just shrugged modestly and hoped that would be the end of it. "Not many farmers can read and write, either, but I can. I don't read much English, but names read much the same in French or English."

"You've caught me out. You see, if I come back this way in a few years, people will be amazed at the tinker who remembers all their names after only meeting them once, and they will be more likely to see if they can find some work for such a friendly fellow. Trick of the trade."

"Mm-hm." Joseph Brossard scratched his mustache. "Funny thing, when you were shouting when the joiner set your leg, or murmuring in your sleep, most of that was in English, too—so far as I could tell."

"Not surprising. Like I said, I spent the last few years a-tinkering in England and hardly heard a word of French. And, where I was a boy we chattered in French and English without knowing the difference. I'm just glad that whatever I said when I was out of my head was in a language no one understood."

"Oh, I understand a few words of English. Words like *sergeant*..."

Cully ran his tongue along the back of his top teeth, then said: "In England, like most other countries, a vagabond tinker sometimes finds himself thinking about officers of the Crown more than he would like."

Oddly, instead of pressing his suspicions any further, Joseph Brossard suddenly looked down at the floor and muttered: "You've had a hard life." Odder still, Eulalie

La Tour looked down, too, as though she and her stepfather had intruded on something they shouldn't.

Cully said: "I don't know how I can thank you."

Joseph Brossard looked up confusedly. "For what?"

"For *what*? For taking an invalid stranger into your home for the good God knows how long!"

Joseph Brossard said as though the facts explained themselves: "You had a broke leg and a cracked head and half-drowned and we were the nearest house."

Eulalie La Tour said: "What else would anyone do?"

Cully refrained from saying: *I'd* probably ask the nearest sergeant if he cared and then go on about my business.

V

ulalie stepped out the door to throw kitchen scraps to the chickens, and was surprised to find the tinker Cully Robin sitting in the sun with his splinted leg stretched out in front of him and his back against the front wall of the house. She'd expected to find him there—given that she and Henri had helped him hop out the door, and he certainly wasn't going far on his own—but she'd expected to find him occupied in trying to fix his carbine. She hadn't expected to find him sitting there with the gun propped slackly across his lap, and his eyes agog as though he'd just seen a night-rider crossing the sky. He looked up at her and said: "I heard of miraculous cures, but..."

"'Cures'...?"

He pointed at the barn, where Beau-père was pitching the last forkful of hay off a cart up to Jacques in the loft. As Henri came up with another cartload from the rick in the far field, his father bounded off the emptied cart and up onto the full one before it stopped moving.

Cully Robin said: "Two days ago he could barely hobble across the room!"

She laughed. "Oh, *that* cure. He is only a broke-down old man for strangers, or for people he has to call 'sir'. The rest of the time, all three boys together can barely keep up with him."

The tinker laughed so hard she thought he was going to slap his broken leg. When he'd caught his breath, he said: "Your stepfather is a very wise man." Then he looked up at her and added oddly: "Thank you."

"For what?"

"For telling me I'm not a stranger."

She didn't know what to say to that. She didn't know what to say to him about a lot of things, ever since she and Beau-père had peeled the tinker's sopping shirt off in his delirium, and found a back webbed with puckered whip scars. Beau-père had told her she mustn't ever ask the poor man where they came from, or let him know she knew.

So instead of saying anything, Eulalie just called the chickens, threw the contents of the slop pail in their general direction and went back inside. After the tinker had had a few hours of sunshine, she got Hélène to help her help him back into the house. She unwound the bandage on his head and changed the poultice of plantain leaves. It looked like most of the poison had been drawn out already, and the gashes were sealing themselves together. Then she brewed up a tea of dried goldenrod to make him sweat and put him back to bed.

His eyes closed as soon as his head hit the pillow, and his lips parted slackly in instant sleep. His upper lip had a slight twist on the left side, as though his mouth had once been bumped hard enough for a tooth to come through. He had an odd nose—somehow hooked and snubbed at the same time. His eyelashes were surprisingly thick and long for somebody with such thin hair.

Eulalie became aware that Hélène at the washtub was looking at her looking at the tinker. She closed the bed doors abruptly, just catching herself before they slammed and woke him up.

The tinker slept and sweated until suppertime. Eulalie was going to give him a bowl of soup in bed, but he said now that he was awake he'd rather sit up at the table, with his splinted leg propped on a chair. After supper, she sat down at her loom. Beau-père called gravely from behind her: "But it's Thursday, Eulalie!"

"I know that."

"But I see no pitcher and cup! Do you want André Melanson to ride all this way just to turn around and go back to Piziquid for good?"

She felt herself blushing. "You know perfectly well, Beau-père, that André had to go off on his father's boat till the end of the week."

The old idiot laughed happily at teasing a blush out of her, and explained to the tinker, which made her blush even more. "You see, when a young man is coming to visit, the young woman sets out a pitcher of water or dandelion wine or some such, and a cup beside it. After the young man has talked a while with her mother and father and brothers and sisters—pretending that he gives a damn about their conversation—he gets up and fills the cup from the pitcher and goes to sit beside who he has really come to talk with. If there is no pitcher and cup, he knows she is tired of him visiting.

"But, as Eulalie says, tonight André is off on his father's boat keeping up an old Melanson family tradition: smuggling. The Melansons were Scottish at first, but now they are as Acadian as anyone, and Acadians have been smugglers since Charles La Tour's day—or what is *called* smugglers. In times when we had a French governor, it was called smuggling to trade with Boston. In times of an English governor, it's called smuggling to take a few barrels of salt fish north to Louisbourg, or across the bay to what is still French Acadia. The only difference the change makes to us is which port we head for in daylight and which at night."

Eulalie wondered whether Beau-père wasn't saying too much to someone who, although not exactly a stranger anymore, still wasn't Acadian. But Cully Robin just laughed and said: "Where I grew up, I doubt there was one man with a fishing skiff didn't do a bit of smuggling. The Channel Islands are so convenient between England and France."

"So, your father, then..." Beau-père probed discreetly, "He was a smuggler, too?" Among Acadians, you didn't really know someone until you knew who his father was—and mother, and great-grandparents, and second cousins...

"No." The tinker's voice had suddenly taken on a tang of the iron she'd seen in his face when he'd first tugged off his hat to say *bonjour.* "No, my father was an eminently respectable man of business."

"Oh. What business was he in?"

"The business of making money from Monday to Saturday and suffering the little children on Sunday. But, in all justice, he could not have been the man he was without my mother's helping hands."

Eulalie couldn't see the tinker's face without turning around from her loom and making it obvious. But the cold distance in his voice made her quite sure he didn't want to say anything more about the subject, and even more sure she didn't want to know why.

Fortunately, before the silence had a chance to get too long, little, golden-haired Josette came up to Eulalie and said: "Can we have a button to play the game?"

"Of course, my dear. Bring me the tin and you can pick one out."

As the younger children started forming two lines to play "Button, button, who's got the button?" Cully Robin surprised everyone by asking if he could play, too. The children dragged their chairs up around his and he "Button-buttoned" as enthusiastically as they did and laughed along with them.

When the game of *bouton* wound down, he entranced them by showing them how he could make the button disappear with a snap of his fingers. Then he entranced them even further by showing them how the magic worked—that the button held between his thumb and second finger shot up his sleeve when he snapped his fingers. All the children, even the older ones, had to beg a button from Eulalie so they could try it. By the time it was time for the littler ones to go to bed, they were all calling the tinker "Cully."

As the children climbed up to their loft, Beau-père brought out the dominoes and asked the tinker if he thought he could give him better competition than Jacques and Henri, who always played as a team. The clicking of the pieces on the table joined the clicking of her loom, and the room grew easy with the scent of tobacco and the sound of soft, deep voices behind her:

"Thought you had me there, didn't you, Cully?"

"And I do, Uncle—try this on."

"Jesus-Mary-and-Joseph!"

When the game was over, Eulalie and her stepfather helped the tinker into her bed. Beau-père said: "Sleep well, Cully."

"Good-night, Uncle. Good-night, Eulalie."

"Good-night, Cully." They pushed the bed doors closed.

"Well, *petite-mère*, I'm for bed, too."

"Good-night, Beau-père."

She banked the fire low and unrolled the quilts and blankets that would be her bed on the floor until the splints came off the tinker's leg. Her nightdress was in the middle of the roll. Normally she would change into her nightgown sitting up in her closed-in bed, and hang her day clothes on the pegs inside. Last night she'd just stepped outside, but there was a late frost in the air tonight.

She assured herself that everyone was asleep by now, or at least behind their own bed-doors, and that the fire was banked too low to cast much light. But as she began to unlace her corselet out in the open, she got an eerie feeling that the tinker had his eye pressed to the crack between the doors of her bed. So she turned her back to that side of the room while she undressed. The strangest part of the eerie feeling that he might be watching her, was that it wasn't entirely unpleasant.

❈ ❈ ❈

The next afternoon, little Josette grew over-excited and kept running to Eulalie in the garden to ask if she could have a piece of maple sugar candy. Eulalie repeatedly told her no, that it would be suppertime soon and the candies were for Sunday. Josette wasn't used to being told no. Eulalie wasn't sure whether the reason everybody pampered Josette was because she was her mother's last child, or whether it was just because Josette's hair was the brightest gold of all the blond Brossards. Either way, Josette usually got what she wanted.

After an hour or so of Josette periodically running back to the garden to see if the answer had changed, Eulalie happened to glance up and saw Josette sneaking into the house. Eulalie threw down her hoe and ran after her.

When Eulalie came through the door, Josette was standing on a chair reaching for the top shelf of the food cabinet. Eulalie pulled her down, shouting: "There is nothing worse than a thief!" turned her over her knee and slapped her bottom. Josette ran outside crying and Eulalie flopped back into the chair Josette had been standing on, crying herself. She wanted to run after Josette and tell her she was sorry.

"What else could you do?"

The voice had come from the other side of the room. Eulalie looked up to see the doors of her bed open and Cully Robin with his shoulder propped against the frame. She wiped her eyes and sniffed: "What kind of a mother beats her children?"

He shook his head emphatically. "That's not what you did. Not the same thing at all. There's all the difference in the world between a dog who'd got his nose whacked when he was a puppy who pissed on the floor, and a dog who got kicked whenever his master felt like kicking something."

"Children aren't dogs."

"You're right—dogs learn faster."

She laughed in spite of herself, then went and called Henri and Jacques to help her help the tinker out of her bed and into the sun. Cully Robin's hand on her shoulder felt rough with calluses and soft with restrained strength. They were very agile hands, and he seemed discontented when they weren't doing something useful. Josette's doll, which had once been Eulalie's, had developed a crack in its head over the winter, so the tinker had asked for a piece of pine out of the woodpile and was carving her a new face.

His own face still had the hardness that Eulalie had seen at first glimpse: an almost brutal muteness that she'd never seen in any of her many uncles or any other Acadian man. But now it seemed to her that there was something *triste* about that hard look, like someone who'd had the heart cut out of him but was determined to go on living regardless.

She suspected that if she hadn't seen the scars on his back she wouldn't have noticed that he went misty-eyed sometimes when watching the children play, or even when his gaze happened to linger on something as ordinary as the rickety smokehouse off to the side of the barn. She happened to be passing by him when he was looking down the hill at the cattle single-filing their way toward the stream. He said: "So you never have to carry water for them?"

"Only a few times in the winter, when the snow's too deep for them to leave the barn. Even the driest summer, there's still enough of a trickle for them to drink."

He clucked the corner of his mouth and cricked his head, as though that was the most marvellous thing he'd ever heard.

One hot afternoon when she brought the tinker out a cup of water, he said with a laugh in his voice: "The whiffle tree."

"The what?"

He pointed across the yard at Jacques propping up the front of the two-horse cart so Henri could grease the axles. "The shaft the horses get harnessed to. Apprentice tinkers learn more about what can break down on their master's cart than they ever want to know, and one of the weakest spots is where the whiffle-tree is affixed under the cartbed—joined to a cross-brace to make a T.

"Your stepfather—or whoever built that cart there—just found a stout, forked tree branch and cut its ends to make a shaft. No need for a joint that can break—there's a natural Y in the wood. Looks rough, but..."

Eulalie pursed her eyes and her mouth as she got a new look at the cart she never looked twice at. Thanks to the tinker, she saw it now as just lumps of crude, raw timber pegged together by peasants. She said: "We have to make do with what we got."

"You do a lot smarter and better than people who got a lot more."

On Saturday night Beau-père took down his fiddle and Henri and Jacques took out their jew's-harps and Eulalie and the children jigged and sang. The tinker couldn't join in the dancing, but he asked for a couple of spoons and clattered them rhythmically against his good leg.

At one point, Eulalie leaned against the back of Cully Robin's chair to catch her breath and panted out: "You see? We can have our own *fais do-do* any night we want."

He seemed taken aback. He said: "'Fais do-do'?"

"Yes. Didn't they say *fais do-do* where you come from?"

"Um, yes, but it meant, um...'going to bed'."

"It means the same here. To little children, *fais do-do* means 'off to bed, sleepyhead.' When they get a little older, *fais do-do* means: 'The children are asleep now, so we can get as foolish as we want'."

The tinker seemed willing to get as foolish as anyone. He even sang a rather awkward song about a tinker, which he blushingly confessed he'd translated from English himself:

"'Ach away with you, you silly girl,'
"Her mother did implore,
"'How can you love the journeyman
"You never seen before...?'"

VI

⁂

ully awoke on Sunday to find himself in the middle of preparations for a Full Dress Parade. Children were standing in line to have their hair combed, Joseph Brossard was wearing a black coat and breeches and kept squinting at the notches cut into the window ledge that told the time as the sun moved across them, and Eulalie had put on a starched white collar that made her throat look like caramel and her eyes like chocolate.

She was just finishing covering up her hair. Unlike all the other Acadian women Cully had ever seen, Eulalie had always let her hair hang free—except for throwing a quick ribbon around the back when it was falling in the way of what she was doing. Her undressed hair made her seem interestingly half-wild, almost wanton. But now it appeared that her loose-haired ways were only because there was rarely anybody in the valley of Ardoise except her family. She had ribboned her hair back over a little white cap and was knotting a long kerchief over that.

As Henri and Jacques helped Cully out of bed, he said: "Are you going to mass?"

Joseph Brossard laughed: "No, no, Cully—mass is coming to us. Are you of the Faith?"

"I'm afraid not."

"Oh well—so long as you don't start singing Protestant hymns in the middle of the benediction." Cully could've assure him that was highly unlikely, since Corporal Robin was only even a Protestant inasmuch as chapel attendance was compulsory for all the lower ranks. "You see, for so many generations there have been so few priests to serve all of Acadia—and some generations no priests at all—that the Church has allowed for us to hold White Masses led by wise old laymen. But in these parts there are no wise old men to be found, so people have to settle for me."

Eulalie remarked from trying to comb Josette's hair without taking her scalp out with the tangles: "They could do worse than settle for you, Beau-père; they could have an ordained priest like the Abbé Le Loutre."

Joseph Brossard muttered something unpleasant and pretended to spit on the floor. Cully couldn't've been more surprised if the old man had jumped up on a chair and started singing The British Grenadiers. Spitting at the Abbé Le Loutre's name was *de rigueur* in the barracks at Halifax, but Cully didn't expect it among priest-ridden French Catholics. The Abbé Le Loutre was a missionary who occasionally snuck south from French Acadia to preach to Mi'kmaqs and Acadians that God smiled every time a Protestant was scalped. The name of the Abbé Le Loutre engendered as much fear among English colonists as Beausoleil's, but without the grudging respect. At least Beausoleil did his own killing.

Footsteps and jovial voices approached the house as the celebrants of the White Mass began to arrive. There was Benoni and his family, who remembered the tinker who'd mended their tin cups. There was an old man who lived alone at the top of Ardoise Hill, whose twitchy manner suggested to Cully that he never saw anybody except on Sundays. And there was the family from the next farm west of the Brossards. That farmer gave Cully a chill by waggling his finger at him and saying: "I can see you think we have not met before, but we have."

Cully said carefully: "Um, where would that have been?"

"In this very room. I am the joiner who set your leg while your mind was in another country."

No one seemed to think twice about Cully being foist into their little congregation, except to express sympathy for his injuries, or joke that man was obviously not intended to walk on water. As they gossiped among themselves before the service, Cully noticed that they never used each others' last names. Joseph Brossard was "Joseph à Jacques à Thomas"—Joseph the son of Jacques the son of Thomas. Eulalie La Tour was Eulalie à Marie à Pelagie.

The last one to arrive for the White Mass came on horseback—a young man with an open face and small eyes and a neck like a bull. The others made well-worn jokes about how dull the priest at Piziquid must be, to make André Melanson ride all this way for Sunday services.

When André Melanson was introduced to him, Cully said: "You saved my life."

"No, my horse did. I never could've carried you here."

Cully looked at the shoulders like hams and said: "I think you could've." André blushed bashfully and shrugged.

Joseph Brossard took out a book and took up a position in a corner of the room. Everyone else except Cully stood facing him. Cully didn't know much about Catholic masses, but it seemed to him that this one was rather rough-edged and informal. He'd never had much stomach for religion, but he had to admit there was a reverence in the room that had nothing of forelock-tugging in it.

After Joseph Brossard closed his book and drew a cross in the air to bless all who were gathered, Eulalie set cold meat pies on the table and the women from the other farms began to empty out the baskets they'd carried with them. When everyone had eaten a little more than they could, the men took out their pipes and leaned back in their chairs, while the women dealt with the dishes and the children and gossiped with each other.

The men had their own brand of gossip. Cully could see that André Melanson wasn't yet comfortable with being one of the grown men expressing opinions around the table. André said to the others as though he'd been rehearsing it: "My father says he will have to go to Halifax soon, with the delegation to speak to the new governor about the new loyalty oath."

Joseph Brossard shrugged: "Talking to the governor is a good thing for them to do—so long as all they do is talk politely without giving him what he wants. Governor Lawrence can roar and pound the table all he wants to, but the old oath we swore was good enough for old Governor Phillips, and in the end Governor Lawrence will have to see it's good enough for him, too. Why should the English king be unhappy with that? We promise to be his loyal subjects, so long as we can't be made to kill our brothers in his name."

Benoni said dourly: "The English king may be unhappy with that when the war starts."

Joseph Brossard said: "What difference does a war make to us, Benoni? I will tell you the only difference it makes: the more English soldiers come here, the higher goes the price for beef and cabbages and barley."

Benoni shook his head grimly. "The more English soldiers come here, Joseph à Jacques à Thomas, the more the English governor can tell us what to do."

Joseph Brossard threw up his hands and said to Cully: "You see? It's true what they say: 'You can tell an Acadian a mile away, but you can't tell him a damn thing up close.'

"Listen, Benoni, you old woman—what is Governor Lawrence going to do if we will only swear the old oath? Shoot us all, or put us all in prison? Then who will grow food for his soldiers? Who will net fish for them? In all the generations of Acadians, the only times a governor has ever been able to lord it over us—whether an English governor or a French one—was when we forgot that without us, he and all his servants and soldiers would starve to death."

Cully felt a sudden twinge, like someone had stepped on his grave. One of the favourite subjects for humour around the Halifax barracks was the lumpheaded German farmers the colony had been importing by the shipload for the last few years. But those lumpheaded sauerkraut-eaters had done very well for themselves, building farms on free land in the south of the province, and now supplied most of the garrison's provisions. It almost seemed like somebody had been planning for a long time to make the Acadians less necessary.

Cully shook it off and assured himself that Joseph Brossard was right: what was Governor Lawrence to do, imprison three-quarters of the population of his province? Cully had no doubt that there *was* a plan to deal with the Acadians, and he and his list were part of it. The plan was to identify where all of them lived and keep a close eye on them, so that any who lent the French armies a hand could be called to account.

When all the visitors were gone except André Melanson, Cully began to feel the effects of not having had the afternoon nap his body seemed to demand these days. André Melanson boosted him into Eulalie's bed as easily as lifting a pillow, then left it up to him whether or not to close the doors.

Cully watched through half-closed eyes as André filled the cup standing beside the pitcher on the table and went to sit by Eulalie. It seemed to Cully that André Melanson didn't do much but sit there, outside of hesitantly murmuring something from time to time, which Eulalie would nod at without interrupting her crocheting.

Cully didn't have to watch long before deciding it was patently ridiculous. André Melanson was a *boy.* Not that Eulalie was markedly older by the calendar, but being *petite mère* for six or seven years had made her a good deal more than a girl—even if the weight pressed down a little hard on her sometimes.

Although Cully was perfectly willing to admit that André was a big, generous-hearted lad—after all, Cully was living proof of that—it still looked suspiciously to him like André Melanson had hit upon a way to be mothered for the rest of his life.

VII

ndré Melanson climbed up onto his saddle-less plough-horse and started home. The sun was going down, but Daisy had been up and down the path from Ardoise Valley to the road so many times she could find her own way in the dark.

André didn't feel nearly as at ease as he should after a Sunday with Eulalie. There was something about the comfortable way Eulalie joked with the tinker that made André uncomfortable. And the way Joseph Brossard talked to the tinker grated a little. Joseph Brossard had never actually talked *down* to André, but it was always a given that André was, after all, only a very young man with little experience of the world. But when the tinker expressed an opinion, Joseph Brossard would nod and listen like one grown man paying heed to another. In fact, it seemed at times as though white-haired Joseph Brossard thought the tinker could teach him a thing or two.

But the worst of it was the way the tinker looked at Eulalie. André couldn't blame any man whose eyes tended to linger on Eulalie, but there was something domestically intimate in the tinker's gaze. It was obscene: he was almost old enough to be her father.

As if all of that wasn't enough to make André feel a little uneasy, there was something about the tinker that just didn't ring true. André asked himself if he might not be imagining that because of the other things that annoyed him about the tinker. No, when he considered it, the tinker would've seemed a little like a fox in a henhouse even if Eulalie hadn't been the hen.

But André couldn't think of a way to say that to Eulalie or Joseph Brossard without sounding like he was just jealous. He remembered, though, that the joiner had said it would only be two or three weeks before the tinker could be on his way again. André could keep an eye on the tinker until then, and speak up if he found anything to tell Eulalie beyond a vague unease.

By the time André had worked that out, he could see the blockhouse tower of Fort Edward against the moon. He turned off the road onto the side trail to the inlet where his grandfather had chosen to build a farm. There were only a few lighted houses along the trail, and more than a few slump-roofed derelicts barely visible in the gloom. Ever since the founding of Halifax made it clear that the English weren't going to give up Nova Scotia this time without a lot of cannonballs flying around, more and more of the Melansons' neighbours had been following the Abbé Le Loutre's advice to pack up everything that wasn't rooted in the earth and head north into French territory.

The English weren't the only ones who could make Piziquid uncomfortable at times. André could remember peering down from the sleeping loft with his brothers at a dozen snow-crusted French soldiers laying down bedrolls in front of the hearth and pillaging the pantry while his mother and father protested weakly. He hadn't known it at the time, but the same scene was being played out that night in every house and barn along the Piziquid River, with soldiers and bearded men who'd never worn a uniform. The next morning, the soldiers and their un-uniformed friends had been gone. But they'd passed through again a week later, carrying the scalps of 150 English soldiers who'd been snowed-in at Grand Pré. It had been hard to convince the English revenge-squads that the people of Piziquid were innocent, because not all of them were.

But the fact that there were now so many abandoned homes around his parents' place did give André one reason to smile. It would make it so much easier when he and Eulalie were married. Instead of having to build a house and dig a garden, they could just take possession of a place that only had a year or two's worth of cobwebs and weeds to clear out. André had already picked one out, within easy shouting distance of his mother's place if Eulalie needed help. As Daisy ambled him past it in the dark, he could see in his mind the spot on the roof that would need re-thatching, the door that would need new hinges because the Blanchards took theirs with them...

There was still a light burning in his parents' house. He slipped down off Daisy at the pasture gate, slipped his feet into the wooden shoes he'd left beside the gatepost, took Daisy's halter off and slapped her rump into the pasture. His mother and father were still up, his father whittling a new rung for the rocking chair and his mother sewing a new shirt out of linen she'd woven last summer. He sat down to a piece of cold *tourtière* and answered their questions about his day in the valley of Ardoise, trying to say as little about the tinker as possible. Then he yawned his way up to the sleeping loft and the wide straw mattress he still shared with his younger brothers, wondering what it was going to feel like to share a bed with Eulalie for the rest of his life.

In the morning, he was up and moving long before everyone else, so he could do his share for the family and still have a little time before breakfast to do something for himself. The tide was coming up the rivermouth; within a few hours his father's boat wouldn't be stranded on mudflats but floating in ten feet of water. He felt over the net his father had hung out to dry, but it was still too damp with dew to roll up. So instead he milked the two cows that weren't pregnant, split and stacked a few days' worth of firewood, and decided that that was enough to allow him to go to work on his cart wheels.

No Acadian man was considered old enough to start a family of his own until he'd made a serviceable pair of cart wheels with his own hands. No Acadian woman was deemed old enough to marry until she'd woven a serviceable piece of cloth, but Eulalie had been weaving the Brossard family's blankets and clothing ever since her Aunt Marguerite died.

André took down his father's draw knife and went to work shaving a spoke, humming the little song Eulalie had made up: "Three hills home, my dear, three hills home..."

VIII

⁓⁓⁓⁓⁓

Eulalie opened the door to shake the supper crumbs off the tablecloth, and her breath caught in her throat. The light from the doorway fell on a snarling, painted Indian brandishing a knife over his head. She found her breath again and said flatly in Mi'kmaq: "You're too late for supper."

He lowered his knife and looked disappointed that his joke hadn't worked. There were other Mi'kmaqs coming forward behind him, along with a few ragged-bearded men in buckskins and homespun, and a trim-bearded man in a priest's cassock. She said over her shoulder: "Beau-père...?"

"I see, Eulalie." She could hear in his voice that he'd become a wheezing old man again. She took his cane down from the peg beside the door and brought it to him. He looked down at Rouge and Noir and muttered: "Some watchdogs."

The priest and one of the Mi'kmaqs and one of the buckskinned men stepped through the doorway, the rest stayed outside. The priest paused to raise his hand and say: "I bless thy house, Joseph Brossard." His cassock was made of the finest woollen cloth Eulalie had ever seen, but had a few burrs clinging to the hem. He looked a little old and soft to be tramping along Mi'kmaq trails.

Beau-père wheezed: "Thank you, Father. Monsieur l'Abbé, this is my daughter, Eulalie La Tour; my son, Henri..." He introduced all the children and ended up with Cully Robin sitting at the foot of the table with his splinted leg propped on a chair. But Beau-père never mentioned the name of the Monsieur l'Abbé they were being introduced to. Eulalie didn't have to make many guesses to know why. It was the Abbé Le Loutre.

Beau-père said: "Sit down, if you will, Monsieur l'Abbé. Eulalie, perhaps Monsieur l'Abbé would like a cup of your fine blackberry tea." Eulalie went to the hearth to ladle a cupful out of the pot, as the Abbé Le Loutre sat down in her chair. "I would offer some to all your friends, Monsieur l'Abbé, but we have only so many cups."

"There is no need. They are accustomed to making do with the good God's clear, flowing wine in the streams and rivers of Acadia. But a few chickens would be appreciated…" A panicked squawking from outside, suddenly choked-off, told Eulalie that a few chickens were already finding their way into the Abbé's friends' food pouches.

Beau-père said: "But of course, Monsieur l'Abbé."

The Abbé took off one of his boots, started massaging his foot and added: "And some flour. And a steer to herd along with us until the chickens have been eaten."

"I will gladly give what I can, but I am not a rich man, and have so many mouths to feed—"

"Now is not a time to be thinking of earthly riches, my son. The heretic whoreson English are preparing to send an army against Fort Beauséjour—on the pretext that Fort Beauséjour doesn't truly mark the border between Nova Scotia and French Acadia. If Beauséjour falls, there will be nothing to stop the English from marching through French Acadia all the way to Quebec."

Eulalie said: "Nothing but Beausoleil." Monsieur l'Abbé threw her a glance meant to remind her of her place.

Beau-père added: "And Louisbourg."

The Abbé said to him, as though Eulalie hadn't spoken, "Louisbourg can only guard the seaways. And Beausoleil can't fight all the English armies." Beau-père shrugged as though that had yet to be proven. "This is not just a matter of kings and flags, Joseph Brossard. If it were only that, do you think that at my age I would put myself sneaking through the backwoods of a province that has a price on my head?

"You Acadians of Nova Scotia think the English have tolerance for your faith—because they allow you a few priests. How long do you think that tolerance will last once England is at war with His Most Christian Majesty?

"Any Acadian foolish enough to stay in an English province will someday see his grandchildren lose their faith and their language and their souls. You should move your family to French Acadia as soon as you can. But in the meanwhile, the message I am risking my life to spread is that all true sons of the Church must hurry immediately to Fort Beauséjour, to help stop the Antichrist from raping New France."

Beau-père coughed and slapped his chest and gasped: "Would to God I was a few years younger, Father, and my lungs not so rotted out. I am sure our friend the tinker wishes he could march with you, too—perhaps he can find his own way to Fort Beauséjour when his leg heals."

"Your oldest son looks big enough to shoulder a musket."

"Henri?" Beau-père laughed. "Yes, he is big enough—but terrified to death of gunpowder. The one time I tried to get him to fire my musket, he shook so hard he couldn't hit the barn!"

Eulalie had once seen Henri lean out the house door and drop a wolf lurking by the sheep pen, but she decided not to mention it. She shot her eyes at Henri to make sure he had the sense to swallow his father's insult.

The Abbé Le Loutre said: "Boys can be trained out of their fears. For far too long, Joseph Brossard, some Acadians have been growing fat on their farms while others have done the fighting for their rights."

Cully Robin suddenly laughed, slapping his forehead, and crowed: "*Musket!* Chucklehead that I am! How many days, Uncle, have I been promising to clean your musket to make myself a little useful? And I never remember till I'm falling asleep at night. Eulalie, would you reach me down your father's musket? And you might was well bring mine, too, so's I can clean them both while I'm at it. Chucklehead..." He chuckled like the village idiot, grinning at the Abbé Le Loutre glowering at him like he must be the village idiot.

Eulalie had no idea what had taken possession of Cully, but she moved to bring him the guns anyway, and the pouches that went with them. The Abbé shrugged off the fool's interruption and spoke intently to Beau-père. "And there is another message, Joseph Brossard, I want you to pass on to the people of Piziquid. I would carry it there myself, except that the stinking Protestants have a garrison there now. You don't sell provisions to Fort Edward, do you?"

"Certainly not. Well, maybe sometimes an English soldier steps up to Eulalie at market to buy an egg or two, and she can't say no without causing trouble, but other than that..."

Eulalie's eyes dwelt on Cully's clever hands playing over the carbine and the musket. It seemed to her that his hands were making an exaggerated show out of working the cleaning rod down the barrels and inspecting the flints. Her eyes travelled up to his face. His eyes had gone bright and hard and his cheeks pale with a streak of a flush across the cheekbones. He was breathing in a slow and steady rhythm, as though counting out the beats for each breath.

She looked down at his hands again. He wasn't cleaning the guns—he was loading them with buckshot and cocking them. For all the cleverness of his hands, anyone who looked closely would see that that's what he was doing.

Eulalie snatched her eyes away and said loudly: "Would you like some more tea, Monsieur l'Abbé?"

"Yes, bless you, child. Joseph Brossard, the message you must pass on to the people of Piziquid is that I *will excommunicate* anyone who sells provisions to the English—beyond, of course, the egg or two someone like your daughter must sell to avoid trouble.

"Tell them at Piziquid that if they are not wise enough to pay heed to the judgement that will come down on them in the next life, they should pay heed that my

Mi'kmaqs—who are truer servants of His Most Christian Majesty than some French-men—will make them pay for it in *this* life. Now, I have many leagues to cover before daylight..."

Beau-père wheezed: "Give me a hand up from my chair, Eulalie. No, no, Monsieur l'Abbé—the least I can do is walk you to the door. May your holy work accomplish what it deserves."

Monsieur l'Abbé paused in the doorway. It seemed to Eulalie that his eyes lingered on Henri and then shifted to Cully. Then the Abbé Le Loutre and his friends were gone and Beau-père was closing the door behind them.

Eulalie opened her mouth, but Beau-père held up his hand and stayed by the door, listening. Finally he nodded and hung up his cane. Eulalie let out a long breath and heard Cully doing the same. Beau-père pointed at the loaded guns leaned across Cully's splinted leg and laughed: "The English would've paid you one hell of a re-ward—if his friends had let you live to collect it."

"I was praying like hell he wouldn't make me use them. Not that I had any intention to shoot him—suicide's a sin. I was just going to stick one muzzle in his guts and point the other at his friends in the doorway, and make him swear the sacredest oath you could think of to leave peacefully and without Henri."

Beau-père shrugged: "He would've gave you his word and then broke it. But as it is I think you made him think twice about things."

There was a kind of breezy giddiness in the air that Eulalie recognized from times when herding an angry bull or rooting a skunk out from under the henhouse came off with no harm done. She slowed the trembling in her hands enough to pick up the guns to put them back where they belonged. She knew that the trembling wasn't just from stretched nerves going loose again. Part of it was because the tinker with the whip-scarred back had been willing to chance his life for no reason but the good of her family.

As she carried the guns away, she heard Cully say to Beau-père: "You don't seem fond of Monsieur l'Abbé."

"I wouldn't piss down his throat if his heart was on fire." From the way Cully laughed, that old Acadian expression hadn't yet found its way to the Channel Islands or France. "There was an Acadian village called Beaubassin, on the Nova Scotia side of Fort Beauséjour. I say 'was' because all the king's men in Fort Beauséjour and Quebec kept telling the people of Beaubassin to move to French Acadia, but the people wouldn't leave their homes. So, five years ago—"

"Six," Eulalie put in.

"Six?" *Beau-Père* looked doubtful, then shrugged acquiescence. "Mi'kmaqs came in the night and burned Beaubassin to the ground, so the people had no choice but to move to the French side, where I hear they've been starving since then. Maybe there was some French soldiers with the Mi'kmaqs, too, and maybe it was on orders from Quebec or France, but there is no doubt it was Le Loutre who sent the Mi'kmaqs to burn Beaubassin. The ship that brought him here from France was called *The Bizarre*—sometimes the good God tries to send us warnings in funny ways."

Eulalie said, in all fairness, "They do say The Abbé loves the Mi'kmaqs dearly, and that's why he hates the English."

Beau-père said: "Oh, yes, he loves *his* Mi'kmaqs dearly—so dearly that he makes them kill Englishmen whenever they can, which makes the English keep up the bounty on Mi'kmaq scalps."

Eulalie handed Hélène a candle to light the younger children out for their *fais dodo* trip to the outhouse. Beau-père said: "But I guess he must have a good side to him hidden somewhere—they say he and Beausoleil are great friends."

"That doesn't follow like the night the day, Beau-père. Maybe it means Beausoleil has a bad side to him. You know why they put him in jail at Annapolis Royal."

"Which time?"

"Marie Gonsile."

"Oh, that was thirty years ago, Beausoleil was a young man."

"That's no excuse."

Beau-père puttered his lips and waved his hands. Cully said: "I don't know why they put Beausoleil in jail at Annapolis Royal."

Eulalie looked around the room to make sure the younger children were still outside, then said: "He fathered a child and refused to pay even a little allowance for the mother to raise the baby."

Beau-père said: "The child wasn't his."

"He *said* it wasn't. You think a woman wouldn't notice who fathered her baby?"

"You think a man wouldn't notice there was no chance it was him? You shouldn't pass judgement, Eulalie, on things that happened before you were born. I heard the story when it happened, and there was more to it than someone told you at market thirty years after. Marie Gonsile's mother and father said they would rather raise the child themselves, and with no allowance to them, than have their daughter raise it. That's the kind of woman Marie Gonsile was."

Eulalie was quite sure there had to be more to it than Beau-père's "more to it". But he was right that it was foolish to argue judgements over something that happened thirty years ago to people they'd never met. And there was no point arguing with Beau-père about Beausoleil anyway—even though he'd never met the man who carried his same name, he wouldn't hear a word against him.

Beau-père turned to Cully and said: "I shouldn't let Monsieur l'Abbé leave a heretic whoreson Protestant with the notion that all our priests are like that. The parish priest at Piziquid would no more threaten excommunication for politics than bite the head off a dog. Le Loutre is a mad dog."

Cully said: "Um, if you'll forgive an ignorant heretic confessing his ignorance... Before I—came to Nova Scotia..." It seemed to Eulalie that he'd just caught himself from saying 'before I' something else. "...everyone told me that Acadians were all slaves to their religion and their priests. Goes to show you what 'everyone' knows."

"But..." Eulalie said perplexedly—perplexed that someone who'd seen so much couldn't see something so obvious, "...religion and the Church are not always the same thing, thank the good God."

s summer ripened in the valley of Ardoise, Cully began to have dangerous thoughts. In fourteen years of soldiering he'd seen a few executions of deserters—and the colonel of his regiment was particularly inventive when it came to making examples. But Nova Scotia was an easier place to disappear in than England. He'd heard stories of deserters who'd been taken in by the Mi'kmaqs. The stories suggested that those deserters would likely live to a spry old age with their brown grandchildren playing about their knees.

If a man could lose himself among the Mi'kmaqs, why not the Acadians? He could grow his beard out, take another name, pretend to be an immigrant from another part of Acadia... He could see no reason why the Brossards and their friends should find it any more difficult to lie to the British authorities than to the Abbé Le Loutre.

The Acadians had a way of fitting themselves into the world that appealed to him. One morning at breakfast, Joseph Brossard announced: "Well, I'd say we're between the getting-ready seasons now. Spring is getting-ready for summer, fall is getting-ready for winter, and in between we do what we like. So, today I think I'd like to go down to my pole garden and harvest a few for the calf pen."

Cully said: "Pole garden?"

"You know the stand of poplars down by the hollow the stream flows through?"

"I certainly know the hollow the stream flows through."

"Well, some people will tell you the poplar is a nuisance tree—because the wood is so soft and they grow so fast. If you let a pair of poplars grow tall, they send out shoots with saplings growing all around. You have a garden of living poles—just pick the size you need today. And just by harvesting the ones you need when you need them, by coincidence you keep them from growing into a forest of poplars marching up the hill.

"If you think something's a nuisance, it's a nuisance. But if you think: 'Maybe the good God is trying to do me a favour somehow...'"

Cully's leg was only splinted along the calf now, instead of up past the knee, and he was able to get around with a crutch he'd cobbled together. That still didn't enable him to do much useful beyond carrying baskets of fresh-picked peas for Eulalie, but that gave him an excuse to go out in the garden with her.

Eulalie La Tour had brought something back to him that he'd forgotten long ago. In the world where he'd lived all his adult life, the only three forms a woman could take were a ha'penny whore, a crick-backed laundry drudge, or a soldier's wife with nothing but a blanket on a string to separate herself and her squalling brats from the rest of the barracks. Some women existed in all three forms at once. But Eulalie had reminded him that a woman could be something more than that—just as a man could be something more than a bloodybacked marching machine who could only tell one month from another by whether he'd pissed away his pay in one night or two.

He had a fancy that he and Eulalie had a private bond, since both of them had had their childhood stolen away. In her case it had happened by being orphaned young and then becoming mother to seven children before she was old enough to bear one of her own. Anyone who'd had the chance to be a child could never truly understand someone who hadn't.

The family was just sitting down to their mid-day meal when Rouge and Noir set up a racket outside. Joseph Brossard went to look out the door and said: "We have visitors," and went back to his chair. He left the door hanging open and left his cane still hanging beside it, so Cully assumed the visitors must be friends.

There was the sound of several horses approaching, and a moment later four Mi'kmaq men walked through the door. They were in off-duty dress, rather than Full Parade Uniform—no face paint, and very little ornament to break the mud-coloured anonymity of their deerskin shirts and leggings.

They sat down on the floor and Eulalie filled four plates for them. In between bites, they and Joseph Brossard carried on a conversation in a mixture of French and Mi'kmaq. From the parts that Cully could follow, he gathered that there were more fish in the Piziquid River this year than last, and that these particular Mi'kmaqs were no fonder of the Abbé Le Loutre than Joseph Brossard was. Cully also got the distinct impression that some of the conversation in Mi'kmaq was curiosity about the splint-legged stranger—although he couldn't catch any of the four looking directly at him.

There seemed to be something familiar about the Mi'kmaq who was doing most of the talking. Cully finally placed it, more by the voice than the face. The last time they'd met, the top half of the gentleman's face had been painted black, and he'd been bobbling a tomahawk in his hand.

Cully couldn't think of anything to do or say, though, about the fact that one of the horses he'd heard approaching might well be his stolen Maudit. He just hoped the French-speaking Mi'kmaq wouldn't ask him if he were still planning to join Beausoleil, which would give him one more thing to lie about to Eulalie and her stepfather.

When the Mi'kmaqs took their leave, the one who'd done most of the talking paused in the doorway just long enough to turn his eyes on Cully and say in French: "Since you friend to our friends, we give you back you horse. *Natoa-nsen* can walk."

The heads around the table turned from the empty doorway to Cully. When he told them more-or-less what had happened, there was much jolly laughter. Cully didn't join in the laughter. Getting his horse back meant he had to face reality. Although his leg still wasn't healed enough to walk to Fort Edward, he could ride if he took it slow. Captain Namon was undoubtedly there by now, but might not be for much longer.

Cully looked down at the table and saw his ridiculous fancies evaporating out of the pores in the wood. The rest of his life had been determined from the instant he'd reached out his idiot hand to take the recruiting sergeant's shilling. Since that instant, the only decision left in his own hands was whether to summon up enough wit to make that life as comfortable as possible—which in this case meant making damned sure he kept his rendezvous with Captain Namon.

Cully looked up from the table and said: "Well... Well... As I said, there is a man I have to meet at the end of the road..."

Eulalie La Tour crossed her arms under her breasts and looked down at her knees.

ulalie and Beau-père and all of the children helped the tinker load his tool sack onto his horse and helped him up onto the saddle. Beau-père handed him up his gun, and then said: "Now, children, say good-bye to Cully quickly and come inside. I have something very important to tell you."

The children protested, but did as they were told—Josette holding up her new-headed doll for 'the surgeon' to kiss good-bye. Eulalie watched the door close behind the rest of the family, then looked up at Cully Robin, who was looking down at her. He said: "I never thought I'd regret it that broken bones don't stay broke forever. I will think of you wherever I am."

He looked so sad it made her eyes wet. He leaned down carefully, cupped his hand on the back of her head and kissed her. It wasn't a brotherly kiss, or a fatherly kiss, or a kiss from one cousin to another. Then he straightened back up and said: "Good-bye, Eulalie."

"Good-bye, Cully." She knew better than to ask him if he'd ever be passing by this way again. She watched the horse carry him out of the valley of Ardoise and out of her life. Just before he disappeared into the woods around the stream at the bottom of the pasture, he turned and waved.

Eulalie turned back toward the house, telling herself not to be so foolish. After all, she'd only known the tinker for a few weeks, and saying good-bye to him was nothing compared to what she'd had to learn to live with when she was just a girl. She'd had to say good-bye to her entire family when her mother and father were put in the ground and her brothers and sisters scattered among various aunts and uncles throughout Acadia. And she'd had to say good-bye to her second mother, Aunt Marguerite, just when she was getting used to calling her *Maman*. Losing a tinker who'd been part of the household for a few weeks was nothing to cry about.

When Eulalie opened the door, the children were all sitting around the table, and it was obvious their father had been driving them to distraction by skirting around the 'something important' he had to tell them. When he saw her come through the door, he said to them gravely: "What it is I have to tell you, my little cabbages, is this: I know it seems to you now that the summer will last forever, but it won't. So you'd best enjoy it while you can. So hurry along with you now to all the chores and games you have to do outside."

They howled in fury at yet another of his so-called 'jokes', but he shooed them outside and closed the door behind them. Then he turned to Eulalie and raised his hand to gently coast one crack-callused fingertip under the corners of her eyes. He said: "I had got used to having him around, but I'm glad he got his horse back and could leave before we expected. I was growing afraid you might do something you would regret."

"Regret...?"

"He is a hard man not to like, but it isn't by accident that a man his age has no home of his own. You could bring a coyote pup into the house, and raise it up just like Rouge and Noir, but it would still run for the woods when the moon is high. You know as well as I do that for all Cully's funny stories about his travels, there are some things he never spoke of."

"I do, Beau-père."

"We Acadians have a blessed life. I may have only seen a little of the outside world, but enough to make me know that. There are things out there I hope you will never have to see. Whether or not you like it, or he likes it, that is the world he lives in."

"Yes, Beau-père."

But when she went to change the linen on her bed, the bed-cabinet smelled of him, and she knew it still would when she closed herself into it for the night.

XI

ndré Melanson looked at his finished cart wheels and sighed. Last night he'd lain awake picturing himself riding out of the woods behind Joseph Brossard's farm, with Daisy's harness mate following behind carrying the cart wheels. But in the cold light of day he had to admit that one wheel was more oval than round, and the axle hole in the other was slanted. But he could see where he'd gone wrong, and it wouldn't take nearly as long to do it right the second time—especially since most of the spokes and one of the hubs could be used again.

He took down a mallet and knocked the wheels apart. Then he saw by the sun that it was time to catch and halter Daisy if he hoped to be in the valley of Ardoise in time for his regular Tuesday evening visit.

He hadn't got far down the road when he saw another horseman coming toward him, on a scruffy saddlehorse two hands shorter than Daisy. The man rode oddly, with one foot in the stirrup and the other leg hanging stiffly. A little closer and André saw it was the tinker.

They reined in when they came up to each other. The tinker told him the story of his horse, in such a way that André found himself laughing even though he was hardly fond of the man. André said: "So, will you be back this way next year, when the pots you mended are ready to be mended again?"

"I'd call that doubtful—not doubtful that my mending might turn out to not be worth a tinker's dam; doubtful that I'll be back again. The man I'm supposed to meet in Piziquid has promised to pave my way to places I've not seen before. No, I'd say I can say for certain, that after today no one in Nova Scotia will ever see Cully the Tinker again."

André just nodded, pursing his mouth to keep it from breaking into a grin.

"André—I hope you won't take this amiss, but you know I've seen more of the world than you have..." André refrained from saying: *Yes, Father Time.* "I hope you know what a lucky man you are."

"I do." André leaned out from his horse to shake the tinker's hand. "Go safely."

"Well, if I don't, I hope there's another great lunk of a farmboy to pull me out of what I step in."

André clapped his heels against Daisy's ribs. She broke into a trot that bounced him up and down like a cork on a spring, but he didn't mind. He hadn't noticed before that the wild apple trees were already beginning to show green nubs of fruit, and that the roadside was bright with fireweed. The only shadow in the bright haze of summer was that he was a little ashamed of his own jealousies and suspicions. The tinker wasn't such a bad fellow after all.

XII

⸙

The sun was setting by the time Maudit's reined-back walk plodded Cully to Fort Edward. Long before he saw the fort, he could see the Union Jack floating above it and smelled salt water. He came to a hill perched between two rivers flowing into an inlet of the bay. The road climbed the hill and ended at the gates of Fort Edward. The "fort" could've been plunked down in Halifax market without disturbing anything, but looked like a place where a soldier could sleep securely: sloping, green earthworks topped by log ramparts, with a dry moat and a drawbridge.

The drawbridge was down and the gates hadn't been closed for the night, but a sentry blocked Cully's way. "State your business."

Cully started to reply in French, then caught himself. After six weeks, English felt a little awkward in his mouth. "I was appointed to meet an officer here. Captain Namon."

The sentry suddenly grew less obstructive, even nervous. "In the blockhouse, sir. Anyone there will know where to find him."

"Thank you."

The inside of Fort Edward wasn't any more monumental than the outside: a couple of squared-log barracks buildings, a powder magazine and a two-storeyed blockhouse like a whittled mushroom, the second storey wider than the first. Most of the open space between the buildings was taken up with tents. Fort Edward seemed to be housing a lot more troops than it was built for.

A couple of off-duty loungers helped Cully down off his horse and up the blockhouse steps. He wanted to tell them he was one of them, that they didn't have to hold up that wall that soldiers maintained for ignorant civilians. But he didn't know whether Captain Namon wanted him to reveal that.

Inside the blockhouse, a rough-planked set of stairs led up to the second storey. The private stationed at the foot of the stairs clattered up to the top, rapped on the trap door and called: "A Mister Robin to see Captain Namon."

Cully didn't hear the reply, but the private heaved the trap open with a bang, clattered back down the stairs and helped Cully to hobble up them. The big trapdoor looked new and temporary, pink against the gray railings it hooked to.

The second storey of the blockhouse was a gun battery, with cannons on three sides poking out through loopholes at the rivers and the bay. Captain Namon had set up shop in the open space in the middle. There was a traveling trunk, a cot and a small desk. Sitting behind the desk was the back of a large map, unrolled like a sideways scroll, with a pudgy hand at either end.

The map stayed in place until Cully was standing in front of the desk, leaning on his crutch, and the private gone back down to his post. When the trap door thumped down again, Captain Namon lowered the map and rolled it up. The yellow eyes flicked over Cully and his crutch, and Captain Namon said: "Ah, that explains it."

"Explains what, sir?" Their voices echoed in the room made to accommodate several gun crews rolling cannons back and forth.

"What took you so bloody long. Another two days and I would've been gone."

"I broke my leg, sir."

"So I can see. Not before you accomplished your purpose, I hope."

"No, sir. Most of it, at least. There was a few places I didn't get to, but..." Cully reached into his shirt for the waterproof-wrapped notebook, struggling to maintain his balance on the crutch and one foot.

Captain Namon leaned forward to take the notebook and waved Cully toward the cot. "You'd best sit down and put your leg up, while I peruse your handiwork... It's smeared!"

"I fell in a creek, sir."

"The same time you broke your leg?" Captain Namon spoke without raising his eyes from riffling through the notebook.

"Yes, sir—trying to wade a flood I shouldn't've tried to wade."

"You should've ridden your horse."

"My horse was stolen, sir. But I got her back."

"Lucky for you—that horse is Crown property." Captain Namon still hadn't looked up from the notebook. "But this still seems legible. Yes, this should do nicely." He closed the notebook, opened one of the desk drawers and tossed out a small canvas bag that clinked when Cully caught it. "I believe I said ten."

"You did, sir."

"I'll see that you are quartered, and attended by the surgeon, *Sergeant* Robin."

"Thank you, sir."

"You'll have Fort Edward almost to yourself while you knit back to marching condition. The reason I'll be gone in two days is that all but a skeleton guard will be sailing to join a flotilla from Boston and Annapolis Royal."

"Making for Fort Beauséjour."

Captain Namon leaned back in his chair and raised one puffy eyebrow. "Well, well... It seems you were cut out for a spy."

"It was only a rumour I heard along the road. The French seem to know nothing more than that there *may* be an assault on Beauséjour sometime this year."

"I see. And what do the Acadians propose to do about this rumoured assault?"

"Nothing, sir, so far as I could tell. They don't seem to be getting their sporrans in a knot about it—except for worrying what a battle at Beauséjour might mean for the Acadians who live around there. The French have sent out agents to try and drum up volunteers, but they don't seem to be having much luck."

Captain Namon had suddenly grown very still. "Which...'agents'...?"

It occurred to Cully that if he mentioned the Abbé Le Loutre's visit to the valley of Ardoise, Joseph Brossard and his family would be guilty of not reporting it. "As I said, sir, all I heard was rumours." After all, punishing a few hapless farmers caught in the middle wasn't going to help His British Majesty defeat His Most Christian Majesty.

"I see." Captain Namon propped his elbow on the desk rim and his chin on his fist and looked at Cully with such detached interest that Cully felt like a naturalist's specimen. After the yellow eyes had pinned him to the wall for what seemed like a very long time, Captain Namon said: "You are new to the spying business, Sergeant Robin, and seem unlikely to pursue it to further experience. So I will tell you something you likely won't get the opportunity to learn. The greatest danger to a spy is not that of getting caught out and shot, or strung up by an annoyed mob."

"It isn't?"

"No. The greatest danger is that he will play his part so well, he begins to feel more sympathy with the people he is pretending to be one of than where his true allegiance lies. Has anything of that sort been happening to you?"

"Not at all, sir. I ain't forgot I volunteered to spend my life serving my king and country. But I can tell you, now as you've paid me for that list, I do think you're going to get less use out of it than you think you might."

"Why is that?"

"Because I don't think you're going to have to root out a lot of Acadians trying to help the King of France. There's no doubt the Acadians would find it more convenient having a governor who spoke their language and went to the same church, but they'd rather live with the inconvenience than die for the *fleurs de lis*. It seems to me all they really want is to be let alone."

"Oh, is that how it seems to you?"

"Yes, sir."

"Well. So that is how it seems to you. *Corporal of the Guard!*" Cully flinched at Captain Namon's sudden bellow, and at the boots thundering up the stairs and stamping to attention. "See that Sergeant Robin is settled into a quiet bed to convalesce in. Even if he recovers completely before I return, he is not to be assigned any duties, as I still have a use for him."

"Yessir, Captain Namon. Just put your arm on my shoulder there, Sergeant Robin—upsy-daisy. Just down the stairs and across to barracks. Accident, was it, Sergeant, or a brush with the enemy—?"

The corporal's fraternal chatter was cut off by a drawl from behind: "Oh, and Sergeant Robin...?"

Cully and the corporal paused on the stairway and Cully looked back across a floor now level with his chest. Captain Namon seemed to make a technique of 'Oh, and...' to people about to escape his presence. "Yes, sir?"

"You will find, Sergeant, in your newly-elevated rank, that you will occasionally come across a corporal who will occasionally fail to report to you that he found a young recruit asleep on sentry-go. You will find you have to exercise your discretion as to whether to discipline said corporal, or whether there's been no harm done and let sleeping dogs lie—so long as they don't lie to you too often."

"Yes, sir."

As the Corporal of the Guard gently shuffled Cully down the stairs, the corporal murmured: "Meaning no disrespect to our betters, Sergeant, but *that* one'd put a cold sweat up a polar bear's arse."

"Bugger disrespect—he'd take it as a compliment."

When Cully was settled into a curtained-off bed in the sergeants' quarters, with his ten guineas and new uniform in the footlocker, the fort surgeon came to look over his leg. The surgeon pronounced somewhat frostily that the joiner had done a surprisingly competent job for a man without benefit of formal training, but that Cully must stay confined to his bed because the ride to Fort Edward had set back the healing.

Cully lay dozing in the gathering gloom, listening to the murmurs of the other sergeants and thinking of all the reasons he should be pleased with the way things had turned out. But whenever his eyes opened on the halberd propped in the corner of his cubicle, he couldn't help but think of the reason a sergeant carried a ten-foot pike as his badge of office—so he could hold it crosswise across the backs of his men and shove them forward into the enemies' guns. No doubt it was much better to be one of the shovers than one of the shoved, but it didn't feel much better.

XIII

ndré Melanson was malleting a peg into the first of his new pair of cart wheels when his father stuck his head in the shed and said: "Leave that for now, André—the tide is going out. Time for the *corvé*."

André stepped out into the yard where his mother and younger brothers and some of the neighbour women were setting out trestle tables for the *corvé*. In a *corvé*, everyone in the community contributed food and work for a day, or until the job at hand was done. Hand-me-down stories had told André that back in France *corvé* meant an all-hands task demanded by the whims of the *seigneur*. In Acadia, *corvé* had come to mean a task demanded by the whims of nature.

André followed his father down the bank and into the barley field that had been a tidal marsh in his great-grandfather's day. At the far end of the field was a long, green, sloping wall. André could see that the ragged cleft in the top of the wall had grown wider since yesterday, and that the high tide had bearded the cleft with seaweed.

Other men from all over Piziquid were heading in that direction. Some of them were André's older brothers, some of them were cousins so many times removed that only an Acadian would consider them relations. Although the break in the levee was on André's father's property, the dike protected all their fields, and it was up to all of them together to keep it sound—just as it had been up to all their grandfathers and great-grandfathers together to build it.

Like the other men, André kicked off his wooden shoes before climbing up the levee to look down into the hole. All agreed that it looked to be the work of the *petite bête maudit*—their far-from pet name for the muskrats who liked to dig dens in the base of the levee that would eventually cave in.

André's father said: "Well, cursing won't mend it," and no one had to say anything more for the work to organize itself. Some of them went back to what once had been the shoreline to start cutting sods, some relayed the sods to the levee, and some stayed at the cleft to lay the sods in place and weave them together so they would hold until their roots grew down into each other.

André enjoyed it. It was hard work, but that was what arms and backs were for. He liked the well-worn jokes in the air. And he liked the gambling feeling that there was something urgently needing to be done before the tide came back in, but that there were likely enough hands who knew what they were doing to get it done in time.

André's father called: "André, the seaweed that washed in might've clogged the *aboiteau* when the seawater washed back out." André waved to show that he'd heard and went back to the barn. Propped across the rafters were several very long poles with the bark still on, trimmed to leave a fork at the thin end. He carried one of the poles back to the levee and crouched down beside what a stranger would think was just an open-ended wooden box sticking out of the base of the grassy slope.

The *aboiteau* was actually a square wooden tunnel running from the inland side of the levee to the outer side, with a wooden flap in the middle that was hinged to only swing outward. Rainwater or snow-melt draining off the fields could flow out the *aboiteau* at low tide, but when the tide came in, salt water trying to invade would press the gate shut and seal itself out. André had a reverence for *aboiteaus*. Much of what he'd learned over the years of helping his father had to do with *aboiteaus*: building them, mending broken ones, and replacing ones that had caved in with age. Many people took them for granted, but André knew it was only that simple invention that allowed Acadians to have rich, level fields in a country that was mostly thick-treed, rocky hills.

André pushed his pole in until it touched on something soft jammed against the hard surface of the gate. He pushed with a little more strength, flapping the gate open, and kept on pushing until his end of the pole was in as far as his elbow. He left it there, climbed over the levee, squelched his toes in tidal mud and tugged out the tongue of seaweed dangling from the mouth of the *aboiteau*. Then he went back and pulled his pole out and pushed it back in at another angle. His father always said that it was better he push his pole in too many times than not enough.

The sun was going down, and the last sods being stamped down, when a male voice called to André's father from the inland edge of the field. André looked in that direction and saw that it was Uncle Thomas from Grand Pré, on the bayshore near Cape Blomidon. André's father called back: "Well, Thomas, it is good of you to come all the way from Grand Pré to help us mend our levee, but as you can see you show up just as the work is finished—as usual." The other men laughed, but Uncle Thomas didn't laugh with them or call back a friendly insult of his own, which was unusual. Neither did Uncle Thomas climb down off the bank and cross the field toward them.

Even through the salt smell of the incoming tide, André could smell the *tourtières*, fish stew, fresh-baked bread and other good things on the trestle tables in the yard behind Uncle Thomas. The other men picked up their tools and headed in that direction. André fell in beside his father, already tasting *bouillabaisse* in the depths of his stomach.

He suddenly remembered it was Thursday, but far too late to set off for the valley of Ardoise. He would have to explain to Eulalie on Sunday. One of the many things he liked about Eulalie was that he knew she would understand immediately when he said there'd been a *corvé* to mend a break in the levee. One of the other things he liked about her was that he knew she would also understand, without him having to embarrass himself by saying it, that he was proud his hands had been needed as much as any other man's in Piziquid.

When André and his father came up to Uncle Thomas, Uncle Thomas said: "No, I didn't come to help you mend your levee. I came to get my gun back from Fort Edward."

André's father said: "What the devil is your gun doing at Fort Edward?"

"Last night, two English soldiers came to my house, saying they'd got leave to go fishing and could they spend the night? It happens from time to time, you know, and they often leave a few pennies for their breakfast, or bring you a fish on their way back to the fort—the good God knows the army doesn't seem to feed them much but sour bacon.

"What I didn't know was that last night there were two soldiers 'going fishing' in every house at Grand Pré. At midnight, they all got up from their beds on the floor, took down the guns hanging over our fireplaces, and woke us up to tell us the governor had decreed that all our guns must be taken to Fort Edward. Whoever thought that plan up was very, very clever—no one could come to the aid of their neighbours, because we were all disarmed at once."

André said: "Why would they want your guns? They have plenty of their own."

Uncle Thomas looked at him like he was an idiot. "Because they think that when the war starts, we would use our guns to shoot them in the back for the glory of the King of France." As far as André was concerned, if that's what the English thought, they were the idiots.

André's father said: "*Merde*. How are you supposed to keep wolves from killing your cattle, or skunks from eating your chickens?"

"That is what I mean to tell the commander at Fort Edward—that our guns are no more weapons of war than our felling axes or scythes."

But André's father said more than *merde* the next day, when a proclamation was posted that all the "French Neutrals" in and around Piziquid must surrender their guns, and that all those who owned boats must surrender them as well—to prevent provisions being smuggled to Fort Beauséjour or the French outposts across the bay.

When André set off along the path to Fort Edward, carrying his gun and his father's, he met up with a neighbour he'd run with since they were old enough to run. The neighbour said: "You should tell them to take their proclamation to hell. There's so few of them here now, with so many of them gone to fight at Beauséjour, we could easily fight them off if they tried to take our guns."

André said perplexedly: "But we don't want to fight them. That's what we've been trying to tell them all along."

"Some of us do."

"Then some of us are fools. How many soldiers do you think we could shoot before a warship sails in off the bay and starts blowing up our houses?"

André and his father hid their rowboat in the woods behind the farm, but they couldn't very well pretend they'd never owned a fishing skiff. By standing on the levee in front of the farm, André could catch glimpses of their skiff out in the harbor, looped together with the other impounded boats like a flock of wooden sheep rising and falling with the tide.

André scratched his mark on a petition from everyone at Piziquid and Grand Pré, telling the governor that their obedience to his order should prove they were all good and loyal subjects, but they needed their guns and boats back if they were to keep on feeding themselves and His British Majesty's soldiers. It turned out lucky that André's father decided there was too much to do at home to be one of the delegation that took the petition to Halifax. Governor Lawrence was so insulted at having one of his decisions questioned that he locked up the delegation on an island in Halifax harbor.

In every other summer of André's life, he could always look to people like his mother and father, or old Joseph Brossard, to tell him what to expect of the season by comparing it to all the different kinds of summers they'd seen before. This summer, they all seemed as baffled as he was.

<h1 style="text-align: center;">XIV</h1>

 hen Fort Beauséjour fell to the English, stories about the siege and its sudden ending even found their way to the valley of Ardoise. Eulalie quickly discovered that she didn't like war stories, particularly ones where some of the unnamed people killed had been Acadians. One of them could've been Henri, if the Abbé Le Loutre had had his way.

The one happy story from Beauséjour was that the Abbé Le Loutre was gone from Acadia. He had preached to the defenders that they must fight to their last drop of blood, and then slipped out the back gate for Quebec. Beausoleil, of course, had acted differently. The story went that he and his *couriers de bois* had attacked the English camp from the woods on the day the fort surrendered, to let the English know that even with Beauséjour gone it still wasn't safe for them to venture into French Acadia.

The part of the war stories that seemed to interest Beau-père most was that the troops who'd taken Beauséjour would be holding over at Piziquid for a while on their way home. He took a ham out of the cellar and bundled some pullets into a wicker cage. Eulalie put on her market shawl, tied her white cap under her chin, and Henri and Jacques helped her carry the extra load out to the road to wait for Uncle Benoni.

When they got to Piziquid, Uncle Benoni had to slow his ox to a crawl and manoeuver carefully. The marketplace was choked with red-coated soldiers, slouch-hatted militia from the Boston colonies, and even a few tattooed and scalplocked warriors from a tribe Eulalie had never seen before. When Uncle Benoni told her they were Mohawks, she laughed out loud. He said poutily: "Well, they *are*. You think I don't know?"

"I believe you. I'm not laughing at you, Uncle Benoni. But how many times have you heard a Mi'kmaq say that the reason his canoe went missing or her wigwam caught on fire was because the Mohawks sneak up here and cause trouble? Well, now they can point and say: 'You see? The Mohawks *do* come up here!"

Uncle Benoni angled his cart around to transform it into a market stall, then went off to join the knot of Piziquid men drinking cider in the shade, while Eulalie hiked herself up onto the cart-rim and called out: "*Jambon! Poulets!*"

Beau-père was once again proved wise in the ways of money. In no time at all she had sold her ham and pullets for twice what they would've fetched last week. She even managed to sell a couple of Uncle Benoni's little wood-carvings to Boston militiamen looking for souvenirs to take back to their families. Trade wasn't inhibited by the fact that the only English she knew was the numbers from one to twenty and the difference between a shilling and a penny.

"Eulalie!" It was a laughing young Acadian woman on the arm of a New Englander. The woman slipped her arm free and came skipping over to Eulalie.

A lot of Acadians around Piziquid weren't inclined to smile back at Barbe Thibodeau, because they thought her far too friendly with the English soldiers. It would've been the same if it were French soldiers, or Basque fishermen. But Eulalie didn't particularly like the feeling of looking down her nose at someone she used to play *bouton* with, and she didn't particularly think her own nose long enough for looking down. One of the many things Eulalie never regretted about living on a farm tucked away in the backwoods, was that she never had to concern herself with the neighbours' opinions of anyone or anything.

Barbe Thibodeau exclaimed: "Have you ever seen so many men at Piziquid market before?"

"No. It's certainly good for business."

"It certainly is!"

Eulalie decided that she didn't want to know exactly what Barbe meant by that, so she just said: "Beau-père will be disappointed that he didn't send more chickens with me, and that all these hungry men will be gone by the next time I come to market."

"Oh no they won't. *Les Bostonais* are all grumbling that they have to stay here for they don't know how long."

"Why? They came to take Fort Beauséjour and they took it, what's left for them to do here?"

"They don't know. Those are their orders. Oh! There's that captain who wanted to flirt with me. Say *bonjour* for me to old Joseph à Jacques à Thomas—and ask him if he and his money don't get lonely out there in the valley of Ardoise...?"

The next time Eulalie went to market, she found that Barbe à Judith à Marie hadn't been entirely right about all the soldiers and militia being ordered to stay at Piziquid. Some of them were still there, camped around the base of the hill Fort

Edward stood on. But some of them had gone to Grand Pré, and some of them had gone further down the bay to Annapolis Royal, where the first Acadians had taken root in the long-ago days of Charles La Tour. But none of them had gone back to Boston or Halifax.

Eulalie didn't like it. They'd done what they'd come to do, why didn't they go home?

XV

ndré and his father and brothers had just finished the last haying of the summer when a proclamation went out from the commander at Fort Edward to all the people of Piziquid and the surrounding area. *"All men both young and old, including the lads of ten years of age,"* were to assemble at Fort Edward *"on Friday, the fifth September, at three of the clock in the afternoon."* At that time, the Officer Commanding would *"communicate to them in person"* the resolution which His Excellency the Governor had formed *"respecting the matter proposed to the inhabitants."* It seemed that His Excellency the Governor was *"desirous that each of them should be satisfied with His Majesty's intentions, which he has also ordered us to communicate to you, as they have been given to him."*

It wasn't an offhanded invitation—*"no excuse will be admitted on any pretence whatsoever on pain of forfeiting goods and chattels, in default of realestate."*

It didn't take long for word to come to Piziquid that the commanding officers at Grand Pré and Annapolis Royal had issued the same proclamation, ordering an assembly in the church at Grand Pré and the fort at Annapolis Royal on the same hour of the same day as the assembly at Fort Edward.

Neighbours gathered in André's parents' kitchen to try and puzzle out what the proclamation might mean. Pretty much everyone was in agreement that *"the matter proposed to the inhabitants"* had to be either the loyalty oath or the order that had confiscated their guns and boats. One thing certain from the wording of the proclamation was that the king had sent some orders to the governor, and the governor had to obey them whether he liked them or not. Maybe the king had told the governor to give them back their boats and guns, so they could keep on feeding his soldiers. Or maybe the king had told the governor to stop trying to force an unconditional oath of loyalty down their throats, because the king didn't mind having loyal subjects who would rather grow food for his armies than join them.

André said: "If it's the loyalty oath, Joseph à Jacques à Thomas has always said that if we all kept telling the governor politely we will be glad to re-swear the old oath, eventually he would have to settle for that. After all, the old oath gives everyone what they want—the king gets subjects who have sworn to be loyal to him, and we get to live in peace."

André's father said: "Joseph à Jacques à Thomas is too stubborn in many ways, but no one ever said he didn't know how to bargain."

They chewed it over for a while longer and then the neighbours all drifted home. Abraham Landry was the last to go. He paused in the doorway and smirked at André's father. It seemed that what Abraham had to say was difficult to say with a straight face. "Maybe... Maybe the king wants us all to gather together because... Because he wants us to tell his officers how to get red horses to go with their red coats." Then he stepped out quickly and closed the door behind him, but André could hear him chuckling as he made his way across the yard.

André's father glared at the door and muttered darkly: "*Merde.*" Then he turned to André with an evil glint in his eyes and said: "Well, maybe Abraham wasn't the one that done it, but he seems to want to take the credit. I think tonight, André, you and me will put an end to jolly stories of red horses."

Practical jokes were an Acadian art form, and André's father had been the butt of one that had become legendary. For years, André's father had made mock of people who believed in *les lutins*—the little people—or in will-o'-the-wisps or *loups-garous*. But then, one summer, an odd thing began to happen to his horses. Although he was just leaving them out to fend for themselves in the pasture, as he did every summer, they began to take on a sleek, glossy appearance—as though they were getting a steady diet of oats and mash, and being brushed and curry combed every night. People commented that *les lutins*—the little people—must be riding them at night. It was well known that when *les lutins* took a fancy to a particular farmer's horse, they would feed it and pamper it.

André's father had scoffed at the notion of *les lutins*, but not quite as heartily as he had before. He stopped scoffing entirely the morning he discovered that parts of Daisy's and her partner's manes had been braided into tiny stirrups, just as *les lutins* were said to do to give them a firmer seat on a horse's neck. He became so converted that he took to leaving a dish of milk outside the door for *les lutins*, even though he'd used to say that such nonsense only served to spoil the barn cats.

The culmination had come when André's father went out to the pasture one morning and found that both his horses had turned bright red overnight. He had approached the bewitched horses cautiously, and finally worked up the nerve to reach out and tentatively touch one of them. His hand came back red with fresh paint. Very human laughter had come from the woods, but by the time he'd charged across the pasture the laughers were gone.

The paint hadn't done Daisy and her partner any harm, but it had made André's father famous in a way he didn't care to be. No one ever told any Melanson who had perpetrated the long, elaborate joke, but no one forbore to tell every Melanson that it was too bad the culprits hadn't been caught red-handed.

As Abraham Landry went chuckling on his way, André's father squinted out the window and said: "Sun's almost down. It's well known that Abraham à Mathieu à Bernard sits up later than most people, smoking his pipe and sipping blackberry wine to get his bowels moving. Come along, André. And leave your shoes behind."

André followed his father out the door, down through the barley field, over the levee, and then along the tidal mud, with the dike ridge hiding them from anyone inland. By the time they drew parallel with the Landry farm, the sun was down and they had to feel their way through Abraham's cornfield. There was still a light burning in the Landrys' window. André's father tapped him on the arm and pointed to the dim silhouette of the outhouse.

When they'd snuck their way to the outhouse, André went to one side of it and his father to the other. They rocked the little shed back and forth to loosen its base frame in the ground, then André crouched down and worked his hands in under the corners while his father did the same on the other side. His father hissed: "Up!" and André put his back and legs and arms into it.

It was like lifting a horse, and not a very well-balanced horse at that—once it was lifted, André had to press his forehead against its side to keep it from overtoppling. His father gasped: "Back!" and André started shuffling sideways.

When they'd moved it back as far as its width, André's father gasped: "Down!" and they lowered it onto the weed patch behind the pit. Once they'd caught their breaths, André's father gave the little house a tentative push to make sure it wasn't going to topple over and spoil everything, then hissed: "Home!"

André was just settling into bed when he heard a distant bellowing that echoed pleasantly over the water. One of his little brothers woke up and said: "What was that?"

"Nothing. Just Abraham à Mathieu à Bernard howling at the moon. *Fais do-do.*" But the 'go to sleep' didn't take. It was difficult for anybody to sleep in a house shaking with their father's laughter.

Two days later was Friday, the Fifth of September. André spent the morning scything the weeds down where his mother wanted him to dig a new garden, beheading a couple of chickens for his mother to cook for supper, and working on his cart wheels. After a big mid-day meal of clam *chaudiere*, he and his father and the two oldest of his younger brothers stepped out the door and into their wooden shoes for the walk to Fort Edward.

André's mother caught his father by the arm and raised her hand to his cheek. His father laughed and patted her hand against his cheek and said: "There's nothing to worry about. It is only going to be some more threatening noises, or a windy way to give us back our boats without apologizing. We'll be home in time for supper and I'll tell you which it was. Maybe we'll *sail* home." He kissed the palm of her hand, turned to his sons and said: "*En avant, mes braves.*"

Along the cart trail to Fort Edward, men and boys came sifting out from every farm that hadn't been abandoned. The road passed through the village of tents the militia from New England had been living in for weeks now. All of *les Bostonais* except a few sentries seemed to have found somewhere else to be today.

The fort gates were standing open, and a hundred or so Piziquid men were already standing in the parade square waiting. The inside of Fort Edward wasn't a strange place to them. They'd been coming there every Sunday for three years, ever since the parish church burned down and the commandant offered one of his barracks buildings to hold mass. Today, though, André felt something in the air that wasn't exactly nervousness, but an anticipation of nobody knew what.

That air of uncertainty didn't prevent André's father and several other men from forming a group within hearing range of Abraham Landry, and gravely discussing whether there might be a *loup-garou* in Piziquid—they'd heard it howling night before last. André just stood at the edge of the group nodding with his mouth clamped shut. He knew he wasn't good at keeping laughter in when it wanted to get out.

The Major in command of Fort Edward stepped out onto the blockhouse steps, glanced at a huge pocketwatch and nodded at two red-coated drummer boys standing nearby. The boys began rattling their drums, the gates swung shut and streams of soldiers and militiamen poured out of the barracks and blockhouse. They clattered up the steps to the palisades and lined the walls, facing inward with their muskets at the ready. Another file of red-coated soldiers took up a position in front of the blockhouse and fixed their bayonets to their muskets.

André looked at the older men around him for some explanation of what this might mean. They were all looking at each other for the same thing.

The Major held up a rolled parchment with a red ribbon around it. He looked grim. But then, they all looked grim always, when they weren't filled with rum and chasing honest women. He began to speak loudly in English, translating himself into stiff, Parisian French as he went along.

"Gentlemen, I have received from His Excellency Governor Lawrence the King's instructions, which I hold in my hand. I have been *ordered* to inform you of His Majesty's final resolution concerning the French inhabitants of his province of Nova Scotia, who for more than half a century have had more indulgence granted to them than any of his subjects in any part of his dominions. What use you have made of it, you yourselves best know."

The Major paused and flicked his eyes around the men up on the firing ledge, and the line of bayonets in front of him, then directed his gaze again at the unarmed men and boys boxed-in between them. The gold-braided chest of the Major's coat grew wider, like a man filling his lungs before diving into deep water. In a louder voice than before, with a brass edge to it, the Major blared: "Your lands and tenements and cattle and livestock of all kinds are hereby forfeited to the Crown, with all your other effects except money and household goods."

Voices around André whispered confusedly: "Did he say 'forfeited'...?" and other voices hushed them fiercely as the Major went on.

"All French inhabitants of Nova Scotia are to be transported and dispersed throughout His Majesty's other American colonies from Georgia to Massachusetts, beyond the reach of influence from France or French possessions.

"I am directed to allow you as many of your household goods as you can take without overloading the vessels you go in. I shall do everything in my power to see that whole families are placed on the same vessel. Your families are free to continue their lives outside these walls until such time as transport can be arranged. But *you*, gentlemen, shall remain confined here, under the security of these troops which it is my honour to command.

"When the ships are ready to embark, you and your families will be reunited. I hope that in whatever part of the world your lot may fall, you may be faithful subjects and a peaceable and happy people."

There was a silence like André had never heard before. The distant whisper of the outgoing tide seemed to be sucking the air out of the world.

Someone shouted: "*Bâtards!*" But it was a weak and hopeless shout, and the surge toward the Major and his ribboned parchment came to an abrupt halt as the bayonets in front of him sloped forward. The men up on the parapet had all cocked their guns and pointed them down into the courtyard.

Even while André was still wrestling himself into believing that the Major's elegant words had actually said what they seemed to have said, he saw what a sickeningly clever plan it all was. The English would be spared the trouble and expense of herding in all the Acadian women and children, and keeping them fed and housed and guarded "until such time as transport can be arranged." The women and children were already manacled to Fort Edward by stronger chains than any jailer could devise, and when the time came they would herd *themselves* in, rather than be separated from their husbands and fathers and brothers and sons.

André saw the Major make a gesture towards a pale and puffy-looking officer standing behind the line of bayonets. That officer beckoned over his shoulder at a tallish soldier who wasn't holding a musket, and the soldier fell in behind him toward the blockhouse steps. There seemed to be something impossibly familiar about the soldier—"impossibly" because how could anyone tell one of them from another with their identical white, clubbed hair and red coats? Then André saw it was the tinker.

XVI

⁂

hen Cully heard the bull-roar of fury off to his left and getting closer, his feet automatically swung around to plant his back against the block house wall. André Melanson was charging toward him through a gap in the crowd—a gap that was quickly growing wider as his fellow Acadians scrambled out of his way. André seemed oblivious to the fact that there was a line of forward-pointing bayonets between him and Cully. The two soldiers directly in front of him braced themselves for the impact.

Cully bellowed: "No bayonets!" He blessed the British Army's training to jump without thinking, as both bayonets immediately pointed to the sky. The next soldier in the line reversed his musket and swung it against the side of André Melanson's head. André's charge turned into a sideways stumble, but he kept his feet and swung a wide right at the nearest powdered head. That soldier dropped like a rag doll, and another musket butt took André in the stomach, doubling him over.

The musket butts continued to come down on André Melanson's back and shoulders, or up against the side of his head, and he continued to swing his fists and try to grapple. There was nothing Cully could do but stand there and scream in his mind: *"Don't fight them!"*—as he wished someone had screamed at him on that long-ago day when he took the recruiting sergeant's shilling.

Finally André Melanson went down and his friends dragged him back into the crowd. Captain Namon turned to Cully and remarked: "Someone's husband?" then beckoned Cully to continue following him toward the blockhouse steps.

Cully followed in a daze. He'd had no more idea than the Acadians of what was going to be in the proclamation the Major read out to them. He suspected that no one in Fort Edward today had had any idea, except the Major himself and Captain Namon. Somebody very meticulous had been aware that if the secret leaked into the barracks, it was bound to find its way to some soldier's Acadian girlfriend or cider-supplier.

Once Cully and Captain Namon were up on the blockhouse steps, Captain Namon said to him: "Are all the men present whom you met on your tinker's foray?"

Cully looked out over the crowd. Some of them were looking up at him, but he was quite sure that no Acadian except André Melanson or the family in the valley of Ardoise had seen enough of "the tinker" to recognize him in uniform. He spotted Eulalie's Uncle Benoni, and the joiner who'd set his leg, and the boy who'd cheerfully rowed him across the Piziquid River and refused to take a farthing's payment... But neither Joseph Brossard nor any of his sons were anywhere to be seen.

Cully said: "It's difficult to say in such a crowd."

"I wasn't expecting a perfect headcount—just the best you can estimate from a cursory surveillance. Do you notice any of them missing?"

Cully swallowed the acid crawling up his throat and said: "None but those too old and broken-down to make the journey."

"Well and good. You are dismissed, Sergeant. Tomorrow you go back on active duty."

Cully wandered back to the sergeants' quarters and then wandered out again. He couldn't seem to stop walking, but he had nowhere to go. Finally he muttered: "Bugger it," and his aimless ambling became a purposeful march into the blockhouse.

A bench and a clerk's desk had been set up at the foot of the stairway to the second storey, to serve as a kind of improvised ante-room. The corporal doing door-keeper duty stood up from the bench as he saw Cully approaching. "You can't go up there, Sergeant, Captain Namon is—"

"I know what he is." Cully brushed the corporal aside and mounted the stairs, holding his right arm up to raise the trap door on the way.

Captain Namon had taken off his coat and powdered wig and was lounging on his cot with a leather-bound book and a tumbler of something amber. He looked up from his book and raised an eyebrow. Cully let the long trapdoor crash shut behind him and said: "*Ten guineas?* I thought the going rate was thirty pieces of silver."

Captain Namon took a swallow from his tumbler, smacked his lips open, exhaled and said: "Well, well—I can see I was wrong that you have the temperament for a spy. A mere three weeks out of uniform makes you forget that I could and should have you flogged for raising your voice to an officer."

Cully stood rooted to the floor as Captain Namon set down his tumbler, inserted a bookmark and closed his book, sat up, picked up his tumbler again and leaned back against the wall with his legs crossed at the ankles. "However, Sergeant, you have done me good service. And when a tool has been twisted out of shape by being used for a purpose it was not made for, the least the user can do is try to put it right.

"Those poor innocents you think you've betrayed are not near so innocent as you seem to believe. If I calculate the calendar correctly, you would still've been confined to quarters by your mending leg the day the rest of the garrison celebrated the news of the capture of two French warships off Newfoundland...?"

"I was."

"I do hope one of your fellow sergeants had the good grace to bring you up your extra measure of grog, instead of drinking it himself. Well, in the hold of one of those two French warships were found twenty large, leather bags, each containing five hundred scalping knives."

"I heard that rumour in the barracks."

"It was no rumour. Believe me, Sergeant, people do not send me *rumours* in dispatches without identifying them as such. At least, they do not do it twice.

"The careless captain of that French warship neglected to destroy the list of twenty names accompanying the twenty bags of scalping knives: various Mi'kmaq chiefs, the Abbé Le Loutre, Joseph Brossard *dit* Beausoleil... And several prominent 'innocent' Acadians of Nova Scotia."

Cully felt less sure of himself, seeing in memory the scalped corpses of a wood-cutting crew being carted back into Halifax. But he said: "Just because the French tried to send them scalping knives, doesn't mean they would've handed them out and used them. The only reason they ever helped the Abbé Le Loutre was he threatened them into it, and now he's too far away to make threats."

Captain Namon cocked his head to one side, like a hunting dog who's heard something, and said: "And just what exactly makes you so certain about the Acadians' relations with the Abbé Le Loutre?"

Cully could feel the yellow eyes pinning him to the wall again. Since he'd already lied once about Le Loutre's visit, to protect the Brossards and Eulalie, he was even more guilty than they were. The wise and careful voice of the survivor Sergeant Robin whispered inside his ear: *Cully my lad, you've gone and stepped in it again.*

Cully said: "Only what I heard the Acadians say amongst themselves in their kitchens, sir. Most of them seemed to feel no allegiance to the Abbé Le Loutre—or to the King of France, for that matter."

"If the Acadians have so little loyalty to the King of France, why do they refuse to swear loyalty to the King of England?"

"They *have*—and they'll be glad to swear the same oath again! They swore to be loyal subjects, and the king swore they'd never be press ganged."

"Yes, I'd heard that story."

"It's no *story*! I spoke to men who signed the oath, or made their mark!"

"It never happened." Cully's mouth flared open to protest; Captain Namon raised a finger and an eyebrow; Cully's mouth closed again. "I don't doubt they told you so. And I don't doubt they spoke the truth. But it never happened.

"You see, the governor of that day was an accommodating man. He found himself in a terrible position, for an accommodating man. The Lords of Trade in London wanted an unconditional oath of loyalty from the Acadians; the Acadians wanted to swear an oath which contained that one condition. Eventually, the old governor came up with a way to accommodate everyone: he told the Acadians they were swearing an oath with that one condition attached to it, and he told the Lords of Trade the Acadians had sworn an unconditional oath.

"So, our present situation, as it appears to the Lords of Trade, is this: the Acadians swore an unconditional oath of loyalty in the past, but are refusing to reaffirm it in the face of a war between England and France."

"But—"

Captain Namon raised a forefinger again. "Harken to the tides, Sergeant. The Lords of Trade believe no conditional oath ever happened. If London believes it never happened, it never happened."

Captain Namon stood up and carried his tumbler over to his desk, saying: "You and I are both soldiers, Sergeant. That means we are in the business of solving our sovereign's problems. The Acadians were a problem. They have been solved. You would be very wise indeed not to make yourself into a problem. Even a minuscule one, which is all that you would be."

The captain opened a drawer and pulled out the notebook containing the tinker's list. "The active duty you will be assigned to tomorrow will be to lead a squad of men back along the road that brought you here. As you said on the blockhouse steps: it's difficult to be certain, looking out over such a large crowd. There may well be some Acadians who thought themselves sufficiently unknown to us that they could safely ignore the order to appear today. You will bring in all the males over the age of ten."

Cully looked down at the notebook held out in the captain's puffy hand. Captain Namon said: "Take it. Take it like a soldier." Cully reached out and took it, then turned to go. He'd heaved the trap door up and got his foot down on the first stair when the drawl came from behind him: "Oh, and Sergeant Robin...?"

Cully stopped and turned back, propping the trap open with his shoulder. He had to swallow before he could say: "Sir...?"

"I made a copy of that list."

Back in the sergeants' quarters, Cully sat on the edge of his bunk slapping the notebook against his thigh and staring into the fireplace kindled against the coming night. In the dancing flames he saw the little farm in the valley of Ardoise, and he saw Eulalie La Tour washed-up like driftwood on the shore of some distant colony where no one spoke her language and everyone hated her religion.

He told himself that even without the tinker's list, the patrols that would be sent out tomorrow to scour the countryside would've eventually stumbled across the valley of Ardoise. After all, the Halifax-Piziquid road actually ran along the south slope of the valley—all some enterprising soldier had to do was climb a tree to get his bearings and he would see the farm.

But then, that "eventually" would've given Eulalie and the Brossards time to get wind of what had happened at Fort Edward and escape. Maybe north to Louisbourg, or maybe just disappear into the woods with the Mi'kmaqs until the patrols stopped hunting for Acadians.

Cully didn't doubt that the Major had meant his humane promise that families wouldn't be separated in the deportation. But neither the Major nor any other British soldier except Cully Robin knew what an Acadian family was. Cully knew that Eulalie's family didn't just mean the people who slept under the same roof as she did, but all her other uncles and cousins and aunts who were threads in the fabric called Acadia. He couldn't imagine her being able to breathe without it.

He told himself that he was twisting his own lungs into knots for nothing. Because come tomorrow the friendly tinker was going to march into the valley of Ardoise and arrest Joseph Brossard and his two oldest sons, to be held at Fort Edward until it came time for Eulalie and the children to join them on a ship bound for God knew where. Either that, or Sergeant Robin was going to have to march back to Fort Edward with some damned good explanation of why his list wasn't complete.

"*Cully, my lad,*" the voice of reason said in his head, "*don't go standing yourself up in front of a firing squad.*"

"Sergeant Robin," he replied, tossing the notebook into the fire, "*Fuck yourself.*"

He stood up and stripped off his uniform coat and headed for the washstand, unknotting the leather band clubbing his hair. He'd just got started at scrubbing out the greased powder when one of the other sergeants stumped in and leaned his halberd against the wall. "What's this, Cully? Old Creepy sending you off on some other secret something-or-other?"

"The less you know about it the better." Which was decidedly true.

"Well at least let me give you a hand, even if I don't know what for. Here, bend down, let me give you a good pour of the pitcher... You know, some of the other lads get their backs up a bit 'cause you seem to be Captain Namon's pet hunting hound. Me, I'd rather be Lucifer's lapdog. Let's see if we can get a comb through there now. *Don't* fidget—it only makes it worse."

Once his hair seemed something like hair again, instead of a greased leather helmet, Cully changed into his tinker's garb and sat waiting. When tap-to brought all the garrison to bed except the night watch, he strapped his ordnance belt on under his civilian coat, picked up his civilian carbine and his Crown-issued Long Land Pattern musket and started for the door. He paused there and turned back to his fellow sergeants, who were pretending not to notice what they weren't supposed to notice. He wanted to say good-bye—to them and to fourteen years' worth of his life, and likely to the rest of his life. But a fervent farewell would've been a bit too suspicious, so he just said: "Good luck, lads."

"You too, Cully."

"Come back in one piece, Cully, from whatever the bloody hell you're going to do."

"Watch your back, Cully."

The parade square was dark, except for the watchlights. A soft, hopeless old hymn was wafting from the tents and awnings set up to keep the rain off the prisoners. Fort Edward hadn't been built to house two hundred prisoners. Some of the tents had been edged out into the dry moat, which wouldn't stay dry for long if the rain kept up.

Cully headed for the stables, feeling with every step the whip on his back, the noose tightening around his neck, the firing squad's bullets... But he also felt more than a little lightheaded, almost jaunty—as he suspected he would've felt in the few seconds between jumping off the blockhouse tower and hitting the ground.

He told the ostler: "Captain Namon instructed me to take a horse."

"Which horse?"

The ostler's lantern glinted on the Major's corn-fed, glistening Irish hunter, and on the head-high rumps of two other splendid mounts. Regretfully, and pragmatically—given Cully's horsemanship and the likelihood of rough forage—Cully pointed to the ragged tail of Maudit twitching over a stall gate. "That one."

The sentry at the gate thrust his bayonet up toward Cully's nose and barked: "Where the hell do you think you're—Oh, Sergeant..."

"I'm on orders. Open the gate. But watch that none of them tries to sneak out while it's open."

"Yes, Sergeant."

When the gate thumped shut behind him, Cully propped his hands on the slowly-rolling pommel of the saddle and taught himself to breathe again. When he looked up, Maudit had already negotiated her way through the militia camp and was looking around to see where to go next. He pointed her nose east along the Halifax road and dug in his heels.

XVII

⸻⸻⸻⸻

Eulalie was brushing out her hair when there came a tapping at the door and Rouge and Noir jumped up barking. Beau-père went to the door, taking down his cane before opening it. He exclaimed: "Jesus-Mary-and-Joseph! Eulalie, look who's this," and stepped aside to usher in Cully the Tinker.

Eulalie almost crossed herself, it was so much like seeing a ghost. Over the summer she'd accustomed herself that she would never see him again, and that the two weeks he'd been part of her household were just a curio that Madame Eulalie Melanson would dust off and glance at from time to time.

He said grimly and quickly, keeping his voice low so as not to wake the children, "*Bon soir*. There is no time for niceties. There is something I must tell you." He sat down at the table without waiting for an invitation. Eulalie and her stepfather glanced at each other confusedly, then sat down as well.

As Cully Robin told them what the English had done at Fort Edward a few hours ago—and presumably at Grand Pré and Annapolis Royal—Eulalie felt like someone was plucking out her insides strand by strand. By the time he was done, her sleeves were soaked from wiping her eyes. Tears were coming out of Beau-père's eyes as well, but he wasn't wiping them, just leaning his head back to stare at the roof beam and let the streams run down into his white hair.

Eulalie whispered: "André...?"

The light brown eyes across the table from hers twitched and dropped away, and the lank-haired head nodded. For a moment there was no sound but hoarse breathing, then Beau-père rasped at the stars beyond the roof beam: "How can they do this?"

Cully Robin said: "They can. What matters now is you have to get away."

Beau-père lowered his gaze from the roof thatch. "'Get away'...?"

"Before they come to take in you and your sons."

"But... They don't know where we are. You see...?" He gestured at his musket and powder horn hanging over the door. "When they sent out the order to bring in our guns, I kept mine. No one came to take it."

Cully Robin shook his head. "This is different. I know some of the soldiers, from doing some tinkering for them. They say tomorrow morning at first light they'll be ordered out to start scouring every forest path and waterway. They *will* find you." It seemed to Eulalie there was something inexplicably bitter in his 'They will find you.' "You must get away by morning."

Beau-père said: "To where? We have no boat to take us across the bay to French Acadia. We could try to go north to Louisbourg, but there is nothing there but a big fort on a rock—how would we live? Fort Beauséjour is English now, and they are probably doing the same thing to the Acadians around Beauséjour as—"

Eulalie interrupted him, "The Petitcodiac and the Miramichi."

Beau-père scratched his beard and looked thoughtful. Cully Robin looked confused. Eulalie told him: "The Petitcodiac River and the Miramichi River are west of Fort Beauséjour—or what was Fort Beauséjour. If we can be safe anywhere, it will be there."

Beau-père nodded, and said to the tinker: "The Petitcodiac and the Miramichi are the stomping grounds of Beausoleil."

Eulalie nodded back at Beau-père. He rubbed his eyes, planted his hands on the table and said: "We'll leave the crying for tomorrow; tonight we have many things to do. We can't take a cart on Mi'kmaq trails, but we have two horses we can load as packhorses—"

"Three," the tinker interjected. Eulalie looked at him. "I would go with you, if you'll allow."

She could feel Beau-père's eyes slide onto her and then back to Cully. Beau-père said: "Why would you want to do that?"

"Many reasons. I can't go back to Fort Edward, in any case. When I realized I had to come to warn you, I happened to notice a soldier's musket and ammunition belt leaning in a convenient place. I thought they might be useful to people taking to the woods, so I took them. The soldier will know who it was."

Beau-père said: "I thought you had planned to be in Quebec by now...?"

"Plans don't always come through. Can it be enough for me to just say I have reasons to come with you, and leave it at that?"

Beau-père said: "It would be enough for me, Cully, if you said you had *no* reasons. It will be a very, very long walk, and another man to carry one of the little ones when they get tired will be a blessing for my back."

Eulalie said: "Cully... I would try to thank you for coming to warn us, but how could I say -?"

"It seems to me I once tried to thank some Acadian farmers for taking in a stranger with a cracked leg, and they wouldn't let me."

Beau-père stood up and said: "Well, much to do. Eulalie, wake up Henri and Jacques, and Hélène and Marie, but let Jean-Marc and the younger girls sleep as long as they can. Burn as many candles as you want, we can't carry them all. Come out to the barn with me, Cully, and help me with the packsaddles."

Eulalie woke up the older children, explained to them as quickly as possible, told them that now was not the time to ask questions and sent them scurrying to fetch things from the cellar or outside. As the pile on the floor grew larger, she tried to see in her mind how many things would fit on the backs of three horses and of ten people whose shoulders ranged from half as wide as hers to almost twice as wide: smoked hams and slabs of bacon, a sack of flour, the small stewpot and large skillet, the big canvas sheet used for covering the haystack, blankets, a leather bottle of maple syrup and another of rum, jerked beef, a sack of carrots and turnips and another of cabbages, the small axe and the short-handled shovel...

She heard horses by the door. Beau-père came in carrying the long-handled shovel and said: "Henri, dig a good, deep hole by the big elm tree, as wide as you. Marie, so soon as there's enough light, dig up a few chives with enough roots to plant. Eulalie, I need an armful of candles."

She fished them out for him and then carried on with filling out her list as it occurred to her: a pouch of salt, spoons, the big kitchen knife, the firebox with flint and steel and tinder...

She saw through the open door that Beau-père had stuck a ring of candles in the ground around the tethered horses. He and Cully began to ferry the pile she'd built out to the horses. It was all going too fast. She was sure she was piling up too many things, or forgetting something essential. She told herself to cry about it tomorrow and went on flicking her mind and hands at what mattered: Beau-père's holy book, fish hooks and line, needles and thread, a coil of rope, pigs of lead, bullet moulds, the stubby keg of gunpowder out in the shed, the roll of smoked moosehide and the moccasins she and the girls had already made for next winter...

By the time the flicker of candles outside was getting washed out by the brightening sky, the horses were loaded and the remnants of the jumbled pile on the floor had been transformed into ten blanket-wrapped bundles of varying sizes. Beau-père came back inside to say: "Time to wake the little ones, *petite mère*. Don't be afraid if you hear gunfire—I asked Cully to fire a few blank shots in the air."

"You wake them—I'll see to breakfast." She went outside to gather eggs. As she passed by the waiting packhorses, she saw that Beau-père had leashed a couple of calves to their tails to butcher along the trail.

Her nerves were so taut that, even though she'd been warned, the sudden sound of a gunshot made her jump. She looked down the hill as the gun-crack echoed and re-echoed through the valley.

Cully was standing in the orchard, re-loading. It seemed to her that she was watching a clockwork doll: a complicated series of mechanical movements performed without thought. He fired into the air once more and then went through the exact same dance again. The oddest part of it was that although she knew he was only firing off blank charges, his hand still went to the shot pouch on his stolen belt and then to the muzzle. It put her in mind of the dance called The Oats Song, where at the end of every verse you automatically raised your hand to your mouth and pretended to chew, even though you had no oats in your pocket.

She clucked at herself for dallying and hurried along toward the chickens' favourite roosts. When she got back to the house, little Josette and the others were all up, looking rumpled and lost. Eulalie said: "Sit down at the table and I'll soon have breakfast for you."

Beau-père said: "Not yet. Everybody come outside, by the big elm tree."

The big elm tree dominated the farm, fanning its leaves up to the clouds. More than once, high winds had carried its broken branches through the barn roof—the valley was a playground for high winds, which kept the biting flies down. But Thomas Brossard, Beau-père's grandfather, had decreed that since the big elm tree had miraculously survived the forest fire that cleared the land for him, it wasn't up to human hands to cut it down.

Everyone else stood beside the hole Henri had dug between the elm tree's roots, while Beau-père went into the barn. Rouge and Noir kept jumping up against Eulalie, aware that something had gone wrong with the state of the world.

Beau-père came out of the barn carrying his strongbox. Cully helped him lower the strongbox into the hole. Beau-père straightened up, handed Eulalie a small purse, patted the clinking bulge in his shirt and said: "We take a little with us, but we won't have much use for money where we're going. The rest stays here for when we get back. Marie, when Henri and Jacques finish filling in the hole, you plant the chives you dug up, so it will look like just a new bit of garden."

Eulalie felt an eerie twinge, then realized why. After all those years of hiding his strongbox from all eyes but his own, Beau-père was now making certain that everyone in the family knew where it was. And that made her realize something else. He had included Cully Robin in the family.

Over breakfast, Beau-père kept glancing out the door and muttering things like: "I would've thought, with the gunshots..." When the girls got up to clear the table, he said: "No, leave the dirty dishes for the English. Everyone, put on your coats and shawls and hats—if the day turns warm you can carry them."

When the family all trooped outside carrying their bundles, Rouge and Noir went frantic with confusion. Eulalie asked her stepfather: "What are we going to do with them?"

"I don't know. I thought I did, but—Ah, finally." Two Mi'kmaqs were emerging cautiously from the woods at the base of the pasture, holding their guns at the ready. Beau-père went down the hill to talk to them. As she stood watching old Joseph Brossard confer with the Mi'kmaqs, Eulalie suddenly laughed, although it was a choking kind of laugh.

Cully said: "I missed the joke."

"Oh... Oh, it just came to me that it will be harder on him than any of us. Ever since I grew old enough to do the marketing, I don't think he's stepped foot outside the valley of Ardoise more than twice a year."

Cully didn't laugh, but gave out a little grunt that showed he'd heard her. Then he picked up his two guns and said to Henri: "I can only use one at a time, and I know you can shoot. The carbine's the better gun, but I think the musket's a bit too long for you." Eulalie could see Henri's eyes slavering as his hands closed on the carbine. And she could see Jacques's eyes doing the same—if Jacques's big brother had a gun, then they both had a gun.

Beau-père finally came back up the slope with one of the Mi'kmaqs, while the other one loped back into the woods. Eulalie wanted to get moving and get it over with. It only got worse the longer she stood there looking around at the grazing sheep she'd lambed, at the swing hanging from the pine tree, at the well that had never run dry...

Beau-père said: "Henri, you and Jacques tie Rouge and Noir to the fence," then turned to Eulalie. "I told our friends they could have a fine feast here and take whatever they want, and they told me a few things about the trails north. Rouge and Noir will try to kill them when they start killing our cattle, but once enough meat's been thrown to them they'll be glad to become Mi'kmaq dogs."

The Mi'kmaq who'd come up with him looked around at the family and said confusedly: "You are like the rocks and the trees here, like us. How can it be that the English would pull you up out of the earth and put you on a boat to another land?"

Eulalie whispered back to him: "I don't know, but so it is."

Beau-père said: "Well..." He looked around and Eulalie could see his beard trembling as his lower lip pushed up into his mustache. "We waste daylight standing here."

They set off in single file up the deerpath that wound north over Ardoise Hill. When the path passed the little graveyard that Joseph Brossard had kept fenced and weeded for so many years, he said: "You go on, I'll catch up with you," and handed Eulalie the lead of the train of packhorses and calves.

Eulalie herded the children in front of her, with Cully Robin bringing up the rear. Some of the children were crying—the older ones holding it to silent tears—but the other ones were too dazed to do anything but put one foot in front of the other. All except little Josette, perched atop one of the packhorses, who began to sing as though they were going on a picnic, "Three hills home, my dear, three hills home..."

Eulalie didn't join in on her song. The one thing she knew for certain was that it would be a lot more than three hills before any of them saw home again.

XVIII

⁂

ndré Melanson sat under canvas drumming with rain in the courtyard of Fort Edward, along with every other man of Piziquid. For all
of them, it was the first morning in their lives they'd woken up to a
gate barring them from roaming where they would.
André was the only one, though, who was propped up against a cushion of blankets with a bandage around his head and another wound around his ribs. The fort
surgeon and the joiner had argued with each other through a translator, but they'd
eventually agreed that he had a couple of cracked ribs and his skull wasn't cracked.

André had tried to make his father and Benoni and the joiner understand about
the tinker. But he could see from the way they'd looked at each other that they thought
he'd just gone a little unhinged with confusion and rage—as they all had—and had
mistaken some anonymous soldier for someone he'd met before.

Two pairs of soldiers' shoes and gaiters appeared among the rain spatters beyond
the lip of the awning. One of the soldiers bent his head in and said: "André Melanson?"
André nodded and the soldier beckoned.

André's father started to protest, but the soldier shook his head and waved his
hand to show André wouldn't be harmed, even holding out his arm to support André
grunting upright and out of the awning. In the short time André and his fellows had
been prisoners, they'd already learned that their jailers came in different varieties. Some
of the soldiers hated Acadians, some of the soldiers were indifferent, and some of the
soldiers actually seemed to feel some sympathy. But all of the soldiers would shoot
them at the drop of an order.

The rain turned out to be softer than it sounded on the awning. The two soldiers
walked André across the courtyard to the blockhouse, and up a set of stairs to the
second storey. There was a wide, open room with a desk and a cot. Behind the desk
sat the same puffy-looking, gilt-collared officer who'd beckoned to the tinker yester-

day. Up close, André could see that he had yellow eyes, like the wolf-dog André's father had kept until it started killing chickens.

The officer said something in English to one of the soldiers. The soldier replied briskly—André caught the word "captain"—and ran down the stairs, running back up an instant later with a chair that he set down in front of the desk.

The captain smiled up at André, "*Asseyez-vous, Monsieur Melanson. Un peu du vin?*" He poured a glass and proffered it. André reached out for it carefully and very carefully took a sip. He had heard there were people who drank out of glass, but it seemed a fragile undertaking.

"Monsieur Melanson, yesterday you tried to kill one of my soldiers. Why?"

André wasn't sure what he should say. There was something about this captain that put him in mind of a priest who says 'Have you anything to confess?' without letting you in on what is or isn't a sin.

The captain said: "I have no intention of punishing you any further than you already have been. I can perfectly understand why you'd feel moved to try to kill a British soldier yesterday. The question is: why *that* one in particular? And it seemed you didn't much care if you got yourself killed in the process."

"I..." It seemed wise to know as little as possible. "I thought I knew him. I was wrong."

"Oh were you, now? Are you so sure of that?"

André shrugged.

"Where did you think you recognized him from? Are you acquainted with many soldiers?"

"No. I thought... I thought he looked like a tinker."

"And that put you in a killing fury? Do you hate tinkers so much?"

"No... But... You see, if this tinker was a soldier, then he was a spy. As I said, I was mistaken."

"Tinker, soldier, spy... Are you sure he wasn't a tailor? A little more wine, Monsieur Melanson?"

André was more than a little wary of getting too relaxed around this captain. But the wine did make his head throb a little less, and make his jaw not quite as painful to answer questions with. So he shrugged and held the glass out for a little more.

"Where did you become acquainted with this tinker who maybe was a soldier and maybe wasn't?"

André thought of the murmur that had passed back and forth among the prisoners last night—that Joseph Brossard and his sons hadn't obeyed the order to come in to Fort Edward. And he thought of the patrols that had marched out of the fort at dawn. He said: "At the farm of my father's cousin Benoni. And not 'acquainted'—I only saw him the once... when I took some fish to Benoni's and the tinker was mending a pot."

"What a remarkable memory you have for faces—only saw him the once and still recognized him done up like a soldier."

"Not so remarkable—like I said, I was wrong."

"You may well be wrong that you were wrong. The man you tried to kill yesterday is now a deserter. If you can remember information that will lead to his capture, there is a reward of ten pounds sterling—and I would see to it that you and your family were placed on a ship bound for Catholic Maryland, rather than one of the Puritan colonies."

André just shrugged as though he would do his best to get his slow head to eventually remember what it could. He would've been more than glad to cause the tinker to be shot or hanged or whatever it was they did to deserters. But he couldn't think of a way to say any more without bringing Eulalie and the Brossards into it. And he'd got the distinct feeling that this captain was sniffing for more than just a deserter.

"I can see I've tired you, Monsieur Melanson. You need to rest and recover." The captain gestured André's guards to take his glass and give him a hand up to his feet.

"Oh, and, Monsieur Melanson...? I will give you a piece of advice that you may well already have taken in the hard way. But I will tell it you nonetheless, and hope you take it to heart and pass it on to your *confrères*. There is nothing you nor anyone else can do to stop what has been put in motion. Let it carry you where it will. Only if you flail against the tide will you be pushed under."

XIX

ully was more than a little chagrined that a family of Acadian civilians seemed to have no trouble keeping up a pace he didn't have to slow down for. He had deployed himself as rearguard, and sometimes he had to bustle to narrow the gap between himself and the tail of the last packhorse. He consoled the honour of the British army with the thought that he was out of condition from the weeks he'd spent laid up, and that tiptoeing along forest paths was hardly the same as road-marching.

Their first night's camp was on the side of a hill within sight of a vast stretch of open water, which Eulalie told him wasn't the Bay of Fundy but an inlet called the Minas Basin. As the sunset painted the waves red, Eulalie pointed to a misty, distant, black shape tonguing into the water and said: "That is Cape Blomidon, where Glooscap lives."

Cully said: "'Glooscap'?"

"He is a giant who is the Mi'kmaqs' great friend, so I guess he must be our friend, too. Most of the time he stays on Blomidon with his two watchdogs and his friend the rabbit and his messenger the loon. But sometimes he comes down to help the people or play tricks on them. The missionaries tell the Mi'kmaqs Glooscap is dead now. The Mi'kmaqs nod their heads and say 'Yes, Father,' but they know better."

Little Josette squeaked from the blankets she and her sisters were curled up in: "Tell us a story, Eulalie!"

"All right, but only one. Would you like the one about how the rabbit lost his tail?"

"Yes, please."

Cully leaned back against a tree and puffed a cloud out of his pipe to mask that he was staring at Eulalie. There was no question it made a pretty picture: the brown maiden in the greenwood storying children to sleep. But parts of him would've preferred the children weren't in the picture.

Cully woke up stiff and sore, wondering if there was a square yard of Nova Scotia that didn't have a pine root sticking out of it. Old Joseph Brossard creaked to his feet in groaning stages. He shrugged at Cully: "Yes, it's bad to be old and have pains in the body, but it's better than being young and have pains in the brain."

In the afternoon they came across a bramble thicket, and stopped to stuff themselves and a sack with blackberries. The thorns were diabolically clever, finding a way to score stinging scratches across the backs of Cully's hands no matter how cautious he thought he was being. Joseph Brossard said: "You see, Cully, what wise and good families blackberries are."

"How's that, Uncle?"

"There are always three generations of blackberry in a thicket. The old ones have no sap left in them, and are so dry and brittle next winter's winds will break them down—but that makes their thorns sharp and hard for protecting the younger ones. The youngest, green ones will have no fruit until next year—too busy growing. And the red ones with fat berries will next year be dry and brittle, good for nothing but bearing thorns to shelter the young ones growing to bear fruit. So the thicket stays alive and never changes."

Eulalie said grimly: "Ripe blackberries already."

Joseph Brossard said: "I know what you mean, Eulalie," then apparently saw that Cully didn't. "The distance from Ardoise to the Petitcodiac and the Miramichi would be no trouble to walk before winter—if we could go in straight lines, straight north and then straight west. But the long arm of the Minas Basin pushes way inland north of us, so we will have to circle east."

Eulalie said: "And Cobequid."

"Yes. You see, Cully, there is—or was—an Acadian village at the head of the Minas Basin. There might be British patrols there looking for strays, so we will have to circle even further. Well, come on, children, enough blackberries. We still have a few hours to walk before sundown."

As they put more and more miles and days between themselves and the valley of Ardoise, Cully noticed the forest air tasting increasingly sweeter, and that his arms and legs felt like they had springs in them—despite the aches from sleeping on the ground. He knew that by all the rules of sense he should be feeling worse, not better. If it hadn't been for one crack-brained decision he would still be a sergeant with a relatively comfortable life laid out ahead of him, instead of a fugitive with the standard price on his head. But the deserter had one thing Sergeant Robin never would've had. He was free. At least until they caught him.

Even though Eulalie and Joseph Brossard looked increasingly worried at the yellowing leaves, they still had to pause to forage from time to time. Where the trail wound along the side shore, they walked out at low tide to pick up lobsters among the rocks and drop them in the pot that Eulalie kept boiling. Cully was embarrassed that even Marie and Hélène were more adept at snatching up lobsters by the part of their backs their claws couldn't reach. But Joseph Brossard said: "Better to be too slow and careful, Cully, than lose a thumb."

When the path moved back inland, they came to a trickle of a river with wide, red mudflats, and whiled away a morning digging clams. Cully was on his knees furiously scooping away mud above a clam who was furiously burrowing deeper, when Joseph Brossard called out: "Cully, the tide comes in."

Cully called back: "All right," but kept on digging. A bit of salt water soaking into his breeches would be a small price to prove that human hands were superior to clam necks, or whatever it was the little bugger was digging with.

A moment later, Eulalie called from the riverbank: "Cully, the tide!"

"Yes, I heard," and he kept on digging.

Eulalie shrieked: "Cully! The *tide!*"

He raised his head and heard a high wind rising in the west. He looked in that direction. It was an odd wind. He could hear it rushing and growing louder, but he couldn't feel it.

Around a bend in the riverbed came a chest-high wall of churning water, with bits of driftwood dancing on the foam. Cully jumped up and ran for the shore, mud sucking at his bare feet. Eulalie, Joseph Brossard and Henri reached their arms down from the bank. He grabbed hold of as many hands as possible and scrambled upward as the wall of water took his legs out from under him.

Once he was safely on his feet again, Eulalie flung her arms around him and gasped: "You great *fool!*" Then she dropped her arms and stepped back, blushing. Cully cleared his throat and tried to find something other than Eulalie to look at. He could still feel the imprint of her breasts against his ribs. After ten days living in the woods she looked more Indian than ever, and the pink blush lit up her sun-browned cheeks.

Cully looked at the river choking the banks that a moment ago had looked like a ravine with a few mud puddles in the bottom. Joseph Brossard said: "You don't seem to have much luck with water, Cully," and everyone laughed. "You see, the tides in our bay are very high—especially at full moon, like now—and when all that water gets squoze into a narrow channel... We take it as a matter of course, but we should've thought to warn you."

Cully shrugged and nodded as though paying attention. What he was really thinking of was that if a woman had flung herself on Corporal or Sergeant Robin like that, he would've had her on her back before she could squeal Jack Robinson.

A few days later, they were walking along a cart track in a light rain when the procession Cully was rearguarding suddenly began to peel off into the woods. Eulalie looked back at him, put her finger in front of her mouth and scooped her hand urgently for him to follow. He did, until he was far enough into the woods to not be seen from the road. Then he turned around, unslung his musket and crouched down.

He began to hear what had sent the ones in front of him scurrying off the cart track: the approaching sound of heavy shoes marching in cadence. Joseph Brossard and Henri came up from wherever the rest of the family had gone to ground, and crouched on either side of him with their guns cocked.

The marching grew louder. Peering at the red coats through the yellow and orange leaves, Cully counted a dozen, with a sergeant in the lead. They didn't appear to be as nervous as he'd expect of such a small squad marching along a forest road. Apparently, the fall of Beauséjour had convinced them there'd be no more raiding parties. He did find it strange, though, to find himself thinking of them as "them".

Once the marching had faded into the distance, Cully straightened back up and Joseph Brossard gave a birdwhistle that brought Eulalie and the others forward with the packhorses. Brossard said: "I'm afraid we'll have to struggle along through the woods, instead of the open road, in case they come marching back and catch up with us."

"They won't," Cully told him. "They were marching in full kit. They'll bivouac tonight before they start back."

"You're sure?"

"I'm sure." Unless they had a prig of a commanding officer who insisted on full kit even for day patrols, which was possible. The rearguard of the Ardoise Fusiliers would just have to keep his ears open.

Brossard said: "You seem to know a lot about soldiers, to be so sure."

"Oh, the kinds of taverns tinkers can afford to drink in are the same ones soldiers go to. Sometimes they'll buy you mugs of ale all night, if you sit and listen to them grumble about full kit and forced marches."

Joseph Brossard looked down, the same as he had the day Cully woke up with a broken leg and had to explain his notebook and being delirious in English. Cully got the distinct feeling that Brossard knew he was lying, but that the old man considered it his own fault for asking questions he shouldn't.

Joseph Brossard looked up again, 'though not at Cully, and said: "Then we'll follow the cart trail a few leagues further. But after a few leagues we must turn off along the first path we find, before we stumble into Cobequid Village, or what's left of it."

There wasn't a green leaf left in the forest by the time the refugees from Ardoise Valley got far enough north to turn westward. They followed a well-worn footpath along what Joseph Brossard said was the north shore of the Minas Basin, and would soon become the north shore of the Bay of Fundy. They came to a rivermouth and a smattering of birchbark huts. Pulled up on the riverbank were a half-dozen of those eccentrically-shaped Mi'kmaq canoes that Cully's old messmates had always found so amusing, with the hulls upswept at the mid-thwarts as high as the stern and bow.

There weren't only Mi'kmaqs there. A dozen raggedy-looking Acadians came forward, and there was much handclasping and "Joseph à Jacques à Thomas!"; "Moïse à Jean à Mathieu!" It seemed they were refugees from Annapolis Royal, and that the British plan for September Fifth hadn't been executed as neatly there as at Piziquid and Grand Pré. Several bloodybacks and several Acadians had been killed, and many Acadian families had got clean away. Some of them had headed straight north, hoping to get to Louisbourg or maybe Ile St. Jean. But some of them, like these, had only one name for the refuge they were seeking: Beausoleil.

Joseph Brossard said to the grizzledest of the Annapolis Royalites: "You must have run all the way, Moïse, to get here before us."

"We were not so heavy-loaded as you." Cully could believe that—they looked like they'd been living on berries snatched from bushes as they ran. "And maybe, Joseph à Jacques à Thomas, I know a little more about straight paths than you."

"So you decided to stop here to fatten up before going further?"

"No. We decided to stop here because we don't know if we *can* go further. The English have re-built Fort Beauséjour bigger, and christened it Fort Cumberland."

Brossard shrugged: "I expected they would do something like that. It should be easy enough to sneak around it to the north."

"No. Because the English have built another new fort, a little one, on the seacoast straight north of Fort Cumberland."

Brossard said: "*Merde*," and then explained to Cully. "What joins Nova Scotia to French Acadia is only a narrow neck of land. If the English have a fort on one side of that neck, the bay side, and another on the other side, the sea side, they can easy keep up patrols between them that no one can sneak through. At least, no one with a train of packhorses and children."

They sat down around a fire with several of the Mi'kmaqs to puzzle it out. Apparently Eulalie spoke Mi'kmaq better than her "Beau-père", because she was called upon to translate some of his questions and some of the Mi'kmaqs' explanations of the lay of the land. Or maybe Joseph Brossard was just trying to take advantage of the fact that the Mi'kmaqs had smiled when they heard her name was La Tour.

Either way, her translating meant that Cully could follow at least part of the conversation. It seemed that the river they were on had its source halfway across the isthmus. From there, it was possible to carry canoes and baggage to another river running north to the sea.

Joseph Brossard rubbed his beard and said: "We could paddle along the north shore till we come near their little fort. Then we wait for a calm night, paddle out to sea and head straight west till morning. By the time we have enough light to make a landing, or for anyone to see us, we should be in French Acadia. Moïse...?"

Moïse nodded and Brossard said to Eulalie: "Tell our friends here we will trade our three horses for canoes..." He interrupted himself to see if it was all right with Cully to bargain his horse away. Cully nodded and the bargaining began.

It was finally agreed that the Mi'kmaqs would trade two canoes for the three horses—they had less use for horses than canoes. But two canoes would never carry two dozen Acadians and their gear.

The head Mi'kmaq made a long speech that seemed to have some genuine sadness in it. Eulalie translated: "He says there is nothing he would rather do than give up more canoes to help his friends—he and his sons can always make more canoes. But just now they need the canoes to fish with, so they can trade the fish for the gunpowder and other things they need to live when they go into the deep woods for the winter."

A glumness descended on the Acadian side of the fire. Two canoes just might manage to carry the party from Ardoise, but it was obvious to Cully that neither Eulalie nor Joseph Brossard were even considering saying: "Well, it's our three horses, so our two canoes, so *adieu* Moïse *et famille*." He could see Eulalie weighing in her mind the paltry little purse her stepfather had handed her when he buried his strongbox. And Cully could almost hear Joseph Brossard re-hearing himself say: *We won't have much use for money where we're going.*

Cully surreptitiously reached one hand into his coat pocket, loosened the string around the little canvas bag he'd got from Captain Namon, and held up one gold guinea. "Would this be enough to buy them what they need for the winter?" From the glint in the black eyes reflecting the gold glinting in the firelight, it would be more than enough. "And some provisions as well as the canoes."

Once the bargain was sealed, grizzled Moïse from Annapolis Royal said to Cully: "What was your father's name?"

"Gilbert Robin."

"And his father's name?"

"Gilbert Robin. The Robins were never inventive."

Moïse held out his hand. "I thank you, Cully à Gilbert à Gilbert."

As Cully shook the callus-cratered hand, and caught a glimpse of Eulalie beaming mistily at him, he felt like a thief. The more these people welcomed him, the more it ate at him that they had no idea who they were welcoming.

XX

~~~~~~

ulalie contrived that she and Cully would paddle the same canoe. It only made sense. Cully had said he'd never paddled a canoe before, so his strength and her experience would make a balanced team—just as Henri's and Jacques's fairly equal strength and experience made a balanced team. She took the stern position and Cully the bow, with Josette and two of the Annapolis Royal children perched among the baggage in between.

She pushed the canoe off from shore, splashing her bare feet in the river until the water was deep enough that she could climb in the stern without grounding. Then she waved her paddle at the Mi'kmaqs and turned her canoe to fall in line with the others.

But no matter how hard she tried to keep the canoe pointed straight, its progress was a zig-zag—steadily falling farther behind instead of falling in line. She laughed and called to Cully: "It isn't enough just to shovel at the water. Turn your paddle sideways at the end, to keep *us* from going sideways."

He looked back and she showed him, "Like this. You see? Yes, that's right, just a twist of the wrist. It feels clumsy at first, but after a while you don't have to think about it."

He turned forward again, but she didn't have to see his face to see he was applying himself studiously to the lesson and putting his back into it. She still found it surprising that someone who'd been so many places and had so much experience of life could be ignorant of so many things. He didn't know that when a loon sang in daylight it was time to get under cover before the clouds opened up; he didn't know the difference between mushrooms that were good for feeding your friends and ones that were good for poisoning your enemies...

But his ignorance was endearing in a way, especially since he made no bones about it and seemed more than happy to have her teach him. She would've thought her head was growing too big for her cap, trying to tell a full-grown man how to do things, except that she never forgot he knew many things about the world outside Acadia that she never would.

Watching the sinewy shoulders and back rise and fall with the rippling of the paddle, she shuddered at suddenly remembering the snakes' nest of whip scars hidden under his shirt. It was easy to forget them, now that his beard had grown in enough to cover the hard lines around his mouth and make his eyes seem larger and softer. But no matter how many campfires he shared with her family, it still seemed to Eulalie that there was something a little distant about him, like he was hiding more than his whip scars.

She shifted her eyes from the tinker's back to the gilded riverbank rolling by, feeling a twinge of guilt about André Melanson. André was either still imprisoned at Fort Edward or in the hold of an English ship taking him the good God knew where, and here she was thinking about another man and enjoying his company.

But she reminded herself that it was hardly her choice that she and Cully and her family were paddling up a river on their way to French Acadia. And what harm was it doing André that she had a friend while governors and armies forced her and André into different corners of the world? What good would it do André for her to spend all her time weeping at the thought of his oak-slab wrists in chains? And after all, she and André weren't married, or even affianced. If they had been, she would have stayed to go into exile with him, like the wives and fiancés of all the other men of Piziquid.

Nevertheless, she still felt like a bit of a betrayer the more things she found she liked about Cully Robin. One of the things she liked about him was the way he went about working. When the canoes hove into shore at what appeared to be the path the Mi'kmaqs had described, and Henri and Jacques came back from exploring to announce that there was indeed a river flowing north at the other end of the path, Cully just stood up without a word, loaded himself down like a packhorse and started walking. But that matter-of-fact attending to the task at hand, such as trudging across the portage with one end of an upturned canoe on his shoulders, didn't stop him from spouting resonant nonsense at the children for the pure fun of how his voice echoed with a canoe over his head.

It was at the camp at the other end of that path, while Eulalie was applying river sand to the flatbread flakes stuck to the skillet, that Beau-père came up to her and murmured: "Cully says he has something to tell us. Just you and me." She looked up quizzically, but he just shrugged his white eyebrows and looked as mystified as she.

She called Hélène over to finish up the skillet and followed Beau-père into the woods. Cully's voice called from up ahead: "I'm here." He was sitting with his back against a pine tree and his hands stuffed in his coat pockets, puffing his pipe and chewing on its stem. He said: "Sit down, this may take a while."

When they sat down, he stood up. He took the pipe out of his mouth, sucked his lips and chewed on them, shot his eyes at Eulalie and then away, then heaved out a breath and said: "You may have noticed that I know less than most twelve-year-old children about farms and forests and canoes and horses and such…"

Eulalie and her stepfather both spoke at once, Beau-père saying: "Now, Cully, that's nothing to be ashamed of," and Eulalie: "You know a lot of things we don't."

"Yes. Yes I do know a lot of things you don't. And that's why I don't know much useful. I know how to get along in barracks, how to keep the sergeant from paying too much attention to me, how to get an extra measure of rum out of the sutler, how to stick a bayonet in a man's guts without a qualm… I'm a deserter from the British army."

"Your back!" flew out of Eulalie's mouth before she could throw her hand up to close it off. She looked guiltily at Beau-père for breaking her promise. But then, he'd only sworn her not to ask Cully about it, not to pretend ignorance if Cully offered an explanation.

Cully was looking at her confusedly. She peeled her hand away from her mouth and said: "When we… When your leg was broken and we had to take your wet clothes off to put you into bed… The scars on your back… They say that English soldiers are whipped all the time."

"Well, not *all* the time. But they don't call us the bloodybacks for nothing, or the Blood Red Roses. I didn't know any scars still showed. Last time I was stupid enough to get myself flogged was a long time ago, and I don't see my back very often.

"So, I told you the truth when I said I was born on the Channel Islands and ran away to follow a tinker. What I didn't tell you was that when I'd finally learned enough to set up as a journeyman on my own, I fell for a recruiting sergeant's trick and woke up with a bludgeoned head and a red coat on my back. Fourteen years. Those soldiers we hid in the woods from, and the ones who were marching toward the valley of Ardoise as you were hurrying to escape—I'm one of them."

Eulalie said softly: "No, Cully—you *were*."

That didn't seem to lighten what was pressing down on him. He carried on as though she hadn't said anything, "So, you see, when I offered to come with you, I wasn't being generous or helpful. It was the only hope I saw to save my own hide."

Beau-père said: "None of that makes any difference to us, Cully. If you'd told us when you first came up the pasture with your tinker's pack, we would've told you where to find other deserters hiding safe among the Mi'kmaqs."

"But, you see, I wasn't a deserter then."

Eulalie's head cocked itself sideways—just like Rouge and Noir when Jacques and Henri walked on their hands. Beau-père said: "Huh?"

"When you first met me, I was still a soldier. A good soldier. I did not become a deserter until the Fifth of September."

Beau-père said: "But how—?"

"Do you remember my notebook you dried on your hearth, with its list of tinker's customers?"

"Yes."

"Do you remember the gold guinea I gave the Mi'kmaqs for the canoes?"

"But of course, but—"

"That gold guinea was part of my payment for making that list. You see, His Excellency the Governor knew there were Acadians whose homes were away from settlements like Piziquid and Grand Pré, who might be able to avoid what he had planned for the Fifth of September. But he didn't know where they were or how many. One of his officers offered a handsome reward to a soldier who could lie in French well enough to sneak among the Acadians. That wasn't a tinker's list. It was a spy's list." Then he closed his mouth, as though all that was left to him to do was wait for what he'd said to sink in.

"*All that time...?*" The words rose up out of Eulalie as she rose to her feet. "All that time you lay in our house...? In *my* bed...? And sang songs with the children...? And...? *All that time* you were—?" She took two steps toward him, cocking her right arm back as far as it would go, and swung her hand across his face as hard as she could. She turned her back on him and ran back toward the camp. The stinging in the palm of her hand was nothing to the stinging in the rest of her.

XXI

ctober found André Melanson and the rest of the men of Piziquid still under canvas in the courtyard of Fort Edward. They had to sleep with their feet in each others' faces; Fort Edward hadn't been built to house two hundred prisoners. André could see his father growing grayer-skinned and more slack-handed as—just beyond those wooden gates—the time for harvesting flax and barley came and went, the apples fell from the trees, and the time for slaughtering and sausage-making drew closer.

The tents and awnings had become even more crowded since the Fifth of September, as patrols brought in more men who'd thought their homes were hidden-away enough to ignore the order. But there was still no sign of Joseph Brossard or any of his sons. André could only assume that the Brossards and Eulalie had taken to the woods before the patrol got there. He had no doubt that the English soldiers knew how to find the valley of Ardoise; that had been the tinker's mission.

It seemed obvious that the commander of Fort Edward had had no wish to keep his prisoners for so long. But the ships that were supposed to take them off his hands still hadn't appeared. The long delay made for plenty of time to make a plan. It started with André and the younger men, but eventually they persuaded the older men as well.

The plan grew out of two predictions that seemed certain. The first was that when the ships did arrive to take them away, the human cargo on each ship was bound to vastly outnumber the crew. The second was that, with a war on, the ships were bound to want to travel in as large a convoy as possible, maybe with an English warship or two as escort.

Before the ships from Piziquid, Grand-Pré and Annapolis Royal could form a convoy together, they would first have to rendezvous out on the bay. Once the ships were all rendezvoused and riding at anchor, it should be easy enough for the prisoners to shout innocent-sounding messages from one ship to another—messages that would mean something entirely different to an Acadian than to even a French-speaking Englishman. Before the fleet weighed anchor, the Acadians on all the ships would all rise up at once and overwhelm the crews, then sail across the bay to French Acadia. Even if there were English warships guarding the convoy, they would hardly fire their cannons at ships filled with English sailors, even if those sailors had become prisoners instead of crew.

The plan not only gave André a glimmer of hope, it also gave him something to think about other than things that stung his eyes. But he couldn't think about the plan every hour of every day. He was sitting with his back against the palisade, in one of the last patches of warm sunlight the year would see, when his memory betrayed him into a daydream of Eulalie at her loom. She was smiling over her shoulder at him. A curl of dark hair peeked out from her white cap at the temple. She laughed like a spring brook, without interrupting the dance of her quick, small hands—small compared to his—darting the shuttle through the threads.

He was rescued from his weepy-making memory by the rattle of a drum. The fattest of the sergeants bawled from the blockhouse steps in his fractured French: "All prisoners to be assembling!"

André and all the others got up and drifted toward the blockhouse. Some of them—like André's father—moved with a listless shuffle. André could hardly blame them; the past five weeks had been the first time in their lives they'd ever been confined by anything except the weather or a bout of fever.

Once they were all assembled, the Major came out onto the blockhouse steps. He didn't look happy. He said: "Gentlemen, the ships we have been waiting on have arrived, but not near so many as I'd been led to expect. Nevertheless, I believe it is better to try to fit all of you and your families onto what ships we have at hand, rather than hold you here the good God knows how long with winter approaching. Your families have been informed to present themselves and their household possessions on the beach tomorrow morning, when you and they will be embarked."

André headed back toward his patch of sunlight, hearing stilted murmurings among the other prisoners. He understood why they were having trouble knowing what to say about tomorrow, because he was feeling the same two horses pulling his own heart in opposite directions. Tomorrow he would finally see his mother and sisters and younger brothers again. And tomorrow they would all be put on a ship sailing away from Acadia.

He didn't sleep much that night, and neither did any of the other men around him. As the sun rose, sounds came in over the parapet: sounds of horses, oxen and cartwheels, sounds of women's and children's voices shouting confusedly and male voices barking back at them. Squads of soldiers kept forming up in the courtyard and marching out the gates, and the gates swinging shut again. Finally the gates stayed open. The fat sergeant thumped the butt of his halberd on the platform at the top of the blockhouse steps and shouted: "*Allez! Allez!*" pointing at the gates.

André tucked his coat and blankets under his arm and joined the herd funnelling out of the gates. There was an aisle of soldiers and militia leading down to the beach, and a long line of red coats and duller coats along the bank above the beach. The tide was going out and clumps of soldiers were patrolling the receding waterline. There were four ships in the harbour and boats were rowing out to them. Four ships for a thousand people and their household possessions.

The English had organized matters like a careful swineherd moving pigs from the pen to the cart: the prisoners were blocked from going anywhere except down to the beach and onto the boats. The beach itself wasn't organized, though. It was a riot of wailing women and children, bawling oxen, barking dogs and panicked cart-horses.

Through the storm of noise, André heard his mother's voice call his father's name. He looked and saw her running forward from a cart piled high with things that belonged in their kitchen or barn. André and his father and André's oldest little brother ran toward her and the rest of the family running toward them. There was a whirl of hugging, hand-clasping, eye-wiping and: "You've grown so thin..." And then their reunion and everyone else's was chopped short by a shriek that cut through the din.

André swung his head toward where the shriek had come from, but along the way his eyes hit against what had caused it. From somewhere back beyond the line of soldiers, a line of black smoke was rising into the sky.

André's father whispered in a voice like broken glass: "That would be Abraham à Mathieu à Bernard's place."

Other gray-black plumes rose up and joined together, until the morning sky was dark. Behind the line of bayonets along the bank, other soldiers and militiamen came through the smoke, coughing and laughing and herding cows, steers, pigs and sheep toward Fort Edward, whipping the cattle's rumps with neck-wrung chickens.

For a moment, André became just a pair of eyes, blinking and flicking around the smoke-wreathed beach from one picture to another. Up on the bank, the soldiers' friend Barbe Thibodeau was trying to flail her way off the beach but was being pushed back with musket butts. On the beach, two soldiers were arguing over a horse hitched to an empty cart. Out on the water, Benoni and his wife were squeezed into the bow of a boat being rowed away, holding each other's hands and keeping their faces stiff.

André's eyes caught on one picture and held. On a knoll were several men in dark coats and two men in goldbraided red coats. The dull-coated ones looked like Boston sea captains. The red-coated ones were the Major and the icy Captain who'd asked André about the tinker. The Captain didn't look icy now: he was flourishing a sheaf of papers in the sea captains' faces and growing as red-faced as his coat. Finally he threw his arms up, turned away, ripped his papers to pieces and threw them to the wind.

A soldier stepped up to André's father, shouted: "*Allez!*" and pointed at a boat coming in to shore. André took hold of Daisy's headstall and led the cart down to the boat. As they unloaded bundles from the cart, the sailors snatched them from their hands and threw them into the boat. The boat filled up quickly. A man with a belaying pin in his hand slapped it against André's mother's spinning wheel and barked: "No!" then against his father's toolchest: "No!"

André's father bellowed: "*Tabernac!*" and started to raise his hands. André grabbed him and pointed out the soldiers and militiamen hovering around with their muskets cocked.

His mother and father climbed into the boat and André handed them his youngest brothers and sisters as the sailors took their places. When all the crew and all the family except André were aboard, the waves were lapping over the gunwales. André raised his foot to climb in, but the belaying pin slapped against his shin: "No!" and pointed toward the next boat loading up.

André's mother shrieked: "André!"

"It's all right, *maman*—I'll meet you on board."

He took his place in the next boat and sat waiting for it to push off, watching his family and their possessions being handed up the Jacob's ladder of the first ship in the line. As the oarsmen on either side of him put their backs into it, the ship grew larger and André could see she was a sprung-ribbed old tub that wasn't fit for hauling coal.

He could also see his mother and father waving from the rail. He waved back eagerly, then realized that the boat wasn't turning in toward that ship but heading for the next ship in line. He lunged at the steersman, shouting: "No! *That* ship!" The steersman put a boot into his chest and shouted back at him in English, as the boat rocked from side-to-side shipping water.

André sat back down and called to his parents: "We'll meet again when we make land!"

As soon as André's feet were on the ship's deck, he was tapped on the shoulder and pointed toward a hatchway. The hold was already full of Acadians and getting fuller. André finally found a place to squeeze his blanket onto and headed back up the ladder. A sailor pushed him back down. So he sat among the rest of the huddled driftwood, with his knees hugged to his chest, listening to the capstan wind the anchor chain and the sails crack into life.

Once they'd been underway a while, he thought maybe they wouldn't mind him going out on deck now. No one stopped him this time. They were just rounding Cape Blomidon.

André stood at the rail watching the smoke from Piziquid and the smoke from Grand Pré form a pair of curtains framing Glooscap's home. He wondered if Glooscap was sleeping while the people who lived around the footings of his mountain were being torn away.

A sound came across the water—a sound that made André wonder whether he should cross himself or decide he was going crazy. It was a many-voiced, wordless wail of pain and loneliness. He got the eerie feeling he was listening to the land itself crying out for its people.

Then his ears managed to separate some of the voices and he realized what he was hearing. It was all the cows of Grand Pré bawling to be milked, and all the dogs howling around the empty houses.

He turned away from the land and looked ahead at the gray waves. Up until the Fifth of September, the shape of his future had been laid out clearly. Now it was a void. But there were two things in that void he could hold onto. Someday he would find Eulalie La Tour and marry her, as the good God had intended. And he would someday find the tinker and kill him. He'd never married anybody or killed anybody before, but he had no doubt he would know how to do both when the times came.

PART TWO

BEAUSOLEIL

I am in hopes our affairs will soon put on another face...
and I rid of the worst piece of service that ever I was in.
– COLONEL JOHN WINSLOW,
COMMANDER OF NEW ENGLAND MILITIA AT GRAND PRÉ,
SEPTEMBER, 1755

XXII

꧁ ꧂

ully sat on the dawn-lit seashore staring glumly at the wreckage: broken canoes, scattered cooking gear, soaked blankets spread out to dry...

Last night they'd tried to make their run for French Acadia, but they hadn't even got within striking distance of the border before a sudden squall drove them into a rocky landfall.

He supposed they could call themselves lucky. If the storm had come up a couple of hours later, it would've driven them straight into the arms of the garrison in the little fort the British had built on the north side of the isthmus. And no one had suffered anything worse than a soaking and a few scraped bruises. But the canoes that hadn't been stove-in completely all had gashes in their fragile birchbark skins, or cracked cedar ribs.

The Mi'kmaq chief had thrown mending materials into the bargain, and apparently the Acadians knew how to use them. But squatting on the isthmus for several days sending smoke up from a fire for boiling spruce gum seemed like a splendid way of attracting British patrols.

And then there was the other wreckage, the one Cully couldn't blame the sea for, which made him even glummer. Ever since he'd told Eulalie and her stepfather his secret, she never spoke to him except when absolutely necessary, and then only in his general direction without speaking his name.

Joseph Brossard had let it be known among the others that "the tinker" was in fact a British deserter, but hadn't told them any more than that. As far as Cully could tell, it hadn't altered their opinion of him. But there was only one opinion that mattered.

He cursed himself up and down once again for being so stupid as to tell her. If he'd kept it to himself, there was no way she could ever have found out. "Ah well," he consoled himself, looking again at the shattered canoes, "it makes little difference now."

The way things were going, Eulalie would soon be in the hold of a transport ship and he'd be standing in front of a firing party, if any of the bloodybacks at Fort Cumberland or its outpost happened to recognize their old messmate.

A council was convened to determine what to do next. Cully didn't contribute any opinion, since it seemed patently obvious to him there was only one choice left to them: pick up everything they could carry, start walking west and hope they were lucky enough to slip between the pickets.

When everyone else finally reached that conclusion, Cully stood up and slung his musket over one shoulder, his improvised backpack over the other, and looked around for something else to carry. Eulalie appeared to be wishing she could grow another arm. She was standing with one hand holding the skillet, the other on the hoop-handle of the stewpot filled with what was left of their provisions, looking down uncertainly at a blanket-wrapped bundle in front of her feet.

Cully stepped forward, put his hand on the pot handle he'd mended in the spring, and said: "I can carry that." She just let go of it without looking at him, scooped up the bundle and turned away.

They angled inland a few miles before starting west, to keep the bookends of Fort Cumberland and the little fort as far on either hand as possible. The country they were walking through was sparsely wooded, with spits of sand between the trees. It made for easier marching than a forest, but didn't offer many places to hide.

Near sundown, Henri and Jacques came running back from scouting ahead and panted: "Papa, soldiers!"

"How many?"

"Six! In a poplar grove straight ahead of us! Sitting around a campfire drinking."

Cully said: "Drinking?"

Henri said eagerly: "Not drunk, no more than a little, but passing a little bottle around and laughing loud—too loud to hear anyone sneaking up on them. We have five guns, we could drop almost all of them if we fired all at once."

Cully shook his head, "And bring every soldier from both forts running. Let's take a closer look. Those with guns, come with me—everyone else wait here."

He could see Eulalie looking insulted that he should presume to give orders. She could go to hell: for the last six weeks he'd been a babe in their woods, now they'd finally encountered a situation he knew more about than they did. Being a relatively old hand, though, didn't prevent his blood from starting to race as though his heart was drumming "Stand To".

There was a meadow of shoulder-high marsh grass. The Acadians called it elephant grass, even though no Acadian had ever seen an elephant. Cully hunched his head down and followed Henri through the elephant grass, with Joseph Brossard and Moïse and Moïse's oldest son tagging behind. They came to a thicket of alders on the edge of the poplar grove. Cully peered through the sparse remaining leaves.

Henri had counted right: there were six of them, at their ease around the fire, with their muskets neatly tripoded out of reach of flying sparks. Unfortunately, the bottle they were passing around didn't look large enough to incapacitate them, even if it was pure Jamaica rum. They weren't talking loud enough to pick out words at thirty yards, but from the tone of their voices Cully could clearly hear the kind of conversation he'd taken part in ten thousand times:

"I fooked old Annie the laundress!"

"Go on!"

"I did. Only cost me tuppence. She wanted more, but I'd drunk the rest."

"You must've drunk six months' pay to get drunk enough to fook old Annie. Bloody wonder you could get it up."

"Well the smart thing, you see, about fooking old Annie, is you don't have to fooking worry about getting the fooking pox, 'cause you know fooking well nobody's fooking fooked her for twenty fooking years."

Cully reached down to his ordnance belt, drew his bayonet and fixed it to his musket as quietly as possible, hoping he wouldn't have to use it. Then he took two deep breaths to prime his Parade Ground voice and bellowed: "What's this, what's this, what's this? On your feet, you slovenly soldiers! At Attention! If you're bloody drunk on bloody duty I'll have your bloody guts for garters! Eyes front, damn you!" Then he waved Joseph Brossard and the others to follow him and stepped out into the open with his musket at the ready.

One of the soldiers quivering at attention gaped at him, "You're a bloody deserter!"

"I'm your bloody *murderer*, old son, if you don't do what you're told. Down on your asses, all of you, with your hands behind your heads. When's your relief due?"

"Any minute now. They were supposed to be here by—"

"Don't bloody lie to me—you wouldn't be passing a bottle around if you expected your sergeant coming up with your relief any minute. I'm just asking 'cause I'm trying to decide if it's safe to leave you trussed-up here, or whether we should cut your throats and take your scalps for the bounty."

"Our relief's due tomorrow morning."

"Good. You won't starve to death by then, and we'll be long gone." He switched into French. "Henri, cut one of their blankets into strips to tie them to trees. We'll take the rest of the blankets with us, along with anything else useful." By way of illustration, Cully slung one of the stacked muskets over his shoulder and picked up the ordnance belt that went with it. "These are bound to be useful to the people we're going to meet—or to any of the rest of us who can shoot but don't have guns."

Joseph Brossard nodded, "Eulalie."

Cully said: "Eulalie?"

"She can shoot a gun. Oh, not like Henri, but better than most soldiers."

Brossard whistled and the rest of the band of refugees came up to join them. They all laughed happily at Joseph Brossard's colourful description of the trick Cully had played. All except Eulalie, who just wordlessly slung one of the ordnance belts around her—like a bandoleer belled out by her breasts—picked up a musket and trudged on westward.

Cully could feel himself slumping again, as though his back had stiffened itself to deal with the matter at hand, and now that it was over the starch had all gone out. As he picked up his burdens to fall in as rearguard, one of the trussed bloodybacks spat at him: "How much did the King of France pay you to kiss his arse?"

"I don't give a damn for the King of France. Or the King of England."

But when Cully glanced back over his shoulder at six of his one-time brothers-in-arms sitting with their backs against poplar trees and their hands tied behind the trunks, he wondered if Eulalie La Tour's opinion of him wasn't that far wrong.

XXIII

s they left the border zone behind them, Eulalie expected to find Acadian farms and fishing stations along the shoreline. What they found were charred stone chimneys standing out of piles of ashes, and starved-looking watchdogs still nosing around the wreckage and whining.

Beau-père declared: "It's only that we haven't come far enough yet. Beausoleil would never let this happen on the Petitcodiac or the Miramichi." Eulalie wasn't sure whether he was as certain as he sounded, or was just trying to keep spirits up.

Either way, there was nothing they could do but keep on walking north as the nights grew frostier and the last leaves blew off the trees. Their only other option was to backtrack to Fort Cumberland and give themselves up for deportation, and no one wanted to talk about that yet.

The children grew colder and hungrier and more bad-tempered. One morning Josette woke up with something in her eye. She'd rubbed it red before Eulalie could stop her. Eulalie wetted the corner of her kerchief and dabbed at the eye, but could find nothing. There was definitely something in there, though, which by all reason should've been washed out already by the tidebanks of tears. Josette was starting to panic and everyone else was impatient to get moving.

"Got something in your eye, Josette?" The voice came in over Eulalie's shoulder. It was the tinker. Eulalie wanted to tell him to mind his own business, whatever that was. But that would've meant speaking to him.

Josette whimpered: "Yes, Cully." As though any fool couldn't see she had something in her eye.

The tinker said: "Well, luckily for you I have an eyestone."

Eulalie snapped: "This is no time for stupid games."

"It isn't a game." He crouched in front of Josette, set down a tin cup filled with water and opened his hand to disclose a tiny, leather pouch nestled in his palm. "Where

I come from, Josette, on the Channel Islands, every family has an eyestone or two. The people of Guernsey say they invented them, but we of Jersey disagree. I just have to wash the sugar off it…"

Josette sniffled: "Sugar?"

"An eyestone has to be kept in brown sugar to keep it from going stale." He plucked something out of the pouch, swirled it in the water and held up his forefinger. Stuck to the tip of his finger was something shiny and opaque. "Now open your eye as wide as you can. This will feel funny, but it won't hurt…"

Josette twitched as his finger touched her eyeball. He said: "Now close your eye and tilt your head to the side—that's right—now blink your eye and keep on blinking…"

Josette squealed: "It's moving!"

"That's good."

"It feels funny…"

"I told you it would. Has it reached the other end of your eye yet?"

"Yes."

"Then open wide again." He dabbed the eyestone out, glanced at it and said: "A speck of soot. You shouldn't sit downwind of the campfire," then stuck his finger in the cup again.

Josette said: "Thank you, Cully."

Eulalie stood up with her back to the tinker and called to Beau-père: "All right, we can start now."

Once they were on the move again, Josette said to her: "Why are you so cruel to Cully?"

"Someday I'll tell you." But Josette's question got Eulalie thinking again about the one piece she couldn't fit into the picture of the tinker who'd betrayed them for money. It nagged at her all day as they trudged along another footpath that led nowhere but another pile of ashes.

When they camped for the night, she went up to the tinker—trying not to look at him directly—said: "I have to ask you a question," then turned and walked into the woods.

She could hear him following her through the mat of brittle leaves. When she judged they were out of earshot of the others, she turned around and said brusquely: "I only have one question. Will you promise to answer it truly?" She realized how ridiculous that was as soon as it had left her mouth. How could she trust his promise?

He said: "After what I've told you already, what would I have left to lie about?"

That was more convincing than any oath he could've sworn. But maybe he was clever enough to know that. She went ahead and asked her question. "Why did you come back?"

"Come back?"

"To Ardoise valley. You'd done your job and got your reward. Why didn't you stay at Fort Edward with your friends?"

"I didn't know."

"Didn't know what?"

"I didn't know what the list was for. I thought it was just so we'd know where to find anyone who turned into a troublemaker once the war started. I don't think a dozen people in Nova Scotia knew what the governor had planned for the Fifth of September. The soldiers at Fort Edward, including me, found out the same time as the Acadians did: when the Officer Commanding read out the king's proclamation.

"After I heard the proclamation, I looked over the crowd and saw that Joseph Brossard and Henri and Jacques weren't among the prisoners. I thought you could all get away if you were warned. So I put away my uniform and went over the wall."

Her impulse was to cry out: *You did that for us?* But she only had his word for it, so she held it in.

He said awkwardly: "Eulalie, you don't know what it is to be a soldier: you do what you're told, or they make you wish to Christ you had."

"You're not a soldier anymore."

"No, I'm a bloody deserter."

"They hang deserters."

"They have to catch them first."

"Well... Well... I have to help Moïse's wife try to make some supper from what food we have left." She turned and walked quickly back to camp.

The next morning brought a blessed last-gasp of Indian summer, with people shucking off their coats or cloaks as they walked. But the sun only warmed Eulalie's skin. Inside she was chillingly calculating whether they had one more day or two before they had to face the choice of turning back for Fort Cumberland, or keep on walking north until they starved to death.

They were straggling along a path that wound along the edge of sea cliffs, when a voice called from the forest: "*Bonjour!*"

Eulalie almost fell into the breakers. A dozen hard-looking *couriers de bois*, dressed in buckskins and homespun and armed to the teeth, stepped out of the woods. Beaupère called to them: "*Nous somme Acadiens!*" and the two groups melded in a cheerful babble—deliriously cheerful on the part of Eulalie and the others she'd walked so far with.

After they'd all got a start in on figuring out who was whose second cousin twice removed, the roughest-looking of the *couriers de bois* said: "Well, I guess we best take you to Beausoleil."

They came to a riverside farm with tents and lean-tos clustered around it, and Acadians of all shapes and sizes bustling around them. Away from the bustle, a kitchen chair had been set out in the sun. Sitting on it was a meaty-shouldered, big-jawed man with a pewter flagon in his hand. He was wearing only doeskin breeches, and the hair on his massive chest was as grizzled as the matted thatch on his head.

Eulalie could see Beau-père's face getting that happy pucker which signified there was a joke he'd been waiting to tell for a long time. He thrust his hand out at the man in the chair and announced: "I am Joseph Brossard."

The man squinted up at him confusedly, tilted his chair back to get a better angle, and muttered thickly: "No... I am Joseph Brossard..." The chair teetered too far and toppled backward, taking its occupant with it. The great Beausoleil's head hit the ground, emitted an unconcerned grunt, closed its eyes, lolled sideways and began snoring.

XXIV

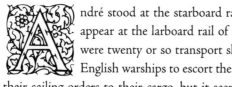

ndré stood at the starboard rail at sunset, waiting for an Acadian to appear at the larboard rail of the ship anchored closest to his. There were twenty or so transport ships rendezvoused to convoy, and three English warships to escort them. The English captains didn't mention their sailing orders to their cargo, but it seemed likely that their plan was to weigh anchor tomorrow morning, when the outgoing tide would speed them south out of Fundy bay.

A white mobcap poked over the rail across the waves from him. He waved his arm over his head and called: "*Bonjour, cousine!*" She waved back, he shouted his name and she called back hers. He called out questions that would sound to an eavesdropper like just passing the time of day, and discovered that she was from up around Fort Beauséjour and that her ship was carrying eight hundred Acadians, twice as many as his.

He cupped his hands around his mouth to make his voice louder, "Are you all women and children, then?"

"No, many men as well."

"Do you know the story of Charles La Tour and the Mohawks?"

"Which one?" The tone in her voice suggested she suddenly suspected she was conversing with an idiot.

There were many stories about Eulalie's great-great-great-grandfather—so many, in fact, that André was sure they couldn't all be true. At the moment, though, it didn't matter whether this particular story were true, only that most Acadians knew it. The story went that some English fur traders had offered a big reward for his capture, and some Mohawks had come up to Acadia and ambushed him and his companions. The Mohawks had been pleasantly surprised that the bold La Tour made such an easy prisoner. But in the night, when they were camped at the base of Cape Blomidon, La Tour had slipped his ropes and made his captors captive.

André called across the water: "The story about La Tour and the Mohawks and the reward and Blomidon. Do you know it?"

"Yes..."

"Tomorrow is the anniversary of when that happened. We on this ship mean to have a little celebration of that anniversary tomorrow, for luck. The crack of dawn is when we of Piziquid always celebrate that anniversary. It would be good if *all* of us on all the ships did the same. The more people that celebrate, the more luck there is. And if there's one thing we of Acadia need now, it's luck."

There was a long pause, then she called back: "I'll be sure to tell my father."

André stayed at the rail a while longer, asking her opinion of the weather, and whether she was acquainted with his mother's brother-in-law from up around her way, then bid her *bon soir* and *bonne chance*. As he made his way back to the hatchway to the hold, he avoided meeting the eyes of the New England sailors going about their business. But none of them seemed in the least suspicious. Maybe he was finally learning how to lie.

Long after the dog-watch came on duty, André sat on his cramped blanket listening to the anxious murmurings around him. The prisoners outnumbered the crew by so many times that it should be easy to overwhelm them in one rush, before the captain could get out of his bed and issue weapons. But saying it would be easy was one thing, doing it another.

Because the name André Melanson had long been a Piziquid byword for "strong as a bear", even since before he got his full growth, he had naturally been picked for the group that was supposed to silence the night watch. He sat on his blanket wondering what he would do if they fought back. Seeing the tinker at Fort Edward was the first and only time in his life he'd wanted to kill someone. He knew he had the strength in his hands to crush a man's neck, but could he? The men on night-watch had never done him or his family any harm, except to sail where their captain told them.

The bobbing shadows from the lamp chained to the ceiling of the hold began to bounce and elongate. The floor beneath André's blanket began to slide crazily up and down, instead of rocking gently. Even from the hold, he could hear the wind rising, and then pellets of sleet driven against the hull. Seaboots and bare feet drummed across the deck overhead, and voices bellowed into the wind. The windlass clattered frantically to draw up the anchor chain before it snapped. All the hatches thumped shut and were battened down.

Someone in the hold had the sense to jump up and blow out the lamp before it scattered fire. Children screamed in the dark, as people and bundles of possessions began to collide. André remembered that the family next to him had one small child too many to shelter them all. He shouted to them and fumbled with his hands, scooped up a bearcub-sized girl and held her in his arms while their wooden whale-belly reared up and down and sideways.

When the sea finally calmed and the hatches were thrown open again, daylight streamed in. André squinted against the brightness, patted his smooth-skinned bearcub back to her family, and creaked stiffly to his feet to climb out into the open.

Although the state of the ship was hardly André's responsibility, he'd been through enough storms on his father's boat that his eyes automatically searched around for damages as soon as he stepped on deck. Some sailors were up on the mainmast yard-ärm, taking down a tattered topsail, but otherwise the storm seemed to have done no damage except shattering the hope he'd been holding onto for two months.

He went to the rail and ledged his hand to his forehead to see better. They were out on the open sea, with no land in sight to the east, north or south. Which meant that the wind and tide had already carried them out of the bay and past the southern boundary of French Acadia. The hazy black line on the western horizon was the coast of the Boston colonies.

A few of the other sails of the convoy were in sight, but scattered far too wide for clever messages to be shouted from one to another. If only one of the transport ships mutinied, it would be an easy matter for the warships to come alongside and board her. André squinted at the ships that he could see, wondering if one of them might be the one carrying his family.

He tried to think of some good reason why the good God would have decided to let a storm come up on the bay last night. The best he could come up with was that maybe the plan wouldn't have worked, and a number of Acadians and sailors would've been killed to no purpose.

But even with that possible good reason in mind, André still couldn't put aside the feeling that if it hadn't been for an accident of nature, he and everyone else in the convoy would now be sailing for French Acadia. He had decided back at Fort Edward that as soon as he set foot on French Acadia he would start walking north to the Petitcodiac and the Miramichi. Knowing Eulalie and Joseph Brossard as he did, he had no doubt where they had run to: Beausoleil.

XXV

eausoleil wants to see *l'Anglais*."

Cully looked out from under the corner of the old sail that he and Eulalie and the Brossards were trying to rig into a tent. As his eyes lit on the rough-looking, extremely well-armed gentleman who'd delivered the summons, his ever-wary mind leaped to a very unpleasant possibility.

If Beausoleil wanted to see "*l'Anglais*", someone had obviously told him Cully was a British deserter. Maybe Eulalie or Joseph Brossard had also told him about the tinker's spying. They might've innocently assumed that it was something Beausoleil should know and that he would more or less put it in the past, as they had. Well, not very far in the past in Eulalie's case.

But maybe Beausoleil had come up with a very different answer to Eulalie's question of why Cully had come back to the valley of Ardoise. An ambitious English spy could earn a tremendous reward by smuggling himself in with Acadians fleeing to Beausoleil, and then informing his masters where to find him.

The messenger added: "And he wants *l'Anglais* to bring his musket and bayonet."

That didn't sound like an invitation to a throat-cutting. Cully picked up his musket and ordnance belt and started off. Joseph Brossard called after him cheerfully: "Lucky again, Cully—we'll have all the work done when you get back." Cully waved over his shoulder and refrained from replying: "*If* I get back."

Beausoleil and several dozen other men were gathered in a clearing by the river. It was a drizzly, overcast day, which Cully saw was a stroke of luck for Beausoleil. His long nap in the sun yesterday had left a painful-looking, bright red border along the top of his forehead and his temples. He was a good deal taller than he looked sitting in a chair or stretched out on the ground—taller than most Grenadier Guards.

Beausoleil said: "Ah, *l'Anglais*—we're hoping you can teach us something. You see, whenever we fought English soldiers before, we fought like our brothers the Mi'kmaqs—a quick ambush and then back into the forest..."

Cully said bitterly: "I know."

"But now, if they come marching into our home country, we may have to stand and fight them toe-to-toe. So, show us how the English soldiers will use their bayonets if they come at us."

"Well... I can show you how we're—they're—*taught* to use them."

"Good, yes, show us that."

Cully buckled on his ordnance belt and stood Brown Bess—the only reliable bedmate in a soldier's life—on her butt in front of him. He performed the seven distinct motions involved in *Draw Bayonets, Fix Bayonets and Recover*, ending up with Brown Bess's neck propped across the crook of his left arm and his right hand on her bottom. "This is the stance for the front rank. For rear and centre ranks..." He shifted his feet and his grip, so the musket was balanced on his left hand instead of the crook of his elbow, and the bayonet was further forward. "*Whether front, centre, or rear, all ranks on the order will push their bayonets three times while advancing three steps.*"

He demonstrated and the clearing erupted in laughter, with *couriers de bois* and outlaw-farmers mimicking his shuffling steps and mincing push-pull on the musket butt. Beausoleil called out: "You won't laugh so loud to see a wall of steel coming at you," which managed to sober one or two of them. For all his woodsy joviality, there was an air of gravity to Beausoleil, as though he were always considering things a bit more carefully than those around him.

Cully said lamely: "Well, that's the method for an orderly advance. If the enemy doesn't give way, and it turns into tooth-and-nail, every man has his own method."

Beausoleil said: "*Anglais*, do you shoot as good as most English soldiers, or better...?"

"Passable average."

"Good, we'll see what 'passable average' is. Someone set me up a mark on that stump over there."

Cully looked around for a stump and couldn't see one. Then he saw a boy about Jean-Marc's age running toward the far end of the clearing. There was a stump there, all right, at least fifty yards away. The boy set a white rock on top of it that Cully could barely see.

Beausoleil gestured at Cully to shoot the rock. Cully said: "No one could hit that from here."

Beausoleil said: "No one?" He picked up a long rifle leaning against a tree, clicked back the cock, dropped to one knee, took aim in the flick of an eyelash and fired. The rock jumped off the stump. No one applauded or seemed to consider it a remarkable shot, at least not for Beausoleil.

Cully said: "That's with a rifle, not a smooth-bore musket."

"You're welcome to borrow my rifle for a shot."

"I'm not used to it."

"Well… Show us what the English soldiers *can* hit with their muskets, then. How about that oak tree?"

The tree he pointed at was four feet wide and twenty yards away. Cully went through the prescribed motions of *Present And Aim* and pulled the trigger. He missed it cleanly.

The laughter this time threatened hernias. Cully muttered: "It would've hit the next man in line," which made them laugh even harder—whooping at the notion that Acadians would be standing shoulder-to-shoulder patiently waiting to be shot at.

Cully could feel his cheeks getting hot. He raised his voice over the laughter: "All right—so now the bloodybacks have fired at you and missed, and you've knocked a few of them on the head while they were brainlessly pushing their bayonets forward. And now it's come to face-to-face and hand-to-hand… I need three men who don't mind a bit of rough-and-tumble, and I need a strong green stick a little longer than my bayonet."

They all jumped eagerly at the prospect of a bit of rough-and-tumble. Beausoleil picked out three of the biggest ones. A fourth man came forward with a very long knife and a length of poplar sapling.

Cully worked the stick down over his bayonet, telling the selected three: "Take up your muskets or rifles, but don't cock them—we'll say you haven't had time to re-load." He was wishing he'd thought before he'd shouted. Three made rather long odds, and all three of them were very large—one of them almost as large as Beausoleil. But he was damned if he was going to leave these shoot-from-ambushers with the impression that a Regiment of the Line was something for them to laugh at.

He waved his arm to shoo the spectators back, gripped Brown Bess at Advance, turned to the three volunteers leaning on their guns and bellowed: "All right you whoreson, pissant, frog-licking shitdiggers—come get yourselves killed so we can fuck your wives and daughters! How can I stick a bayonet in your guts if you don't have any? We'll fuck your mothers, fuck your sisters, fuck your priest in his black dress!"

One of them lost his temper an instant before the others, which would make it a little easier. He came on at a run with his musket clubbed and the other two a step behind. Cully rammed his bayonet-stick into the first one's midriff, then pivoted his musket to drive the butt against the second one's head.

The third one was swinging his gunbutt down like a splitting axe at Cully's head. As the voice of Sergeant Robin said in Cully's inner ear: *Told you you should've said "two"*, Cully flung Brown Bess up braced two-handed and just managed to catch the blow. They were frozen for an instant—Cully's arms and the woodchopper's numbed by the shock—and then Cully kicked him squarely in the yarbles. The poor man went down on his knees and Cully held up his musket like a canoe paddle poised to stroke, to show how easy it would be to dash the kneeling man's brains out, then lowered it and turned away.

A large body slammed into him from behind and came down on top of him as he hit the ground. A hand in his hair wrenched his head back, a knife flashed and a gasping voice jeered: "So what's to stop me from cutting your throat now, you—?" There was a thump and a grunt and the weight on Cully's back was gone. He looked sideways and saw the man he'd knocked the breath out of with his bayonet-stick rolling away, and Beausoleil's booted foot coming back to the ground.

Beausoleil shouted: "What's to stop you from cutting his throat is he already killed you with his bayonet! That's enough lessons for today." He reached his pie-sized hand down and helped Cully to his feet. "But you, *Anglais*, you come with me."

"Wait!" Cully called out to the buckskinned and homespunned men starting to drift away. They stopped and turned. "Something you should take to heart... At one time or another, you all must have seen British soldiers drilling, stupidly repeating the same movements over and over all day as their officer calls out the orders. Well, one of those orders—just as matter-of-fact and by-the-numbers as *Shoulder Arms*, or *About Left*—is *Wipe Your Bayonets.*"

Beausoleil nodded approvingly at the lesson in that, then beckoned Cully into the woods. As Cully followed him down a forest path, Beausoleil said over his shoulder: "My son has too much of a temper—good for fighting, but not for learning."

"Your son?"

"The one you killed with your bayonet. I have four sons grown big enough to do all the fighting for me, now that I'm too old. I just go along for show." Cully highly doubted that, but didn't argue.

They came to a stream with a small campfire beside it and an Indian woman pottering about. Beausoleil flopped down on the carpet of leaves, with his back against a hollow log, and gestured Cully to make himself comfortable. As Cully found himself a perch, Beausoleil reached into the log and came out with a leather bottle. He pulled out the stopper and handed the bottle to Cully, saying: "You have to be careful with this cider, it's stronger than it tastes. Saved from last winter, when we sat a barrel out in the snow overnight and drained off what didn't freeze."

"You didn't seem very careful with it yesterday."

"Every man needs a holiday from time to time. And I won't see another one soon. In a day or two we have to be back on the war road, even if we have to go on snowshoes. I can't do much about Fort Cumberland, except keep them nervous about sticking their noses out. But the little fort north of it is almost in my backyard. I don't like strangers moving into my backyard. So, I intend to keep on making life at the little fort as miserable as possible until they go home. You could pass that bottle back from time to time—I don't mean to be *that* careful."

Beausoleil began to ask questions. He seemed to know a surprising amount about which elements of which regiments were stationed at Fort Cumberland and the little fort. But all that that information meant to him was names and numbers. To Cully, the names and numbers meant the difference between green recruits and veterans; the difference between officers who were reputed to barely have the brains to parrot the manoeuvres their grandfathers practised in the Dutch war, and officers who were reputed to actually march into battle in front of their troops instead of behind them; the difference between soldiers who'd been living through Nova Scotia winters since Halifax was founded and ones freshly posted to North America...

The one thing Beausoleil's information was obviously dead wrong on, though, was the cider. Cully was perfectly willing to admit he knew next to nothing about canoes and mushrooms and such, but he certainly knew the taste of alcohol, and there wasn't much in this stuff. He did find himself finding it increasingly hilarious, though, that Beausoleil should consider his brains worth picking.

XXVI

N ight had come down, and all the younger children asleep in the new tent made from an old sail, by the time Eulalie heard the singing approaching. One of the voices was Cully Robin's, loudly singing a very slow version of his Tinker's Song. The other voice was male as well, la-la-ing along underneath. Into the campfire light came Cully and Beausoleil, each with an arm around the other's back. Cully looked like he definitely needed the support, Beausoleil not necessarily—it would've taken at least two Cully Robins to hold him up.

Beausoleil brought them to a halt and said cheerfully to Eulalie and Beau-père: "I think this one here is ready for a sleep."

Eulalie got under one of Cully's arms, Beau-père took the other and they helped Cully into the tent. Along the way, Cully's head bobbed down toward hers and he let out a cider-steeped whisper: "Eulalie..." then turned it into a rising and falling trill, as though it were a la-la-la chorus, "Euu—la-lee, Eu-la-lee..."

They laid him down on his back on his blanket. His hand fluttered up toward her left breast, then fell back down and his eyes fell shut. Eulalie didn't feel particularly embarrassed to see him so drunk. Once or twice she'd had to load Beau-père into his bed in the same condition. It was just one of several ridiculous things men seemed to have to do from time to time—as long as they didn't make a habit of it.

She stayed kneeling beside his blanket a moment longer, looking down at the snoring, hooked-snub nose and the lines around the closed eyes. His face looked so much darker now, after two months of living in the open. She wondered if she'd ever make up her mind about him. One moment he was the companion who'd walked so many miles with her and her family, the next he was the traitor in her bed. She felt stupid and cruel to be constantly clicking back and forth like a loom shuttle—stupid when she caught herself forgetting what a cunning liar he could be, cruel when she suddenly turned cold to him in the middle of some family playfulness. But whatever cloth some unseen hand was weaving with her, she couldn't stop herself shooting from one side to the other and back again.

When she and Beau-père came back out to the fire, Beausoleil was still standing there. He waggled his finger toward the tent and said: "You take good care of that one, he is a mine of gold to us." Then he scratched his peeling forehead and said: "Funny, though—when he got too much cider in him to get any more sense out of him, he kept muttering the same thing and laughing and winking, 'You think I'm a tinker, but I ain't.' What did he mean?"

Eulalie didn't know whether she should tell him. Beau-père wasn't jumping out with the story, either—which meant that he, too, wasn't sure whether it would be wrong not to tell Beausoleil, or wrong to tell him. It would be so easy for anyone to pass judgement on what the tinker had done in the spring—anyone who hadn't spent the autumn fleeing through the woods with Cully Robin.

Eulalie said: "He told us he was a travelling tinker before they made him become a soldier. I don't think he ever wanted to be a soldier."

"Ah. Yes, I *thought* he seemed too smart to volunteer. Tomorrow morning, I want to speak to you and all our other homeless ones. We have to make some plans. Well, *bon soir*. I hope you enjoyed your supper of dried fish. Me, if I never see another damned dried fish again I won't cry."

After Beausoleil was gone, Beau-père said: "I think you did right to not tell all the truth, Eulalie. He wouldn't've understood."

"Do *you*?"

"Oh yes. It seems simple enough: they gave Cully his orders and shook a bag of gold under his nose. And he didn't know what his list was going to be used for."

"You believe that?"

"Oh yes. When a governor has such a big, secret plan, he doesn't go telling it to common soldiers. I think probably if Cully had known, he still would've done it, *then*— before he broke his leg and became friends with us and... other things. I told you once he's a coyote; coyotes live how they can. And," he laughed, "I was glad we had a clever coyote along when that camp of English soldiers blocked our path."

"We wouldn't've needed to be on that path if it wasn't for him."

Beau-père shook his head. "The soldiers from Fort Edward would've found the valley of Ardoise sooner or later. The tinker's list only made it sooner. I don't say I forget what he did, but I can understand."

Eulalie pushed a stick into the coals and stirred them around, then said: "Maybe I can understand *why*, but not *how*. How he could smile and lie to our faces..."

"Isn't that what *you* just did, with Beausoleil? And very well you did it, too, I thought. Makes me wonder what kinds of things you and the children got up to back home that I never suspected. Well, *bon soir, petite mère.*"

She sat up a while longer, stirring the coals into their last flames. She wondered if maybe she stared into the fire long enough she might see whatever foreign place it was that André Melanson had been set ashore. But Cully Robin kept interposing among the pictures in the flames.

It was hard to keep her mind from worrying at Cully Robin. He had become like a will-o'-the-wisp that kept revealing itself in new and different shapes as it lured her further into the woods. All her life she'd heard stories of Beausoleil, but never expected to meet him; and now here was Beausoleil himself singing drinking songs with Cully Robin and calling him a mine of gold.

In the morning, Eulalie and all the rest of the refugees assembled in front of the farmhouse. There were two hundred of them or more. Standing off to one side were a French officer and a couple of dozen white-uniformed soldiers. Eulalie tried not to stare; she'd never seen French soldiers in her life. They didn't look all that different from English soldiers, except the colour of their coats.

Beausoleil stood up on the chopping block beside the farmhouse door and said: "Me and my *couriers de bois* and Lieutenant Boishébert are heading off to meet some Mi'kmaqs and pay a little visit on the English before they get too snugged-in for the winter. *L'Anglais* will come with us, but the rest of you men have something else important to do: getting yourselves and your families away from here before the snow flies."

Eulalie's stomach turned over. She'd thought that once they'd found Beausoleil they'd have found a resting place.

"This place is too handy to the sea—much too easy for an English warship to sail in here and drag you all away to the English colonies. And the few little farms here can hardly feed so many people. Even the dried fish is almost gone—thanks be to God.

"The fishermen here will ferry across anyone who wants to go to Ile St. Jean. Ile St. Jean will be safe as long as Louisbourg stands. Some of you may rather walk north to the Miramichi, or west to my own home country on the Petitcodiac. Well, that's all I have to tell you."

Beausoleil jumped down and threaded his way through the crowd to where Eulalie was standing with her family and the tinker. "*Anglais,* you look a little green this morning."

"Not so bad. At least the stuff was pure. But it sounds like I got drunk enough to volunteer."

Beausoleil shrugged, "I can *say* you did, and how could you say you didn't?" Then he turned to Beau-père. "It seems only fitting, Joseph Brossard, that you should take your family to the Petitcodiac, where lives Joseph Brossard."

Eulalie said: "Is there room there to have a roof over the children? I can already smell snow in the air."

"A lot more roofs than the Miramichi. As for Ile St. Jean—it's true that the English will never land an army there while Louisbourg still stands, but there's no saying they won't make raids along the coast. Yes, I'd say the Petitcodiac is the best place for you to be. I'll leave a good man behind to guide your way.

"*Anglais*, best be fetching your musket and blanket. And take the stick off your bayonet."

Cully turned to Eulalie and the family and said: "Well, um…"

Beau-père stuck out his hand and said: "*Adieu*, Cully. We see you again on the Petitcodiac."

Eulalie shook Cully's hand as well and said: "*Bonne chance.*" Then all the children from Henri down to Josette stuck out their hands.

When the tinker had shaken all their hands, he looked down at his cracked boot-toes, said: "Well, um…" and walked away from them, wearing his shoulders for earrings.

Watching Cully's back recede, it crossed Eulalie's mind that Beausoleil's insistence that she and her family winter on the Petitcodiac might be because of *l'Anglais*. She wondered what else Cully might have muttered in his cups last night, besides his dangerous joke about tinkers and soldiers.

The trail west wound under naked trees with trunks as wide as Eulalie could stretch her arms, and across streams that already had a thin skin of ice. Back home in the valley of Ardoise, there would have been a few hard frosts by now but the days would still be warm.

They walked in a straggling line with half-a-dozen other Acadian families who looked as raggedy as them. Eulalie could see the children growing thinner, and Beau-père leaning more heavily on the staff he'd cut at their first night's camp. It was one journey too many for all of them.

Eulalie woke up in the middle of one night to discover that the blanket nest she shared with the girls had a crust of snow on it, and big, fat flakes were wafting down. She pulled the top blankets up higher to cover their heads and huddled in tighter. From then on they didn't carry their blankets, but wore them over their coats or cloaks. Eulalie lost count of the days.

They came to a big river with a network of creeks running into it, and little farms and hunters' cabins dotted along the waterways. People came out of the cabins and farmyards, calling out curiously in Acadian French. But the guide kept leading onward, so the curious ones fell in beside the newcomers, gabbling back and forth and shaking hands on the move.

The guide finally stopped in a farmyard that looked no different from any of the others, except the house was a little bigger. A weary-looking woman with white-streaked blonde hair came out of the house. The guide said to her: "They escaped from the English. Your husband sent them here."

Beausoleil's wife looked up and down the line of refugees, with her cheeks puckering like she'd just drunk vinegar, and said: "He *would*."

❊ ❊ ❊

It turned out that almost all the spare space in the settlement was already filled with fugitives. Eulalie and her family were relegated to Beausoleil's brother's hayloft.

When Eulalie helped Madame Beausoleil—Agnes *dit* Anne à Jehan à Pacifique—divide up the provisions the neighbours had brought in for the new arrivals, she saw why Anne had looked so sour. There was little more than a few sacks of flour and cabbages, and rag-ends of stewing beef.

Anne said: "People give what they can, but you see, Eulalie, the country here is nowhere so good for farming as the old, diked lands on your side of the bay. Not that no one gets fat here—what with hunting and fishing to fill out the corners. But we are getting to be too many here; I think when my youngest sons start their own families they will have to move to another part of the country. And now suddenly this winter we have twice as many mouths to feed as last."

Eulalie said: "I'm sorry."

"What for? What was my husband to do but send you here? What were you to do but come here? Are we to leave our cousins to starve in the snow? Would you do that to us? But, that doesn't mean it's going to be easy."

Eulalie put herself and her family to work providing what they could for themselves. She sent Jean-Marc and Louise scouting for cranberry bogs. Henri and Jacques took Cully's carbine along with some of the local boys going moosehunting. Eulalie, Beau-père, Hélène and Marie went digging cattail roots and Jerusalem artichokes, with Josette tagging along to stay out of mischief.

But the digging turned out to use up more food than it provided. First they had to scrape away the snow, then make a fire to thaw the ground. By the time they'd dug up three or four roots, they each could've eaten a dozen.

Eulalie had been at Petitcodiac three weeks when Beausoleil came home, trailing a line of raffish-looking men on snowshoes. The people along the Petitcodiac were in need of something to celebrate, and now they had more than something: their men had all come home safe after seeing to it that the English soldiers weren't going to venture far from their forts this winter.

Eulalie reveled in the stories of Acadians finally giving the English second thoughts. At the little fort, Beausoleil's band had ambushed a woodcutting party of soldiers, and sniped at the fort so accurately that the sentries grew afraid to stick their heads above the palisade. Then they'd gone on to give the same treatment to the big fort. The commander of Fort Cumberland had sent out a troop to teach the Acadians a lesson, but that had only resulted in a lot of red coats making fine targets against the snow, and a few greased and powdered scalps for the Mi'kmaqs to take home.

The celebration centered in Beausoleil's house, but radiated out into several of the houses nearby. Eulalie shepherded the younger children from house to house, enjoying the music and the dancing and the laughter. But in one house she came across someone who wasn't singing or dancing or laughing. Cully Robin was sitting in a dark corner drinking cider and staring through the wall.

Eulalie went up to him and poked his shoulder and said: "Aren't you happy you came away from the shooting with no bullets in you?"

He looked up at her and then away. He said flatly: "They were my brothers."

XXVII

ndré's ship and one other were the only transports left in the convoy. The others had all peeled off singly or in pairs as they'd passed by Massachusetts, Connecticut, New York, New Jersey, Maryland, Virginia... André had no idea where the ship carrying his family had turned aside, only that it wasn't the other one still left.

Even out on the open sea, the air had been growing steadily warmer. The hold had become a steampot of human odours, but there wasn't room on deck for all the prisoners all at once, so they took it in turns.

André had just reached the end of his quarter-hour of fresh air when the captain started shouting orders and sails were trimmed to swing the bow toward the shoreline. André knew his allotment was up, but he stayed on deck. From the look of things, there would soon be plenty of fresh air for everyone.

Other Acadians began to scuttle out on deck, until there were as many of them as could crowd together without blocking the crew. The hold hatch filled with heads craning around and shouting questions.

The captain took a moment from bellowing orders to call out: "*Mes amis!*" All Acadian heads turned toward the quarterdeck. The captain pointed ahead with his spyglass and said: "Charleston, South Carolina."

The ship passed between two headlands, into a sheltered harbor with a town at the other end. As the anchor dropped, André joined the flow crowding the rail to see where they'd been taken.

Charleston, South Carolina, was a long, stone quay with warehouses and stone buildings and, beyond them, roofs and church spires fading into the distance. The largest town André had ever seen was Halifax. Charleston looked like it could lodge the entire population of Halifax, garrison and all, in its outhouses.

The ship lowered her boat and began ferrying the cargo ashore. André hadn't brought his possessions along for his stroll on deck, so he had to work against the current surging out of the hold. By the time he'd fetched his coat, blanket and wooden shoes, and been allowed a place on the boat's next shuttle, the quay was a kicked-anthill of confusion. A hastily-assembled line of redcoat soldiers blocked the landward end, and all the Acadians who'd already been ferried to the dock were milling around with increasingly less room to mill. Men were yelling at each other in French and English and not seeming to understand either.

The next boatload after André's included the ship's captain. The captain and a man in a satin coat and white wig began to roar at each other nose-to-nose, waving their arms.

The woman standing next to André suddenly spat out: *"Tabernac!"*

André whispered to her: "What is it?"

"I know a little English," she whispered back. "Enough to know what they're—" She paused to swallow and inhaled through her teeth. "Governor Lawrence of Nova Scotia, you see, wanted it kept secret what he had planned for us. So secret that he didn't even tell the governors of the colonies he sent us to."

The satin-coated man finally gave up yelling at the captain and went to yell orders at the soldiers. The red line hinged open at the middle, forming a cordon to a long, low shed off the quay. The satin man turned back to the Acadians and shouted something in English, pinwheeling one arm and pointing the other at the shed. The soldiers stood vigilantly on guard at first, then relaxed as they saw that the flotsam plodding between them knew there was nowhere to run away to.

When André stepped into the shed, he saw it wasn't low-roofed after all—just so vast and long that it looked low. After two months crammed into the hold, this place seemed like it had room for every Acadian ever born to stretch out comfortably. But comfort obviously wasn't what the building was intended for: what windows there were had bars on them, there were iron rings fixed to some of the wallposts, and the door thumped closed with a ramming of bolts as soon as the last Acadian was through it.

There was a smell about the place that made the backs of André's hands squirm. It was a smell of fear-sweat, blood and herded panic. It would've put him in mind of the smell of a holding shed beside a slaughtering pen, except that the smell was human.

As darkness came down, the shed was filled with soft murmurings of unanswerable questions: *How long do you think they'll keep us here? What do you think they mean to do with us?* The morning had barely begun to cast shadows of the window bars when the door flung open and a squad of soldiers marched in to form a line along the front wall. A number of well-dressed men followed the soldiers in and fanned out through the slumped flock of Acadians. One of the men, a little quicker than the others, came in André's direction with his eyes darting about. When his eyes lit on André they lit up and the man pointed: "You! *Ici*," beckoning him forward.

As André got up and came forward, the man with the darting eyes picked out two other young men and beckoned them as well. When all three were standing in front of him, the man said in perfectly fluid French: "I am Monsieur Kenney."

Even though 'Kenney' sounded like an English mangling of some French name, André was so overjoyed to find someone in authority who spoke French as though he spoke it at home, that he stuck out his hand and grinned: "*Bonjour, confrère.*"

Monsieur Kenney looked down at André's hand like it was a dead cat, then said: "I am not your *confrère*. My family are Huguenots, whom your Catholic *confrères* hounded out of France—the few they didn't burn at the stake or massacre on St. Bartholomew's Day."

André said lamely: "A lot of the first Acadians were Huguenots."

"And what did you do to *them* to make it 'were'? I have no intention of persecuting you as my grandparents were persecuted, but speaking French does not make you my brothers.

"The three of you are to work for me, to pay your families' keep. A thousand destitute people suddenly thrust among us will quickly drain the public purse. So, those who can work will, to pay for those who can't."

It didn't cross André's mind to say that his family wasn't here, so the only keep he had to work for was his own. Among the thousand were more than a few who were his cousins, second cousins, uncles' sisters-in-law...

"The wages you earn," Monsieur Kenney went on, "I will pay to the public purse, less what it costs me to keep you."

André said: "*You* to keep us...?"

"Yes. Your families will stay in Charleston; you will work and live on my plantation."

A hovering old woman shrieked: "No!" and flung her arms around one of the young men standing beside André. All throughout the shed, pockets of voices were rising in rage or horror. A lone voice from the doorway cut through them.

Neither André nor most of the other Acadians understood what the voice had barked, but something in its tone turned their heads in that direction. The soldiers had all drawn their bayonets. Their officer barked another order and a sibilant clicking echoed down the shed as the bayonets were fixed.

The officer gave no further orders and the soldiers made no further moves, but that was enough to turn the shouts of anger into tearful *au revoirs* and promises to meet again soon. André felt a little removed from it all; he'd already been through it in Piziquid Harbor.

Monsieur Kenney beckoned to follow him outside. There were a number of wagons drawn up on the swath of flagstones between the shed and the blue gleam of Charleston Bay. A man with a double-barrelled fowling piece was leaning against one of the wagons. Next to him stood a wizened black man holding the bridle of a very tall, glossy saddlehorse. The man with the shotgun pointed at André's wooden shoes and laughed so hard he had to hold onto the wagonwheel. The black man stooped and cupped his hands for Monsieur Kenney to put his boot on and boost up onto the saddle.

Monsieur Kenney looked down at André and the other two as though they'd just proven themselves bone-stupid and said: "Into the wagon! Up, up!" then prodded his horse with his spurs and trotted away.

The black man drove the wagon, with the man who found wooden shoes hilarious perched beside him. As they clattered through the miraculously stone-floored streets of Charleston, André gawked at the rows of brick and clapboard buildings, at the spit-polished carriages rattling by, at the filigreed ironwork gating pink and blue houses whose colour seemed to be somehow imbedded in the plaster, at the bright-silked ladies with their parasols and the brocade-waistcoated gentlemen greeting them with elaborate bows: one hand cocked elegantly on a goldheaded walking stick while the other fluttered down a lace-trimmed hat like a dancing swan...

When the wagon left the town behind, André could just make out Monsieur Kenney cantering along the open road ahead of them and widening the gap. The road passed stands of lazy-looking, bearded trees with moss and ferns carpeting the ground and even the trunks and branches. The shades of green were moister and hazier than in Acadia. André had to remind himself that it was the middle of December; it felt like a fine spring day in Acadia, although the air was heavier.

The trees ended for a while and there was a long row of black men clearing a field, watched by a white man with a whip coiled around one shoulder. André stopped looking at the roadside and turned his attention to the other two Acadians in the back of the wagon. Although their homes had been on the far side of Piziquid from the Melansons', André had known them since they'd all grown old enough to roam beyond the sound of their mothers' voices.

At the moment, Phillipe à Jacques à Ti-Pierre was unashamedly wiping his eyes and sniffling; Patrice à Bernard à Moïse was peering about eagerly and pointing out every new and strange sight. André suspected that Patrice's daylight fascination with the new would only make it worse for Patrice come nightfall, when he closed his eyes to sleep and the old came sneaking up on him.

Since André had already had two months to accustom himself to the feeling that had sprung on Phillipe and Patrice only this morning, he wanted to tell them they'd get used to being separated from their families. Except he knew it wasn't true. It was like what an uncle who'd long ago lost his leg had told him once. Sometimes the uncle would still reach down to scratch an itch in the foot that wasn't there. Sometimes André would stumble across something funny or pretty and would turn around to tell his father and mother, or brothers and sisters. Or Eulalie.

The sun had climbed up to the top of its hill and started down the other side by the time the wagon turned off the road to a sprawling farm with a huge, white house and many barns and sheds. The man with the shotgun led André and Patrice and Phillipe to a cluster of sheds where black men and black women and their children were filling bowls out of a pot over an open fire.

"   It was no surprise to André that there were black people in the world. He'd seen black people in Nova Scotia, running errands for their masters at Halifax market. In fact, it was well known that a black man had been on the ship that first brought French colonists to Acadia. But these ones had a different air to them than the domestic slaves in Halifax. Some of the men and women had tattoos on their faces like Mi'kmaqs.

The man with the shotgun showed André and Patrice and Phillipe into a shed with straw on the dirt floor, and gestured that this was where they were to lay down their blankets. As they were mounding the straw into mattresses, Monsieur Kenney appeared at the door, with a pipe in one hand and a flagon in the other. He said: "Tomorrow, my overseer will pair each of you with a fieldhand who knows his business. If you work hard, you will eat well, and your families in Charleston will be taken care of—*well* taken care of, given what it cost me for your indenture.

"It is true you are white men, and not slaves. But if you try to run, my hunting hounds will smell you black."

XXVIII

E ulalie!"

Eulalie looked up from the pot of twice-boiled soup bones on the firepit in front of Beausoleil's brother's barn. Little Josette was standing in the barn doorway, twisting her pale hair around her fingers like maybe she'd done something wrong. Over the last two months, Josette's dark blue eyes had grown bigger as her face grew thinner. "Eulalie... Papa says come see him. I think he is annoyed."

Eulalie looked back into the bubbling pot. It wasn't going to boil over, and those bones would have to cook for hours to get anything out of them. She set her stirring spoon down in the snow, went into the barn and climbed the ladder to the loft. Josette tagged along behind her—not as though she wanted to, but as though she were under orders. They both moved slowly and dully, as everyone along the Petitcodiac seemed to these days.

The loft wasn't exactly warm, but it wasn't exactly cold, thanks to the cattle below. There weren't as many cattle as there had been, though. Alexandre Brossard had slaughtered all his steers and even some of the cows. Any more and he wouldn't have a herd left.

Penned human body warmth also helped to keep the loft from freezing. A family from Annapolis Royal had straggled into Petitcodiac in December and since then had shared the loft with Eulalie's family. At the moment, most of both families were sitting slackly in the straw, even though it was the middle of the day. Moving about outside any more than absolutely necessary would have been foolish. For now, life meant very slowly smouldering whatever fuel you could get in your body, and hope to keep the fire burning until spring.

The only members of Eulalie's family not in the loft were Henri and Jacques, who'd gone to inspect their rabbit snares and try their luck at the fishing hole they'd chopped in the ice. Eulalie didn't expect them to have much luck at either. With three times as many people hunting and fishing around Petitcodiac as ever had before, the woods and streams were just about cleaned out.

Not that anyone was in danger of starving to death before spring. With very careful rationing, there was enough for everyone to get a little nourishment every day. But bodies nourished just enough to keep from starving didn't have much strength to spend on fighting off sickness, especially when trying to live through an Acadian winter in haylofts, or woodsheds, or sleeping head-to-foot on kitchen floors. Marie and Hélène were currently wrapped up together in every spare blanket, and covered up to their necks with hay, in hopes of sweating out their hacking coughs. And when Beau-père looked up at Eulalie, his eyes were watery and pale and his face looked whiter than his hair.

He wheezed out: "Is this true, Eulalie? Josette tells me you told her, and all her brothers and sisters, that when I've ate all I can of my dinner, and hand the rest to one of them, they're to tell me they can't eat any more?"

Josette wailed at Eulalie: "I didn't know it was a secret!"

Eulalie said: "That's all right, Josette, we don't keep secrets from your papa," although she'd just as soon this one hadn't come out to create a *contretemps* when she could barely muster enough resources to meet the dull round of the days. She turned back to Beau-père and said: "Yes, I told them to say that."

"Well where is the sense in that? If I have ate my fill, what is the sense of wasting what's left over?"

"Because you haven't ate your fill. No one in Petitcodiac has ate their fill for weeks now. But you just take a couple of spoonfuls and give the rest away."

"That isn't true. I eat all I can. My bones stopped growing before you were born, and I don't do much to burn up food these days."

Eulalie caught herself seeing her uncle and stepfather as a petulant child, and asked herself who she thought she was. But his hands *were* fluttering about and his lower lip sticking out, just like Josette's when she got overtired. Eulalie said flatly: "Whatever you leave in your bowl, I'll throw to Beausoleil's dogs."

He closed his eyes and murmured: "Eulalie, Eulalie..." shaking his head and waggling the palm of his hand at her to make her stop. He opened his eyes again and said: "Josette, go see if Marie and Hélène need a sip of water they can't get for themselves when they're all bound up in blankets."

"Yes, Papa."

When Josette had moved away, Beau-père beckoned Eulalie closer and lowered his voice, although trying to whisper brought out a rattle in his throat. He began: "Eulalie, I am an old man—" then suddenly broke into a laugh that turned into a wet choking sound. Eulalie snatched hold of his upraised hand with her left hand and slapped his back with her right.

He spat into the hay and caught his breath, then said: "But it *is* funny, you see. All those years I thought it so clever to pretend to be a broken down old man when it suited. And now..."

"You're not a broken down old man. The winter is doing this to everyone. Come spring your sap will start running again—if you eat enough to keep alive till then."

"I *am* an old man. I've lived my life. I'll never see the valley of Ardoise again. But my gold is still buried there. *All* my gold is buried there—except her children and you. I was so sure I'd lie beside her one more time... There's no sense in wasting food on me, but you and the children must live to go back, when the English king and the French king grow tired of killing each other's soldiers."

"So must you. I meant what I said—any food you don't eat I'll throw to the dogs. And keep your head warm—here, we'll pull your shawl up like a wise old woman. I'll bring you a cup of spruce tea."

He sighed: "As you say, *petite mère*," then plucked at the hay between his knees and muttered sulkily: "Why doesn't Cully come to visit anymore? Spends all his time making war plans with Beausoleil."

"He does come visit. He was here just the day before yesterday and brought Beausoleil's dominoes. You remember? You had to clear a space on the floor and played all afternoon."

"That wasn't day before yesterday."

"It was."

"Wasn't."

"Well... I'll go make you a cup of spruce tea."

But she didn't, at least not immediately. She looked into the pot of bones, threw on a few more precious scraps of wood to keep it boiling, then walked down the path between Beausoleil's place and his brother's. She knew that Cully's quarters were a corner of Beausoleil's harness shed, but she'd only seen it from the outside. He'd taken off a few shingles to make a smokehole, and had turned the shingles into an open-ended box sticking out of the hole, to give at least some sort of draw. A few wisps of smoke were coming out of it now. She knocked on the door.

"*Entrez.*"

She pulled the latch string. He was sitting cross-legged in front of the fireplace he'd rigged up out of a rusted-out stewpot. He had a blanket shawled across his shoulders over his coat, and a tin box and pair of pliers in his hands. Even with the smokehole and drawbox, the air inside stung her eyes.

"Eulalie! Come in and close the door—it's warm by the fire." He shifted sideways and patted the folded blanket he was sitting on. "Down low the smoke ain't so bad."

She closed the door but stayed where she was. "No—thank you. I have soup to take care of. I only came to ask you... Beau-père, you see, he shouldn't go outside much until he's better, but he has no one in the loft for company but women and children, and a man who talks of nothing but that the English driving us out is God's judgement for not always listening to the priests. Beau-père wouldn't like it if he knew I told you, but..." She remembered that it hadn't worked out too well the last time she'd told someone something Beau-père wouldn't like. But Cully Robin was a much better liar than Josette. "He wishes you'd visit him more."

"Of course." He started to rise to his feet. "I'll come back with you now and—"

"No," her voice stopped him partway up and he stayed there, resting on one knee. "That'd seem too much coincidence. Come a little later. Thank you."

"It ain't a favour. I'd've come every day but I was afraid I'd tire him out." She was about to turn to go, when he said with a strange intentness: "How are you?"

It seemed an extremely foolish question. She said: "Oh... Oh well, the children have just enough to eat. Marie and Hélène will lose their coughs, I think, with enough hot tea, if I can find some rose hips—"

"I didn't ask how *they* were, I asked how *you* were." He rose the rest of the way to his feet and moved slowly toward her. "While you are taking care of the soup, and taking care of Joseph Brossard, and taking care of his children, who is taking care of Eulalie?"

"Oh... I take care of myself. The children who aren't sick help out." But she couldn't keep a bit of a tremble out of her voice. The tinker was betraying her again: luring her into feeling sorry for herself when she knew she was no worse off than ten thousand other Acadians.

He put his hands on her shoulders. She looked up. His eyes slid away from hers as soon as they touched, then came back abruptly and held. He lowered his head and kissed her. She had never been kissed on the mouth by a man with a beard before—Acadians believed in shaking hands, and no amount of cheek-peckers from Quebec could convert them. Her lips stayed limp at first, then began to move on their own accord as his moved against them.

He took his mouth away and raised his head, so that the side of her head fit in against the side of his neck. He held her to him, one hand stroking her hair. With the warmth of his body against hers, she felt the cold seeping out of her for the first time since the snow came. She could feel the stiffness in her spine starting to melt away, but too many people depended on her keeping her back straight. Her arms wanted to lift up and close around his back, but she held them glued to her sides.

He said softly: "You can't spend your whole life being *petite mère*. When was the last time you laughed?" His voice grew hoarser. "I tell you what—I'll give you something to laugh about... I've never been much good at taking care of other people, but I swear to God I'll do the best I can. Will you marry me?"

A sob thrust up into her throat, but she bit down on it. She pushed away from him and said without looking at him, "Oh, Cully—in *these* times?" She pushed the door open and went out into the snow, raising her shawl over her head and looking down at the path so no one could see her face, dabbing at her eyes with the corners of her shawl.

The water in the pot was half boiled away, so if there'd been anything left in those old bones it was leached out by now. She stirred in the last handful of hulled barley and stood beside the pot watching Henri and Jacques shivering their way up from the river with nothing in their hands.

Later in the afternoon Cully came up into the loft with Beausoleil's dominoes. Luckily, Eulalie happened to be sewing another patch onto Jean-Marc's coat, so she could just nod her eyes at Cully without meeting his and then lower her gaze to her fingers as though whip-stitching an old piece of wool onto an older piece of wool was complicated work.

Beau-père perked up with the company and the game. Listening to the click of the dominoes and the low, male voices Eulalie could close her eyes and almost imagine she was back in the valley of Ardoise, working at her loom while Beau-père and the tinker whiled away the evening with pipes and dominoes.

At one point, Beau-père's mind seemed to drift away from the game. He said: "You know, Cully, Eulalie does a very good job of raising my children. But there are things that a boy needs a father to teach him."

Cully said: "What sort of things, Uncle?"

"Oh, important things. Useful things. Things even the best of mothers wouldn't know to teach her sons. Things like... 'Never piss uphill, unless you keep your feet wide apart.'"

Cully laughed, then said: "The only thing I ever learned from my father was to stay the hell away from him." Beau-père laughed and Cully surprised Eulalie by laughing, too. After the bitter cold that had come over him when Beau-père had asked the tinker about his family, Eulalie had never expected to hear him laugh about it. It seemed as though his past life had become more distant to him. But then, all of their past lives were distant now.

❊ ❊ ❊

Beau-père grew worse and Marie and Hélène didn't get any better. Beau-père's chest pained him constantly and he had to struggle harder to breathe. Anne brought over a little dried yarrow to steep into a tea for him, but only a little. Anne's stock of medicines hadn't been planned to accommodate so many sick people. A few older women came up to the loft to give what help they could, and murmured about secret medicinal plants that Eulalie already knew of from her mother or Mi'kmaq women. Eulalie also knew that all those plants were dead and buried under the snow. She didn't begrudge that she got little help. Most of the women in Petitcodiac had their own sick to tend to or were sick themselves.

In the end, all Eulalie could do for her *beau-père* was boil spruce needles and carry the water up to him in a cup for him to tent his blanket over and breathe the steam. When his breathing sank to shuddery gasps, she wrestled his shoulders up onto her lap and rocked him back and forth, stroking his clammy hair and crooning: "Three hills home, my dear, three hills home..."

He interrupted her singing once with a whispered: "Eulalie...?"

"Yes, Beau-père?"

"Do you remember the dead apple bush back home?"

"Yes." Years ago, one of their old apple trees had blown down in a winter storm. For a year after, Beau-père kept vowing he was going to saw it into pieces and roll it out of the pasture, but never got around to it. The next spring, the dead, grey wood had sprouted new shoots growing straight up out of its trunk. The next summer, and for every summer since, the 'apple bush' had given more and sweeter fruit than any of the standing trees.

"When we first met the tinker," Beau-père rasped, "I thought he had a dead soul."

The last words he said that seemed to have any connection to each other were: "Eulalie... the world is sliding into the sea... grab what you can."

XXIX

ully helped Henri and Jacques burn a bed-sized mat of brush and straw to thaw the ground to dig their father's grave. Father La Brosse came up from Fox Creek, where an Acadian farmer had been putting him up ever since the victors of Fort Beauséjour burned the village his church had stood in.

As Father La Brosse droned on about immortal souls, Cully gazed across the grave at Eulalie and the children. She was standing with one arm pressing Josette against her leg and the other arm around Jean-Marc's shoulders. Cully wanted to be on the other side of the grave, holding *her* up, but he wasn't part of the family. He didn't think old Joseph Brossard would've taken it amiss, though, that what his mind kept drifting back to on this solemn occasion was that it was impossible to say whether Eulalie's hair was exactly black or brown.

When Father La Brosse was done, Cully went over to Eulalie and the children and mumbled that idiotic formula: "I'm sorry."

Eulalie said: "I know," and reached out her hand to touch his arm without looking up at him. "You were a good friend to him, Cully. You've been a good friend to all of us. I must see to Marie and Hélène. Come along, my dears."

As everyone else around the grave drifted away, a low voice above and behind Cully pronounced: "There'll be plenty more before the winter's out."

Cully turned back to see Beausoleil tugging his sealskin cap back on. "Come along, *Anglais*—time we did something to make sure next winter ain't the same."

"You don't think the war will be over by then?"

"Ha! Do you?"

"No." From the information that came to the Petitcodiac through Lieutenant Boishébert on the seacoast, Great Britain and France had finally officially declared war and were going at it all over the world. Last year's unofficial campaign in North

America had been a disaster for the British. Outside of taking Fort Beauséjour, and winning a small battle in the backwoods of New England, the only memorable feat of British arms had been getting two entire regiments wiped out in one day by a force of French and Indians. But Cully had been a soldier long enough to know that the massacre of a few thousand bloodybacks wasn't about to make the Lords of Trade give up one square foot of the Empire. The crimps and press gangs could always scour the gin shops for more heroes.

Cully ambled back down the path toward Beausoleil's place with Beausoleil and his big brother. Alexandre Brossard wasn't only older than Beausoleil, but actually even bigger. Alexandre was technically "Beausoleil" as well, since "Beausoleil" was a nickname for that whole branch of the Brossards. But in this generation the name had come to refer to one man. It put Cully in mind of what a Black Watch soldier had once told him about the Highland Clans: there were thousands of MacPhersons of Clan MacPherson, and then there was The MacPherson.

It didn't seem to bother Alexandre. In their younger days, his little brother had followed him—marrying the younger sister of Alexandre's wife—and now everyone followed his little brother.

Cully didn't let it swell his head that the Officer Commanding hereabouts seemed to have a fondness for his company. He knew that his experience of the inner workings of the British army made him useful to have around. And he suspected Beausoleil found him even more useful in another way. To everyone else along the Petitcodiac, and to most Acadians everywhere, Beausoleil was the wiliest, the bravest, the best shot with a rifle, the terror of their enemies, the reincarnation of Charles La Tour and then some... Although Cully had no doubt Beausoleil enjoyed his reputation, it must've been a relief sometimes to have someone around him who'd only heard of him as a sneaking outlaw.

Anne had gone ahead of them and set out a small pitcher of cider and a quillpen, ink and paper. Cully knew enough to water his cider now—besides, it stretched it out more. Alexandre took up the pen and Beausoleil said: "You see, *Anglais*, when the rivers are open, Lieutenant Boishébert and his thirty soldiers get supplies from Quebec. They get enough gunpowder and lead to supply us, too—but only enough food and blankets and such for them.

"It don't seem right, since if it wasn't for us the English would've easily stomped down Boishébert's thirty last summer. But, to the silk hats in Quebec we are just doing what we've always done: living fat off our farms and taking the occasional long shot at an English soldier to while away our lazy days.

"So, Quebec has to be told different..." Beausoleil began to prowl around the kitchen, tossing out phrases that Alexandre laboured to turn into sentences: The little homesteads along the Petitcodiac and the Miramichi had always been barely able to support themselves, much less hundreds of refugees from Nova Scotia and the country around where Fort Beauséjour used to be... The suffering and starving would only get worse next year, as the men who should be spending the summer growing crops and netting fish would be too busy keeping the English from taking all of Acadia... If the English took French Acadia they'd be on Quebec's doorstep... The entire reason the Acadians were suffering and starving was their unswerving loyalty and love for His Most Christian Majesty, Louis XV...

Cully interjected: "What about the Mi'kmaqs?"

"What about them?"

"You told me that come spring, when the Mi'kmaqs come out of their winter hunting grounds in the deep woods, they'll bring us food and hides and such."

"So they will, but hardly enough to keep as all fed and warm."

"The quartermasters in Quebec don't know that—or they can *pretend* they don't know that. I'm not acquainted with French sutlers, but if they're anything like the English breed they're always looking for excuses to sell their stores for profit, instead of wasting them on men who might get killed tomorrow anyway. And why would Quebec throw away perfectly good supplies to keep Acadians in the field, when the Mi'kmaqs will join Boishébert's little army for only a few beads and scalp bounties?"

"Because they won't. Not many of them, anyway, and not for long. Boishébert is a good fellow, but he doesn't understand how our cousins of the country fight their wars. No more than the English understand."

"I'm not talking about the truth; I'm talking about quartermasters."

"Ah. You see, Anne...? I told you he has his uses. So... 'The savages in this part of the country are... lazy and... perfidious... and...'"

By the time the letter was drafted, it was dark. Anne started setting out supper and invited Cully to join them. He didn't need to be asked twice: Beausoleil's family ate better than the refugees, though not much. When supper was done, Beausoleil plucked a candle out of a wooden wall sconce and said: "I'll light you to your mansion."

Cully knew his way from the house to the harness shed blindfolded, but he didn't argue. When they'd gone a few steps out the door, Beausoleil blew out the candle and grumbled as they crunched through the snow, "What the devil's the matter with you and that woman?"

"What woman?"

"Well she sure as hell ain't a *girl* anymore. The La Tour. I never seen two people make such moony eyes at each other and do nothing about it."

"I *have* done something about it," although the words didn't taste very good in his mouth. "I asked her to marry me."

"Son of a whore!" Beausoleil slapped Cully's shoulder, almost knocking him into the snow. "Maybe you're not so English after all. Why keep such a secret?"

"To save embarrassing myself."

"The bitch said no?"

Cully had to laugh at the way 'The La Tour' became 'the bitch' the instant Beausoleil thought she'd hurt one of his *confrères*. Beausoleil was overly endowed with the characteristic that most inspired loyalty to an officer: he himself was loyal to a fault. Cully said: "I'm not sure if she said no. She said 'In *these* times?'"

"Huh." Beausoleil rubbed his jaw. "Seems to me one thing these times *ain't* for is putting things off. But, no one should ever try to tell a woman what to think. Or a man, for that matter."

Their last few sentences had been spoken standing at the harness shed door. Beausoleil flapped his arms a couple of times and muttered: "You'd think the nights'd be getting warmer by now. Well, sleep well, *Anglais*."

"You, too, Beausoleil."

Watching Beausoleil trudge away through the cold moonlight, it seemed to Cully that it must be a pleasant thing at times to be Jack The Lad, known far and wide as *un homme sans foi ni loi*—which English could only feebly translate as "without fear of God nor man." But not so pleasant when the people who looked up to you were starving and freezing and dying all around you.

XXX

⟡

ithout Beau-pére to nurse, Eulalie's duties didn't get any lighter, and she was dimly aware of being pressed down into a flat world where everything was reduced to its bones. Marie and Hélène's racking coughs turned overnight into a fever with diarrhoea. Eulalie stripped off their skirts to wash them out, then decided she might as well use the skirts to wipe their thighs and asses while she was at it—the cloth was soaked in shit already. Then she laid the girls down in the hay wearing only their blouses and covered them with blankets. Marie complained that the hay prickled her bare skin, but Eulalie told her: "Better that than you have no blankets, because any I put under you I'll only have to take away to wash. Now you stay covered up and I'll make you something to stop the diarrhoea."

Henri and Jacques were off in the woods again, so there was only Jean-Marc to send to beg some lye soap from Anne, and Eulalie had to take the axe herself to go looking for a stand of sumacs. She came back dragging a branch with several galls on it, set the skirts and soap to boil in the big pot, cut out the galls, put them in the little pot, filled it up with snow and squeezed it onto the corner of the fire the big pot didn't cover. Then she trimmed the rest of the sumac branch to make a long stirring-stick, keeping one eye on the little pot to make sure to scoop in more snow as it melted down.

She was stirring the skirts around, not looking forward to the moment she would have to start lifting them out and scrubbing the worst spots with her hands, when a hand yanked on her skirt—almost pulling it off, her hips had grown so thin—and a voice squealed: "Eulalie!"

Eulalie spun around and screamed down at Josette: "What? What do you want? You want me to wipe your ass? You want me to make a roast beef out of cowshit? You want new shoes or a fur blanket? Did you ever think maybe *I* want some things, too?"

Josette didn't cry, just backed away with her hands up to her mouth and her eyes wide with terror. Eulalie dropped to her knees and held her arms open to her. "I'm sorry, my dear. I'm not angry at you, just at the world." Josette stopped backing away, but didn't move forward. Eulalie kept coaxing her, like trying to convince an orphaned fawn to come eat from her hand, and finally Josette edged closer. When Eulalie flung her arms around her, Josette tried to jump away, but then settled down and tentatively put her arms around Eulalie's neck.

When night came down, bringing closer the blessed escape into sleep, Eulalie sat in the hay with her blanket around her shoulders, listening to the human sounds mingling with the lowing and crunching of the cattle down below. Jean-Marc and Josette were getting Marie and Hélène's cough, and Louise was whimpering to herself about a sore stomach. And then there was the inevitable, endless drone of the man of the family who shared the hayloft with them, on his knees in the corner praying—and praying, and praying, and praying...

XXXI

ully settled a burl of frozen wood onto his fire and arranged his bed for the night: blanket folded over a mat of spruce boughs, coat on top of him, second blanket on top of that and pulled up to cover the top of his head, curled on his side with his hands between his thighs. The burl was just beginning to hiss nicely, promising to someday start giving off heat, when the door blew open.

He sat up muttering curses, then stopped. Eulalie was standing in the doorway, framed by the stars, with a blanket across her shoulders and the wind lifting her hair. Before he could say anything, she crossed the threshold, closed the door, stepped around the fire, knelt beside him, put her hands on his shoulders and kissed him.

It didn't take him long to start kissing her back. As he shifted his lips from her mouth to her cheek and eyes and neck, his torso shifted sideways and she shifted as well—as though it were a dance step they'd practised—and she was leaning on one hip with her breasts pressed against his chest. She took her hands off him for just long enough to drape her blanket around them both. He could only use one hand to touch her, his other arm was propping them up, but when his hand rounded her back to settle over one wool-sheathed breast, she sighed and so did he. Stupidly, he couldn't think of anything to whisper to her but: "Eulalie." Even stupider, he could feel tears in the corners of his eyes. Corporal Robin would've laughed himself sick at the notion of a man getting teary over bedding a woman.

He slowly turned her around and settled her down on her back—or perhaps she led and he followed, he wasn't sure. He was hardly in any position to lift or lower anyone at the moment: his propping arm had gone dead asleep. It began to tingle back to life as he unbuttoned her blouse. Her eyes were closed and her hands blindly caressing his hair and shoulders.

When he'd undone the last blouse button, he pulled the blanket up to his shoulders before folding her blouse open. He could see the tongues of her breasts poking through the threadbare linen of her shift. Her shoulders had grown so thin.

As her hands went up and down his sides, he unfastened the neck slit of her shift and furled it down. Even in the dim and smoky light, the haloes around her nipples were clearly more brown than pink. He kissed his way around the puckered circles of soap-bubble-thin skin, then raised his head to whisper: "I'm afraid I may be a little awkward; this is my first time."

She shot bolt upright, pushing him away and spitting: "If you think that's *funny*—!"

He grabbed her shoulders to keep her from jumping to her feet, and said softly: "If it is, the joke's on me. This *is* the first time I've ever lain down with a woman I loved."

XXXII

Eulalie jerked awake and panicked: she was wearing only her shift, and a half-naked man was spooned against her back. Then she remembered. The memory was woven of contradicting tides. There was remembered pain, and a remembered pleasure that made her understand why the church had to call it a sin. There was a deep well of embarrassment, and an artesian spring of laughter. There was a feeling that she'd made the mistake of her life, and a feeling that she wasn't alone now for the first time since Beau-père got sick. But there was one feeling that didn't carry a contradiction—although it seemed so much like something from another life that it was disorienting in itself. The tip of her nose was the only part of her that was cold.

She knew there was a parchment window on one of the harness shed walls, but she could see no glow except the embers in the firepot, so it was still night. Cully stirred. The arm that was draped slackly across her fumbled to life, and the hand attached to it cupped her left breast. It startled her, then made her blush, warming the tip of her nose.

She had no idea how people were supposed to go about speaking to each other in such circumstances. She tried out: "Cully...?"

"Hm?"

"I have to get back to the loft before the children wake up and don't know where I am."

"You could send a letter..."

"I wish I didn't have to, but I do."

"Hm. Well..." His voice grew muffled by her hair and neck as he shifted his body. "First you'd best pull your clothes in here and warm them up. I think your skirt's over here..." She could hear his right hand fumbling on the floor behind him, while his left hand stayed cupping her left breast.

She said lightly: "You're just trying to fool me into staying." It wasn't so difficult after all to talk to someone who had his hand on her naked breast—at least not this someone. In fact, it was easier.

He muttered into her neck: "Well, so long as you leave your blanket when you go..."

Once her skirt and blouse were under the blankets with them, she eased over onto her back—or was eased-over, she wasn't sure—and he propped himself up on one elbow to look down at her. He traced one finger along the line of her jaw and said: "So, Eulalie—now will you marry me?"

"Have you made a pair of cart wheels?" It just jumped out of her of its own volition. Maybe it had intended itself to be some sort of joke, but on the way out it turned bitter and caught in her throat.

Cully looked confounded. She breathed deeply and wiped her eyes with the hem of her blanket, then reached one hand up to the patch of cheek between his beard and eye and said: "Yes, Cully." She added: "Thank you."

He looked like he was going to say something clever about that 'Thank you,' but thought better of it. Instead, he just took hold of her hand and said: "Thank *you*. We can tell Father La Brosse on Sunday, when he comes up from Fox Creek to say mass."

But Father La Brosse came up before Sunday. On Friday morning he poked his head in the barn, called: "Eulalie!" and beckoned her outside. When she stepped out of the barn, he started walking toward the river, with his hands behind his back and his cassock flapping around his ankles. Eulalie caught up and fell in beside him.

Once they were away from the barn, Father La Brosse said: "So, Eulalie, I hear you are going to be married."

"He didn't tell *me* he'd sent a message!"

"Hm? Oh, he didn't send a message. Didn't need to. You see, Eulalie, there are hundreds of people packed like herrings along the Petitcodiac this year—as you well know—all of them with nothing to do to pass the winter but murmur around the fire. They are always happy to find something new to murmur about. I'll hear your confession before the wedding."

"Yes, Father. But... there is also..." It was a problem she hadn't considered, what with all the other problems she had to cope with, until kneeling in front of a priest loomed on the horizon.

"Yes, daughter...?"

"He isn't Catholic."

"Oh. Would he convert?"

"I'm sure he would." That sounded more politic than: *I'm sure he doesn't give a tinker's dam one way or the other.*

"Well, in these times neither he nor I nor anyone else can afford to wade through all the Instruction. We don't even have a church to post banns. I'm sure the good God will understand; He understands a good deal more than He's given credit for.

"Besides," Father La Brosse added brightly, "you are a good Catholic, and it is usually the mother more than the father who guides the children into religion."

His talk of children made Eulalie more than a little embarrassed to have a priest take as a given what she'd done with her body, and fully intended to do again. The possibility of children was something she'd thought about a great deal since the first night she went to the harness shed. Mostly what it made her think about was giving birth in a hayloft reeking of sickness and hunger and death.

The wedding took place in Beausoleil's house. When Father La Brosse said: "Do you, Cully—?" Cully interrupted him.

"Gilbert."

"Pardon me?"

"My Christian name is Gilbert. I had a baby brother who couldn't manage 'Gilly,' so he made it 'Cully.' It stuck because it fit—'cully' in English means 'fool.'" He turned his glittering eyes on Eulalie. "But if there is any fool here today, it ain't me."

Eulalie felt a twinge that maybe he wasn't that far wrong. It seemed to her that if there was one day in a woman's life she should feel no uncertainty, it should be her wedding day. But if there was one thing she'd learned from the last half-a-year, it was that no one could be certain of anything. Part of her half-expected that André Melanson would come crashing through the door before she finished her vows. But the reasoning part of her knew that she and André Melanson would never meet again in this life.

XXXIII

❦

Spring planting came early in South Carolina. André had to take people's word for it that winter had come at all, much less gone. He stepped out of the line of slaves hoeing around sprouting indigo bushes and signalled to the overseer that he needed to pause to sharpen his hoe. Well, not *his* hoe—Mister Kenney's hoe. Everything belonged to Mister Kenney.

When he'd handed the sharpening file back to the overseer and started hoeing again, a tall slave with shoulders as broad as his own murmured: "You workin' too hard again, Li'l Bull." André kept forgetting that the rhythms of work he'd learned in Acadia would kill a man in this steamy sun. And he kept having to be reminded that the amount of work he got done in one day would be no benefit to him or anyone he cared about, only to Mister Kenney.

André glanced to make sure the overseer was out of earshot, and whispered back one of the scraps of English he'd picked up: "Sho'nuff, Abraham." 'Abraham' wasn't Abraham's real name, but the slaves on Mister Kenney's plantation had been taken from so many different tribes in Africa that the only words and names they had in common were the ones used by their masters.

When the heat of the day came on, the fieldhands were herded back to the slave compound. André sat in front of the shed he shared with Patrice and Phillipe, munching his mid-day rice and trying to find something else to think about besides home.

His eyes latched onto movement at the front of the big, white house. Madame Kenney and the children came out onto the porch, all dressed in peacock silk and velvet. The family carriage, not the little one that Mister Kenney liked to sport around in, drew up in front of them and waited. Along with the carriage came two mounted overseers with double-barrelled guns propped across their saddles, and belts bristling with pistols.

The outriders gave André something else to think about. He still found it strange that the whites and blacks of South Carolina were so terrified of the local Indians, the Creeks—as terrified as the English of Nova Scotia were of the Mi'kmaqs. No Acadian had ever been more than mildly nervous of any Mi'kmaq or Maliseet since Charles La Tour's day. Well, except when the Abbé Le Loutre threatened to stir up his converts. André wondered whether the difference was between French colonies and English ones, or whether it was just Acadians. Maybe the French in Quebec were just as terrified of the Mohawks, or whatever the tribes were there.

He didn't wonder about it long. The thought was like an odd-looking pebble that he picked up and glanced at and tossed over his shoulder. A mockingbird in the magnolia tree began to show off its collection of stolen voices. André set his empty bowl aside and listened. He'd learned to grab hold of anything that could distract him for even a moment from the ache where so many things had been torn out of him.

Abraham wandered over and sat down beside him—two plough-horses in the shade. Abraham flapped a finger toward the footman loading luggage onto the carriage and said: "Guess Massa Kenney and the family bees goin'-a Charleston for a visit."

André wasn't sure what a 'visit' was, but he said: "Yassuh, Abraham, I guess."

"Uh-huh." Abraham plucked a stock of grass and rolled it between his teeth. "You Christian, Li'l Bull?"

"Huh? Sho'nuff, Abraham."

"If you-all Christian, how come you an' Patrice an' Phillipe don't come out when the minister come visit Massa Kenney an' call us out to hear the Bible?"

"Um... *Acadiens* bees... diff'ent Christian. We gots... priests and..." he laboured to find the English word for *blanc*, "...white masses."

"Huh? I thought you bees free back home."

"Yassuh, Abraham, we beed free."

"How you be free and got white masses?"

"Huh?"

"We got white masses here, and sho to hell we ain't free."

"No white masses here."

"You crazy? Got all kindsa white masses here. Massa Kenney, and li'l Massa David, and—"

André started to laugh. It took him a moment to get control of his breath enough to say: "Not white Massas, Abraham, white mass*es*. It, um, to say, um..." Then he saw that Abraham wasn't offended or confused or even aware that he was there anymore. Abraham's face had turned into carved granite and his eyes were fixed straight ahead.

André followed Abraham's eyes to the front of the house. The loaded carriage and the outriders were trotting away, and Mister Kenney was standing on the porch steps waving *au revoir* to his family.

Abraham stood up abruptly and walked away. André started to call after him, but the head overseer clanged the triangle to get back to work.

There was no joking or singing in the fields that afternoon. No one spoke except to say: "Yassuh, boss," when the overseer barked. When they got back to the slave quarters, two high-nosed men in tailored riding clothes were trotting up from the high road. Mister Kenney and two other men came out of the house to greet them with bottles and laughter. A little later, another planter in a wide straw hat came cantering his tall horse. When he dismounted he patted the cheek of the liveried, white-wigged, black boy who'd scuttled out of the house to hold his horse.

The sun was turning pink when Mister Kenney and his friends came ambling down to the slave pens. Most of them were in their shirtsleeves over their doeskin breeches and riding boots, but one still wore his brocade waistcoat, and another still held his riding crop in his hand. They all carried swords or pistols.

They looked over the women and girls and made their selections, making grand fun of each others' tastes. One of those picked was Abraham's woman.

As the women were herded toward the house, with the aid of an occasional jolly slap on the rump with the flat of a swordblade, André wondered what he would have done if one of them was Eulalie. If he'd tried to stop it, all he would've accomplished was getting himself flogged half to death, or branded, or gelded. Or killed in as gruesome a manner as possible, if Mister Kenney decided he'd become too troublesome to be worth much except as an example.

As the sun went down, the slave men gathered in a circle around the cooking fire and began to sing, clacking sticks together and slapping their bodies. André didn't need to understand their language or strange music to know that it was a war song sung by helpless warriors. He also knew that part of the reason for the singing was to drown out the sounds from the house.

André's shack was halfway between the circle and the house, so he could hear both. At first, the sounds from the house were of boisterous male voices and the occasional high-pitched plea when one of the women forgot her place enough to raise her voice to her masters. But after awhile the whooping and laughter became female as well, as more dark rum was forced down brown throats.

When André said his prayers that night, he included a plea for mercy on *all* human cattle herded across the earth wherever the dogs drove them. The singing outside had sunk lower and slower, without the clacking rhythms, but the softer song was even less soothing than the roaring songs had been.

André dozed on and off, and then suddenly found himself fully awake. It was still night, but something had changed. The singing had stopped. In place of it, there were stumbling footfalls and women's voices approaching. Some of the voices were whimpering, some laughing and crowing, some retching or belching. They were met by male voices: some wailing, some struggling to maintain a comforting tone like to a maimed child. But some of the men began to take out their ground-down fury on their whoring, drunken woman.

André threw back his blanket and started to get up, but then asked himself what he thought he was going to do. The sounds outside had become a babble punctuated by shrieks and blows and men yelling at each other in tones of *Stop that!* and *Mind your own damn business!* He could no more change their lives than he could his own.

He lay back down on his side, pressed one ear against his pillowing arm and covered the other with his hand. But he could still hear the sounds.

The slaves slunk through the next day like beaten dogs. André made a point of trying not to meet anyone's eyes, then realized there was no danger of that happening. As he was eating his evening rice, one of the women who'd been up at the house last night stole up beside him. Her name was Rachel, she was barely more than a girl, and she seemed to be always pushed to the fringes of the life that went on in the slave pens. She murmured in English: "André, you know boat?"

"Boat?"

"Boat." She made rowing motions, then arced her hand down through the air and blew, which he supposed was meant to indicate a sail. "You can do?"

"Yes. Some."

"You," she pointed at him, "follow." She walked two fingers across the palm of her hand, then tapped her chest and put a finger to her lips. She glanced around warily, then wandered away from the shacks and into the woods. André waited a moment and followed after her.

She was waiting just beyond where the forest turned impenetrable to outside eyes. She beckoned and led him over the ferny moss and rotting deadfalls toward the sound of running water. A little river ran through Mister Kenney's property on its way down to the sea. Washed up on its bank was an old skiff that must have broken its moorings upstream. It had shipped some water through a cracked plank, but the keel was still intact. Best of all, the oars and sail were still on board, and the sail had only suffered a little rot.

Rachel said: "You, me—run?"

He managed to get across to her that the cracked plank would have to be mended, that a few of the other planks didn't look too sound, and that they would have to sneak a store of food. "*Alors,*" he nodded, "we run—you, me, Patrice, Phillipe."

"No! You, me!"

"No Patrice, no Phillipe—no me."

She didn't look happy about complicating her plan with extra bodies, and extra mouths, but André knew she didn't have much choice if she wanted somebody who knew how to manage the boat. He stuck his right hand out. She looked at it confusedly. He gestured her to put out her right hand and shook it, then got her to help him drag the boat into the woods, turn it over and cover it with brush.

When he told Patrice and Phillipe, Patrice said: "Run *where?*"

"Straight north along the coast until we get to French Acadia, then through the woods to the Petitcodiac and the Miramichi. The English may have taken Fort Beauséjour, but they'll never get any further so long as Beausoleil is alive." He didn't mention that he had a personal reason to try to get to where Beausoleil was.

Phillipe said: "Easy for you to talk of getting away from here—your family isn't in Charleston."

Patrice said: "We never see our families anyway, Phillipe. It won't do them any harm if we get away back to Acadia. And maybe if we can help Beausoleil hold off the English, we'll be helping make it easier for our families to come home some day."

They argued it over for a while, and decided that escaping to Beausoleil wouldn't really be deserting their families. But André still had to solve the problem of making the skiff seaworthy, and that meant getting his hands on tools and planking. He thought about it hard, and came up with Mister Kenney's disappointing rice field.

A far corner of Mister Kenney's plantation was a tidal marsh which Mister Kenney had sensibly decided could be diked to make a rice field that didn't have to be irrigated. Sensibly, except that the salt accumulated in the marsh couldn't leach out through the dike. According to the other fieldhands, for three years running they'd been planting and tending that field, and only a few clumps of spindly plants survived to harvest.

André went up to the house and convinced the servant at the door that he had something to say which he could only say to Mister Kenney himself, since only Mister Kenney understood French. When Mister Kenney came to the door, puffing a long-stemmed pipe, André said: "Your south rice field, *monsieur*, it has too much salt in it."

"You dragged me away from my *digestif* to tell me *that?*"

"In Acadia, *monsieur*, we have something called an *aboiteau*. It goes into the dike and lets salt water drain out, but keeps more salt water from coming in."

Mister Kenney looked less annoyed. "How does it work?"

"I can't explain it, *monsieur*—I think better with my hands than with my head. But I could build you one, if I had tools and wood, working a little bit each evening after my work in the fields is done."

"Good. That's good, André, that you show ambition. If this device works, I will increase what I pay to the public purse to support your family in Charleston. I will instruct the overseer that you are to have the use of whatever tools and wood you need."

"Thank you, *monsieur*."

"Thank *you*, André—if this device works."

"Oh, I will make it work, *monsieur*, no fear of that."

He used strips torn off his blanket to caulk the scraps of plank he patched the skiff with. It was easy enough to convince the overseer he needed tar to seal the seams of the *aboiteau*, but complicated to sneak it from the slave pen to the woods before it cooled. As the repairs crawled along, he and Patrice and Phillipe squirreled away what bits of food they could—a sweet potato here, a handful of rice there...

André was squatted in front of their shack one evening, very slowly planing the *aboiteau* gate he'd been planing for a week now, when Abraham sauntered up and sat down beside him. Abraham said out of the corner of his mouth: "You goin'-a run, Li'l Bull?"

André didn't know what to answer. He didn't *think* Abraham would tell the overseers, but Abraham might threaten to if André didn't offer to take him along, and there was barely room in the skiff for four. André decided to tell the truth, a decision he didn't used to have to weigh. "Yassuh, Abraham, I goin'-a run."

Abraham held out his fist and opened it. In his hand was a folded square of cloth. He gestured with his eyes for André to take it. When André unfolded it, he found a fish hook and a coil of line. Abraham said: "Man gets hungry runnin'. Run good, Li'l Bull. Run like the goddamn hurry-cane."

"Abraham, I—"

"Don' be thankin' me today, Li'l Bull. When you gets home, gets you own plantation back, *then* you thanks me—buy me, my woman, my childrens. We work hard for you."

"Not *too* hard...?"

Abraham laughed so hard tears came out of his eyes.

By no coincidence, the boat and the *aboiteau* were finished at the same time. Mister Kenney instructed the overseer to let André have a work crew—Patrice, Phillipe, Abraham and a few other field hands—for the chancy job of breaking open the dike, putting the *aboiteau* in place and rebuilding the dike before the tide came back in.

They got it done. The next day was a heavy rain and Mister Kenney was delighted to see the run-off pouring out of the *aboiteau*, and the sea sealed out when the tide rose again. He promised to double the wages that André had never seen. André didn't tell him that the hinges he'd put on the *aboiteau* gate were so flimsy they wouldn't last a month, and then salt water would flood the field. It went against André's grain, and against every word he could remember his father saying to him, to build an *aboiteau* that wouldn't last. But maybe the next time Madame Kenney and the children went away on a visit, Mister Kenney and his friends could spend the evening digging out the *aboiteau* and figuring out how to fix it.

On an evening with no threatening clouds, André walked past Rachel in the line for the rice pot, caught her eyes and nodded. When night came down, he and Patrice and Phillipe met her at the boat. The moon was almost full, which wasn't good for hiding but good for avoiding snags in the river. André took the oars, Phillipe the tiller, and Patrice knelt in the bow with a long pole. Rachel sat amidships with their paltry provisions and possessions and the gourd of fresh water.

When they pushed off, André started rowing straight for the opposite shore. Phillipe angled the tiller to turn them downstream, but André said: "No! Hold her straight."

"But—"

"Hold her straight. Mister Kenney's hounds are going to help us."

It took only a moment to reach the other riverbank. André shipped the oars and said: "Phillipe, you hold the boat here. Patrice, we'll go into the woods—you one way and me the other—just a little ways in and then come back. Hurry." He beckoned Rachel to come with him.

Once they were on their way downstream, the current and the oars made for a good pace. The moon was going down by the time the river spilled them out onto the sea. They set the sail and André took the tiller and found the pole star. Phillipe was pretty good at trimming the sail, but Patrice proved next-to-useless in a boat— his father had preferred to trade turnips for what other people brought home from the sea. Patrice could help Rachel bail, though, and there was a lot of bailing to do.

The sea air tasted to André like the first real air he'd breathed since the wagon rolled inland from Charleston Bay. As the sky lightened to gray, Patrice called from the bow: "There's one," and pointed ahead to starboard. André steered in that direction. After a while he could make out a darker shape rising out of the dark waves. The island turned out to be little more than a sand dune, but it gave them a place to lay up for the day, in case the trick played on Mister Kenney's dogs might not have stopped him from spreading the word to watch the sea.

At nightfall they set sail again, and kept on sailing even after the sun rose. André figured they were far enough away by now that the only danger was of stumbling across a ship with a curious captain. He kept the coast just barely in sight, changing tack as the winds shifted on- and-off shore. When he had to sleep, Phillipe kept them more or less on course.

There came an evening with a mackerel sky, but André decided to keep on sailing nonetheless. He'd sailed in the rain before, and it would give them a chance to collect a little fresh water. But a little wasn't what they got. He finally gave in to the fact that the boat was filling up faster than they could bail, and turned her nose to see if the wind would carry them into shore before the rain sunk them.

It wasn't the first time he'd made a landfall by flashes of lightning—smugglers couldn't afford to wait for the skies to clear. After dodging only a few snaggle-toothed rocks, and skimming safely over who knew how many hidden reefs that the good God had allowed to be just below their keel, the skiff's nose lodged on a sandy beach.

Once André had his feet on land again—wet sand between his toes—he laughed and laughed that he wasn't drowned. He figured he must look as soaked-through as Rachel, whose calico dress looked like a pattern tattooed on her apple breasts and over her belly, thighs and what lay in between. She was laughing as hard as he was.

Patrice and Phillipe were looking at Rachel as well, and murmuring to each other. They moved toward her and she stopped laughing. Patrice reached his hand out to the mounded, calicoed triangle at the base of her belly. She slapped at his hand, squealing: "No!" Phillipe grinned and reached his hands out.

"No!" André shouted over the wind.

Patrice shouted back at him: "Why the hell 'no'? She sure as hell ain't the Virgin Mary! She came back laughing and singing from Mister Kenney and his friends!"

"So would you if he put that much rum in you! The only reason we got away from there is she wanted to get away from that. You want to be like them?"

Phillipe chortled: "Sounded like they had more fun than we ever have," and made a move to get around behind Rachel to cut off her escape.

André roared: "I said *no!*" Or rather, it roared itself, and he was just the instrument. Patrice and Phillipe stopped moving. André knew that his hands could crush both their necks at the same time. Unlike the night he'd sat up waiting for the mutiny that never came, he also knew he *would* as well as could, if they didn't leave Rachel alone.

Patrice and Phillipe backed away. Phillipe said: "You think you are our priest or something?"

"I don't think I'm anything. But you don't touch her if she don't want you to."

Patrice snorted: "You think you can take us both?"

"No. I know it. And so do you. You're better men than tonight makes you seem. Let's us all go find some trees to sleep out of the rain." They didn't move. "Let's us all go do that *now.*"

They did. André ended up not finding a tree, but a hollow worn away at the base of a sand bluff. He was dead asleep when a hand on his neck jerked him awake. Rachel whispered: "Ssh—just me," and crawled in beside him.

She began to kiss his ear, and her hand roamed down his chest and lower. He caught hold of her wrist and stopped her hand. She said: "No want?"

He most certainly did want, and then some. She smelled like seawind, spices and rain, and her lips on his neck felt like steamed velvet. But too many pictures rose up in between. He could see his own face wearing the leer of Mister Kenney's friends, or the fox grin of Patrice and Phillipe a few moments ago, and he could see the pictures his mind had painted from the sounds on the night the women stumbled back from the big, white house. And he could see Eulalie. He said: "I gots... wife."

"She never know."

"I know." He patted Rachel's hand against his chest. "Rachel bees my good, good friend. Sleep." She did, and he did eventually.

When the sun brought him and Rachel out of their den, Patrice and Phillipe were perched on the bow of the beached boat like a couple of singed crows. Phillipe cawed: "Not for *us*, just for *you!*"

André said: "We just slept."

"And pigs just fly!"

André didn't feel nearly as confident about facing down the two of them as he had last night. He couldn't seem to get as angry in the cause of protecting himself as protecting Rachel. Especially since he could see that Patrice and Phillipe had good cause to be angry at him, even though they were mistaken.

Patrice suddenly choked out: "Phillipe—!" and then had to cover his mouth with his hand for a moment to get control of his laughter. "Phillipe... I think he's telling the truth!"

They had a good wind for the day's sailing, but it gradually became undeniable that the strain of last night's storm had turned one of the patches on the hull into little more than decoration. There were still a few hours of daylight left when the tide carried them ashore. André, Rachel, Patrice and Phillipe sat looking at the hulled-up skiff, trying to think of what to do. They were still sitting there at sunset when a dozen men with muskets at the hip came out of the red light behind them.

XXXIV

As soon as the frost was out of the ground, Eulalie and her husband went to work building a house out of fences. It was Eulalie's idea for how to quickly put up a cabin that might not last many years but would be snug through the winter. Acadians didn't build fences by planting posts and fixing rails to them. Acadians dug a narrow trench and laid the posts out beside it, then wove saplings and supple branches between them like oversized wickerwork, stood the finished fence into the trench and filled it in. Eulalie's idea was to build a square of fence ringed by another square of fence about a handspan wider, and fill in the gap with sods and river clay.

The house wasn't much bigger than a shed, but it would only have to house the two of them and three children. Sure-handed Hélène, sweet-singing Marie, Louise—who'd just been learning to use her dead mother's loom when the Fifth of September came—and Jean-Marc, who used to try to cheat at *bouton*, all slept beside their father on the hill above Beausoleil Creek.

Henri, Jacques and little Josette had fattened up quickly once the Mi'kmaqs came out of the deep woods on their way down to the bay shore, and the spring run of gaspereau had filled Petitcodiac with the smells of frying fish, boiling fish, drying fish and smoking fish. Eulalie's skirt was no longer in danger of falling off her, and Cully's face no longer looked like wind-scoured driftwood—although she knew that part of that had to do with her trimming his overgrown beard. Tree frogs, crickets and songbirds now filled the evenings with music. All the world that had survived the winter was bursting back to life.

The little clearing where they were building their cabin had soil too thin for growing anything but alder bushes. But Anne's garden was big enough to keep two families busy, and getting bigger. All along the Petitcodiac and the Miramichi, men were furiously breaking new ground on the edges of fields and gardens before they had to put away their ploughs and pick up their guns.

Eulalie and Cully and the children were thatching the cabin with bundles of elephant grass when Beausoleil came sauntering out of the woods. Cully and Henri jumped down off the roof, and Eulalie put down the bundle she was tying together. Beausoleil looked the place over and pronounced it at least as snug as his brother's hayloft. He added: "But you only have tomorrow, *Anglais*, to finish putting on the roof—'though maybe Eulalie would be just as glad you don't finish, so she can get your clumsy hands out of the way and do it right."

Cully said: "What's happened?"

"Oh, our people watching Fort Cumberland say a troop is marching out to look for more villages to burn and Acadians to ship south. Stupid of them. We'll shoot them from the woods and skip away, and then shoot them from the woods and skip away, until the ones that are left give up and turn back. Maybe we'll keep on shooting them from the woods all their way home. Once that's done, the fellows who've been making life unpleasant for the little fort need someone to take their place for awhile, so they can remind their families who they are."

Cully's arm had settled around Eulalie's shoulders while Beausoleil spoke. For the first while after they were married, she'd found it embarrassing the way he was always putting an arm around her waist in public, or leaning against her. She still wasn't entirely comfortable with it, but she rather liked it. She reached her hand up to take hold of his draped on her shoulder.

"But, *Anglais*..." Beausoleil scuffed his boot-toe on the ground and looked down at the mark he'd made. "I know last year it didn't sit well on your stomach, shooting at men wearing the same uniform you used to wear. Not that you were likely to *hit* any of them... I would like to have you come along with us, and bring your bayonet. But if you'd rather stay behind, no one will blame you."

"No. No, it ain't the same as last year. I still don't know if I'll be able to pull the trigger when I get a red coat in my sights—not that me pulling the trigger'd be likely to hurt anybody. But now I know I'm not a traitor. Because I'm not fighting for the King of France."

"Don't tell Lieutenant Boishébert that. Well, day after tomorrow morning. Eulalie, don't wear him out before then. *Abientot*."

As Beausoleil sauntered away, Henri said tautly to Cully: "I'll go with you."

Eulalie said: "No!"

"I have a gun."

"For shooting ducks! You're too young!"

"Cully...?"

Cully's eyes flicked at Eulalie and then settled on Henri. "Fifteen, Henri?"

"Fifteen last month," as though Cully didn't know that perfectly well.

Cully's arm dropped off Eulalie's shoulder. He scraped his fingernails across his mustache and said: "There will be soldiers in the British column who're no more than fifteen."

Eulalie shouted at him: "It isn't up to you! You're not his father!"

"No. No, I'm not. I'm just telling you the truth. What you and Henri choose to do with it is your affair."

She beckoned Jacques and Josette to start helping her again, and did her best to bind grass stocks into bundles without tearing them to pieces. She had to keep reminding herself that she'd get her chance at speaking her mind to Cully when the sun went down. Enough of the roof was on for her and Cully to sleep in the cottage, but the children would spend one last night in the hayloft. Or more likely two, now that tomorrow night would be the last she and Cully would have for a while.

As soon as Josette and the boys were gone, and a fire kindled in the clay fireplace, she said: "You must tell Henri tomorrow that the only reason there's boys his age in the English army is because they were tricked into it like you were, and they're really too young to fight."

"But that isn't true. The young ones are more likely to've been stupid enough to volunteer."

"*Fifteen?*"

"He has a gun and he can shoot. Better'n me, if that's anything to brag about."

"That doesn't mean he has to go to war! *You* don't even have to go. Beausoleil said no one would blame you."

"If you think I want to go, you're crazy. I think Beausoleil's right that we can chase them back to Fort Cumberland before they get anywhere near here, but that doesn't mean it'll be easy. An extra man or two could make the difference. If we can keep them out of this country until France and England make peace again, there'll be no more reason to deport Acadians, and we can build something solider here than this cosy little shed.

"As for Henri, like you said, it isn't up to me to tell him what to do. But I won't lie to him. I did enough lying to you and him last summer."

Eulalie doubted it was up to her to tell Henri what to do, either. Josette might look upon her as her mother, but to Henri she was no more than an older sister, and one who hadn't even come into the family till he was already six years old.

She crossed her arms and looked up through the cage of unthatched roof poles at the moon. In the valley of Ardoise the apple blossoms would be shining in the moonlight now. She said: "When the war ends, we won't have to build something solider *here*. Beau-père made sure the deed was kept up and registered in the parish records. He was always very careful about anything that smelled like money." The land would legally go to Henri, but she was sure he wouldn't mind another farm next door. The more hands, the easier it would be to rebuild and clear off the wild growth that was no doubt already invading the fields.

Cully said: "I'd have to change my name... Maybe to La Tour. Maybe we'll start a fashion—men taking their wife's name when they marry. But other than that, I don't think we'd have to worry much about me getting found out. By the time this is over, I don't think the British army is going to want to waste much effort combing through Acadians for long-gone deserters. Who knows—by the time this is over, Nova Scotia might be Acadia again."

"I don't care, as long as we can go home."

"Neither do I."

She sighed and went and sat down beside him on the blankets laid out under the finished portion of the roof. She ran her hand through Cully's straight, lank hair—so much finer-spun than her own—and he kissed her and swivelled her down onto her back. He pulled a blanket over them and they undressed each other as their hands and mouths roamed. When he slid into her, she forgot for a while the graves on the hill beside Beausoleil Creek and the farm on the side of Ardoise Hill.

When they were dozing warm and naked and coiled together, Eulalie whispered: "Cully...?"

"Hm?"

"You will be careful...?"

"No fear. The only danger is I'll be so careful I might as well've stayed home. This is the first time in my life I've had a home and family. I don't want to lose them."

"Nor we you."

Beausoleil's war party set off down-river in a motley collection of fishing skiffs, pirogues and canoes. Eulalie stood on the bank with the other women of Petitcodiac, and the children and old men, watching the boats disappear into the morning mist. Henri sat in front of Cully paddling one of the canoes. Eulalie was pleased to see that Cully remembered to angle his paddle like a knife in the water at the end of each stroke, instead of shovelling.

When the boats were out of sight, Eulalie sent Jacques and Josette back to the cabin and went to do something she hadn't been able to bring herself to do while Cully was around. She'd been meaning to do it since the first Mi'kmaqs of the spring passed through, but she'd always found an excuse to put it off—knowing full well that the real reason was that she didn't want to have to argue about it or lie about it. She was afraid she might've waited too long already; another week or so would tell.

A very late-migrating family of Mi'kmaqs was camped in Alexandre Brossard's woodlot. There was an old woman smoking a pipe and weaving a splint basket. Eulalie said: "*Kwahee, noogumee,*"—'Hello, Grandmother.' *Noogumee* was a word that carried even more respect than 'Grandmother'; it was also the name of Glooscap's housekeeper.

The old woman looked up at her suspiciously. Eulalie said: "My name is La Tour."

The old woman didn't exactly smile, but she looked a little less suspicious. Eulalie sat down near her and said: "These are bad times to be Acadian. The English hate us."

"The English hate everybody."

"I became a wife not long ago."

"Does it stand up straight like a poplar tree like a man should?"

"Um... I, um, I don't know what any other man is like."

"Well, if you're not curious, then your man must stand up straight like a poplar tree."

"These are bad times. We must live through the winters in cowhouses, or out in the woods like... rabbits." She'd almost said 'like Indians.' "This winter my father and three sisters and one brother died."

"I feel sad for you, granddaughter."

"I don't want to bring a baby into the world to die in the cold. I want my man and I to have children, when better days come, but not now. I know something about medicines, but there are secrets only *noogumee* knows."

"Do you want to stop a child that is started, or stop one from starting?"

"Is there a medicine that can do both?"

"No, one medicine can't do both. I can give you one to stop a child, but only take it if you are sure—it's hard, hard medicine. And I know of something that will stop a child from starting—a tea you must drink every day except when you are bleeding. But, if I give you those medicines, what will you give me?"

Eulalie held up one of the coins from the aggregation made up of the purse Beaupère had handed her the day they left Ardoise and the one he'd died clutching. The old woman shook her head. Eulalie held up another one alongside it. The old woman nodded, "Come back tomorrow and I will give you enough medicines to keep you until I pass this way again."

"What are they?"

"If I told you that, you wouldn't have to give me anything, would you? Maybe after a few seasons I'll tell you, if you still want to know. Is your man a white Frenchman, too, or are you wiser than your mother?"

"He is English."

"Well, maybe they don't hate *everybody*. Give me the money now and I will give you what you want tomorrow."

"No, I will give you the money tomorrow."

"Well, if you aren't wiser than your mother, she was pretty wise."

On the way back to the cabin where Jacques and Josette were binding the last few bundles of reeds and elephant grass together, Eulalie debated whether she'd tell Cully when he came back—*if* he came back. She had no idea how he'd feel about it. It might make a *contretemps* over nothing. For all she knew, the old woman's medicine wouldn't work at all. Or it might well be that the fact Cully would be gone for much of the summer, and she might be on starvation rations again next winter, would make the medicine irrelevant.

He wasn't the one who would have to risk carrying a child to term with snow blowing in under the door and barely enough food to keep the cold out of a person's bones. He rarely talked about the times he'd had to stand up with a gun in his hands and cannonballs crashing around him. She didn't expect him to say much about it this time, unless she asked. That was his risk, this was hers.

She decided she wouldn't lie to him about it. If he asked, she'd tell him.

XXXV

ndré sat in the back of a wagon with Patrice and Phillipe again, only this time they were manacled and they were travelling inland through Pennsylvania, not South Carolina. But at least this countryside seemed to be in the same universe as home. In the woods along the roadside, André spotted the occasional frayed-barked, homy birch tree showing white among the darker trunks. And here there wasn't that feeling that damp moss would start growing on anything that stayed still for longer than half an hour. The road wound past comfortably-aged, family-sized farms, instead of the new-looking, sprawling plantations of South Carolina.

Rachel had been separated from them on the beach. André's English wasn't enough to tell whether the men who'd captured them meant to send her back to Mister Kenney for a reward, or sell her, or keep her for themselves. André didn't like to remember his last sight of her: the white-rimmed eyes in the brown face pleading over her shoulder as she was hustled away. But protecting her from Patrice and Phillipe was one thing; a dozen men with muskets was another.

André's English was enough, though, to make the men with muskets double over with laughter when he said things like: "Yassuh, we bees Acadian mens sho'nuff."

The road came out onto the bank of a wide river with a city up ahead. The city looked even bigger than Charleston. André craned his neck from side to side as the wagon rolled through aisles of houses with barely room for a flower garden between them, and past tall buildings made of brick and stone. The streets and the neatly-planked footpaths on either side were bursting with a bustle of people and a babble of languages. Few of the people were dressed in the bright silk and brocade he'd seen on the streets of Charleston, although some of the ones wearing black or brown looked like they could afford to buy any colour they wanted.

Among the babble of languages, André recognized the cadences of English and of the German he'd heard from farmers in Halifax market. There was at least one other language that didn't sound like English or German. But none of the languages was French.

The wagon turned a corner, and up ahead André could see and hear a market square that made Halifax market seem like Piziquid's. But before they got there, the wagon stopped in front of a high, wide building with a flat roof. The man beside the driver gestured with his gun for André, Patrice and Phillipe to climb down.

The entrance to the building was a pair of huge, iron-bound doors at ground level. The wagon driver banged on the doors with his whip, a slot opened and words were exchanged. There was a sound of locks and bolts, one of the doors swung open and André obeyed the barked: "Inside!"

The building wasn't flat-roofed after all; it was a high, stone wall surrounding a courtyard with a building inside it. A man with a thick stick in his hand and a pistol in his belt herded André and Patrice and Phillipe to the building and into a room with bars on the windows. Their manacles were taken off and the door slammed and locked. André had never seen even the outside of a jail before, but he'd heard of them.

But all worries and confusion vanished for a while when a man came to the door with three bowls of soup and a loaf of bread. The soup was thick with chunks of beef, cabbage and potatoes. After nothing but stolen scraps on the boat, months of slave food before that, and two months of ship's biscuit before that, André could've eaten all three bowls and the whole loaf.

The next day, two other men with guns led André and Patrice and Phillipe out of the jail and through the market. Despite the roar of market noise all around him, André could still hear the clumsy clacking of his wooden shoes on the round stones of the street. In the middle of the market square was the strangest, vilest flagpole he'd ever seen. It was a thick mast with the English flag on top, and partway down a round platform like a crows-nest. Fixed to the mast above the platform was a wooden rectangle with holes in it. The holes on one side of the flagpole were empty, but the holes on the other side were closed around the neck and wrists of a man standing on the platform. There were stains and garbage on the man's face and the wood around it, as though some stall in the market had been selling rotted vegetables to throw at him.

The guards brought André and Patrice and Phillipe up the high steps of a building facing the market, and inside to a very large room very much like the inside of a church. Pewfuls of people faced a tall, wooden altar and a couple of long communion tables in front of it. Behind the altar sat a man in black robes and a long, white, curled wig. A man in smaller robes and a shorter wig stood up from one of the communion tables as the guards ushered André and Patrice and Phillipe toward him.

The man in the shorter wig said to them in French: "Well, gentlemen, exceedingly fortunate for you that the magistrate has no manner of comprehension of the language of Molière—hence the county has to pay for a translator, and hence you get an advocate thrown into the bargain."

The advocate's French was very strange and very hard to follow, as though he knew a great many words but wasn't exactly sure how they were supposed to sound. He went on: "Were you aware of the fact that it is a grievous crime indeed to assist an escaped slave? Shake your heads. Attend me—I said *shake your heads*."

André shook his head, and the advocate turned to address the magistrate in English. André could only pick out a word or two in their conversation. When the magistrate turned his eyes on him, André looked down, so as not to seem impudent by staring back, then quickly looked up again, in case not meeting the magistrate's eyes seemed a sign of guilt.

The advocate turned back to André and switched back to French. "Well, ignorance of the law may be no excuse, but the fact you had no awareness you were committing that grievous crime does encourage the magistrate toward the conclusion that it would cost the county less to house you with the other Acadians who were shipped here from Nova Scotia, rather than in prison.

"For very good reasons, which you three are suspected to exemplify, the province of Pennsylvania, like our sister colonies, has made it a policy to disperse the Acadians foisted upon us as far inland as possible. Although Pennsylvania has no standing militia and will take no part in this or any other war, we would suffer as much as any other English colony if the French are victorious. Consequently, we would prefer that the French Acadians thrust among us not be presented with the opportunity to steal a boat and sneak north to join the French armies and pass on information as to our defences and the British army's movements.

"And *that*, you see, gentlemen, is the other charge levied against you. The question in the magistrate's mind is whether you are simply ignorant farmers seeking to make your way back to your homes in Nova Scotia whence you were exiled, or whether you are spies. I think that now would be a very good time to look confusedly at each other and shrug your arms and make protestations."

André had no difficulty at all doing exactly what the advocate suggested; it seemed less a suggestion than a licence to follow the natural inclination he'd been holding in. The advocate spoke with the magistrate again, then turned back to the prisoners. "Well, gentlemen, it seems you will have to make do with the thin gruel of charity instead of hearty prison fare. One of you will stay in Philadelphia and the other two will be parcelled out to separate counties, to even the burden on the public purse. I advise you not to cultivate the company of our Irish and German Catholics, as there is more than a little nervousness hereabouts about a catholic conspiracy in a colony with no military capacity."

André said: "We are very much in your debt for helping us, *monsieur*."

"Pardon me?"

André repeated himself more slowly, trying to pronounce each word separately and reminding himself to use the formal *vous* instead of *tu*. Acadians called anybody and everybody *tu*, but André's father had warned him that educated people would get offended.

The advocate shrugged, "Nothing to thank me for—as I said, the county pays the bill. Are any of you familiar with the works of Voltaire and Rabelais?"

André looked at Patrice and Phillipe, who looked at him. André offered uncertainly: "I've heard of Rabelais. They say he comes from the same part of France as most Acadians."

"*Came*," the advocate looked pained. "He's been dead two hundred years. Have you read him?"

"No, *monsieur*. I've heard he told funny stories, but blasphemous."

"Pity. It would've been interesting to discuss with someone who learned the language in the cradle. I believe the magistrate wants you to move along so he can get on with the next case."

They were held in the cell overnight again and then put into the back of another wagon, this time without manacles. The wagon carried them away from the bustle of the market and down a street that parallelled the river—André could see the tops of ship masts over the buildings on his left—then turned right. A few minutes more and they came to a halt in front of a row of low, wooden houses with sagging roofs. The guard beside the wagoneer took out a piece of paper and read: "Andrew Melanson?"

"*Ici*."

The guard pointed at the row of houses. André shook hands with Patrice and Phillipe, assuring each other they'd meet again. Phillipe said: "I'm sorry about Rachel."

André said: "I know."

The guard said: "Move!"

André climbed down and the wagon rumbled away. The guard hadn't specified which house in the row he was supposed to go to, so he headed for the nearest one. The fence in front of it had pickets missing and the gate was hanging from one hinge. André knocked on the door and a parchmenty voice called: "*Entrez*."

The room beyond the door was bare of furniture. There were a few blankets laid on the floor, and an old man and two old women were sitting on them. One of the women was making a broom out of willow twigs, and the old man was trying to make a chair with nothing but cut saplings and a knife. The old man looked like Eulalie's Uncle Benoni, only ten years older.

The old man squinted up at him. "André...?"

As Benoni started to rise, André stuck out his hand to help him to his feet while making it look like he was only shaking his hand. "André—it *is* you! Where the devil did you come from?"

André told them. Benoni said: "Well, you won't be going any further north from here. You see, the governor of Pennsylvania wanted to spread us out through all his counties, but it didn't quite work out the way he planned—we didn't want to be separated and the counties didn't want to take us. Still, some got sent to counties outside Philadelphia County, and each county is very jealous that they not have to be troubled with even one more Acadian than they were allotted. So we can't go into another county but with a written pass, and they won't write us a pass unless a cousin is dying or some such—maybe not even then.

"But you are lucky this is the county they put you in. At least there is a Catholic church in Philadelphia, and a priest who speaks a little French. There are a dozen more of us living in this house, but in the morning a wagon comes to take the young men and women off to work for the county. I guess tomorrow you'll go with them."

André looked around at the broken windows and the sunlight seeping between the wall planks. He said: "How did you live through the winter here?"

"We didn't. They only brought us here a month ago. The governor of Pennsylvania didn't know what to do with us, so we sat on an island in the harbor all winter long while he made up his mind. What little food they brought out to us was bad, and then there was the smallpox. Three hundred of us when our ship dropped anchor, a hundred and fifty when spring came. Abraham à Moïse à Bernard, Henri à Marc à Laurent, Judith à Marie à Marie... But, maybe we would still be sitting on that island if the governor hadn't seen that a hundred and fifty would be much easier to manage than three hundred."

André said: "My family...?"

"No, no, they weren't on our ship. The good God knows where their ship went." Benoni gummed his tongue and looked into the distance. "All last summer—was it only last summer?—I tried to warn people that this war was going to bring the English to do something evil to us. No one would listen. Not your father, not Joseph Brossard... 'Just Benoni being an old woman again.' There's little joy in being a prophet. But not even *I* could imagine they would..." The old man wiped his eyes and his nose. "Do you see any children here, André?"

As a matter of fact, he hadn't, but he hadn't thought of it till now. "No."

"You won't. They're gone. One here, two there... To live with English families, and learn to think in English, and go to English churches, and be brought up to forget they were ever Acadian. They took our children, André."

XXXVI

ully spent his summer living in forest camps and skirmishing with His British Majesty's Land Forces. The population of the camps kept changing, as other men came and went to their families on the upper Petitcodiac or the Miramichi. But Beausoleil stayed in the field, so l'Anglais did, too.

There was only Beausoleil's shifting band of Acadians and Mi'kmaqs left to defend north Acadia now. Early in the summer, Lieutenant Boishébert and his troops had been evacuated to Quebec, along with Father La Brosse and a lot of the Acadian refugees. Cully guessed that the ones who'd stayed all had their own versions of what Eulalie had told him when the evacuation rumours started circulating in the spring. "I am *Acadienne*, not *Quebecoise*. If we run away to Quebec, we might just as well have let the English take us south, and Beau-père and Marie and Hélène and Jean-Marc and Louise will have died in vain."

Cully had barely stopped himself from replying: "Everybody dies in vain." He didn't much want to go to Quebec, anyway.

Beausoleil's war band had succeeded in driving the column of bloodybacks back to Fort Cumberland, and only lost two men doing it. Neither of the two was Henri, and Cully managed to persuade him that he'd done his part and should go home to help Eulalie get ready for winter. Cully whiled away the rest of the summer alternating between harassing the little fort and much more cautiously taking potshots at Fort Cumberland.

When the leaves turned to flame, so did the little fort. The garrison set it ablaze before quick-marching across the isthmus to Fort Cumberland and slamming the gates shut behind them.

That was cause to break out the cider in Camp Beausoleil, but an even better cause introduced itself a few days later. They had moved camp to within a few miles of Fort Cumberland, for one more spate of snipe-and-scamper before heading home for the winter. A Mi'kmaq woman in a canoe stopped by and told Beausoleil a story that Cully couldn't follow one word of, but it made Beausoleil laugh and then grow thoughtful.

Beausoleil said: "You see, *Anglais*, the funny story this good woman just told me has to do with an English ship captain who doesn't know shit about the Fundy tides—or didn't until this morning. He anchored a little ways down the coast last night, and when he woke in the morning his ship was sitting in mud. They are having to make a few repairs—to the rudder, by the sounds of what this good woman says—and the captain has let her drift just far enough offshore to still be afloat at low tide. But the ship still sits there, anchored just offshore...

"Now I ask myself, *Anglais*—what would an English ship be doing this far up the bay, except bringing winter supplies to Fort Cumberland? Greatcoats, provisions, gunpowder, brandy, all sorts of good things."

"Unless it's a warship come to sail up the Petitcodiac and cannonade our homes."

"Hm. Seems too late in the year for that. And I don't think the English would waste a warship on the likes of us when they have Louisbourg to worry about. Let's us go take a closer look."

'Us' turned out to mean the whole camp. Along with everyone else, Cully peered out through the leaves of the shoreline brush at the ship out on the bay. It didn't appear to be a warship; Cully could only see three gunports on the side facing the shore. During his years in Halifax, one of the few entertainments available to a soldier between pay calls was to watch the ships come into the harbor and learn to tell them apart. This one was what they called a brigantine, with two masts and a long bowsprit. A work crew in the ship's boat was frantically trying to finish some task at the brigantine's stern before the sun finished going down.

The tide was high and a bit of fog was rising. Beausoleil muttered: "It'd be good if that fog got good and thick, but a person can only expect so much luck. The English seem to think the Baye Françoise has become their private lake that they can sail without convoys. Time we showed them different.

"We'll have to wait until the moon rises and sets, and the tide goes out. The hour before dawn is the best time for surprises, anyway. No fires, and if anyone wants to smoke a pipe go far back into the woods."

There were a few preparations that had to be made, then Cully mounded up a pile of leaves, buttoned his coat to his chin, stuck his hands in his pockets and did his best to sleep. He did pretty well at it, actually—he had to be shaken awake. Beausoleil's voice murmured out of the darkness: "If you'd snored any louder, *Anglais*, they would've heard you on the ship."

They left their coats, hats, and boots or moccasins behind and gathered at the edge of the woods. Beausoleil said: "From here on, not a word, except a whisper in an ear if you have to. On a still night like this, any sound you make will carry far over the water. But, if they sound the alarm, however many of us have managed to get on board had better make as much noise as we can, and the ones still on shore come as loud and fast as you can. Well, let's us go dig some clams."

Cully pointed at Beausoleil, with his rifle slung over his shoulder and a knife and hatchet in his belt, and said: "Must be fierce clams hereabouts." There were stifled snickers and Beausoleil led them out onto the shore.

The shore rocks tortured Cully's bare feet, but after a few minutes there was nothing but soft, squelchy mud—*cold*, soft, squelchy mud. Cully hoped he didn't step on a lobster. The only light was from the stars—patches of them obscured by clouds— and the distant yellow pinprick of the deckwatch lantern. Beausoleil had been right that a thick fogbank would be too much to ask, but there were a few drifting swatches here and there.

It was a long half-mile from the shoreline to the edge of the water. Cully followed close behind Beausoleil, with fifty men strung out behind them, six of them carrying three small canoes. Cully tried not to think about the fact that if the watchman caught a glimpse of them, or heard them, the ship's gunner could easily rake the beach with grapeshot firing blind.

Beausoleil stopped abruptly. Cully moved up beside him and felt a wave lap his toes. One of the canoes was brought forward and set in the water. Beausoleil carefully propped his rifle in the canoe, Cully did the same with his musket, and a half-dozen other men followed suit. Beausoleil was already in the water, wading forward as though he intended to take that ship whether anybody followed him or not. Neither Cully nor any of the others doubted for a moment he would try, which was precisely why they would follow him.

Cully waded in, taking long, slow strides to keep from splashing and to keep his balance. He'd thought the mud had been cold, until he stepped into the water. The water rose gradually to his chest and then his chin. The last few yards he had to swim for it, and he wasn't much of a swimmer.

Beausoleil had headed for the bow and waited for a wave to lift the stern, then lunged out of the water to grab the rigging dangling from the bowsprit and pull himself up. Cully did the same, trying not to gasp or grunt too loud as he hand-over-handed up the ropes. He could hear the sounds of snoring from the fo'c's'le next to his elbow. The ropes felt like wet snakes and his arms felt like wet macaroni, but he couldn't very well give up as long as Beausoleil was still climbing—given that Beausoleil was a good twenty years older and the weight on Beausoleil's arms a good forty pounds heavier.

Once he and Beausoleil were on deck, the men who'd followed them into the rigging relayed up Beausoleil's rifle and Cully's musket. The two of them began to move toward the stern, Beausoleil hunching as low as he could along the starboard rail and Cully hunching much lower by the larboard. Cully took it as a given that the men behind them were getting themselves on board quickly and taking up their appointed positions around the forward hatches.

Cully could make out the man on nightwatch now, silhouetted against the stars. He was moving quizzically from one side of the afterdeck to the other, peering over the rails as though he thought he'd heard something or seen something but wasn't quite sure.

Cully was so intent on watching the watchman, and keeping his teeth from chattering too loud, that he forgot he was carrying his musket. The barrel clinked against the cannon he was sneaking past. The watchman came forward, peering down from the quarterdeck, and said softly: "That you, Joe...?"

Something hissed through the air, and Beausoleil's thrown hatchet took the sailor on the side of the head. The watchman dropped without even letting out a groan— but instead of crumpling conveniently to the deck he went over the rail, making a splash that sounded to Cully like a mountain falling into the ocean.

Cully started moving ahead again cautiously, hoping the crew were all sound sleepers. The half-door to the cabins under the quarterdeck slid open, showing a lantern in the gangway beyond, and a man started to emerge, saying: "Sanders...?"

Without thinking, Cully leaped forward, his musket automatically reversing itself, and drove his musketbutt down between the man's eyes. As the man went down backwards, Cully leaped over him and lunged for the door at the end of the companionway, which he hoped was the captain's cabin. He slid the door open. A man in a nightshirt was sitting up and reaching for a pistol. Cully pointed his musket at him and said: "Don't," then stepped aside to let Beausoleil stoop through the doorway.

The ship was bursting with noise now: voices shouting in French and Mi'kmaq, a couple of gunshots, the clatter of the Jacob's ladder rolling down and whooping men swarming up it. Bare feet slapped down the steps behind Cully, to take charge of the ship's other officers as they bleared out of their beds.

Beausoleil perched himself on the edge of the captain's bed, stuck out his hand and said: "*Bonjour, Monsieur le Capitaine.* I hope you finished repairing your rudder, to save us the trouble."

Cully translated: "Monsieur Beausoleil says that you and your ship and crew are prisoners of war."

The captain said nothing, but his eyes had jerked when Cully said 'Beausoleil'.

Beausoleil looked down at the hand the captain had refused to shake, then up at

Cully. He pointed at Cully's musket, "I don't know why you even bother to load that damned thing. You do all your good work without gunpowder."

By dawn, the ship's officers and crew were all secured democratically in the fo'c's'le. Beausoleil had assured them, through Cully, that they'd be set ashore within a day's walk of Fort Cumberland.

Beausoleil took a lantern and led an exploration of the hold. Cully had to admit that the cargo did look suspiciously like winter supplies for Fort Cumberland: blankets, greatcoats, powder and shot, salt pork, rum...

Beausoleil pried open a coffin-shaped crate and said: "Well, well..." The crate was packed with British army rifles, the kind issued to those elite troops who were actually expected to hit what they aimed at. Beausoleil tossed one to Cully and said: "No more of that smooth-bore miss-a-barndoor for you, *Anglais*. Maybe this winter I'll teach you how to shoot."

As they familiarized themselves more with the insides and outsides of the brigantine *Mary B.*, Beausoleil began to get that wicked grin that meant he was getting an idea. Cully stood on the quarterdeck with Beausoleil and Alexandre Brossard as the brothers pointed up into the rigging and exchanged opinions on squaresails, fore-and-aft sails, lateen sails, scudding sails... Cully's contribution to the conversation consisted of pointing at the bowsprit and saying: "That'd be a spritsail furled up there."

They looked at him and then at each other. Alexandre nodded, "Yeah, I guess it would be, being on the bowsprit and all."

Eventually Beausoleil stopped trading opinions and stood silently with his legs planted wide and his hands in his armpits, staring straight ahead at the waves beyond the nose of the *Mary B.* Cully was willing to swear he could feel a humming transmitted down through the soles of Beausoleil's feet and across the deck.

Beausoleil said: "When Lieutenant Boishébert got ordered back to Quebec, he left me a few little cannons... I'd say the Petitcodiac's deep enough we could sail this little ship up far enough to anchor her in Fox Creek, keep the ice clear around her while we spend the winter re-fitting her... The English have to ship supplies into the bay for Fort Cumberland, Fort Edward, Annapolis Royal... We got as much use for those supplies as they do... And the more trouble we cause them up and down the bay, the less time they got to come marching up the Petitcodiac or the Miramichi...

"What do you say, *Anglais*? When you were a little boy toddling around your mother's kitchen, did you ever say: 'When I get big, I'm going to be a pirate'?"

XXXVII

ith frost in the air, Eulalie went around the inside of the cabin stuffing strips of old blankets into the walls wherever she could feel a draft. She could afford to tear up old blankets now, since Quebec had sent supplies and a promise there'd be more every year until the war was over. She'd even had no qualms about using up an entire blanket to make a curtain for the bed of pine boughs and straw where she and Cully would spend their nights when he came home. It was nowhere near the privacy of a proper, cabinetted bed, but it was something.

The only furniture in the house was a rickety, still-barked table and stools that she and Jacques had made, with a little finishing-off help from Henri when he came home swollen with pride at having done his part in driving the invaders back to their fort. She expected that Cully would make sturdier furniture over the winter. He had such clever hands.

Josette yanked open the door and squealed: "They're home! Beausoleil sent Aunt Anne a message to hurry down and meet him at Fox Creek!"

"Why at Fox Creek?"

"I don't know! Hurry!"

Eulalie threw her shawl on and ran her fingers through her hair—the days of fussing with frilled, white caps and coiled-in ribbons were gone for now. She had no fears that Cully might be coming home wounded, or not coming home at all. Just a week ago, some men who'd wandered back up the Petitcodiac had said that l'Anglais still had a whole skin, and that he and the other men still with Beausoleil only meant to do a bit more sniping around Fort Cumberland.

She grabbed Josette's hand and they hurried down the path toward Fox Creek. A lot of other people were hurrying down the same path, and Eulalie could see through the sparse-leafed riverbank brush that canoes and skiffs were racing downstream.

Everyone kept calling out to each other: "Why did he say Fox Creek?" and getting back: "I don't know."

The wives, children parents, sisters and cousins of the men coming home milled around on the up-river bank of Fox Creek. It seemed to Eulalie that the whole community was like a child being led by the hand with her eyes covered—"No peeking, now!" There was no sign of any band of partisans loping through the woods or paddling upstream.

Then someone shouted: "Look!" and pointed at the treetops on the other side of the creek. Eulalie looked. At first glance, she thought it was just a cloud like all the other puffy, little clouds hemstitched along the horizon. Then she saw it was a sail.

She and everyone else on the creekbank ran to the riverbank. Surging up the river was a two-masted ship, with layers of sails like puffed swans' breasts, and white water curling from her prow.

The sails began to furl as the crew trimmed to turn her into Fox Creek. Eulalie flicked her eyes from one to another of the men up in the rigging, or hauling at the ropes on deck. Then she muttered to herself: "Idiot," and looked to where she should've looked in the first place. Standing next to Beausoleil on the quarterdeck was her man, with his hair bound back by a ribbon and his shirt belled out by the breeze.

The last sails were furled and the anchors dropped. But there was no need to haul forward the ship's boat leashed to the stern, like a calf following its mother's tail. Even before the anchors touched the bottom of Fox Creek, the ship was already surrounded by canoes and boats. People scrambled aboard to get a closer look, incidentally leaving boat-room for anyone who wanted to get ashore.

Cully was in the first boat. Josette, Jacques and Henri flapped their arms and shrilled: "Cully!" but Eulalie just stood still and silent, seeing more as the boat drew closer. He'd draped on a heavy-looking, grey coat she'd never seen before; some of the other men were wearing soldiers' red coats with the tails cut off. He was holding a new rifle instead of his musket. He didn't look as thin as she remembered, despite a summer of living off the country. He looked darker, rougher and looser, and like his mouth had forgotten how to form: "Yes, sir!" He looked Acadian. But not like an Acadian farmer, like a *courier de bois* like her roguish great-great-great grandfather.

When he stepped out of the boat she stopped standing still. He dropped his rifle to fling his arms around her. He smelled of woodsmoke, pine trees and salt water. And he felt like the only man who'd ever held her naked in his arms.

Like everyone else who'd watched the ship come in, Eulalie fountained-out questions. Like everyone else who'd come in on the ship, Cully parcelled out nonchalant answers, as though people picked up ships or clamshells on the beach every day. A keg of rum from the ship got its head knocked in and people ran to fetch their fiddles and drums. Bonfires were built to keep the dancers warm between jigs and to roast potatoes.

Eulalie was in a swirl even before a drink of rum. She'd happened to be at Piziquid once on the day all the fishing boats came home from the last run of the season, and today at Petitcodiac had something of the same feeling only much more so. But today she was as much a part of it as anyone: rolling her eyes sideways at the winks of the other summer widows, and thanking the good God that her man had come home safe.

Cully, too, had become as much a part of it as anyone, giving and getting shouted tidbits such as "Where's your knife, *Anglais*?" or "Going swimming again, Jean?" Eulalie had no idea what the jokes meant—no doubt she'd hear all the funny stories over the winter, again and again—but she knew they referred to things that had happened while the men were thrusting themselves into danger for the sake of everyone around the bonfires.

Cully let go of her for a moment and she saw him over by the other bonfire talking to Henri. When he came back, he said: "Let's go home."

When the noise of the celebration faded behind them, she said: "What did you say to Henri?"

"I told him to keep Jacques and Josette there for at least an hour."

Eulalie laughed, "He'll be lucky to pry them *away* from there before sunset, if then." For that matter, Henri, Jacques and Josette might not come home that night at all. Some thoughtful woman whose husband hadn't been gone all summer might well scoop them up with her own children for the night.

Eulalie and Cully gabbled at each other all the way along the path to Beausoleil Creek, snatching crumbs of what each others' lives had been for the last three months. But when they came into the little clearing behind the waterfront farms, he went silent. She watched him go over to the shoulder-high stacks of firewood banked against two walls of the cabin and run his hand along the top layer, watched him stoop to lift one of the green logs covering the pit she'd dug to keep root vegetables through the winter, watched him open the door and step inside.

She followed him in, went past him to the fireplace, stirred the coals alight and laid down some twigs and split wood. When she looked back, he was still standing in the middle of the room looking around. She saw through his eyes the kennel-like pile of blankets and straw in the corner where Henri and Jacques slept, the one in the other corner where Josette would have to sleep now that Cully was home, the moth-eaten blanket pretending to be a curtain for her and Cully's bed, the table and stools that were really just sticks splinted together... She said: "I thought... I thought maybe... over the winter you might make a better table and chairs than me and Jacques and Henri ever -"

He turned away from her and went back to the door, saying nothing. He raised his arms and set his rifle on the two pegs fixed over the lintel.

She stood up as he came back toward her. He put his hands on her shoulders, then raised one to her hair and whispered: "Thank you."

She wrapped herself around him, yanking at the back of his shirt to tug it up out of his breeches, balancing on one leg so she could cock the other one up behind his hip.

He seemed at least as ravenous for her as she was for him, but once they were in their pine-scented bed and he inside her, she found she wanted him to go very slowly. He seemed to want the same without her saying so, like lenten fasters not wanting to wolf away their first real meal since Mardi Gras. But going slowly didn't stop her from forgetting herself to the point where she suddenly realized she was scraping her fingernails across the furrowed scars on his back. She flung her hands up like she'd grabbed a hot skillet and gasped: "I'm sorry!"

He stopped moving and said: "Sorry for what?"

"Your back—the scars—I didn't mean to hurt you..."

"They don't hurt. All I feel of them is they itch a little from time to time, and scratching's good for an itch. I told you that when you asked before. Forgot already?"

"No, but I thought maybe you were just saying it."

"No, I'm never polite when it comes to something hurting me. A lot of things someone outside might think hurt don't. Like *this*!"

"Oh!"

"Did that hurt?"

"I wouldn't say *hurt*..."

"How about *this*?"

"Um. Not exactly. How about this...? Did that hurt?"

"Uh, I'm not sure. Maybe you'd best try it again and we'll see—*Uh*... Hm, still not sure..."

The children didn't come home that night, which was just as well. What with dozing and waking up again and one thing and another, an hour wouldn't have done it. Eulalie knew she could keep herself from making loud noises if she had to, but she didn't want to have to every time.

Just before they drifted off for the last time, Eulalie giggled: "I have baby hands again."

"Hm...? 'Baby hands'...?"

"I can't make a fist."

In the morning, she boiled water for blackberry tea and for the medicine she'd got from the old Mi'kmaq woman. Last night she hadn't thought of the fact that this morning would be the first time he saw her drinking it.

He said: "What is that, some sort of tonic?"

"Yes... A women's tonic." That wasn't exactly a lie.

He sniffed at it, said: "Remind me to thank the good God I wasn't born a woman," and never said another word about it.

Eulalie couldn't be sure whether it was because of the Mi'kmaq medicine, but fall passed, the snow grew higher, the year turned and still she didn't become pregnant, even though there were plenty of opportunities. She thought it might just as easily be because her body wasn't getting enough sustenance to be fertile—not starving wasn't the same thing as being well-fed. Or maybe it was just luck.

She was happy, and wise enough to know it. It didn't take her a lot of looking back over the last year-and-a-half to see she was one of the lucky ones. She didn't look ahead beyond next month, or next week, or next summer. There was no sense in anyone thinking beyond that until the war was over. For now, it was enough to find herself singing with Josette over the cooking pot while Jacques and Henri helped Cully fit the legs onto the new table, or to lower her mending into her lap when she heard him coming up the path from Beausoleil's attempts to teach him to shoot like a hunter instead of a soldier.

But there were times she found herself thinking of André Melanson, and of how different things would've been. André was her own kind, and they would've had no trouble understanding each other. There were things about Cully Robin she would never know, and didn't want to. Sometimes when he put his hands on her she couldn't help but wonder how many other women, and what kinds, those hands had clutched, or how many men those hands had thrust a bayonet into. Beau-père had been right that a coyote couldn't wipe away its past, even if he were her coyote. She certainly never complained when he encouraged her lovemaking to resemble a bitch in heat, but she blushed remembering it in daylight.

She told herself that every wife, even Beausoleil's Anne, must occasionally daydream of what life would be like married to another man. But that didn't stop her from getting tears in her eyes when she remembered pictures like André holding a barn beam on his shoulders while Beau-père pegged it into place, and imagined André doing the same thing in the house she and he would've lived in.

At first, André would only come into her mind once in a while, and not for long. But as the winter wore on it began to happen more and more often. She was afraid that Cully would ask her what she was getting so misty-eyed about, and afraid there must be something missing inside her heart, that she couldn't appreciate what she had. With Beau-père gone, there was no one she could talk to about it. She certainly couldn't talk about it to Cully.

Every now and then Cully would go with Beausoleil to Fox Creek, where the trading ship *Mary B.* was being turned into a privateer. Cully might not know much about ships, but he was good at tinkering with things. On one of those days, Eulalie went looking for Anne.

In Eulalie's first winter on the Petitcodiac, it hadn't take her long to learn that Agnes *dit* Anne à Judith à Pacifique had more thoughts of her own than might be expected of someone married to as dominant a man as Beausoleil. The first piece of land Beausoleil and Anne had lived on, before moving to the Petitcodiac, had belonged to Anne. And none of the people living along the Petitcodiac would've had title to their land if it weren't for a lawsuit Anne's family had fought against a French officer who claimed he owned it all.

Eulalie found Anne in her kitchen, cutting up a muskrat and popping the bits into a bubbling stewpot. Anne glanced at her, pushing a wisp of gray-blonde hair out of her eyes with the back of her knife-wrist, and said: "Oh, Eulalie, I'm up to my elbows in—" then glanced at her again. "I was just about to put my knife down for a while and make a cup of tea. Would you like one?"

"Thank you."

Anne hefted the stewpot off the firehook, replaced it with the kettle, reached down a pewter teapot and ladled in a few spoonfuls of the tea that had been part of the *Mary B.*'s cargo. Then she set out two cups and a bowl of maple syrup, sat down across the table from Eulalie and said: "Tell me."

Eulalie told her, while Anne kept one eye on the kettle, filled the teapot, waited for it to steep and poured. Anne sipped her tea and pursed her mouth, reached across the table to touch Eulalie's hand and said: "This André Melanson, I'm sure he is a nice young man, but he isn't what you're yearning for when you find yourself yearning for him."

"He isn't?"

"No. He is like... When Beausoleil is away—and been away for long enough for me to forget that he thinks sticking his hunting knife in the table beside his dinnerplate makes for a handy way to cut up his meat—I will notice the empty peg where his coat should be hanging, and feel a pang. But it's not his smelly, old, smoked-moosehide coat I'm missing.

"This André Melanson is a peg you are hanging something else on. When you see André Melanson in your memory, you are seeing all the things that might've been—that *would've* been—if there hadn't been a Fifth of September. There is nothing wrong in your heart to feel a yearning for that; you'd have to have no heart not to feel it. But don't mistake the coat for the man. There, you see—I made up a proverb!"

Eulalie went home feeling lighter, but still not entirely convinced that her pangs about André Melanson didn't have at least a little bit to do with André Melanson.

Cully came home from Fox Creek, and the family was just sitting down to a supper of ship's biscuit floating in salt pork boiled with cabbage, when a raucous singing erupted outside:

"*Monsieur, madame mariés,*

"*N'ont pas encore soupé...*"

Eulalie jumped up shouting: "Candlemass!" There'd been no real Candlemass last year, so she'd relegated it to the place with all the other things that had ceased to be. "Josette, open the door for them. I need to find some food..."

Cully said: "There's plenty of food on your plate," and, as usual, didn't look displeased at getting laughed at for saying something foolish. He seemed to think that being a joke was as good as making a joke, as long as people had something to laugh about.

Eulalie said: "Not food for *today*, you cully," and scooped a bit of flour into a hank of patch-cloth and tied it up. Outside the door were half-a-dozen men, two of them holding the tow-ropes of toboggans that had a few things piled on them already. Some of the men had their hats on backwards, some had their faces painted, and one was wearing a mask made out of a skinned bear's head.

Eulalie handed them the flour. The one wearing the bear mask said: "There'll be half-a-dozen feast houses, but this goes to Beausoleil's."

On Candlemass morning, Eulalie took Josette to Beausoleil's house and joined in with the women preparing all the food that had been collected, and a great deal more besides: the contributions were only a priming for all that Beausoleil and Anne had stored up for the occasion. Josette kept chirping the little rhyme her father had taught her:

"Candlemass day, Candlemass day,

"Half your wood and half your hay."

Around mid-day the men and boys began to arrive, and each took his turn flipping the Candlemass pancake he had to eat before he could eat anything else. When Anne called: "*L'Anglais*," Eulalie didn't think to warn him. His hands were so agile at most things, it never occurred to her that he wouldn't easily flip a half-done pancake and catch it neatly in the pan.

She was wrong. The pancake came down on the lip of the skillet and fell on the floor. There was silence, and then much laughter. Cully sidled his eyes around suspiciously. Beausoleil said gravely: "You know what that means, *Anglais*."

"Um... No? No, I don't." Cully's eyes found her out in the crowd and Eulalie shrugged apologetically.

"What it means, *Anglais*, is very bad luck if a man who drops his Candlemass pancake joins in the feast. What he would've eaten should by rights go to the dogs. Unless, of course, he is the dog who eats the pancake."

"Huh?"

"If you get down on all four paws and eat your pancake like a dog would eat it, then you can eat all you want of the rest of the feast and there is no bad luck."

Cully's eyes found Eulalie again. She covered her mouth with her hand and nodded that it was true. He crossed his arms, looked at the ceiling and sighed, then said: "Ruff. Rrrruff! Woof woof." He got down on his hands and knees and proceeded to tear at the pancake with his teeth, gobbling it down and wagging his hindquarters happily, snarling at anyone who made a move toward his pancake. Anne's shouted: "You see? my floors *are* clean enough to eat off!" barely penetrated the wall of laughter. Eulalie laughed so hard Henri had to hold her up. She wondered how she could be such a cully as to think she could ever love another man like her own Cully.

The feast was demolished and the fiddles clawed the rafters. After dancing yet another *escaoutte*, Eulalie planted her back in a corner and sank down on the floor, while Cully went to fill their cups again with water and a few drops from the last barrel of rum from the hold of the *Mary B*. Beausoleil flopped down beside her, pointed at Cully's back weaving through the dancers, and panted: "You know what it is about your Englishman that makes him useful?"

Eulalie could think of a few things, but she didn't think any of them could be what Beausoleil had in mind. So she said: "What?"

"He don't think."

"He don't think?"

"Oh, he does when there's time for it—maybe thinks too much for his own good. But when it's time for doing, he don't spend even the blink of an eye thinking: 'Should I hammer that man between the eyes with a musketbutt or shouldn't I?' You'd be surprised how many men pause to wonder whether they got enough good reason to do someone a damage. With *l'Anglais* it's just *bang*—" he slapped his fist into his palm so sharply it made her jump, "and think about it later. I tell you, if I had two hundred like him I could take Halifax."

"Oh." She looked up to see Cully coming toward her with two cups in his hands and a grin on his face like a coyote who'd just bitten the throat out of a lamb.

XXXVIII

ndré climbed into the wagon along with the other men and women deemed not too old to earn the keep of the Acadians allotted to Philadelphia County. One of the women should by rights have been still in bed, but the county believed that a good day's work was the best thing for whatever ailed an Acadian.

The big oak trees along Third Street were finally starting to bud. Spring could sometimes fool other trees into budding when winter still had one more frost left in him, but oaks weren't gullible—so at least there'd be no more heaving cobblestones about with frozen fingers. Some charitable citizens had made a Christmas collection of old woollens and boots and such, but worn-out mittens only kept out the cold for so long. André did have to admit, though, that the round-heeled, square-toed boots he'd pulled out of the pile were better for getting around in than his wooden shoes.

When the wagon rumbled into Market Street there were already a few citizens waiting on the courthouse steps to make their pick for the day. Sometimes the Acadians worked directly for the county, sometimes they were rented out to private citizens. André recognized the brown bonnet of the widow Ames. She'd employed him a few times to split firewood or hoe in her garden. Today she wanted a quick-handed young woman to help her with spring cleaning, and a strong-backed young man to dig a pit for her new outhouse.

André climbed up onto the widow Ames's carriage and she handed him the reins. "Thee remembers the way, André?"

"I think me I do, Mrs. Ames."

"Thy English is improving, André—getting better."

"I thee thank, Mrs. Ames." At least he'd learned not to say 'yassuh'.

As André guided the carriage along the hemmed-in streets, the widow Ames good-morninged passersby. Depending on someone's place in the order of things, she might call out: "Good morning, Mr. Smith," or just "Good morning, Smith." It hadn't taken André long to learn that Pennsylvania, for all its thees and thous and citizen assemblies, had a system of who bowed to whom just as clear-cut as the planters and sharecroppers of South Carolina. In Acadia, the only people who had to be deferred to were the old people—and an old woman who lived in a shanty was due just as much respect as an old man who owned a hundred acres and three fishing boats.

André couldn't for the life of him understand why people would want to organize their lives so that everyone had a rank and the ones below had to salute the ones above. If that's what they wanted, why didn't they just join the army? He knew it wasn't only an English sickness. He'd heard stories that it was just as bad in Quebec, and even worse in France. He had often been told that one of the reasons the first Acadians left France to take their chances in a new land was to get away from that sort of nonsense.

But André wasn't in Acadia now, so he obediently dug the widow Ames a new outhouse pit and said: "I thee thank, *ma'am*," when she brought him out a bit of bread and cheese. He considered telling her the funny story of Abraham à Bernard à Moïse's outhouse, but thought better of it. Not only was she unlikely to see the humour in it, it put him too much in mind of his home and family, and he didn't like those kinds of emotions taking hold of him in front of the English.

On the way back to the courthouse and the rendezvous with the wagon, the widow Ames said: "I think, André, thy English has become good enough—not perfect, but nothing thee should be ashamed of—to help in a small way the work of gentle Jesus in this world."

"Yes, ma'am...?"

"When thee were in South Carolina, thou were housed with the African slaves, and thee worked in the fields with them..."

"Yes, ma'am."

"The Society of Friends believes that slavery is wicked and must be abolished—stopped. But some among us do not truly understand how horrible it is. If you could come to meeting, and speak of the depths of suffering you saw among our poor, black brothers and sisters, it would be a blessing."

"Thee and thy... friends, thee does not to believing in slaves?"

"No, we most surely do *not* believe there should be slaves."

"What do thee call *us*?" He thrust the reins at her. "I can walk." He jumped down and started heading down a side street. He could hear the widow's voice pursuing him from the carriage, calling out something that sounded like a Bible verse about ingratitude, but he couldn't follow all the words. He kept on walking. What was she going to do: have the magistrates throw him in jail? At least he'd get three good meals a day there.

He turned to left and right as the alleyways dictated, heard a rising tide of sound

ahead of him and came out into Market Street. People were singsonging from behind stalls hawking everything from live piglets to lace tablecloths. The channel between the rows of stalls was a swirling current of multicolored parasols, flat, black
hats and fur-trimmed tricornes.

André stepped into the current and let it carry him. The back of his mouth was
flooded repeatedly by the smells of maple-cured hams, fresh-baked fruit pies, roasted
chestnuts... He passed a stall selling smoked sausages, and his eyes and nose almost
broke his neck by staying fixed to the stall while his legs kept on moving. He hadn't
tasted a smoked sausage since the day he stepped onto the ship's boat on Piziquid beach.

The crowd ahead of him opened up for just long enough to catch a glimpse of
something he'd never expected to see there: Eulalie's Uncle Benoni. Benoni should be
back in the row of so-called houses on Pine Street, whittling or hunkered by the fire.

André called to him, but the noise around was too much for his voice to pen-
etrate. He moved toward Benoni, grinning in anticipation of the old man's surprise
when a voice would suddenly ask him in French what the devil he was doing there.
Then he saw what Benoni was doing there. He was begging.

André spun on his heel and went back the way he'd come, hoping that Benoni
hadn't seen him see him. He could feel his face growing hot with shame for Benoni,
and for himself and all Acadians. He passed by the sausage stall again, then stopped
and stepped out of the current and looked back.

The sausage stall was at the end of a shoulder-to-shoulder line of stalls. Beside it
was a big, wooden crate with a stone on its lid. André guessed that the crate was
where the sausage maker kept his stock, and that the sausage maker didn't bother to
keep much of an eye on it—since the stone looked too heavy for most men to lift
without making it obvious that that was what they were doing. For most men.

André had been brought up to believe that stealing was something neither he nor
anyone he knew would ever do. Not so much because there was a Commandment against
it as because life would hardly be worth living if everybody had to be on the lookout for
what a neighbour might walk off with while their backs were turned. But then, André
had also been brought up to believe that no one he knew would ever have to beg for food.

André wandered back near the sausage maker's stall, plunked himself down beside the crate and pulled one boot off as though there was a pebble in it. He shook
the boot, set it down and rubbed his foot, glancing up to make sure the sausage maker
was busy haggling. Tingling with the certainty that someone in all that passing crowd
was bound to notice him, André put one hand on the lip of the lid and heaved as
hard and gently as he could, trying to open it just enough to steal his other hand in
without raising it so high as to overbalance the rock. His fingers grasped the ends of
two sausages. He snaked them out and tucked them in his coat.

It was hard to pull his boot back on nonchalantly, instead of leaping up and try-ing to run away with one boot on and the other in his hand. As he moved away from the sausage maker's stall, he kept expecting someone to yell "Thief!" behind him. When it became evident that no one was going to, he began to laugh at himself: what had he been afraid of, that they might throw him in jail?

His boots carried him down to the riverfront and then back along Walnut Street to Fourth Street, thinking. When he passed by St. Joseph's church, he thought he should go in and make confession. He didn't. When he got back to the row of low, wooden sheds on Pine Street, a thin *bouillabaisse* of salt cod and potatoes was being served out. Benoni produced a loaf of bread and told everyone he'd got it in trade for a whistle he'd made out of a thumb-length of poplar. André kept his eyes on the floor while Benoni told his lie.

Benoni didn't look at all put out when André trumped his loaf of bread by bring-ing out one of the sausages—or most of one; he'd nibbled the end off it while he walked. When everyone asked him how he'd ever managed to get hold of such a wonderful thing as a smoked sausage, he said defiantly: "I stole it." No one seemed to think he'd shamed himself or them. In fact, they seemed to think it was something to be proud of. He wasn't so sure.

The only one who said a word against what he'd done was Benoni. "But André, to take such a chance! You might've been caught!"

André repeated the joke he'd told to himself: "What are they going to do to me— put me in jail? At least I'd get three good meals a day there."

"The food you get in jail isn't free. If you can't pay for it, you have to work when they let you out. The first day or two you spent working for the county went to pay off what you ate when you were in jail. And jail isn't the worst they can do to you. If they catch you stealing more than once, they can brand you with a hot iron."

That reminded André of the poor man in the flagpole pillory he'd seen on his first morning in Philadelphia. But that didn't stop him from stealing more whenever he got the chance. Some of the things he stole went into the communal dinner pot, but some of them he hid away where he'd hidden the second sausage.

As the buds on the oak trees grew into leaves, André could see Benoni and the others gradually turning into what the English expected Acadians to be: listless, dull-eyed and shiftless, with no thought beyond what was going to be in the supper pot tonight. André didn't blame them—they *had* nothing beyond tonight's supper, and there was nothing they could do to change that. But he was determined that the same thing wasn't going to happen to him. Because there was something he could do. As soon as he'd stolen a few more things he needed, he was going to run like the goddamned hurry-cane.

XXXIX

ully sat stoically in the wave-rolled, captain's cabin of the *Mary B* while Beausoleil and Alexandre Brossard fussed over him with scissors and combs. Beausoleil said: "Don't make his beard shorter, just less raggedy."

"How can I make his beard less raggedy if I don't make it shorter?"

"Well... Only a *little* shorter. Honestly, it's disgusting—only two weeks away from his wife and already his beard and hair look like an old raccoon."

"The captain of the other ship won't see he looks like an old raccoon until he comes on board."

"And what if the captain of the other ship has a spyglass, did you ever think of that? Don't squirm like that, *Anglais*, or how can I comb out the tangles?"

They dressed Cully in a brass-buttoned coat borrowed from one of the crew, and an almost new tricorn hat borrowed from another. When the Brossard brothers escorted him up onto the quarterdeck, the ship the lookout had spotted was within hailing distance. She looked a little smaller than the *Mary B* and carried considerably fewer guns.

Beausoleil respectfully handed Cully the speaking trumpet and he called across the waves in English: "Ahoy there!" He wasn't certain that merchant seacaptains actually called 'ahoy' to each other, but it sounded nautical. "This is Captain Robin of the *Mary Bascombe*, sailing out of Jersey."

Cully would've preferred to use a completely different name for the *Mary B*, in case all captains sailing into the Bay of Fundy had been warned she'd been captured last summer. But Beausoleil had said that re-christening a ship was extremely bad luck. At least he'd managed to convince Beausoleil that the 'B' might stand for Bascombe or Bartlett or even Brossard. As to using his own name, 'Robin' was common enough on the Channel Islands that it was unlikely he'd be caught out, even if the other captain turned out to be from Jersey. One of the first lessons he'd learned from the old tinker he'd run off with was to stick to the truth wherever possible; that way there were fewer lies to remember.

"Captain Smollet of the *Tobias*, out of Boston!"

Cully muttered: "Damn." Being from Boston meant there was a chance Captain Smollet didn't imbibe spirituous liquors. But it was still worth a try. Cully called through the speaking trumpet: "Praise God—Boston is my next port of call, and the blasted owners have saddled me with a chart for these waters drawn by some cross-eyed frog-eater the day after Creation. Would you be good enough to come aboard and bring your officers to share a jug of punch, or a pot of tea?"

"Bugger tea, Captain Robin. We'll be there directly."

The *Tobias* furled sail to drift and so did the *Mary B*. As the *Tobias's* boat came alongside, the *Mary B* rolled down her Jacob's ladder. The first man up the ladder looked around uncertainly at the raffish, woodsy crew, some of them holding rifles. Cully stepped forward, saying: "Captain Smollet...?"

"Captain Robin...?"

"Not exactly. Truth to tell, the *Mary B* is under the command of..." Cully flourished his arm, "Captain Beausoleil. And so is the *Tobias*, if you have any sense.

"Captain Beausoleil, you see, has letters of marque from the Governor of Quebec, ordering him to interfere with enemy shipping. If you count our guns, you'll see that we can easily take your ship by force, if needs be. Better for all of us if you give in to the fact that with you and your officers our prisoners, your ship has no choice but to surrender."

Captain Smollet had sense. They anchored the *Mary B* and the *Tobias* in a hidden cove and proceeded to strip the *Tobias* of her cargo, guns, spare sails and anything else that could be of use on the *Mary B*. The cargo was mostly goods for the Indian trade, including even a bolt of Chinese silk that Cully and Beausoleil flipped pennies for. Eulalie won, but it was mostly a matter of form—the bolt was more than long enough to clothe her and Josette and still leave plenty for Anne.

The *Mary B* sailed on, around Cape Blomidon and into the Minas Basin. Beausoleil had come up with a plan to make the Petitcodiac and the Miramichi safer by doing something a hundred leagues from there: he would raid Fort Edward. The Governor of Nova Scotia would be less likely to spare troops for an expedition up the Petitcodiac if he needed them to guard his own back yard. And the raid would also present an opportunity to take back however many were left of the cattle that had been confiscated two summers ago. The exiled owners would be happier that their beef end up in Acadian stomachs instead of English.

They sailed in at night and anchored out of sight of the fort. In the morning, the *Mary B*'s boat started shuttling her crew ashore. From the quarterdeck, Cully watched Henri and Jacques line up to wait their turn. Eulalie had gone purple when Jacques announced he wanted to go along on this year's campaign. But since he was now the same age Henri had been last year, she hadn't had much of an argument. It was just as well: Henri didn't really know who he was without his little brother at his elbow. Cully had promised Eulalie to keep an eye on them both, but they didn't like him mother-henning them any more than he would've at their age.

Jacques and Henri each were carrying a pair of snowshoes, as was everybody else waiting to climb into the boat. Beausoleil had announced in the spring that every man who came along with him on the *Mary B* would have to bring a pair of snowshoes. Cully had just assumed that Beausoleil was intending a long campaign and just wanted to be prepared in case a freak, autumn snowstorm came up when he wanted to do some inland raiding. But here it was a sunny, summer day and Beausoleil had ordered everyone going ashore to bring along their snowshoes.

When Cully asked him why, Beausoleil just grinned and shook his head. So Cully joined the line of men trying to struggle down the Jacob's ladder with snowshoes slung over their shoulders because Beausoleil said so.

Since Fort Edward stood between the mouths of the Piziquid and St. Croix rivers, the raiding party would have to angle inland through the woods and ford the St. Croix. When they got to the riverbank, the tide was out; the river was just a trickle between two wide swaths of marsh grass, seaweed and red silt that looked knee-deep at least.

Beausoleil, chortling to himself, sat down and strapped on his snowshoes. Some of the others started to laugh and do the same; some just looked at Beausoleil like he'd gone crazy—until he started across the reed-matted quagmire and, instead of sinking, just had to tug a little against the mud's grip on his snowshoes.

Cully hadn't had much practice with snowshoes and fell down a couple of times. By the time he reached the other bank he was covered in mud, but he had to admit that that beat the hell out of still being only halfway across with every step a war to free his leg. They left their mudshoes on the riverbank to dry and followed Beausoleil into the woods. When they neared the edge of the cleared land around the fort, he called a halt and said: "Alexandre, *Anglais*, you come with me. The rest—try not to get in too much trouble while we're gone."

The three of them snuck to the edge of the woods and peered out. Alexandre muttered: "*Bâtards*." Cully didn't have to be told why. Along the riverbanks flanking the fort, where there should've been a rambling hodge-podge of snug farmhouses, barns, sheds, gardens and fishing stations, there was nothing but alder thickets, bramble and fireweed.

The fort didn't appear to have changed much since Cully'd last seen it. With its mounded earthworks, it looked like a hollow, green hill with a pointed tower rising out of its middle. A few cannon mouths poked out of the bastions, pointing out to sea. There was a new addition outside the walls: an acres-wide circle of fencing to pasture about fifty Acadian cattle. Cully had no doubt there'd been a lot more of them two summers ago. Fort Edward must've become a plum posting once word got out how often its quartermaster served out fresh beef.

Cully told Beausoleil what he could remember of the fort's artillery: three nine-pound guns and a half-dozen four- or five-pounders in the bastions facing the rivermouths and the basin. In the upper storey of the blockhouse, where Captain Namon had had his temporary office, there'd been three four- or five-pound guns. It wouldn't take a gun crew long to roll them around to the blockhouse gunports facing inland.

When Cully and the Brossard brothers got back to where they'd left the others, most of them had already scouted out moss beds or tree trunks made for lounging against and were munching smoked meat or puffing their pipes. By now they were all accustomed to Beausoleil's favourite strategy: get in position before dusk, wait through the night and strike at dawn.

Only this time they didn't strike at dawn. They placed themselves along the border of the forest by the parade ground at the base of the hill, and waited in the shade of the woods as the sun grew higher. Eventually the gates opened and a sergeant marched out a couple of dozen men and started putting them through their paces up and down the hillside. Watching the bloodybacks trying to stay in step on a steep slope, Cully hummed to himself: "*The grand old Duke of York, He had ten thousand men, He marched them up to the top of the hill and he marched them down again...*"

When the red ranks right-wheeled and left-abouted onto the flat ground between the hill and the woods, Cully took aim as Beausoleil had taught him: raising his rifle barrel instead of lowering it from the perpendicular. As Cully held his sights on a particularly beefy-looking private, he could remember his own voice joining in the barracks room disgust at savages shooting from ambush instead of standing up to fight like men. He reminded himself that those upstanding soldiers would cheerfully burn every house and garden on the Petitcodiac if they could get there. But he still hoped that Beausoleil would at least pick a moment when the marchers were facing the forest, rather than shooting them in the back.

Beausoleil read his mind. The sergeant was just starting to give the order to wheel back toward the fort when Beausoleil shot him down. Cully pulled the trigger as all the other rifles in the forest echoed Beausoleil's.

The soldiers who were still on their feet didn't shoot back, just broke ranks and scurried for the fort as fast as they could while dragging their wounded with them. Cully wasn't surprised that they didn't return fire. It was usually the practice to drill with unloaded muskets.

Another squad of bloodybacks double-timed out of the fort and formed a firing line on the side of the hill to cover their messmates' retreat. But the edge of the forest was just about at the end of Brown Bess's range, and the side of the hill well within range of rifles.

Not many gaps in the firing line were created, though, before the gunports in the back of the blockhouse tower exploded in smoke and tongues of flame, and the forest exploded in flying branches.

Beausoleil shouted to fall back for now. Cully needed little encouragement to dash away from the sounds of cannonfire and crashing trees. When he was well back in the woods, he heard Beausoleil's whistle and headed in that direction. Beausoleil was sitting beside a stream, panting and scooping water up over his gray-thatched forehead. Other men were drifting out of the forest and gathering around Beausoleil, as always.

Beausoleil laughed, "*Anglais,* I think you even hit the man you aimed at. Well, now we wait till they get tired of wasting cannonballs and then a few of us sneak back there and keep them honest. If they come out to collect their dead we let them, but we drop any redcoat that goes near that cattle fence. Tonight we break that fence down and—"

"*Anglais!*"

Cully looked toward the voice and Beausoleil cut himself off in mid-syllable. It was Alexandre Brossard, coming down the streambank. The front of his shirt was stippled with blood.

Beausoleil started to jump up, but his brother said: "No, no—it isn't mine. *Anglais...* Henri and Jacques—they were both hiding behind the same tree, firing from either side. A cannonball hit the tree head-high. I don't think either one of them felt a thing."

Cully exhaled at the sky and then lowered his head. Even though he'd only known them two years, they'd become the next thing to his sons. The only blessing was that it had happened to both of them at once. Within the family they hardly even had separate names, it was always "*Henri-et-Jacques* went fishing," or "*Jacques-et-Henri* said they saw a caribou."

Beausoleil thumped his hand onto Cully's knee and murmured: "There is no need to say 'Mercy on their souls.' The good God knows that neither of them got the chance to commit any sin worth noticing."

As the cannonfire died down and Beausoleil appointed men to go take up sniping, Cully went with a few other men to the place Alexandre pointed out. If Jacques hadn't been wearing a blue jacket it would've been difficult to tell which was which. They wrapped them together in a blanket, carried them deeper into the forest and dug a hole beside a big oak tree.

When the hole was filled in, Cully didn't go to take his turn at the sniping, but nobody seemed to mind. He stayed at the oak tree, carving into the bark: *Henri-et-Jacques à Joseph à Jacques à Thomas*. The litany of Joseph à Jacques à Thomas would never have another name added to it. As Cully dug his knife through the ridges of bark, he wondered how he was going to tell Eulalie.

Beausoleil's warband harassed Fort Edward for a few more days, plundering everything worth carrying away from the surrounding countryside. A foolish sortie to try to recapture the last of the cattle resulted in a prisoner. Cully was summoned to translate questions and answers.

The prisoner was a corporal who didn't look much at home tied to a mossy deadfall. Cully sat down beside him and said in French: "You loud-bragging redcoats shit yourselves so fast at the sound of a gun you leave your wounded brothers screaming while you run." The corporal just blinked at him. Cully said to Beausoleil: "He doesn't understand a word of French."

"Good enough. Ask him how many men are in the fort."

Cully did. The corporal gawked at his easy English, then spat: "Renegade!"

"That may be true, but you're the one tied to a log, so if there's any name-calling done around here I'll be the one to do it."

"If you think I'm going to fucking tell you anything you can fucking fuck yourself!"

Cully translated that to Beausoleil, who shrugged and said: "Call the Mi'kmaqs."

Three Mi'kmaq warriors had elected to spend their summer as part of the crew of the *Mary B.* Beausoleil gestured at the corporal and said to them: "This young fellow needs to be scared."

The Mi'kmaqs drew their knives and howled, circling the corporal, pinching his flesh and licking their lips, sawing off pieces of his hair for a closer look. Cully said offhandedly in English: "They have a belief—fucked if I can say whether it's true or not—that a scalp taken live lasts longer than one cut off a dead man."

The corporal shouted: "It doesn't make any fucking difference what I tell you, because you fucking frogs are fucking finished! By the time you get back to Louisbourg there'll be a British flag flying over it! Lord Loudon is sailing from Halifax with enough ships and guns and troops to crack Louisbourg like a walnut!"

Cully didn't bother to correct the corporal's impression that they'd come from Louisbourg, just translated the gist of his outburst. Beausoleil looked away and rubbed his wide, round jaw, then scrubbed one hand back through his gray thatch of hair, picked up a fallen twig and looked at it.

Cully knew what he was thinking. If Louisbourg fell, there was no base for the French army and navy east of Quebec. The British would be free to sail as many troops and gunships up the Miramichi or the Petitcodiac as they wanted.

Beausoleil scratched the twig against the loam and said distantly, "Funny that this Lord being sent against us should be named Loudon. Loudons, you see, is the part of France most of our ancestors came from. Some say that's why we Acadians don't bow to the church as much as we should. Because our ancestors were there to see the Devils of Loudons, and pass the story on to us: of nuns rolling about like dogs and tearing their clothes off and screaming Satan raped them, and people from all over France coming to pay to see the show—especially the show of the priest being burned alive. Ridiculous. Even more ridiculous than that nonsense among the English in Salem. Even more ridiculous than the English coming to burn our homes to teach the Pope a lesson."

Beausoleil bowed the twig almost to the snapping point, looked at it closely and then let it spring out of his fingers and fly away. "Well, *Anglais*, we'd best be getting home before someone else gets there first."

"What about him?" Cully indicated the corporal.

"Oh, we'll send out a white flag to ask the fort what they'll give us in trade for him. If his friends don't think he's worth anything, we'll give him to the Mi'kmaqs."

XL

⚜

On Sundays after mass, the Acadians of Philadelphia would generally drift toward the county lines. There they would meet up with the Acadians of neighbouring counties and sit and trade news of who was ill or who had found a penny on the street, pass on rumours about the war and reminisce about the days before that Fifth of September. Since the day he stole the sausages, André squeezed in as many innocent questions as he could about the roads in the neighbouring counties and the counties beyond.

When he'd first decided that he was going to run like the goddamned hurry-cane, he hadn't thought about the fact that he would have to start by running across the Delaware River. But he heard that where the river narrowed, in the shadow of the castle the founder of Pennsylvania had built for himself in Bucks County, there was an old fishing shack. In the shack lived a broken-down, old fisherman who would ferry anyone across if they gave him a drink of rum.

One of the citizens André was hired out to for a few days was an innkeeper. André spent the first day trying to think of a way to steal a bit of rum, but at the end of the day the innkeeper offered him a tot. André thanked him wholeheartedly, but said he would prefer to drink it just before he went to bed, if the innkeeper happened to have a spare jar lying around. He worked for the innkeeper for four days, bringing the empty jar back every morning and leaving the day before's tot in a covered cup he hid in the pile of rubble behind the house.

There came a week when André had no intention of being anywhere near the county line come Sunday. When the wagon brought him and the other able-bodied Acadians back from Saturday's work, he took his two blankets out into the yard "to shake them out." Instead, he rolled them up around the things he'd stolen and hidden away. Along with the second sausage, he had a small sack of corn, a half a side of bacon, a little tin pot and—best of all—a clasp knife that the overseer of a road crew had left lying around. A square of canvas folded together was his fire bag: fine sawdust for tinder, a piece of flint he'd spotted while shovelling stones into a drainage ditch, and a length of steel from a broken chisel. And he still had the fishhook and line that Abraham had given him.

He tied the ends of his bundle together with a piece of stolen twine long enough to pass over his shoulder. Then he set it aside for long enough to stick his head in the door and say: "Benoni, I got something to show you."

Benoni shuffled outside and André beckoned him to the gate. From the weeds beside the gatepost, André picked up his bundle and said: "They won't know until Monday when the wagon comes and I don't get on it. By then I'll be long gone. I won't tell you where I'm going—if you don't know you don't have to lie."

"That's good you won't tell me, because I could never guess. Now, an Englishman might guess you were trying to make your way to the sea—but you are not quite such a fool as not to know that with the war going bad for the English they will be watching out for Acadian spies along the seacoast. So I would never guess that you mean to stay as far inland as you can as you make your way north to French Acadia.

"That's a long way to go on stolen food. How far do you think you'll get before you starve to death?"

"I won't have to steal to eat. I have enough food to get a long ways from here, where no one will have heard of an Acadian escaped from Philadelphia. Then I can stop at farms along the road and ask if they want to hire a strong back for a day or two."

"And as soon as you open your mouth to ask for food, they will know you are Acadian."

"No, they will only know I'm not English. I thought of saying I was Spanish, but they say Spain has joined France in the war now, so the English will be as suspicious of Spaniards as Acadians. So I will be Italian."

"Italian? What do you know about Italy—besides that the Pope lives there and it's somewhere near France?"

"Nothing. But no one else seems to know much more than that, either. I will say I left Italy some years ago and now make my home in Philadelphia. I have a sister in Albany, New York who is dying, and I want to see her one last time. When I get near Albany, my sick sister will be in Connecticut, or maybe Massachusetts. I'm not sure which one's north of Albany, but I'll find out from the farmers I talk to along the way."

"You think so? Just how friendly do you think these farmers will be to a strong, young man wandering the roads when he should be fighting in the war to defend them from the French?"

"But I can't fight in any war. I'm a Quaker. That's how I came to live in Philadelphia. I was a sailor on a ship from Italy, and while my ship was docked in Philadelphia I saw that it was better to be a Quaker than a Catholic."

Benoni gummed the back of his lips, as though he'd run out of other things to chew on. André was more than pleased to see that even gloom-crow Benoni couldn't come up with sure reasons why his plan was doomed to fail. Benoni said: "You thought about this a long time."

"I have," André said truthfully. He'd thought about it every day until his head hurt. He wasn't used to making things up.

André stuck out his hand to shake Benoni's and said: "I'll leave my wooden shoes for anyone as wants to wear them. If nothing else, they're good for making Englishmen laugh till they hurt themselves."

Without releasing André's hand, the old man blinked watery eyes at him, raised his left hand to cup the side of André's neck and said: "Tell Eulalie I can still dance Joseph Brossard into the ground."

XLI

⁂

ulalie took Josette into the woods to hunt for blueberries, with Cully's old army musket slung over her shoulder. She didn't think it likely they'd meet up with a bad-tempered bear or a slow-witted deer, but if they did she'd be glad she'd loaded herself down with the musket.

Anne had said that if they followed this old deer trail west, they'd come across a brushfire meadow in an hour or so. It was a pleasant morning for walking, with the late-summer sun slanting golden arrows through the leaves, and songbirds reminding each other to enjoy it while they could. Eulalie let Josette take the lead, even though Josette's legs were getting long enough now to keep up with almost any pace Eulalie would've set.

The path wound through forested flatland and then up the side of a hill that seemed more abrupt than the hills of home. It was a considerate path, twice crossing streams just when a drink of water was becoming an alluring idea. Eventually the path opened up into a slanted meadow mottled with dark green patches of ground-hugging blueberry bushes, just as Anne had said it would. It did seem to Eulalie, though, that it had been more like two hours than one.

Stepping out from the forest path into the bright, hillside meadow put Eulalie in mind of Beau-père's grandfather on the day when the deerpath he was following suddenly opened up into the beautiful, fire-cleared valley he would christen Ardoise. The stab of homesickness didn't twist in her as deeply as it used to. The valley of Ardoise had become one of the many things that existed only in the abstract until the war was over.

She set her musket down against a rock, unfurled the bags sewn out of old sail-cloth, and she and Josette got down on their hands and knees to start combing their fingers through the leaves. For the first while they put as many berries in their mouths as in their bags, laughing at each others' blue tongues, blue lips and the blue dribbles down their chins. Josette said: "Why is it blueberries always grow good where a fire was?"

"I don't know, dear. Maybe they like the taste of ashes."

There was a distant boom that echoed. None of the clouds Eulalie could see looked like thunder. Josette said: "Maybe it's the ship coming home with Cully and *Henri-et-Jacques.*"

Eulalie was doubtful—Cully had said they likely wouldn't be back before the fall. "Well, if it is they'll still be there when we get back. We didn't walk all this way for just half a bag of blueberries."

They kept on picking and didn't hear the sound again. By the time they'd filled four bags they were hungry for something more substantial than blueberries. On the way back they sang a few songs to take their minds off their stomachs, and Eulalie's off the musket strap digging into her shoulder. They even sang "Three Hills Home," even though it was actually only one big hill and a lot of hummocky ground. But at the end of the path was a home of a sort, for now.

When they reached the edge of their own little clearing, Josette squealed: "Cully!" and dropped the bags of blueberries she was carrying and ran ahead. Eulalie sighed and stooped to add Josette's bags to her own load, thankful that the tops were tied, then plodded along in her wake. She saw Cully stand up from his crouch against the front wall of the house and open his arms to receive Josette leaping at him. But he wasn't smiling or shouting *Bonjour!* And when he set Josette down again she ran to peer eagerly into the cabin, then looked back at him confusedly.

As Eulalie got closer to Cully, she could see that his face was tightened rigid. His eyes were fixed on her, but he didn't move toward her. Something made her hands and shoulders go limp. The bags of blueberries fell to the ground and the musket slid off her shoulder. Cully caught the musket and leaned it against the wall, then looked down at Josette like he was thinking of telling her to go inside the house and wait.

He didn't; just raised his eyes to Eulalie's again and said: "Henri and Jacques—a cannon from Fort Edward—it was over in an instant."

Eulalie shrieked: "You promised!" His head snapped back and then slumped forward. The tears were gushing out of her so fast she was hiccuping, but she fought through it enough to touch his arm and choke out: "No—no, I didn't mean..." He started to raise his arms to envelope her, but before he could she dropped to her knees in front of Joseph Brossard's last surviving child and pulled her to her. Josette was crying, too. At barely eight years old, Josette hardly needed the fact of death explained to her.

Eulalie stood up with Josette in her arms, and Cully put his arms around the two of them. After a while, they went into the cabin.

It wasn't until much later that Cully brought out the bolt of silk. Even given the time between, the first thought that leaped to her tongue was that Henri and Jacques were a high price to pay for a bit of silk. But she didn't say it.

She got the feeling that there was something even more than Jacques and Henri that was making Cully sombre. Once she and Cully were in their bed, and Josette banished to hers for the first time in a month, he finally told her why the *Mary B* had come home early. She said flatly: "Ah." A fact was a fact and there was no use trying to negotiate with it. "Do you think the English will be coming up the Petitcodiac soon?"

"I don't know. Beausoleil doesn't know. Probably not unless Louisbourg falls. It might've fallen already. But if Louisbourg beats them off, it'll take the wind out of their sails. We might even see a French expedition come down and take Fort Cumberland."

"Or we might not."

"No, we might not."

The first thing Eulalie did the next morning—intent on getting it done before Josette woke up—was clear away the bed laid in the other corner for Henri and Jacques. Cully helped. He helped with a lot of things in that end-of-summer time when there were so many things that had to be done before it became impossible to do them. He was hopeless at helping in the garden she shared with Anne, but he was good at laying-in firewood and mending fissures in the chimney.

Autumn was always an apprehensive time, but this year Eulalie and the people around her had another reason to look over their shoulders besides gauging the sky and the leaf-fall to guess how many days they had left. This year she felt like a member of a beaver colony furiously dragging poplars into the pond before the ice came while all the while straining their ears for the sound of a snapping twig.

The twig snapped at a moment when she and Cully and Josette were just sitting down to breakfast. There was a flurry of gunfire and shouting from the direction of Beausoleil Creek. Cully jumped up, snatched down his rifle and yanked open the door. Eulalie reached for the musket, then saw that Cully had stopped in the doorway and cocked his head instead of his rifle. There was still the occasional gunshot among the shouts, but with the door open it was now clear that the voices were whooping with laughter.

Cully said: "That's no battle," and put his rifle back. Eulalie and Josette followed him out the door and the three of them followed the sound to Beausoleil's place.

There were people milling and jigging in Beausoleil's yard, some of them firing their guns in the air. Beausoleil was beaming, standing on the boulder behind the house that he liked to use for a podium. Beside the boulder, Anne was taking a hatchet to the head of a captured keg of rum, even though it was barely mid-morning. Eulalie called out questions while she and Cully and Josette moved through the crowd, but the only gist she got back was something about a French ship taken by the English, which didn't seem like much of a reason to celebrate.

As they approached Beausoleil's boulder, he jumped down and said: "Well, *Anglais*—Well, Eulalie—Well, Josette—What do you think of that?"

Eulalie said: "Of what?"

"You don't know? You didn't hear?" Beausoleil's eyes brightened at the license to tell the story again. "A ship going from Louisbourg to France got captured before she'd even got past Newfoundland. In her hold, hidden in a barrel of fish, the English found a packet of letters to high government officials in France. It is very unfortunate that the captain of this French ship was so clumsy a sailor as to be so easily captured... And very, very unfortunate that this barrel of fish was set a little apart from the others, and its head fixed on so hastily that even the English could guess there was something hidden in it...

"One of the letters, you see, carried the very, very secret news—so secret that no English spies had got wind of it before—that a fleet of twenty-four French warships had sneaked into Louisbourg with eight thousand reinforcements, and would stay anchored in Louisbourg harbor until further orders.

"It seems remarkable, don't you think, that a fleet of twenty-four French warships could sail to Louisbourg without the English catching a glimpse of them. But there was the proof in that captured, secret letter.

"Well, when that news was brought to Lord Loudon in Halifax, what could he do but cancel his expedition against Louisbourg and go home...? What do you think of that?"

Eulalie showed him what she thought of that by flinging her arms around Beausoleil's neck and standing on tiptoe to kiss his cheek. He didn't seem to mind. Then she flung her arms around Cully and Josette. Josette couldn't be expected to understand why everyone was suddenly so happy, but she could understand that the air was filled with laughter and the fiddles were tuning up. The beavers dragged no poplar into the pond that day.

But there were still enough days left before the pond froze to do what needed to be done. There were never enough autumn days to do all that you would *like* to get done. You simply attended first to necessities like firewood, digging root vegetables and hoeing manure into the garden for next year, and then turned to things like picking and drying rose hips, or deepening the drainage trench around the cabin, until winter put a stop to it.

Once the snow set in, there was time for things like making dresses out of pirated silk. The bolt Cully had brought back was a pale blue-green, like a spring river on a sunny day. Eulalie only knew one dress pattern: a long-sleeved *blouson* to fit over a collared, white blouse, and a matching skirt gathered at the waist. When she'd finally got it sewn together, and looked at it spread out on the table, it seemed a pity to spoil it with her frayed-collared blouse—even if the buttons on the *blouson* were only pewter ones cut off a decayed coat. So she left the blouse aside and put the dress on over her shift. The neckline seemed a little low without the blouse. She wished she had a looking-glass. Cully and Josette had gone tobogganing on the riverbank, so she couldn't ask their opinion.

She raised her arms and arched her back to see how it fit. The fit seemed fine, but it did seem unfair that her arms could feel the silk on them while the rest of her only felt the worn linen of her shift. She stripped the dress off again, shucked her shift and put the dress back on.

As she walked around the room experimentally, the silk caressed her hips, her back, her breasts, depending on which way she moved. She twirled around to let the skirt bell up. She began to hum to herself and move her body in time to the tune— not exactly dancing, but not exactly going anywhere, either.

She was in mid-step when the door popped open and Cully and Josette bustled in, slapping their mittens together. Their cheeks were flushed with the frosty air, and Eulalie could feel hers turning the same colour—even though she was pretty sure she'd stopped dead before they caught what she'd been doing. One look at Cully's eyes and she knew she did have a looking-glass after all.

Without taking his eyes off her, Cully put his hand on Josette's shoulder and said: "Oh dear, Josette, I went and forgot—silly me... Would you go over to your Aunt Anne's and ask if we could borrow a bit of maple syrup? Tell her I said you deserved at least one of her pumpkin tarts, and a warm-up by her fire, to reward you for running the errand I forgot."

❊ ❊ ❊

Eulalie wore the dress to New Year's at Beausoleil's, but with the shift and the blouse. Wearing new clothes on New Year's Day meant you would have new clothes all through the coming year. Anne's new dress was identical, and Josette's a smaller version of the same, but no one thought anything of that except something else to laugh about.

As she sat back in Anne's kitchen drinking in the smells of roast beaver tail, smoked salmon and rum punch, listening to the fiddles and the murmurs of people going to anyone they'd paid some slight to in the old year and asking their forgiveness, it seemed to Eulalie that more had changed than the number of the year turning from '57 to

'58. Something that once had been had become something else, but she wasn't sure what either of the somethings were.

After Cully had fallen asleep that night, she lay awake drawing her attention to a number of things. The bed they were lying on was no longer pine boughs and straw, but a feather mattress—not a very thick one, maybe, but covered with real sheets that Cully had taken off the captain's bed of a captured ship, and a fur blanket Eulalie had woven out of rabbit skins. Their little cabin wasn't built to last, but it was now chinked together well enough to stay snug until the war came to an end, even if the year changed a few more times before that happened.

They were no longer in any danger of starving, what with the annual supplies from Quebec, what was taken off the land and what was taken off the ships that fell to the *Mary B.* Not only was there much more food now than that first winter on the Petitcodiac, but so many fewer mouths to feed. Even a few fewer than last winter.

Since the English hadn't managed to take Louisbourg—or even come close—there would be no English hunting parties sniffing out the nests of free Acadians. Except maybe more of those feeble attempts from Fort Cumberland, which Beausoleil had picked off so easily in the past as they blundered through the woods or rowed up the Petitcodiac or the Miramichi. In fact, from all the rumours that came in about the war, the English in North America were finding it difficult enough holding onto the territory they had, much less invading anyone else's.

She found it remarkable to look back only three years at the Eulalie La Tour who'd thought herself so rooted in the tilled ground of Ardoise Valley or Piziquid, with the forest only something to pass through on her way from one secure place to another. Well, she'd always bragged that her great-great-great-grandfather had been the first *courier de bois*; now she'd become a *femme de bois*.

As soon as the parchment window Cully had built into one wall began to glow, she snuck out from under his arm and quietly built up the fire. When Cully emerged from behind the bed curtain, he sniffed and gagged: "What the devil are you burning—old stockings and bloodroot?"

"Not exactly." She scooped another palmful out of the pouch of crumpled leaves and buds and threw it on the fire. "My morning tonic."

"What, decided you don't need it anymore?"

"No—no I don't need it anymore."

XLII

ndré woke up shivering in a woodlot a few miles south of Albany, New York. There was a crust of snow on his blanket. He jerked upright in a panic that the snow might've drowned the embers of the fire he'd built last night. Not quite. He blew them alight, fed on some twigs and then some larger sticks. He folded one of his blankets up close to the fire to sit on, cowled the other one across his head and shoulders and sat warming his fingers and toes and chewing on the last of the jerked beef the last farmwife had given him for the road.

His plan to work at farms along the way had turned out just the opposite of foolish. No one asked too many questions, since farm labourers for hire seemed to be a rare commodity and no one wanted to look a gift horse in the mouth. Not many strong, young men were willing to work on someone else's farm when all they'd have to do was clear a bit of wilderness and they'd have a farm of their own.

But although André could be pleased with himself for proving he wasn't such a fool after all, that didn't ease the loneliness. It wasn't just the nights sleeping alone in the woods, or the days walking alone along the road. The times he spent working on English farms, or German or Swedish farms, were just as alone. All his life he'd had people beside him who'd grown up in his same community speaking his same language, up until the night he'd left Philadelphia.

He'd grown adept at calling people up in memory, but sometimes that made it worse. If he spent too long remembering moments with his family, he would run up against the fact that he had no idea where they were or how many of them were still alive.

There was always Eulalie, though. It seemed strange how thinking of Eulalie could make him lonelier and less lonely at the same time. What also seemed strange— although he knew it to be true—was that he knew her better now than the last time he saw her. Since then he'd had two years and more of remembering every gesture of her hand, every tone of her voice... He knew he must've noticed all those shadings of detail at the time, or he wouldn't be able to remember them, but he hadn't noticed he was noticing. Whenever his blind and solitary stumbling north through the English colonies began to seem ridiculous, he only had to remind himself that Eulalie was the pole star he was steering for.

But now when he looked around at the snow mottling the dead leaves, and the naked branches shivering against the gray sky, he had to give in to the fact that he would have to stop steering in that direction for a while. He could barely keep warmth in his body huddled over a fire. If he tried to keep on walking north and sleeping in the woods, it wouldn't be long before he became the object of local ghost stories for years to come—the mysterious stranger found frozen to death by the side of the road. And no amount of farm labouring would make it possible to stay at inns or travel by coach, because the farmers paid him more in food than money.

He decided to go into Albany and see if he could find work for the winter. Come spring he could start walking again. Two years ago he wouldn't've been able to imagine himself walking into a townful of strangers and asking for work, much less planning to spend all winter in a place where he might be found out and imprisoned or worse. He couldn't really imagine himself doing it now, except that the only choices he could see were to try it or die.

He turned his blankets back into a packsack, buttoned up his coat and started walking briskly to get his blood moving. The farms by the side of the road grew closer together, there were a couple of inns, and then rows of houses with no farms attached. As the road became a street, a steadier stream of wagons and carriages passed by, and there were clumps of people walking that André skirted around. He didn't stop anyone to ask where he might look for work; he didn't want to expose his halting English any more than he had to.

He kept on walking through the streets of Albany, not sure what he was looking for but quite sure he'd know when he found it. It was his nose that found it, by a smell of horse manure much too pervasive to come from any family stable. There was a long barn with a wide, trampled yard where two men were trying to wheel a carriage into a shed. André knew he didn't know much about horses, except old plodders like Daisy, but he knew a lot about pitching hay and manure. He called out to the men at the carriage: "Hello! I look for work!"

One of the men lifted one hand off the shaft just long enough to jerk his thumb over his shoulder at the barn and say: "Ask for Mister O'Cail."

Inside the barn was a double row of stalled horses. A black man was wheeling a barrow down the aisle and a white man was brushing a horse. André said: "Mister Cail?"

The white man said: "O'Cail. That's me," but kept on brushing.

"I look for work."

Mister O'Cail glanced at him again, kept on brushing, and said: "Where you from?"

"Italy. And Philadelphia."

"Which one—Italy or Philadelphia? Make up your mind."

"I borned Italy. Sailor. Leave ship to live Philadelphia and be of Society of Friend. I has sister to Massachusetts. Unwell she is, so there I be going."

"If you're going from Philadelphia to Massachusetts, Albany's a tetch out of your way."

André hadn't known that. "I lose my way. Now comes winter, I must stop and work, walk again come spring."

"Huh. Show me your hands." André held his hands out. "No, no—turn 'em over." André turned his hands palm-up. Mister O'Cail looked at them and grunted again, then reached out and felt André's shoulder. "Huh. Yeah, I got work you could do, but... Well, it goes against my grain, but I know someone what could use a strong back a lot worser'n I could. Keep on going along this lane till you come to the end, then turn right until you come to a wheel in the air. Tell 'em I sent you."

"A wheel in the air?"

"Yep. Just like Ezekiel."

"Like who?"

"You'll know it when you see it. Head along, now, I can't stand around here jawing all day."

André headed along, unsure whether Mister O'Cail wasn't playing a joke on him. But one thing he'd learned since the gates of Fort Edward slammed shut was that all he could do was stumble in the direction that someone or circumstances pointed him, and find out what was there when he got there.

The lane ended at a fenced pasture. André turned right and walked along a row of houses. At the end of the row was a high, brick, courtyard wall, with a beam projecting from the top of it. Hanging from the beam was a wagonwheel. André pushed open the gate and stepped inside.

One wall of the courtyard was a squat-shouldered building with barn doors at ground level and a wooden staircase running up the side. The other walls were lined with sheds or awnings sheltering stacked lumber, half-built wagons, chains hanging from block-and-tackle, racks of tools...

A thigh-high girl chasing a hoop around the courtyard looked at André and shouted: "Ma!"

A woman came out of a door at the top of the outside staircase. She called down: "'Morning, mister," and started down the steps. André moved forward to meet her at the foot of the stairway. When she stepped off the last stair, he discovered she was a tall woman, slightly taller than he was—although that still made her shorter than most men. She said: "What can we do you for? You need a new wagon, or repairs...?"

"No, thank thee. I look for work. Mister O'Cail, he send me." He repeated his story about Italy, Philadelphia and Massachusetts.

The woman's eyes pinched in. "You ever been a wagonwright? Or a wheelwright?"

"I did make cart wheels, me." He didn't tell her that he'd only ever made two pairs, one that was botched and one that he'd never got to finish.

"Have you, now? You see that anvil over there?" She pointed across the courtyard.

André followed her point with his eyes. Under one of the awnings was an anvil and a forge. "Yes, I do see that anvil."

"Bring it here."

André went over to the anvil. He bent to pick it up and discovered that it was fixed securely to its stand: a section of tree trunk as wide as his arm was long. He squatted and hooked his elbows under the horn and butt of the anvil, straightened his legs to heave the anvil and the stand off the ground and waddled back across the courtyard. He set it down in front of the woman and leaned his hands on the top of the anvil, breathing himself out.

The woman said: "I'll pay you half a shilling a day six days a week, and room and board seven."

"Good. Yes. Thank thee."

A flicker of surprise crossed the woman's face, but she buried it and said: "What's your name?"

"André."

"I am Mrs. Henderson." She turned to the little girl. "Matty, go fetch your father out."

"Yes, ma." The girl ran to the barn doors, swung one of them open and went inside. A moment later a man came out on crutches, swinging his legs in front of him like slabs of wood. André's one-legged uncle used to go about on crutches sometimes when his peg leg rubbed his stump raw, and he would spring himself around the farmyard as though his crutches were spare legs growing out of his hands. Mister Henderson moved his crutches like they were anvils.

Mrs. Henderson said: "Caleb, this is André. He's going to be our hired man for the winter."

Mister Henderson said: "We don't need to be throwing good money away on hired help. I never needed hired help before and I don't now."

Mrs. Henderson looked like she was going to cry, but she tightened the muscles in her face and said: "André, put the anvil back where you found it, please."

André hauled in and let out a deep breath and hefted the anvil again. When he set it back down beside the forge he stayed leaning on it for a while, waiting for the blood to stop hammering the backs of his eyes. When he came back across the court-yard, Mister Henderson was looking down at the ground. Mrs. Henderson said: "I'll fix you up a bed in the stable, André. Come mealtimes I'll fix you up a plate you can take down with you. Now Mister Henderson will show you what work needs doing."

André became Mister Henderson's hands and arms for any task that couldn't be done sitting at a workbench. Neither Mister nor Mrs. Henderson ever said what had happened to Mister Henderson's legs. But whenever it was necessary to hoist up a wagon box to put on wheels or splice an axle tree, Mister Henderson was adamant that André check the lock-cog on the block and tackle again and again before crawl-ing under.

On the first Saturday, Mrs. Henderson presented André with a two shilling New York Colony banknote. He'd actually started work halfway through Tuesday, which should've made it two and a quarter shillings, but he didn't quibble. He was more worried about what he was going to do come Sunday.

Like Pennsylvania, the colony of New York had a strict law that anyone who wasn't bedridden had to go to church on Sundays. In Philadelphia, André had simply gone to Mass, as he would've without a law. But even if there'd been a Catholic church in Albany, he could hardly attend Mass and still pretend to be a Quaker.

He nervously asked Mrs. Henderson if she knew of a Quaker congregation in Albany—nervously because it seemed unlikely that any congregation of Quakers wouldn't spot him as an imposter within five minutes of the start of whatever kind of services Quakers held. Fortunately, Mrs. Henderson said she knew of no Quakers hereabouts. So he went to the Lutheran church with the Hendersons, lifting Mister Henderson into and out of their wagon. After his first Lutheran service, he under-stood why there had to be a law.

He hadn't been in Albany long before he learned that there were other Acadians there, living in a charity house on the edge of town. But he also learned that it would be very unwise for him to go to see them.

The reason had to do with geography. In Philadelphia he might've been able to get away with pretending not to be Acadian and still visit the local Acadians. But the war was much closer here than it had been in Philadelphia. North of Albany there were only a few small English forts along the Hudson River, and then a big French fort on Lake Champlain. In the three campaigns since the war began, several battles had been fought within a few days' march of Albany: the English had won the first one and lost all the rest. Everyone in Albany was nervous that the coming spring would bring a French army marching down the Hudson Valley. And everyone in

Albany was on the look-out for French spies. If a supposed Italian Quaker aroused suspicions by spending his free hours with Acadians, he'd be lucky if the authorities only threw him in jail or shipped him back to Philadelphia. It wasn't only a matter of what might happen to him, either, but to the Albany Acadians who were already suspect enough just by being French Catholics.

So on Sunday afternoons André would sneak into the woods near the charity house and watch and listen from hiding. He guessed that this batch of Acadian flotsam must be from up around Fort Beauséjour, since he didn't recognize any of them. Then again, he wondered if he would recognize his own family in such ragged and starved-thin condition.

On Sundays with bitter weather there wasn't much to see or hear, since they pretty much stayed inside against the cold, and André couldn't crouch in the woods for long before he started to shiver. But even on those Sundays he could sometimes hear little snatches of songs from home. Not very often, though; they didn't do much singing.

By the time Candlemass approached, the sheaf of banknotes he kept wrapped up with Abraham's fish line had grown to twenty-three shillings. The money would certainly be useful to him when he started travelling again, but by then he would have at least another two months' wages. On the morning before Candlemass he counted his twenty-three shillings over and over, and then asked Mister Henderson if it would be all right if he didn't start work until a little later.

There was a butcher and dry goods store that André passed every Sunday on his way to the woods near the charity house. When he stepped inside the door, the first thing that caught his eye was a fat, plucked goose hanging behind the counter. He said to the butcher: "How much the goose?"

"Two shillings. If that sounds steep, well, everything's been getting steeper every year of this damned war."

"Two shillings... I mean to buy today here many things."

"Like what?"

"Like... That piece big of bacon, some apple from that barrel, some flour if you have..."

"Got corn flour."

"Good. So—a shilling and a half for the goose."

"Done."

André toted up the shillings in his head as the counter piled higher with food and extra things like tallow candles. When he got to nineteen-and-a-half shillings he said: "Enough. I will pay, too, to have it took to... to have it be..."

"Delivered?"

"Just so. But—I buy these foods for some peoples I know who is poor. If they know it come from me, no deal."

"Fair enough, mister. I'll send my boy over and I won't even tell *him* who bought it. Where do you want it to go?"

"There are some Acadian, in a house down this road..." André trailed off as the butcher slapped down his pencil and planted his hands on the counter.

The butcher said: "You some kind of Papist or something?"

"No. I am Quaker, from Italy." He tried to remember whether he'd remembered to say 'thee' instead of 'you' in his dickering.

"Oh. Yeah, I heared you Quakers was big on charity. But you could find a lot better people around here to waste it on. Them Acadians just slough around on the county's money, begging and stealing, don't do any work worth a damn, like a bunch of shiftless Indians."

André found it hard to control his voice. He said: "Mister, what say French army take Albany, send you on boat to Quebec, put you to live in shack, take away you children—how much goddamn shift you think *you* will have?"

The butcher looked André up and down and said: "You ain't no rich man to be throwing money around."

"I have warm bed and work, and good food every day without I have money or no. They have nothing, and tomorrow be Candlemass, when they would be making happy feast on all the good thing they grow on they farm."

The butcher scratched his chin and said: "I'll be a son-of-a-whore. If some of them De Lanceys and Livingstons riding around in their carriages thought even a little bit like you, there'd be no beggars in New York. Do them Acadians smoke tobacco?"

"Some. I do guess."

"Well I got a dozen local-growed leaves out back I got in payment for a ham, and I can't stand the taste of the stuff. I'll throw it in on top of your pile here."

"Thank thee."

"It ain't no Christian charity—like I says, just the smell of the stuff makes me heave like a pig with the shivering shits. Happy Can-doe...?"

"Candlemass."

"Happy Candlemass, mister."

"And you, too, sir."

❊ ❊ ❊

André had accumulated another twenty-one shillings, and the ice on the Hudson River was starting to break, when Mrs. Henderson came into his corner of the stables with a gray-haired woman in a black dress. The gray-haired woman sprang toward him, gabbling an enthusiastic string of words in a language he'd never heard before, slapping his shoulders and pinching his cheek. Her enthusiasm faded in the face of his blank stare. She stepped back and looked confusedly from him to Mrs. Henderson.

Mrs. Henderson said: "It's all right, Mrs. Petroni, it was just a joke."

Mrs. Petroni sniffed: "Some joke."

Mrs. Henderson said, without taking her eyes off André, "Go up and have some more tea, Mrs. Petroni. I'll be up directly, and after we've finished off the cakes I'll take you home."

When Mrs. Petroni was gone, Mrs. Henderson said to André: "You're no Italian."

André didn't know what was safe to say, so he said nothing.

"You're Acadian."

André opened his mouth and then closed it again.

"Do you think Albany's so big I wouldn't hear the story about my hired man and the butcher and the Acadians? Don't worry—I know you're not a French spy. You're just trying to get back home, aren't you?"

André chewed his front teeth for a moment, then said: "Yes. From South Carolina to Philadelphia, and there my boat give out. From Philadelphia to here when winter come."

"You don't have a sister dying in Massachusetts, do you?"

"I do not know. I do not know where my sisters is, or if alive or dead."

"André..." Mrs. Henderson's eyes narrowed. "I know that just because you're a French Catholic sneaking your way north through our English colonies doesn't mean you're a spy. Other people might find that hard to believe."

André waited.

"André, in one more year—the way business has been going—Mister Henderson and I will have paid off the mortgage and the doctors' bills and all the other debts, and then just the bits of work Mister Henderson can do on his own will be enough to keep us going. Just one more year. The war might even be won by then, and no one will care where Acadians travel. You'll have so much more money in your pocket by then. What does another year matter to you?"

"Yes," the words tasted to André like that tobacco to the butcher, "what does another year matter to me?"

XLIII

pring came to the upper Petitcodiac, and the time drew nigh for Eulalie to become a summer widow again. She still wasn't pregnant, despite four months of very carnal relations without the Mi'kmaq medicine. She didn't feel disappointed. It seemed to her that the good God would be doing her a favour if she didn't start a child until the war was over. But by burning the old woman's medicine she'd left it in His hands.

Cully set off down-river with Beausoleil on the *Mary B* again: to make a landing near Fort Cumberland to remind the soldiers there it wasn't safe to venture far, and then to cruise the bay looking for English supply ships. Eulalie and Josette took out their hoes again to help Anne put in her garden.

The pea vines had climbed to the top of their trellises of old fishnet when wandering Mi'kmaqs brought news from the east. The English had mounted another expedition against Louisbourg, and the commander of this one wasn't the type to be scared off by rumours. For weeks now, the big guns of the French and the English had been pounding away at each other from inside and outside the huge, stone fort.

In the bright days of August, the *Mary B* came home again, but this time there was no celebration. When Cully stepped out of the boat and put his arms around her, he did it stiffly, and the first words he said were: "Louisbourg has fallen."

"Will they come here next?"

"I don't know. It's late in the year. Maybe they won't come here at all. Maybe they won't bother with a few *banditti* like us and will go straight on for Quebec."

They came. The leaves were turning when the scouts Beausoleil had posted down-river came running back. A squadron of three English warships, each of them with more cannons on one gundeck than the *Mary B*'s whole complement, was inching its way up the Petitcodiac.

Everyone gathered in Beausoleil's yard. He stood on his boulder and said: "We don't have a hope in hell of stopping the ships—if we shoot at them from the shore, they will blow us to pieces with one broadside. I think the river gets too shallow for them above Fox Creek, so likely they will put in there and land their troops. *Then* we can do something.

"But, the only something we can do is snipe at them from the woods and make them pay dearly for every house they put the torch to. And we can make it unsafe for them to split off into small groups, so they will have to move slowly.

"For those of us who won't be part of the fighting, I think the best thing for you to do is go back to your homes and bundle together all that you can carry—food more than anything else. I don't know which direction the English will march, or whether we can turn them back. If you hear gunfire coming toward your house, then take to the woods in the opposite direction. Those whose homes are along Fox Creek—if the ships do turn in there to anchor, take to the woods as soon as you see them.

"Well, may the good God be with us all today. If we can drive away this batch of Englishmen, and hurt them bad enough, maybe they'll never try sailing up the Petitcodiac again."

Cully walked Eulalie and Josette back to the cabin to get his rifle and a pocketful of jerked venison. Eulalie couldn't pretend she wasn't afraid: for herself, for him, for Josette, and for all those *couriers de bois, femmes de bois* and *enfants de bois* who'd become her family over the last three years.

Cully reached down his rifle from over the door and said: "Maybe we can keep them from coming anywhere this place, but if you hear gunfire coming closer you *will* take to the woods...?"

"We will. And you will be careful of yourself."

"Oh, there's more cause to worry about you and Josette than me. Shooting at British soldiers from behind a tree is safer than sitting in church." He picked at the crumbling edge of the doorpost. "If they do get this far, they might end up saving you and me some work. I was thinking anyway we should tear this place down and build new before winter—poplar's no wood for lasting." Then he looked directly at her and said: "You are my life."

He bent down to kiss the moistened corners of her eyes, then ruffled Josette's hair, shouldered his rifle and marched down the path toward Beausoleil's. Eulalie took Josette into the house and they put together two blanket-wrapped bundles of flatbread, dried peas, the smallest cooking pot, and the other articles that the long trek from Ardoise had taught them would be most useful in the woods.

Eulalie looked around the inside of the cottage one last time, wondering if it would still be standing come nightfall. Then she took down the musket from the wall, checked the powder in the priming pan and beckoned Josette to come outside. They sat down in the goldenrod with their backs against the front of the cabin, their bundles beside them and the musket propped across Eulalie's lap.

There was a sudden roar like the devil demanding his dinner. Eulalie had never heard a broadside from a warship before, but she assumed that that was what it was. Another came, and then another. And then there was a crackling of smaller guns: sometimes one or two at a time, sometimes in volleys. The sky above the gold-leafed trees began to turn black with the smoke of burning homes and gardens.

Eulalie felt like a cowardly fool, sitting there with her musket while Cully and the others were using their guns to protect her. But she knew she would've been more of a hindrance than a help, thrusting herself among a group of men who'd been fighting together in the woods for so long that they could read each others' minds and recognize a complex signal in one whistled note.

Josette was whimpering, but trying to hold it in. Eulalie put an arm around her shoulders. Josette snuffled: "Why won't they leave us alone?"

"I don't know, dear. They seem to be afraid of us."

"Of *us?*"

"I know it's foolish, but people can do terrible things to people they're afraid of, whether they have any reason to be or not. We'll be safe, though, just as long as we keep our eyes and ears open to where they are."

Her own ears told her that the gunfire had been moving steadily up-river from Fox Creek, but way off to the left and not veering to the right. But her eyes suddenly caught a flash of red in the forest that was the wrong shade for an autumn maple. There was another flash of red, and then another.

Eulalie jumped up and shouted at Josette: "Run!" As Josette grabbed her bundle and ran for the woods behind the house, Eulalie hefted the musket and fired at one of the red patches. Then she threw the musket down, snatched up her bundle and ran after Josette.

There was no sign of Josette among the trees, but Eulalie was sure Josette would know enough to keep on running in the same direction until it was safe to stop and call to each other. So Eulalie just kept on bounding ahead, dodging around tree trunks and leaping over bracken, letting her momentum carry her forward.

Josette's voice shrieked from somewhere behind her: "Eulalie!"

Eulalie shouted over her shoulder without breaking stride: "Keep running!"

"I can't! Eulalie!"

Eulalie stopped and looked up at the sky.

"*Eulalie!*"

Eulalie dragged in a deep breath, let it out through her teeth, dropped her bundle and turned back.

Josette had stepped in a rabbit snare. The sapling it was attached to had sprung upright, hoisting her leg chest-high. She was trying to pull her leg down to loosen the snare while hopping around on one foot.

Eulalie grabbed her and held her upright with her right arm, while her left hand fumbled for the loop of the snare. Before she could get her hand on it, a much larger hand took hold of the back of her hair and a rough voice chortled in English: "Well, well—one bitch caught in a trap and another caught trying to get her out."

After two years of being married to a man who peppered his at-home conversation with English phrases, Eulalie could follow the gist. But even if she hadn't understood a word, she would've done the same thing, which was to let go of Josette, arc her hands over her shoulders and rake her fingernails across the back of the hand holding her hair.

The soldier spun her around and cuffed her down to the ground. As she tried to regain her equilibrium, he planted his foot on the hem of her skirt, looked down at her and said: "Well maybe there's *some* use for you. Don't be stupid enough to fight me, now, and you'll get the feel of a good English mainmast instead of slobbery French tongue."

"Private Collins!" a voice barked from behind the soldier.

Without taking his eyes off her, Private Collins said over his shoulder: "Yes, Corporal?"

"You're supposed to be a bloody British soldier, not some bloody Barbary pirate! But you're a pretty lad, I'll grant you that. Anything you do to this woman, I'll tell big Mulligan the coxswain he's free to do to you. He's had his eye on you ever since he saw you stripped down to ride the wooden horse. Take these two back among the other prisoners."

XLIV

For three days and nights, Cully was one of a pack of terriers nipping at the heels of the red behemoth lumbering up and down the creeks fanning out from the Petitcodiac. The nights were lit by the dying flames of houses and fields, and by the occasional flare of sparks when one of the men in the woods fired a useless shot at the floating bivouacs anchored safely in Fox Creek. Although he didn't see or hear anything of Eulalie and Josette, he wasn't worried. They were among hundreds of women and children hiding in the deep woods until the fighting was over, and Eulalie and Josette knew how to live off the land as well as anyone.

On the fourth day, the three ships flying the red ensign sailed out of Fox Creek and away, leaving not one building or crop standing. The people began to drift out of the woods and gather in Beausoleil's yard. Beausoleil sat on his boulder near the pile of ashes that had been his house, staring down at his empty hands and at the lumpy bandage where Anne had dug a bullet out of his foot.

Cully worked his way through the ragged crowd, looking for Eulalie. He couldn't find her, but there were still women and children straggling in. A female voice behind him called: "Cully!"

He turned around. It was Anne, coming toward him with a grim expression on her face. But then, everyone along Beausoleil Creek looked grim today. She put her hands on his chest and said: "Someone saw Eulalie and Josette taken prisoner."

Cully's guts corkscrewed around each other. He said: "Are you sure?"

"I'm sure. That's what the English came here to do, after all—to take us all prisoner and ship us south like our brothers and sisters three years ago. For all their cannons and soldiers, they only managed to capture about twenty—but Eulalie and Josette were two of them. I'm sorry."

Cully turned away and went and sat down by the creek. He was vaguely aware of Beausoleil addressing his people: reminding them that despite the English army's best efforts they were still here and alive, and what they must start to do immediately was put up shelters for the winter. Then Cully was vaguely aware of a bustle going on behind him, and the sounds of axes and saws, as people went to work with whatever tools they'd managed to salvage. But he stayed sitting, looking at the brown leaves on the creek flowing down toward the sea, and everyone left him alone.

Finally Cully stood up, using his rifle to lever himself to his feet, and went looking for Beausoleil. Beausoleil was still sitting on his boulder, with his wounded foot cocked up across his other leg. Nearby, Anne was sitting on the ground with a knot of older women, trying to determine how much food was left in the community. Beausoleil was talking with Alexandre and a knot of older men, pointing out easily fellable trees and making plans.

Beausoleil saw Cully coming and waved the other men aside for a moment. When Cully stopped in front of him, Beausoleil said sadly: "I heard, *Anglais*..."

Cully said: "I'm going in to surrender." Beausoleil's mouth fell open. "Wherever they plan to send her, it'll be easier for her with me along. I can speak English and—"

"You're crazy! The English will hang you for a traitor and then shoot you for a deserter!"

"Not if they don't know who I am. Everything we know about the garrison at Fort Cumberland says there's none of my old regiment there. I doubt if even any of my old messmates would recognize me now, after three years of being turned into a *courier de bois*."

"*Doubt* isn't the same thing as saying you'll be safe for sure."

"I'll probably be safer than you'll be here. How do you plan to make it through the winter? With Louisbourg gone, the Royal Navy'll make damn sure you see no more supplies from Quebec."

"What can we do but try? I think you should think about this some more before you go sticking your head in a noose."

"I've thought about it as much as I can stand. Eulalie was the reason I came here—the only reason I wasn't one of the soldiers that just burned your house. Without her, it doesn't make any sense."

"If you look for sense these days, *Anglais*, you'll only ruin your eyes. Well... there is an old dugout boat I threw into the woods years ago when I got tired of heaving it in and out of the water. It should have enough float left in her to let the current carry you down to the bay shore, and you know your way to Fort Cumberland from there."

Beausoleil stuck out his big, flat hand and Cully shook it. By now Cully had become accustomed that Acadians, like Mi'kmaqs, gave a handshake the same weight that other people gave a kiss or an embrace. Before releasing Cully's hand, Beausoleil said: "I would be very annoyed, *Anglais*, if I did not see you again in this life."

"So would I."

❆ ❆ ❆

When he came to the edge of the woods around Fort Cumberland, Cully stripped off his shirt and coat and tied the shirt to the muzzle of his rifle as some approximation of a white flag. When he shrugged his coat back on, one of the pockets clinked. He still had five of the ten gold guineas Sergeant Robin had been rewarded with. There hadn't been much opportunity to spend money along the Petitcodiac.

He thought about the guineas for a moment. He knew that the original orders had been that all Acadians were to be allowed to keep whatever money they carried on them, but perhaps three years of war had changed that. So he tied a knot between each coin in the little sack, to keep them from clinking, and tucked it down into the waistband of his deerskin trousers.

Just before stepping out into the open, he asked himself: "Are you sure you want to do this?" He hadn't lied to Beausoleil that the odds were very heavy against his being recognized, but they were still only odds. But the thought of Eulalie being washed up alone on the shore of some English colony, or of him sitting alone on the banks of the Petitcodiac, was worse than chancing the odds.

He started across the clearing in front of the fort, waving his white flag over his head and reminding himself over and over that his name was Gilbert Brossard. He'd considered calling himself Joseph Brossard, so he could revive old Joseph Brossard's old joke of being mistaken for Beausoleil. But he'd decided that the less attention he drew to himself the better.

A voice shouted from the gatehouse: "Halt!"

Cully kept on walking, waving his white-flagged rifle and calling: "*Je*—me surrender!"

"Halt!"

The shout was much louder and harsher this time. Cully halted, figuring that it would appear he was responding to the tone of voice rather than understanding the word. He repeated: "Me surrender!"

After a moment, the small gate set into one of the larger gates swung open and a couple of Brown Besses poked out, then a beckoning hand. Cully moved forward, chanting: "Me surrender." When he got to the gates, he was snatched roughly inside and his rifle snatched from his hands. He reached after it, protesting: "*Ma chemise!*"

"'Chemise'? He wants his petticoats!"

"He just wants his shirt back."

"I'll give him back what him and his sneaking friends have been giving *us*!"

"Oh, give him his shirt back. He'll need all the warmth he can get when he gets sat down with His Nibs."

There was much laughter at that. They gave him his shirt back and pushed him along, with Cully protesting meekly: "Me surrender, *oui*?"

"You don't know what surrender *is*, froggy, till you get sat down with the man what knows how to parley-voo."

They herded him across the courtyard and into a squared-log building. They tugged him to a halt in front of a closed door and one of them knocked. A voice inside grunted affirmatively. They opened the door, said: "Another prisoner for you, sir," pushed Cully inside and closed the door.

There was a table in the room, and three chairs. One of the chairs was empty. The second held a uniformed clerk in front of an array of papers, quills, inkbottles and blotters covering his end of the table. In the third chair sat a puffy-looking man in shirtsleeves, with his short-bristled head uncovered. On a stand behind him were a gold-decked uniform coat and a powdered wig.

A pair of yellow eyes flicked up at Cully from the paper they were studying. Captain Namon set the paper aside and said in French: "What is your name?"

"Gilbert Brossard."

"Sit down if you please, Monsieur Brossard. Would you care for a drop of wine?"

Cully was wary of letting his tongue get loosened even a little. But his mouth had gone so dry he'd barely been able to croak out 'Gilbert Brossard'—and bloody glad he was he'd decided not to push his luck with 'Joseph Brossard'. So he said: "*Oui merci, monsieur.*" The clerk poured for the prisoner and topped up Captain Namon's glass, which—by the level in the bottle—had been topped up a few times this morning already.

Captain Namon said: "'Brossard...' Any relation to...?"

"A second cousin, monsieur."

"Ah. Did he happen to come to any harm during our recent expedition up the Petitcodiac?"

"He was perfectly alive when I left, monsieur."

"Pity." Captain Namon proceeded mechanically with a series of formulaic questions, while the clerk scribbled down the fictitious personal history Cully had rehearsed all the way down river. After a while, Cully began to be convinced that if Captain Namon hadn't recognized him by now, he wasn't going to.

He assured himself that if he had changed as much in only three years as Captain Namon had, he was probably safe. If it hadn't been for the setting, Cully would've doubted he was speaking to the same man. Captain Namon had always had a languid puffiness to him, but it used to be a puffiness he looked perfectly comfortable in. The eerie yellow of his irises appeared to have leaked into the whites of his eyes, like eggs with pinpricked yokes. He'd developed a nervous habit of rhythmically scraping the fingernails of his right hand across the palm.

Cully happened to glance up in the middle of describing how young he'd been when his family left Annapolis Royal for the Petitcodiac, and discovered that Captain Namon had gone absolutely still and the yellow eyes were fixed on him expressionlessly. An old Jersey expression suddenly came back to mind: 'Eyes that could hammer nails.'

Cully trailed off. Without shifting his eyes, Captain Namon flicked his index finger at the clerk and said: "Dismissed." The clerk stood up and began methodically gathering together his papers and pens. "No. Dismissed."

The clerk left off gathering his things and said: "Yes, sir. Will you be needing me any more today?"

"You'll be informed."

"Yes, sir. Very good, sir."

When the door shut behind the clerk, Captain Namon cocked his head and focussed on the middle distance for a moment, as though listening for something. Then his eyes jolted back to Cully and he spat out in English: "Good God, man, are you *insane?*"

Cully considered sputtering *Je n'y comprend* and trying to brazen it out. But it would've been ridiculous to try. So he simply said in English: "I am what you have made me." The yellow eyes narrowed. "My wife is among the prisoners taken on the Petitcodiac. The only hope left to me is to go into exile with her."

Captain Namon blinked. "The prisoners have already been embarked for Massachusetts."

❄ ❄ ❄

After the prisoner Gilbert Brossard had been escorted to the lock-up for the night, Captain Namon called for another bottle of wine and sat down to think about the matter. He hadn't mentioned to anyone yet that the prisoner wasn't really named Gilbert Brossard. Captain Namon didn't like to mention anything to anyone until he'd thought it over.

Captain Namon took out his private journal—his *very* private journal; someday he meant to publish it, when sufficient of the powerful names who appeared in it had safely shuffled off this mortal coil—and made his entry for the day. He jotted down the astounding fact that the surrendered Acadian partisan had turned out to be the deserter Cully Robin, and then couldn't think what else to say about it. There really wasn't anything more to say until he'd thought about it more.

So he locked up both clasps on the journal and put it away again, then stretched out on his cot with his bottle and glass and studied the ceiling. The flickers of the hearthflames painted the rafters with the writhing faces on the beach at Piziquid, at Grand-Pré, of the twenty-four half-wild creatures dragged out of the woods up the Petitcodiac...

Well, war was an unpleasant business on all sides. The faces of the scalped British soldiers dragged back into Fort Cumberland weren't pretty to look at, either. Captain Namon did have to admit that the unpleasant business visited upon the Acadians wouldn't have been nearly so unpleasant if it had been executed properly. But it seemed a law of nature that even the most meticulous plan on paper turned into a complete ballocks as soon as human hands took hold of it.

Captain Namon suffered no conscience nor compunctions about doing his duty for king and country. But there was something about the expulsion of the Acadians that the Acadians didn't know. Not surprising they didn't know, since there probably weren't a dozen men in North America that did. Captain Namon knew.

❄ ❄ ❄

Cully spent a sleepless night in the punishment cells of Fort Cumberland. He had every reason to believe that it would be his last night alive. Except that the guards still seemed to think he was nothing worse than just another Acadian outlaw. And from the loosemouthed way they griped to each other around his cell door, they still thought he didn't understand English.

When the door was unlocked in the morning, Captain Namon was standing there in a leather hunting coat. He had a rifle slung over his shoulder, and a pistol and sheath knife stuck in his belt. He said in French: "You and I, Monsieur Brossard, are going for a little promenade," and added in English to the guard, "The prisoner is going to show me the secret paths by which Beausoleil's scalphunters come and go."

"D'ye think that safe, Captain? They might be lurkin' in the woods now."

"It's a little late in the season—they'll all be far away getting themselves denned-in for the winter. And, after all, I'm only a hunter accompanying one of their friends. Monsieur Brossard...?"

Once Cully and Captain Namon were away from the fort, Cully said: "You know bloody well I'm not going to show you any secret paths."

"Maybe I don't give a figgy damn whether you do or not. Keep walking."

Cully had a sudden flare of second sight into the near future, seeing Captain Namon going back through the fort gates and saying offhandedly: "The prisoner tried to escape, send out a burial party." It would save the formality of a court martial which would bring out sticky little details like how Sergeant Robin came to be among the Acadians in the first place. But he couldn't see anything he could do in the present except to keep on walking along the path between the trees, with Captain Namon and his rifle, pistol and knife following behind.

They crossed a stream and went on a little further into the woods, then Captain Namon said: "I think this is far enough," and pointed with his pistol at a moss-covered rock on one side of the path. "Sit down, if you please."

Cully sat down. Captain Namon unslung his rifle and propped it against a tree on the other side of the path, sat down with his back against the tree, propped the pistol in his lap, tugged a silver flask out of his coat and took a deep quaff, then tossed the flask to Cully. Cully sniffed at it and then took a tentative sip of brandy, wondering whether he could spring across the path faster than Captain Namon could raise his pistol.

Captain Namon let out a long, breathy, brandy-fueled belch and said: "There is some element of truth to what you said—that you are what I have made you. It seems only fitting that the creature should know the truth about what he was created from. It would be extremely indiscreet of me, except that it seems highly unlikely you'll live long enough to tell anyone else, and even less likely they'd believe you."

Captain Namon held out his empty hand. Cully looked at it. The fingers beckoned and Cully realized the captain wanted his flask back. Cully tossed it to him.

Captain Namon took another deep swallow and said: "In the summer of 1755, while you were tinkering your way from Halifax to Fort Edward, a dispatch labeled 'Extremest Urgency' was shipped off from the Lords of Trade in London to the Governor of Nova Scotia. It was a response to Governor Lawrence's last report, wherein he'd hinted what he had planned for the Acadians.

"The dispatch said in no uncertain terms that the Lords of Trade saw no reason to uproot and disperse His British Majesty's loyal Acadian subjects—regardless whether said Acadians had or hadn't sworn an unconditional oath of loyalty."

Captain Namon shifted the flask into his left hand and took another drink, while his right hand took up its new habit of rhythmically scraping the fingernails across the palm. "Unfortunately, you see, the ship bearing the dispatch from the Lords of Trade was delayed in Newfoundland. By the time it arrived in Nova Scotia, the expulsion of the Acadians was a *fait accompli*. When the news got back to London, the Lords of Trade reluctantly decided that it would be bad policy to publicly condemn a policy that had already been set in motion. So nothing more was said about it."

Captain Namon sipped from his flask again, although this time it looked to Cully like it was less for pleasure than to wash a bad taste out of his mouth. Cully said: "Well, it wouldn't've made any difference. Even an order from the Lords of Trade couldn't over-ride orders from the king."

"What orders from the king?"

"The orders Major Murray read out to the Acadians at Fort Edward. I was there."

"Major Murray read what he believed to be his orders from the king. What I believed to be his orders from the king."

It seemed that that was supposed to mean something, but Cully couldn't think what. He said: "But—"

"Don't you bloody understand? There *were* no orders from the king! The Governor of Nova Scotia and the Governor of Massachusetts cooked the whole thing up between them and lied to everyone!"

Cully put both hands to the sides of his head, trying to squeeze it back together. After his so-called childhood with his so-called family, and his time on the road with old Giorgio the tinker, and then fourteen years in the army, he'd thought he'd seen enough offhanded insanity to take it as a fact of life. He said: "But... *why?*"

"Why? Who knows why. I suppose that Governor Shirley of Massachusetts found it unseemly that his English colonists have no good land left available to them, while just to the north there were thousands of acres of rich farmland wasted on Frenchmen. As for Governor Lawrence—he's a career soldier; he finds it unsettling and annoying if there are people who don't salute when he farts."

Captain Namon took a last pull on his flask, then screwed the stopper down. He said: "In the end, I'd say the reason why they did it is because they could. Where's the joy in working yourself into a position of power if you don't exercise it?"

Captain Namon tucked the flask away and said: "Well, now you know—for all the good it'll do you." Then he crabwalked his shoulders up the tree trunk until he was on his feet, keeping the pistol trained on Cully. Cully stood up as well, watching the yellow eyes in a desperate hope they'd tell him which way to dodge.

Captain Namon pulled the sheathed knife out of his belt, set it down beside the rifle, shrugged off his powderflask and shot pouch and set them down on top of the knife, then uncocked the pistol and added it to the pile. He pointed south along the path and said: "Massachusetts is that way."

Cully stared at him.

Captain Namon said: "Had I a kind Christian heart, I would see you sentenced to a swift execution, instead of starved or frozen in the wilderness."

Cully said: "*Who are you?*"

"You know perfectly well who I am: Captain Namon of His British Majesty's Land Forces."

"You forget that I can read and write. I know what 'Namon' spells in a mirror."

"It makes no difference. Be off with you before I come to my senses."

❈ ❈ ❈

Captain Namon turned and started back up the path toward Fort Cumberland, hearing the scuffling sounds behind him as the renegade came to his senses enough to scoop up what had been left him and take to his heels. When Captain Namon came to the stream they'd crossed on their way from the fort, he sat down and picked through the shore rocks until he found a sufficiently rough-edged one to scrape across his temple as evidence of the prisoner taking him by surprise.

He laughed at his hesitation to ply the rock, reminding himself that his nerves were numbed with brandy and he'd always been thin-skinned. Sure enough, it only took one scrape to draw blood.

He sat holding the bloodied rock and watching the red and gold leaves swirling down the stream. The leaves put him in mind of the Acadians: torn loose and scattered to the wind and tides. For no good reason. For no reason. For no bloody reason at all.

Captain Namon dropped his stone into the stream and unstoppered his flask. He never heard the musketshot that punched through the back of his skull.

❈ ❈ ❈

Cully heard the gunshot behind him and turned his loping jog into an all-out sprint. Even though he heard no more shots, he kept on sprinting until his lungs forced him to slow down.

He didn't doubt that Captain Namon was right to assume Sergeant Robin didn't have a hope in hell of making it through several hundred miles of wilderness to Massachusetts. But after three years of running through the woods with Beausoleil, l'Anglais stood a chance.

PART THREE

LOUISIANA

*If we can effect their expulsion, it will be one of the greatest things that
ever did the English in America; for, by all accounts, that part of the
country they possess is as good land as any in the world...*
– THE NEW YORK GAZETTE,
REGARDING THE ACADIANS OF NOVA SCOTIA

XLV

E ulalie stood at the starboard rail as the Boston-bound ship rode the outgoing tide down the Bay of Fundy. She held onto the rail with her right hand and rested her left loosely on Josette's shoulder, ready to tighten if the plunging of the deck caught Josette off balance. Neither she nor Josette had said much over the last eight days. It was hard to think of anything besides the fact which would've done no good to voice: that they were now in exactly the same case as if they'd obeyed the English order three years ago, except that Josette's father and brothers and sisters would still be alive.

The western shore of the bay—the last vestige of French Acadia—was just a charcoal smudge along the horizon. Eulalie took her hand off the rail for long enough to point at the smudge line and say: "Somewhere along that shore, Josette, maybe right where I'm pointing, is the mouth of La Rivière St. Jean. That's where Françoise Jacquelin—the first *Acadienne*, and the wife of Charles La Tour—defended their fort for three days and nights against the cannons of their enemies, while he was gone to Boston to get help."

"And then Charles La Tour came back and saved her?"

"Um, no, dear…" Eulalie had only been meaning to point out that the first *Acadienne* had been a fighter, and leave it at that. "No, on the fourth day, when Françoise Jacquelin and her men were at Easter Mass, a sentry betrayed her to save his own skin. *But,* even once the enemies were inside the fort, she and her men kept on fighting. She only finally surrendered when the enemies promised to show mercy to her men."

"And then Charles La Tour came back and saved them all?"

"Well… No, dear…" Eulalie was calling herself several kinds of idiot for thinking children would be satisfied with only the part of a story that was good for them. "The enemies broke their promise, and hanged her men one by one in front of her eyes."

"And *then* Charles La Tour came back and saved her?"

"Um, no, dear. She died before he could come back. Some say she was poisoned, some say she died of a broken heart."

Josette just said: "Oh," as though that was just the way things always turned out.

Eulalie closed her mouth and kept it closed, since all she seemed to accomplish by opening it was to prove that hope was for fools. She watched the seagulls soaring freely and listened to the twangy voices of the English sailors padding around the deck behind her.

It would've put at least some kind of order in the world if she could tell Josette that English Protestants were Acadians' enemies and French Catholics their friends. But the fact was that the enemies who'd besieged Charles La Tour's fort and tortured his wife had been French Catholics, while he'd gone to seek help from his friends among the English Protestants of Boston—the same Boston that this prison ship was bound for. Friends and enemies seemed to change shape from year to year, or even day to day. The one constant seemed to be that to be Acadian was to be a target for anyone who had nothing better to do at the moment but wage a little war.

Eulalie suddenly crouched down in front of Josette and said fervently: "But Charles La Tour *did* come back one day, Josette—and became Governor of Acadia, and married the widow of his great enemy, and they lived out the rest of their lives in Acadia with their children and grandchildren growing up around them. And someday *we* will go back, and build two homes side-by-side in the valley of Ardoise, and you will marry a handsome young Acadian man, and you and I will grow old and fat watching your children and mine grow up around us."

"And Cully, too?"

"Yes..." Eulalie nodded several times to cover up the fact that her voice had got stuck in her throat. "The good God willing..."

When the ship dropped her anchor in Boston harbor, the prisoners still had to stay on board. It seemed the authorities in Boston had no idea of what they were supposed to do with yet another boatload of Acadians, and weren't about to leap to any hasty decisions.

Fortunately, there was enough to gawk at from the ship to keep Josette from getting too flustered as the hours of waiting stretched into days. Eulalie made up a game of pointing out to each other the many church turrets rising over the city on the hill, the spiring masts above the shipyard, the wharf as long as the beach at Piziquid... It seemed impossible to Eulalie that people who had so much could care whether or not someone else lived on a little farm in the valley of Ardoise.

Eulalie didn't quite know what to expect from the people of Boston. "Boston" to an Acadian meant all New England. *Les Bostonais* and Acadians had traded with each other for generations, even during times when the kings of France and England passed laws against it. More than a few shipwrecked Boston sailors had been rescued by Acadians, and vice-versa. But Eulalie had also heard that *les Bostonais* so hated the Catholic faith that every year they paraded a scarecrow of the Pope and burned it in the town square.

On the third morning of waiting in the harbor, Eulalie and the other prisoners were rousted out at dawn and crowded onto the ship's boat. There were two wagons waiting on the quay, and a man with a list who called out names and pointed to one wagon or the other. Eulalie climbed onto the wagon she'd been pointed to and hugged Josette to her to make more room for the others. The wagons clattered along stone streets that quickly filled with more people than Eulalie had ever seen in one place, as the citizens of Boston woke to another morning no different to them than all the ones that had gone before.

At the edge of the city the road ran along a narrow neck of land and then forked as the sea came to an end. One wagon took the left branch and the other the right. Eulalie and everyone else in both wagons shouted *au revoirs* across the widening gap and called each others' names.

The road Eulalie's wagon followed wound through tall stands of bare trees rising out of orange lakes of leaves. The trees gave way to ploughed, fenced fields—but oddly with not a farmhouse or barn in sight. They came to a town of white houses around a green square fronted by a spired building that appeared to be a church, except that there was no cross on the spire or anywhere else. The wagon stopped in front of a house that hadn't been painted for some time. The wagonman read two names off his list and gestured them to climb down.

A woman came out of the house and called out a question in French. Immediately there was excited shouting back and forth between the wagon and the house, and an old man who looked vaguely familiar to Eulalie stuck his head out the door behind the woman. But the wagonman snapped the reins against his horses' rumps and the wagon moved on.

The pattern repeated itself throughout the day. Every hour or two they would come to another town. There was an occasional farmhouse in between the towns, but nowhere near enough to account for all the cleared fields. As the wagon drew further away from Boston, the towns became fewer white houses and more log cabins. Eulalie was also aware that every hour took her and Josette further from the sea.

Eventually only she and Josette were left in the back of the wagon. The sun was going down between the horses' heads when they came to one last town. The wagonman stopped in front of a long, low cabin and jerked his thumb over his shoulder. Eulalie climbed down stiffly, gave Josette a hand, and reached back to scoop up all their possessions: the two blankets they'd been given at Fort Cumberland.

As the wagon rumbled away, Eulalie took Josette's hand and walked to the door of the cabin. She could hear voices murmuring French cadences inside. She knocked on the door and the murmuring stopped. After a moment, the door opened a crack and a large nose poked out. Eulalie said to the nose: "*Nous sommes Acadiennes.*"

The door flew open and a scrawny woman attached to the nose bawled over her shoulder: "Two sisters!" Quizzical faces appeared in the doorway, and hands reached out to pull Eulalie and Josette inside and paw at them tentatively. As the people of the house began to believe that Eulalie and Josette were indeed real and Acadian, there was an excited babble of questions from all directions, which Eulalie attempted to get out answers to. She and Josette were bustled over to the hearth, where the scrawny woman with the fat nose spooned out the dregs of a thin fish soup.

In between trying to answer all the questions about where she and Josette had appeared from, and spooning up the first food they'd seen all day besides some stale bread the wagonman had handed around, Eulalie managed to get in some questions of her own. It seemed that the Acadians in this town consisted of a family with five children, a widow with a grown son, and an old man whose awareness of the world around him appeared to come and go. They'd all been living in the same cabin for three years.

They were all from Annapolis Royal, so Eulalie had never met any of them before. But the widow had a cousin who'd married a sister of Josette's father.

The scrawny woman with the big nose—Celina à Judith à Hélène—seemed to be the head of the household, which her husband didn't seem to mind. Eulalie noticed that while the others pressed her for more stories about Beausoleil and his pirate ship—eager to hear there was at least one Acadian the English couldn't put a leash on—Celina kept her mouth pursed and kept glancing darkly from her to Josette and back again. In a lull in the questions about Beausoleil, Celina said to Eulalie: "Tomorrow the Selectman will come to ask you what you can do."

"The Selectman...?"

"Every town in Massachusetts has its Selectmen and its Overseers of the Poor. In a little town like this, it only takes one selectman to oversee all the poor. People who want to give food or money to the poor give it to *him*, and he gives it out—so that only he will know where it came from. *Les Bostonais*, you see, have a belief that if you give and have it *known* you gave, it isn't charity—it's boastfulness."

If that was an example of how *les Bostonais* thought, Eulalie felt a little safer among them. It certainly didn't seem like any reason for Celina's ominous tone. Maybe that was just the way Celina said everything.

Celina said: "And the selectman has to satisfy the farmers that he's made good use of the money they pay in taxes, otherwise he has to make up the difference out of his own pocket. All the people in this town, you see, are farmers—or almost all. They have their fields outside of town but their houses and barns in town, as though they'd be afraid to go to sleep at night without other houses snugged up around them."

Eulalie said: "Ah." That explained the many tilled fields and few farmhouses. But it still didn't explain why Celina sounded like she was trying to warn her about something.

Celina said: "The reason the selectman will ask you tomorrow what you can do, is because..." There was that sidelong look at Josette again. "*Les Bostonais* have a law for their own people that they use on us as well. Anyone who is so poor they have to live on tax money, and cannot work to pay it back... their children are taken away from them and put to work in households that can pay their keep. In the next township east of here, there was blood on the ground when the selectmen came to take Joseph Landry's children."

"But..." Eulalie found it difficult to speak; she and Josette were all each other had left. "This is different, you see. The selectman can't take her away from me, because Josette isn't my child. That is, I'm only her—"

"It makes no difference. You are the one responsible for her, and if you can't earn her keep... I and my children are only lucky that my man has clever hands for making things people will buy, and doesn't need English to split English firewood. I would go myself to scrub floors or scrub laundry, but I have no English and the English women find it tedious to tell me how they want their work done."

Eulalie said: "I have some English."

"Oh!" The corners of Celina's mouth went up around the wide wings of her nose. "Then I'm sure your Josette will be able to stay with you."

Eulalie wasn't sure how much English she actually had. Some of the words she'd learned from Cully in bed didn't seem like ones a Puritan farmwife would want to hear in her kitchen.

The excitement of hearing two new, French voices in the house kept everyone gabbling at Eulalie and Josette far into the night. Celina's husband sat silently on the edge of the gathering, working pegs into an augured board to make a hay rake. At one point the widow's grown son started a one-sided argument with him: "Have you no pride...? I could make a hay rake, too, to sell for a few English pennies, or weave a fishnet, or whittle hinges. But I have some pride... Why should my hands work for them? We could feed ourselves until they stole all we had; now it's up to them to feed us..."

Celina's husband took it as long as he could, and then said: "All of that may be true. But you have no children. When you do, come back and tell me how much pride a man should have."

Eulalie wondered how many dozens of times they had played out the same argument in the last three years—with the widow's son nipping at Celina's husband's heels until the inevitable slap into the corner. But they had nothing else to talk about.

Eulalie asked if anyone knew what had become of a young man from Piziquid named André Melanson, but no one in the house had ever heard of him. Apparently there were some people from Piziquid in the third township back along the road, but Melanson wasn't among their names.

The excitement of the evening finally wore itself out. Back home in Acadia, the occasion would've been enough to keep these same people up chattering merrily until the dawn declared it time to go to work. But back in Acadia they wouldn't have been living on the occasional spoonful of thin fish soup.

Mattresses made of old blankets and straw were rolled out on the dirt floor. Eulalie and Josette had to make do with just their blankets for now. The cabin looked long from the outside, but by the time twelve people had lain down in it there was barely room to set a foot. With Josette curled up fast asleep beside her, Eulalie lay awake practicing her English by imagining herself talking to Cully.

The next morning the selectman arrived, looking like someone with too many children pulling on his sleeves. He read awkwardly from a piece of paper: "Vous... est... Oolally La Tour?"

"I speaks the English."

"You don't say!"

"But," Eulalie said confusedly, "I did say... I hears more good than speaks, but more I hears more good I speaks."

"Let me see your hands. Well, you know what work is. Maybe I can find a place for you." He turned to go and then turned back. "Oh—you do know that you must stay here...? In this township...? If you are found in another township without a pass from me, it will go the worse for you."

Eulalie nodded, although she wasn't exactly certain what a "pass" was.

"Good." The selectman glanced around at the other Acadians dotted listlessly around the room, and then said to Eulalie—as though it were something he'd been wanting to say for some time, but had had no one he could communicate it to, "We are not cruel people, Mistress La Tour, but we are not wealthy people. It is no small burden to us to find ten, now twelve, landless foreigners suddenly thrust into our little town. Good day."

Two days later, a large man with a thick, grey beard and clean-shaven chin opened the cabin door without knocking and said: "Eulalie La Tour," more like a summons than a question.

Eulalie stood up and said: "Yes?"

"I am the Reverend Mister Buckthorn. I am told you speak a little English and can do domestic work."

"A *little* English. More good make more I hears."

"We'll see. I have a room in the barn where you and your sister can sleep. Gather your things together and come along."

He stepped back outside. Eulalie snatched up her blanket and Josette's, hastily shook Celina's hand and hurried out to where the Reverend Mister Buckthorn was waiting. He set off walking through town with brisk, long strides of his big boots. Eulalie held Josette's hand and bustled along to keep up. Josette had to practically break into a run.

As he thumped along the road, the Reverend Mister Buckthorn declaimed at Eulalie: "My good wife, you see, has given me eight fine sons, but no daughters to help her with the female work. Another pair of hands would be a blessing to her—*if* they be useful hands. If you please my good wife, you will work for your room and board and your sister's, and one cash shilling a week. And my good wife has some worn-out, warm clothing you might patch for you and your sister. When my good wife speaks to you, you will answer 'Yes, ma'am.' When I or my sons speak to you, you will answer 'Yes, sir.' Do you understand?"

Eulalie found it as hard to keep up with his English as his big boots, but she answered: "Yes, sir."

"Good. There will be no work done on The Lord's Day. On that day you and your sister can visit your people at the charity house, where I'm told they hold prayers of their own. In my father's day it would never be tolerated. There is still a law that any Popish priest who enters Massachusetts forfeits his life, but you are only simple people and I hold no truck with the rumours that some of you are priests in disguise."

The Reverend Mister Buckthorn's home turned out to be on the far edge of town from the charity house. The Reverend Mister showed Eulalie and Josette their "room" in the barn—actually only a corner stall with clean straw on the floor—and then took them into the high-roofed, white house to meet his good wife. Madame Buckthorn turned out to be a very worn-out looking woman who worked hard at seeming cheerful. She said to Eulalie: "Can you wash floors, deary?" and made a scrubbing motion.

"Yes, ma'am, Reverend Mrs. Buckthorn."

Mrs. Buckthorn laughed. "Oh, dear me, *I'm* not reverend, deary, just *Mister* Buckthorn is. Now, you see the buckets by the hearth, and the brush and rags, and the dish of lye soap, and the kettle on the fire, and the well outside the window..." Mrs. Buckthorn pointed at each article in turn, to help Eulalie connect the English words with them. "Before the boys went out to the fields I had them move all the furniture in the parlour against the walls, so's you could wash the parlour floor."

So Eulalie got down on her hands and knees and went to work with the scrub brush, Josette following with a rag and a bucket of clear water. They had barely finished when Mrs. Buckthorn called Eulalie to help her set out supper before the boys came home. Once the Buckthorns were all sat down at the table, Eulalie was allowed to take two plates out to the barn for her and Josette. Eulalie ate quickly, so she could be back to wash the supper dishes as soon as the Buckthorns were done eating.

There turned out to be no shortage of work around the Buckthorn house. Eulalie was accustomed to what other people would call hard work, but working in her own home was different from having to listen for footsteps every time she sat down to catch her breath. But one advantage to the long days of scrubbing the Buckthorns' pots, floors and laundry, carrying their water, plucking their chickens and churning their butter, was that she usually sunk straight into sleep at night. On Sundays, when she had too much time to think about the difference between the past and the present, she would try to remind herself that at least she and Josette were still together, that the cows kept the barn warm while the snow howled outside, that even the leavings from the Buckthorns' table made for better eating than the other Acadians in town got, that Mrs. Buckthorn doted on Josette...

The combination of the facts that Mrs. Buckthorn had never had a daughter of her own, and that Josette had big, blue eyes, cornsilk hair and a shy manner around strangers, didn't only produce the occasional piece of rock candy for Josette's sweet tooth. Eulalie had no doubt that Mrs. Buckthorn was responsible for the Reverend declaring at the end of the second week that the wages had been increased to a shilling-and-a-half because Josette worked as well.

But there was one element of the circumstances she and Josette had landed in that Eulalie couldn't conjure up a positive side to. That was the Buckthorns' eldest son, Nathan.

Nathan was as big as his father, with the same bulbous ears and fleshy lips. He was old enough to have a family of his own, but Eulalie strongly suspected that every girl in town was leery of what life would be like in a family of nine males with only two women to take care of them.

Whenever Nathan passed by Eulalie in the kitchen, he always managed to brush up against her. He would stay sitting at the supper table long after everybody else had left, watching her bending over the washing tub. He would say things to her like: "So I hear you had a husband back in Nova Scotia. How long's it been since you... *been* with him?" She got into the habit of always blowing out her candlestub before taking off her dress at night, even though there were no glass windows in the barn and the only sounds around her were the cattle's sleepy lowing and Josette's sleeping breathing.

A few days after New Year's, she was carrying her guttering candle out to the barn when something in the sky caught her eye. She looked up. The western sky was ribbed with thin, sharp clouds. The sun was down, but still cast a glow into the clouds. The picture brought tears to her eyes, but she didn't know why. Then she realized what it looked like. The stream bed in the hollow below the old farm in the valley of Ardoise was scoured, striated slate with sharp ribs. On summer days when the stream was just a trickle, the sun would catch on the slick, raised edges, making gleaming, jagged, gold lines across the black.

Eulalie tightened her mouth, lowered her head and went on into the barn. She waited until she was inside to raise her hand from sheltering the candleflame to wipe her eyes. Josette was sound asleep. Eulalie set the candle on the corner of the stall wall, then stripped off the blanket shawled around her shoulders and laid it down over her and Josette's straw bed. She was about to blow out the candle and start unbuttoning her dress, when she heard the barn door open and close, and saw another rim of light beyond her own.

The cows had all been milked hours ago; she could think of no reason for anyone to come into the barn. She stepped out of the stall to take a look.

It was Nathan, standing at the far end of the barn holding a lantern. He smiled and started toward her. Some instinct made her move away from the stall where Josette was sleeping. She said: "Is there anything wrong? Are one of the cows sick?" He just kept smiling and coming toward her.

When he got near, he hung the lantern on a hook, held out a closed hand and then opened it. In his palm was a large, silver coin. He said: "This'd be more'n a month's wages to you. Won't take you but a few minutes to earn it. All you got to do is lie down on your back and open your legs."

"No."

"'No, *sir*'."

"No, *pig*. Get out of here."

He laughed. "Ain't your barn. You can't tell me to get out of here. But I could tell *you*." He reached his other hand out toward her right breast. She slapped it away. He looked hurt. He said: "You Romish women do it with anybody and then confess to the priest the next morning and forget about it. Why not do it with me?"

He reached his hand out toward her breast again. She slapped it away again and started to say *No!* again. But before she could get the syllable out, the back of his hand crashed across her mouth, turning her sideways. She found her balance, saw a pitchfork leaned against the wall and lunged for it. She managed to get her hands on it, but his forearm came down on the backs of hers and the pitchfork fell to the floor. He punched her in the stomach, knocking the wind out of her.

While she gasped desperately for breath, he pushed her down on a mound of straw and dropped to his knees between her legs, fiercely kneading her breasts with one hand while the other pulled her skirt up. She finally got some air into her lungs and the rafters stopped whirling. She rose up, clawing her hands at his eyes, but he pushed her back down and the hand that had been mauling her breasts turned into a vice pinning her throat. His arm was so much longer than hers were that she couldn't reach her hands to his face, and the squeeze on her throat was making everything muffled and hazy.

He was grunting like a hog, and she could feel him trying to push himself into her as though he thought that was all there was to it. His free hand fumbled with brutally clumsy fingers, trying to open her up. She worked her chin down against the hand holding her throat, until she could get her teeth on his wrist and clamp down with all the strength she could put into her jaws. He tore his wrist free, leaving a taste of blood, and drove his fist down against the side of her head.

There was a dry, searing pain as he forced his way inside her. He shoved back and forth twice and then gasped and flopped across her like a sack of flour.

A thunderous roar came down out of the sky, and the deadweight was torn off her. Eulalie opened her clamped-shut eyes and saw the Reverend Buckthorn tossing Nathan across the barn with one hand while the other reached down a length of harness leather hanging on the wall. Nathan hit the floor, gaped at the buckled leather in his father's hand, and tried to scramble away across the straw and button his breeches at the same time.

The Reverend Buckthorn raised the harness belt high above his head, bellowed: "Jezebel!" and whipped the buckled end of the strap down across Eulalie's abdomen. She flung her arms up to cover her face, and tried to writhe out of the way as the belt came down on her legs, her breasts, her ribs, each blow accompanied by "Whore!" or "Bitch!" or "Fornicatress!"

The Reverend Buckthorn's roars and Eulalie's screams at him to stop were suddenly joined by a third voice, high-pitched and shrieking. The next blow didn't come down. Eulalie parted her arms just enough to see between them. Josette was kicking and punching at the Reverend Buckthorn's leg and howling at him. The Reverend pushed Josette down and stepped back, breathing heavily and looking from Josette to Eulalie and back again.

Josette leaped up and ran to fling herself across Eulalie. Eulalie gasped as Josette's body came down on places where the belt had come down. The Reverend Mister Buckthorn jabbed his finger toward Eulalie and said: "I am going back into the house for five minutes' time. When I come back, be gone."

When they were alone, Josette whimpered: "Eulalie...?"

"Ssh… I'm… I'm all right… But we must hurry now. Run put your dress on. Hurry."

Eulalie waited until Josette had disappeared into the stall before prying herself to her feet, trying not to wince too loud, trying not to vomit. Josette had got her dress and shoes on and was waiting to be told what to do next. Eulalie looked around the stall. Mrs. Buckthorn had given them some old blankets as well as some old dresses. Eulalie used one of the blankets to make a bundle of the old clothes, caped the rest of the blankets around her shoulders and Josette's, and tucked into her waistband the paper shillings she and Josette had earned.

On their way out of the barn, the lanternlight gleamed on something in the scattered straw: the silver coin. It would give her and Josette almost twice as much money as they had now. She left it there.

The snow had grown as high as her hips, but there was a path beaten from the barnyard to the road, and the road had been trodden to mush by the hooves of horses and oxen. Eulalie could think of only one place to go: back down the road to the charity house where the rest of the town's Acadians were kennelled. She stumbled along with one hand on Josette's shoulder, partly to reassure Josette and partly as a crutch. Josette was sobbing, and Eulalie was doing her best to keep her own tears to herself. Every step brought pain out of one part of her body or another. There was something dribbling down the inside of her thigh that might be blood.

As the watchdogs roared in relays to demand what right she had to stagger down their road, Eulalie groped for what to say when she and Josette got to the charity house. She was quite sure that neither the Reverend Buckthorn nor his son would want to noise-about what had happened. But if she told the other Acadians in town, one of them was bound to run raging to the selectman. Celina would kick down his door if that was the only way to get his attention. Once it came out in the open, The Reverend Mister Buckthorn would undoubtedly claim that his innocent son had been seduced by a French whore—and Eulalie had no doubt who'd be believed.

Eulalie took inventory of all the places on her body that felt bruised or welted, and decided they were all hidden under her clothes or hair. She tightened her hand to bring Josette to a halt and knelt down in the snow in front of her. "Josette, you are too young to understand what happened tonight. I'll make you a promise that I'll explain it to you when you're older—if you make *me* a promise."

Josette just kept her mouth screwed shut and kept sobbing.

"The promise you have to make, Josette, is that you promise to say nothing of what happened tonight to anyone. No one. All that happened tonight is that the Buckthorns decided they had no more work for us to do. Do you promise?"

Josette bobbed her chin out of her throat to approximate a nod, then burst out with: "It's my fault!"

"What? How—?"

"If I hadn't got my foot caught," Josette wailed, "we'd still be back safe on the Petitcodiac!"

"No!" Eulalie hugged Josette to her, stroked her hair and whispered: "No, dear, that's not true. The English might've caught us anyway, or the good God knows what else might have happened. None of this is anyone's fault, any more than it's your fault the tide goes out. Now, we'll wash each other's faces with snow so no one will know we've been crying, and we'll both keep our promises, yes? Josette...? Yes...?"

Despite Josette sticking to her promise, and Eulalie sticking to her story, Celina obviously suspected that something more had happened than a sudden shortage of domestic work at the Buckthorns', but let it lie. The selectman came around the next day and told Eulalie that it would be hard to find her another place after the Buckthorns had dismissed her for insolence, but he would try. Eulalie spent long portions of her day huddled in a corner hugging Josette to her and wishing she had a rock to crawl under. None of the other people in the charity house remarked on it or stared at her. They'd all done much the same for periods of the last three years.

Eulalie kept trying to think of other options she could present to the selectman when he would inevitably come back and tell her that if she couldn't pay for Josette's keep, Josette would have to be bound over to an English family who could. But she could think of nothing.

Days past, and still the selectman didn't come back. On a blizzardy afternoon, the door blew open and then flew shut again. Hazy within the inblown dusting of snow stood a clean-shaven man dressed in frost-rimed layers of rags and tags. Everyone else in the charity house eyed him warily while pretending not to be looking at him. They'd learned by now that new jailers or the whims of power might appear at any moment in any guise.

Eulalie blinked and squinted, certain that her eyes were playing tricks on her. But Josette wasn't old enough yet to distrust her own eyes. Josette ran to the doorway, shrieking: "Cully!" and leaped into his arms.

XLVI

E ulalie sleepwalked to the doorway where Cully was setting Josette back down on her feet and straightening up to meet her. She put her hand up to his cheek to make sure he was real, and heard herself stammer out: "Where did you...? How did you...?" Then he put his arms around her. The old blanket that he wore knotted crosswise over his coat was frozen into wrinkles that crunched against her breasts, but she didn't mind.

After a moment she stepped back to look at him again. Not all the damp streaks on his cheeks were from the frost melting out of his hair. She realized that everyone else in the room was staring and even more confused than she was. She turned to them and said: "This is my husband, Cully—"

"La Tour," Cully cut her off. "Cully à Gilbert à Gilbert."

As everyone else came forward to shake Cully's hand and introduce themselves, Eulalie had a moment to wonder why he'd stopped her from saying his name. When she'd been captured by the English soldiers, she'd naturally identified herself as "La Tour," rather than "Madame Robin, wife of the deserter you'd like to hang." But these were Acadians, not English soldiers.

Then again, even though they were Acadians and there were no soldiers hereabouts, they were still in the middle of an English province. She could see the coyote-sense in his thinking that the fewer people knew his real name, the less chance it would accidentally get mentioned in the wrong place. Now that she'd answered that spoonful of confusion, there was only the ocean left to deal with.

Celina sat them down by the hearth and the three of them were a family again, with Eulalie and Cully clutching each other's hands and Josette curled up against them. Along with all the other emotions flowing between them, Eulalie could tell that Cully was tickled by her dumbfoundedness at his miraculous reappearance— the same kind of tickled as the night in the farmhouse of Ardoise when he showed the children he could make a coin disappear by snapping his fingers.

Everyone else gathered round to hear Cully's explanation of the miracle. When he told them offhandedly that as soon as he'd learned Eulalie and Josette had been captured he'd gone in to surrender, Eulalie had to lower her head, and Celina's husband made a choking sound and leaned forward to pat Cully's knee. Eulalie knew that neither Celina's husband nor any of the others knew the half of it; they had no inkling of what a chance he'd taken by putting himself back among English soldiers.

Everyone else expressed amazement when he told them that when he'd discovered he'd surrendered too late to go into exile with her, an English officer took pity on him and allowed him to escape. Eulalie suspected there was more to it than that, but he would tell her when they were alone.

"From then," Cully went on, "the only hard part was sneaking past the English forts on what used to be the French side of the bay. I wasn't in much danger of starving to death in the woods—lucky for me it was autumn, and so many fat and lazy animals getting ready to sleep for the winter even *I* could bag something. And," he winked at Eulalie, "I'm a dab hand at knowing which wild mushrooms are safe to eat.

"When I came to the northernmost New England settlements, I told them I was a tinker who'd had his horse and goods stolen by Mi'kmaqs. They were more than willing to believe that—*les Bostonais* seem to have an unholy terror of Mi'kmaqs. Although they do seem to think the only reason the Mi'kmaqs scalped their grandfathers and grandmothers was they were egged on by Acadians.

"I had some money with me, so I bought some new tools and an old nag, and no one looks twice at a tinker ambling down the road. Especially since I shaved my beard to look more English. Do you like it?"

Eulalie elevated an eyebrow and waggled her head from side to side, as though maybe she liked it and maybe she didn't. Josette said: "I do."

"Thank you, Josette. Well, then all I had to do was amble my way down into Massachusetts and ask at the houses where Acadians were kept, till I found someone who'd heard what become of the captives from the Petitcodiac. So here I am."

He shrugged as though the journey had been a Sunday promenade for a *courier de bois* like him. The shrug also managed to convey—at least to Eulalie—that he didn't really expect anyone to believe that. Then he turned to Eulalie. "And you and Josette...?"

"Oh... Oh, there isn't much to tell. They brought us to Boston and then to here. I had to find some way to earn my keep—because Massachusetts has a law, you see, that anyone who is too poor to feed her children, the children will be taken away to live in someone else's home... So I, we, worked for a while as servants to a family on the other side of this town. But, a few days ago... They decided they didn't need a servant anymore. The selectman said he might be able to find some other work for me, but so far..."

Cully looked down at the gold crown Eulalie had braided and coiled onto Josette's head, and then back up at Eulalie. He said: "Well, if the selectman *has* found you another place to work now, I'm afraid the poor old lad's wasted his time. I have my tools and tin—and that poor, cold, old nag out there I better find some shelter for soon. There's always work for a tinker if he casts his net wide enough.

"I may be married to an Acadian, but being as how I was born on the Channel Islands I'm a pure and simple British subject—no one can tell me where I can or can't go to ply my trade. I still have a bit of money left, and there must be an empty shanty hereabouts we can buy or rent. We can make that home, and I'll amble away on my rounds in the morning and amble back at night."

Eulalie looked down at the hand she was holding and wrapped her other hand around the back of it. She whispered: "Thank you, Cully."

"Don't thank me—if we find a place with a little plot of land you'll have to break your back in the spring putting in a garden so we can have some turnips. You know I'll be damn-all help to you at gardening."

Eulalie looked up to see Celina beaming at her, with the corners of her mouth up around the wide wings of her nostrils again. Eulalie had no doubt that Celina was genuinely happy for, but also genuinely happy that the charity house would only have to hold ten people instead of twelve or thirteen.

When Eulalie and Cully bedded down on the charity house floor that night, his hands began to move across her through the thin cloth of her shift. She shuddered and whispered: "Please. No."

He murmured into her ear: "You're right—not much privacy hereabouts. Soon."

The next day Cully went to see the selectman, and came back with the news that the selectman knew of a disused woodchopper's cabin, which the man who owned the woodlot would be glad to rent out for a few shillings. It took a few days to make the place liveable, with Eulalie and Josette refitting the inside while Cully patched the roof enough to get them through the winter.

On their first night in the cabin, Cully started touching her again. She wanted him to touch her, but she couldn't push the memories away. No matter how gently Cully's fingers glided over her breasts, she felt Nathan Buckthorn's brutal squeezing, and heard his rooting-hog grunts. But tonight she had no excuses; they were alone but for Josette sound asleep on the other side of the room.

As Cully's hands and arms moved around her, and his body pressed tighter against hers, Eulalie bit down on her teeth to keep the sounds of horror and disgust from coming out. She tried to caress him in return, but all she could manage was to drape one hand limply on his shoulder. She told herself that what had happened in the Buckthorns' barn had been no more than ten minutes out of her whole life, from the moment Nathan came into the barn to the moment the Reverend Buckthorn left. That didn't change the fact that everything after those ten minutes was different from everything before. But unless she could find a way to pretend she was the same woman she'd been before, any minute now Cully was going to ask her what was wrong, and she was going to have to tell him.

There was nothing she'd ever wanted to do less than tell him. For one thing, she was ashamed, and knew that he would be ashamed that he hadn't been able to protect her. No matter how ridiculous that was, she knew he'd feel it. And what was the good in making him suffer what had happened to her, when there was nothing he could do to change it?

When Cully's hand moved up between her thighs, she thought she was going to scream. And then she found a way. They weren't in Massachusetts at all; they were still back in their poplar and clay cottage on the Petitcodiac. She'd had a foolish nightmare about being captured and sent into exile; her flailing and moaning in her sleep had woken up Cully and now his comforting was turning into lovemaking. The memories of the Buckthorns' barn were still there, but they were only images from a dream. She wrapped her fingers in Cully's thin, fine hair and rubbed his head against her breast.

❊ ❊ ❊

With what remained of Cully's gold guineas, and the shillings she and Josette had earned, they could buy the basic things they needed to make a home of their cabin in the woods: a pot and skillet, an axe, a good kitchen knife, a few sawn planks, a sack of flour... Les Bostonais were more than eager to sell whatever they could for a little ready money. It seemed that hard cash was hard to come by in Massachusetts and most of their trade was barter for farm produce, which was why anyone without land was doomed to poverty.

Eulalie found plausible excuses to get Cully to go and do most of the dickering and buying. She preferred to stay around the cabin, where she felt safe and didn't have to see anyone except Josette and Cully and the occasional visitor from the charity house. The cabin wasn't much. The table was just some planks fixed into a corner, and doubled as the roof of Josette's bed. The beds were just mats of spruce boughs and straw with blankets thrown over them. But after the last five months, Eulalie was more than happy just to have her own stone fireplace; to have a door she could close, with Cully's rifle hanging over it, and the pistol he'd got from Captain Namon sitting on wall pegs within easy reach of the doorway; to be able to cook enough of a meal that Cully and Josette had to leave a little on their plates to throw to the blue jays; to be able to send Josette over to the charity house with an extra pullet Cully had got for a piece of work.

Cully seemed to have no trouble finding work. Eulalie suspected that some of the farmwives in town and the surrounding townships made a point of finding a knife with a loose handle, just so they could get a look at the man who was said to have given up his freedom and made his way through hundreds of miles of wilderness to be with his wife.

There were increasingly long stretches of hours when she didn't think about that night in the Buckthorns' barn at all. Especially in the mornings, when she and Josette would make Cully breakfast and then kiss him *au revoir*, knowing they'd hear his horse clopping back up the path before sunset.

She did find it difficult, though, the morning he mentioned he was going to do some tinkering at the Buckthorns'. She managed to keep her mouth shut, and shot a look at Josette to do the same. Within a few more mornings, she found she'd got all the way to noon without remembering.

But as March swallowed February, Eulalie had to surrender to the fact that something had happened which meant her island of simple calm had only been a will-o'-the-wisp. She was pregnant. It would've made her happy, except that no matter how many times she counted back over the days and weeks and months, it always added up to the same thing. There was no way to be certain who the father was.

She reminded herself of all the good reasons why she hadn't told Cully about that night. There was no good reason to tell him now. If she only told him she was pregnant, he would go to his grave happily believing that the child was his, and probably it was. The more she thought about it, the more she was certain that the noble thing to do would be to carry the secret inside her like she carried the child. But she couldn't.

On a snowy day when Cully decided he'd be better off staying home and whittling pegs for a real table, Eulalie said: "Josette, you spend so much time here with no company but us grumpy old people. Why don't you go over to the charity house and spend a while throwing snowballs at your Aunt Celina's children?"

"Yes, Eulalie."

"And take along some of that maple rock sugar Cully got in trade."

"Yes, Eulalie."

When Josette was gone, Eulalie sat down at the narrow end of the two-sided table that Cully was taking up the long end of with still-barked birch branches and a pile of shavings. She said: "Cully, I have two things to tell you."

"Mm-hm."

"Put your knife down or you might cut yourself. The first thing is—I am carrying a child." He started to jump out of his chair, but she held her hand up and said:

"Wait! I told you I had *two* things to tell you. You see, there is a chance the child might not be yours."

His blossoming features froze and withered. She looked down at the table and said: "I will tell you why..."

She meant to tell him as quickly and simply as possible, but partway through her voice cracked into sobs and she kept losing the thread. Long before she was done, he got up and came and stood beside her chair and cupped her head between his hand and his belly. When she got to the part about the Reverend Buckthorn and the harness belt, the fingers cupping her head suddenly jerked into claws and then shook with the effort to grow soft again.

When she'd finished telling him, there was no sound for a while except her own weeping and his tortured breathing. Then his voice croaked from far away: "I'm sorry... Just a few days..."

She knew immediately what he meant: if he'd arrived just a few days earlier, she would've been gone from the Buckthorns' before that night. She clutched his hand and said: "No! It could just as easily have happened any night before then. I only thank the good God you came when you did."

He sat back down, holding both her hands in his on the table. His mouth worked as though he was trying to say something. But he kept closing it and looking away, sniffing-in to clear his nose. Finally he said: "I love you."

She could see in his wet-blurred eyes that her biggest argument against telling him had been right. It seemed to her that living with what had happened would be even worse for him than it was for her. It was something that had happened to her, and all she remembered was what had actually happened. Now that she'd told him, his imagination could paint him an infinity of details of the ways it may have happened.

But she also caught a flicker of something else in his eyes—something that hadn't occurred to her as an even bigger reason not to tell him. She'd forgotten that *l'Anglais* was other things besides a tinker.

She clutched his hands tighter and said: "Cully, you mustn't! This is their town, their country. What would happen to you—to us—if you did?"

He looked at her with eyes that could hammer nails. She said: "You have to promise me you won't."

He looked away, heaved in a breath and let it out, then murmured: "I promise."

He never said another word about it. But a few weeks later a knock came at the cabin door when they were sitting down to breakfast. Cully called around his mouthful of egg and biscuit: "Come in."

It was one of Nathan Buckthorn's younger brothers. He took his hat off and nodded: "Mister La Tour. Ma'am." Out of the corner of her eye, Eulalie could see that

Cully's chewing had turned into slow grinding. He swallowed and leaned back from his plate with his mouth and eyes slitted. "Mr. La Tour, Pa says to ask you when're you coming back to re-jig the harness buckle you said was only fixed temp'ry?"

There was a pause, with Cully staring at the young Buckthorn in a way that obviously made the boy uncomfortable. Then Cully said levelly: "You go back and tell your Pa that if my wife ain't good enough to work for him, neither am I. And you tell your Pa that if he's got anything more to say about it, he should come say it to *me*. Can you remember that?"

"Yes, sir."

"Good. Now run along with you."

The Reverend Mister Buckthorn never came around to say anything more about the temporary harness buckle.

As the ice on the creek behind the cabin began to melt, Eulalie's belly began to swell. Cully would put his hand on the swelling and swear he could feel his son or daughter swimming, and gleefully warn Josette that she wasn't going to be a spoiled only child much longer. Sometimes it seemed to Eulalie that he was treating *her* like a child—pretending that he had no doubts or night-thoughts about the baby. But most of the time she was more than glad to let him pretend.

Cully came home one day with a crisp, folded sheet of blotchily-printed paper. He looked like he'd just come from a funeral, but tried to sound like he was making fun of the paper he brandished. "*Les Bostonais* are mad-keen on news-sheets—four weeklies out of Boston-town alone. I could think of better uses for the paper."

He threw the news-sheet down on the table and flopped onto his chair. He rubbed his mouth and said: "But it does take them a hellish long while to get news of anything outside their own back yard. So this is old news... Before Christmas, Beausoleil brought everyone from the Petitcodiac and the Miramichi in to Fort Cumberland and surrendered."

"They say..." He batted his hand at the news-sheet as though to make it stop talking. "They say that the British Army... did such a grand job of burning everything last fall... by December the outlaws and their families were eating soup made out of shoe leather and deershit."

Eulalie put her hand over her mouth and blinked against the pictures of Anne and her children, and all the other children. Cully crossed his arms as though to hold his heart in, then uncrossed them to lean across the table to pinch Josette's nose and say: "So you see, you little stumblefoot, if you hadn't stepped into that snare we would've been a lot worse off."

He crossed his arms tightly again and said to Eulalie: "It seems Beausoleil dickered as good surrender terms as he could, but those weren't very good. Governor

Lawrence is delighted to ship off any *other* Acadians to other English colonies, or the French islands in the Caribbean—but he doesn't want to take any chances with die-hards like Beausoleil and those who stuck with him till the end. So they'll be kept imprisoned on an island in Halifax harbor until the end of the war. Whenever that may be."

Eulalie couldn't imagine Beausoleil living in a prison cell. She whispered through her fingers: "That's the last of us."

XLVII

As André's second spring in Albany ripened, he packed his things together. He had a haversack filled with provisions and camp gear, a bedroll of two blankets wrapped in an oilcloth, and a second-hand fowling piece with a shoulder sling. He had new clothes and new boots, which he'd made sure to break in slowly before it came time to take to the road. And he had two hundred and forty-eight shillings of New York Colony paper money, some in a purse in his coat pocket but most tucked into his left boot.

When he stepped out into the wagonwright's courtyard for the last time, Mrs. Henderson was standing there waiting for him. He wasn't exactly sure what he thought of Mrs. Henderson. She and her family had never treated him like a servant, and there was no question he was now much better equipped for travelling and for getting along in English than if he'd left last spring. But she had stolen a year of his life.

She said: "I hope you can forgive me someday, André. I make no apologies for putting my family ahead of anyone else. We might well've lost this place, and it's all we have." André said nothing. "Are you sure you still want to go all that way, with so many chances of ending up nowhere but a New England jail? Even if you do get back to Acadia, there may be nothing for you there."

André had never spoken to Mrs. Henderson of Eulalie, and didn't intend to now. But Eulalie wasn't all there was to it. He said: "You can not understand. You live in a town, and one town is the same like any other. Me, I belong in the land where I was born."

"Well, if you change your mind there is always a place for you here. I dread to think of Mr. Henderson breaking-in another pair of hands. The road across the Berkshire Hills will take you to Worcester, Massachusetts. From Worcester, you had better say your sister is in New Hampshire and turn north—instead of carrying on East to Boston and the coast roads. People are keeping a watch out for Acadians anywhere near the sea. Go carefully, André."

"Good-bye." He didn't offer to shake her hand, just turned and walked out the gate.

Once he'd put Albany behind him he began to walk with longer, looser strides, filling his chest with clean air. The straps of the haversack and fowling piece didn't weigh much on his shoulders. He spotted a straight sapling by the side of the road and stopped to cut it down with his hand axe and trim it into a walking staff. When he camped that night, he felt like he was free after a year in jail.

He took it slowly for the first few days, so that his feet would grow calluses instead of blisters, and his legs and lungs would stretch instead of tearing. Once he'd worked himself up to walking from sunrise to sunset, he didn't have to think about breaking himself in gradually, since the sun would see to it that he walked just a few minutes longer every day.

The road east became little more than a cow path. As André made his way across the Berkshire Hills, the trees budded and blossomed—new-minted leaves speckling house-high boulders with green sunlight, and ghostly white Indian pipe gleaming in the shadows. He had to admit that these Berkshires were very pretty hills, but they weren't the hills of home.

When the hills shrunk down to hummocks, he guessed he must be in Massachusetts. By the time he came to a town with a store in it, he was out of flour and had used up most of his birdshot. The man behind the counter said: "How do, mister. Walking far?"

"To Worcester."

"That's a ways."

"I have sister ill in Worcester. I come from Albany."

The storeman said, too offhandedly, "Born and bred in Albany, was you?"

"But no. I am of Italy, me. Quaker I become when the ship I did sailor sees Philadelphia."

"Oh. I hear they got some Quakers down Boston-way these days. You just come in for a jaw or can I reach you down something?"

"Beg pardon?"

"You looking to buy anything?"

"Oh! But yes. Two pound of flour and one pound of the small birdshot. And to fill my horn with powder, if you please."

When the storekeeper had toted it up, André handed him a five shilling note. The storeman looked at it twice and said carefully: "This is New York money. You're in Massachusetts now."

"Not good here?"

"Well... No good to most folks, but I do a bit of business from time to time with the other side of the Berkshires. Tell you what, since you're a stranger and travelling for family troubles and all, I'll trade you Massachusetts money shilling for shilling for your New York money. Won't cost me nothing."

"Thank you."

"Hell, like I said, won't cost me nothing. And it'll save me changing money when I go into New York."

André had twenty-three more shillings in his purse. He thought of the two hundred and twenty in his boot, but he didn't like to advertise the fact that he was carrying that much money, and he didn't plan to be in Massachusetts long enough to spend much. Maybe New York money was good in New Hampshire.

The road grew wider again and hilly again. Two days into the hills there was a dilapidated cabin snugged up to the roadside, with a brightly varnished sign of a bunch of purple grapes hanging over the door. André decided that a cup of wine and a meal he hadn't scorched over a campfire would be a good use of some of his money.

Inside the cabin were a woman and a few children going about their day. It seemed that the inn consisted of a pockmarked table in one corner, while the rest of the one-room cabin was the family home. André had barely got out "Hello" before the woman required an explanation for his non-Englishness, just as the storekeeper had. He wondered if the English stayed as suspicious of foreigners when there wasn't a war on.

After satisfying the inn-wife that he was a harmless, Italian Quaker, he said: "A cup of wine, if you please."

She replied flatly: "We got rum. You can have it with water if you want."

"Please. And to eat...?"

"Let's see, it's about mid-day... Mid-day meal'd be eggs and bacon."

"Oh. What if this had be morning?"

"Breakfast'd be bacon and eggs."

"Oh." He didn't ask her what supper would've been.

When she brought him his meal she said: "A tot and a plate makes sixpence." He handed her a shilling note and she came back and plunked down two copper pennies.

He said: "Pardon me, but sixpence tooked from a shilling leave sixpence, no?"

"That was a Massachusetts paper shilling."

"But, this is Massachusetts, no?"

"Has been all my life."

"And I gived to you a Massachusetts shilling..."

"That's what I said. You think I don't know one when I see one? The Commonwealth prints so many of'em I could paper the walls. Whenever Boston wants a new jetty they just print more money. You don't know from one day to the next if Massachusetts paper's worth eightpence hard money or tuppence or six."

"And what if..." André said queasily, "What if I had gived to you New York paper?"

"Oh, New York paper's good as gold. Maybe them high-nosed De Lanceys and Livingstons and such don't let the common people have a say in things like we do here, but at least they're dang careful not to let their money turn into shite-wipe."

André considered going back and having words with that storekeeper. It would be a simple enough matter to hold the storeman over his head and shake him till some New York money fell out of his pockets. But the last thing André wanted to do was draw attention to himself. And a few shillings wasn't worth losing at least four days backtracking, not when he had so much ground to cover before winter. So he ate his eggs and bacon, drank his watered rum and went on his way. But he did wonder how many different ways he'd have to be a fool before he grew a little wise.

The road levelled out and grew better-travelled. André saw another walker ahead of him, going in the same direction but not as fast. As the gap between them narrowed, André saw it was a gray-haired man who was walking with a staff, too—but using it as a prop, rather than something to swing jauntily in time to his footsteps. A little closer and he heard that the old man was singing an Acadian song, the one about the priest and the porcupine.

André joined in on the chorus. The old man stopped in his tracks and turned around. André said: "*Bonjour, grandpère*," and stuck out his hand. "I am André Melanson, from Piziquid. André à Thomas à Mathieu." It was an odd tang on his tongue to be speaking French aloud for the first time in two years.

The old man shook his hand and said: "Claude Bourgeois. Claude à Maurice à Charles. From Beaubassin. Funny... I don't recall hearing of any Melansons hereabouts."

"I haven't been hereabouts. I started from Albany in the spring."

"They gave you a pass from *Albany?*"

"A pass?"

"Yes, a pass like this," the old man took a piece of paper out of his pocket, "allowing me six days to go visit my daughter and new grandson. The English are so terrified that if Acadians are allowed to roam free we will blow up their powder houses or sneak away to guide the French navy into their harbors."

"Oh, but you see," André winked, "I'm not an Acadian. I am a Quaker born in Italy. Or so I say to any Englishman that asks me. You see, when we were loaded onto the ships at Piziquid I got put on a different ship from my family. My ship went to South Carolina, and the good God knows where theirs went. So I made my way from South Carolina to Philadelphia and from Philadelphia to Albany."

"*Formidable!*"

André almost blushed and shuffled his feet. Not since he'd left Philadelphia had he been able to speak to another Acadian about his stumblefooted journey, and now this *grandpère* of Acadia had pronounced what he'd done *formidable*.

"But," the old man went on, "you won't find your family hereabouts. I don't recall hearing of any Melansons hereabouts. Maybe they *were* sent to Massachusetts, but not this part of Massachusetts."

"I'm not looking for my family. I pray to find them someday, but I don't see much chance while the war's on. In the meanwhile, I'm going back to Acadia to join up with Beausoleil."

"You can't do that."

André laughed. "Oh, I think if I can manage to make my way from South Carolina to here, I can manage the little ways left from here to Acadia."

"Maybe so, but you can't join Beausoleil, except in prison. He surrendered last winter."

That knocked the jauntiness out of André's staff. He tried to convince himself that the old man had to be wrong, since he'd heard nothing in Albany about Beausoleil surrendering. But then, why would the people who passed through the Hendersons' wagonyard know or care what happened to some backwoods Acadian outlaw, when there were big doings like the capture of Louisbourg to gossip about?

André said lamely: "And the people who were in the woods with Beausoleil?"

"They all surrendered, too, and are imprisoned with him. Well, all except two dozen who were captured last fall and sent here."

"'Here'?"

"Here and there in Massachusetts, but all to Massachusetts."

"Was one of them... Eulalie La Tour?"

"La Tour? La Tour... A young woman?"

"Yes!"

"It seems to me there was a young woman named La Tour, who was apportioned to the town where Celina LeBlanc is."

André barely stopped his hands from grabbing the old man's lapels. "Where is that?"

"Let me see... If you follow along this road to the next town, there is a path behind the church running north through the woods. A half-day's walk or so along that path will bring you to the town where Celina LeBlanc is. Or you could follow the high roads all the way around, but that's—"

André had already turned to start off. He turned back for just long enough to shake the old man's hand and say: "Thank you," then charged off at a brisker pace than the one that had been eating up the miles from Albany.

The old man called from behind him: "Watch yourself, André à Thomas à Mathieu—*les Bostonais* aren't so easy to fool as other Englishmen." André waved over his shoulder and kept on swinging his boots in front of each other as fast as they could go.

Eventually he had to slow down a little before his head filled with blood. By the time he got to the next town it was nightfall. He wanted to keep on going, but if he tried blundering through the town in the dark, someone's watchdog was bound to bring people out to ask him his business. Even if he did manage to bluff his way through to the path the old man had described, fumbling blindly down a forest path wasn't going to get him anywhere but lost.

He still had enough light left to find a place in the woods to build a campfire that wouldn't be seen from the road. With a blanket wrapped around his shoulders and his oilcloth underneath him, he leaned back staring into that fire all night long.

As soon as dawn appeared, he was up and moving again. He found the church and the path behind it and headed north—sometimes jogging, sometimes holding himself to a walk to breathe himself out. It took him a good deal less than the old man's "half a day" to reach the town at the end of the path.

He walked from one end of the town to the other—his eyes flicking over and dismissing the well-kept houses and big barns—before he found the charity house. It was usually easy to spot a house where Acadians were being kept; it tended to be the most run-down and bedraggled house in town. Most English people took that as proof that Acadians were lazy and dirty. The fact was, why would anyone want to treat their prison cell like a home?

A thin woman with a fat nose was hilling potatoes in the yard of the charity house. André called out to her: "*Bonjour, madame.* I am André Melanson." The woman stopped her hoeing and looked at him quizzically; more quizzically, it seemed, than just because she'd suddenly been addressed by a stranger—more as though she was trying to remember something. But André had no time to wonder about the inner thoughts of signposts along the road. "I look for Eulalie La Tour."

"Ah! *That's* where I heard your name before. The first night Eulalie was here, she asked if any of us had heard anything of André Melanson from Piziquid." That warmed André's belly like a deep swallow of brandy. "But she doesn't live in this house anymore, but in a cabin in the woods. If you follow this road, you will see a red barn on the edge of town. Past there is a path to the left you can follow to her."

André exhaled: "Thank you," and set off.

The woman called after him: "André Melanson!" as though she had something more to say to him. But she'd already said all he needed to hear, so he just waved over his shoulder and kept moving.

He found the path easily enough and started up it. When he came to the end of it, he realized he was running and the haversack and fowling piece were bouncing crazily against his back. He slowed to a walk. There was a small clearing dotted with old stumps, and a cabin with smoke coming out of the chimney. As he crossed the clearing, he vaguely noticed that there was a garden plot hoed among the stumps, and a few chickens scratching about, but his eyes were fixed on the cabin door. As the door grew larger, he unslung his fowling piece and haversack and dropped them without breaking stride.

When he reached the door, he raised his hand to knock, then changed his mind and just pulled the door open and stepped across the threshold. A woman with her dark hair hanging down was standing at the hearth with her back to the door. She said: "Josette?" and turned her head to look over her shoulder.

When André saw those milk-and-hazelnut eyes, and the dream-familiar, sun-browned nose between them, he felt the weight of the last four years slide off his shoulders. Her eyes exploded wider, and she seemed to have some trouble working her jaw. She whispered: "André...?"

He wanted to say: "Eulalie," but couldn't get it out. So he just nodded stupidly and started toward her. As he moved across the room, she turned to face him. He stopped as though his feet had been nailed to the floor. She was pregnant.

She said rawly: "André... André, I'm *married* now."

He gaped into her eyes. Her eyes snapped shut and she angled her head away before opening them again. His mouth kept puffing open and closed like a stranded fish's. Finally a syllable came out of it: "Who...?"

"You know him." Her streaming eyes suddenly focussed past him at the doorway. "There he is now."

André heard footsteps approaching the cabin, and a cheery whistling of an Acadian tune. He turned to look. A man carrying a wooden toolbox appeared in the doorway. It was the tinker.

XLVIII

he roar that came out of André Melanson filled the cabin like a Fundy tide squeezed into a river channel, pressing Eulalie back against the fireplace. She shrieked: "No!" as André dove onto Cully and the two of them disappeared out the door.

Eulalie pushed off from the fireplace and ran after them, cupping her arms around her swollen belly. What she saw when she got out the door was so different from what she'd expected to see that it froze her in mid-step.

She'd expected to see André pinning Cully to the ground, and expected she would have to grab André's hair and try to drag him off before he throttled the life out of Cully. André had come down on top of Cully, all right, but it seemed that Cully had contrived to squirm around in mid-air so that André had only come down on his legs, with the knees bent upward. André was gasping to get his breath back, and trying to claw his way up Cully's chest to get his hands on his throat.

The toolbox and tools lay scattered around them. Cully got hold of the toolbox and slammed it down twice on the small of André's back before the handle broke off in his hand.

Eulalie screamed at both of them to stop. She wanted to do more than scream, but there was no room to get between them, and if she grabbed onto one of them from behind, the other one would keep tearing at him.

She realised what a fool she'd been to assume she'd have to try to save Cully from André. André did have enough strength in his arms to break Cully's back, but the closest he'd ever come to a fight was wrestling with his brothers. Cully had spent most of his life in places that could turn into a riot of broken bottles in an instant. His hard-learned way of simply defending himself was to do as much damage as he could as fast as he could. Eulalie never would have believed it possible that anyone could look like a terrified rabbit and a mad dog at the same time.

André was still trying to get his hands on Cully's throat and Cully was still trying to scrabble away backwards, with his hands scrambling frantically through the grass behind him for anything to hit with. His right hand found a hammer. He swung the side of it against the side of André's face. André went limp for long enough for Cully to get his legs out from under André's chest. Cully leaped to his feet, drove his bootheel down between André's shoulderblades, then planted his feet wide on the ground and raised the hammer high, fixing his eyes down at the back of André's head like it was an anvil.

Eulalie hurled herself forward, screaming: "Cully, no!" Her body hit his and they both went down, rolling away from each other.

Eulalie found her breath again, slowly pushed herself up onto her hands and knees and looked around. André was on his hands and knees as well, not three feet away from her, with blood coming out of his mouth and his cheek. She raised one hand toward him, but he grunted: "Nnn!" and jerked his head away, then staggered up to his feet and stumbled toward the path back to the road.

She levered herself up onto her knees. She saw a packsack and gun that weren't Cully's. She stood, picked them up and called: "André!" But he kept on moving away from her.

She followed after him, calling: "André! Your things!" He stopped but didn't turn around, just held his hands out open behind him. She put the packsack into one hand and the gun in the other and he started stumbling toward the path again. She reached her arm out after him, but he couldn't see it and she had no words for him to hear.

She turned back toward the cabin. Cully wasn't in the yard anymore; he was standing in the doorway with his rifle in his hands and Captain Namon's pistol in his belt, watching to make sure André and his fowling piece didn't turn around before they disappeared down the path. As Eulalie approached the doorway, Cully reached out his hand toward her, the same hand that had wielded the hammer. She pushed the hand away and went inside.

She slumped into her chair, propped her elbows on the table and dropped her face into her hands. From the doorway she heard Cully say: "Eulalie...?" She didn't raise her head. He said again: "Eulalie..." but this time she could hear in his tone that he wasn't asking her for something, he had something to tell her.

Eulalie wiped her eyes and turned toward the doorway. Cully took a couple of steps toward her, wincing with each step and leaning on his rifle like a cane. That explained why he hadn't put the rifle away, but it didn't explain why the pistol was still in his belt, and his shotpouch and powder flask slung over his shoulder.

He said: "Eulalie... That wasn't just because of you. He tried to kill me once before, at Fort Edward. He saw me in uniform. Eulalie—he knows who I am."

Now she understood. She said flatly: "He won't tell anybody."

"How can you be sure?"

"Because *he* wouldn't." She turned and covered her eyes with her hands again. But her hands couldn't stop her from still seeing too many things. Things like seeing André Melanson seeing her married to the Judas.

XLIX

ndré fumbled erratically down the path away from Eulalie. His lower back felt like a knife was going into it whenever one of his feet jarred down against the ground. His vision was blurred and sometimes not there at all. He came to the road and went straight across it into the woods on the other side. He kept staggering blindly further into the forest until he heard the sound of running water and turned in that direction.

He lowered himself gingerly onto the streambank, washed the blood and tears off his face, and scooped up mouthfuls of water. When he stood up and leaned against a tree to relieve himself, there was blood in his urine.

He waited out the day there. He didn't want anyone to see him. When the shadows began to join together, he went back to the road and started walking. He had no idea where he was going, only to get as far away as possible from Eulalie and the tinker. Soon he had nothing but starlight to see by, but all he needed to see was the few feet of road in front of his boots. He came to a town and walked straight on through it. Watchdogs barked, but no one came out to ask him his business.

When the sun came up, he went back into the woods to hide. He went on like that for several days and nights, he wasn't sure how many. The pain in his back and the left side of his face began to fade, but the other pain showed no signs of ever going away. Actually, when he thought about it, it wasn't so much pain as a hollowness. After the burning of Piziquid, and then his family disappearing, he'd been under the mistaken impression that he knew what it was to lose something.

He didn't eat much, but still, in not too long he'd gone through all the provisions in his knapsack and was faced with the fact that he'd either have to buy some food from someone or starve to death—although the second choice wasn't without its appeal. He was leery of talking to anyone face-to-face, afraid his voice would tremble or he might start crying. Nevertheless, when the sun came up the next time he kept on walking along the road instead of heading into the woods.

He came to a farm where a woman was feeding chickens in the yard. He said: "Good morning to you, ma'am. Might I buy from you a little flour and maybe a piece of the bacon or meat dry? I have money."

She said suspiciously: "You ain't from around here."

The old lie tasted dry in André's mouth, now that it had no purpose. "No. Born Italy, me. Now Quaker. I come from Albany to my ill sister by Worcester, but... She die before I do get there."

"Oh, I'm sorry. Sure, I'll be glad to sell you a little food. But if you're heading back to Albany, someone set you on the wrong road. This road loops a long ways around before meeting up with the high road to Springfield and the Berkshires. Once you come this far, though, I guess you might's well keep on a-going."

When he left the farm behind, André thought about what the woman had said: "Once you've come this far, you might as well keep on going." He hated the thought of going slinking back to the Hendersons', but he could think of nowhere else to go. He could stay there safe and earning a living until the war was over. Once it was over, whoever had won was bound to make some sort of decision about where Acadians would be allowed to live the rest of their lives. Not that the rest of his life meant much to him anymore.

On his way back across the Berkshire Hills, he saw the occasional twisted pine tree or pretty waterfall that he remembered from before. But now he was seeing them from the other side. The other side of a lot of things.

Not far from Albany he came upon a real inn, not just a cabin with a spare table in the corner. He'd passed it by on his way east, but now he had no reason to horde his money. The inn turned out not to have cider, but they did have beer, and a roast of beef spitted over the hearth. André surprised himself by actually enjoying the taste of food.

At another table, four men were talking loudly and banging their tankards down. One of them said: "Well, no, they ain't said nothing outright, but any dang fool can cipher out where we're going: up to kick the froggies out of Oswego and then over to Niagara to do the same. While the main army's whaling hell out of Quebec, we'll be finishing off the Frogs in the west. By the end of the summer it'll all be over except sweeping up Montreal."

One of the other men said: "Maybe. *Saying* it's one thing, doing it's another."

"Hell, it'll be like fish in a barrel. What with all the militias, and a regiment of bloodybacks, and the Iroquois, we'll be four—five thousand. The Frogs won't even know we're coming till we get there. Three years they been sitting in Oswego and we ain't done spit. They'll still be sitting there scratching themselves and yawning when we come over the walls."

André felt a twinge of life for the first time in weeks. From the war rumours he'd heard during his year in Albany, he had a rough idea of where Oswego was. At the upper end of the Mohawk River Valley was a portage to another river running north to Lake Ontario; where that river flowed into the lake was Fort Oswego. If an English army could march from Albany to there, he could certainly walk there, or buy a canoe from some Indians along the way. He could be the one to deliver the warning that saved the fort. Or he might die in the fighting. Either one would be better than drudging out his days making wagons that someone else would ride in.

When the war began, he'd only had a vague, traditional preference that the French might win. But since then the English had done so much to him, and to all Acadians, and here he was being given a chance to pay them back. And at least it was *something* he could do with his life.

He spent the night in the woods outside Albany, then skirted around the town, crossed the Mohawk River on a ferry and started walking up the Mohawk Valley. He was amazed at how much better he felt now that he had a purpose. Not that he felt *good*, but at least there was somewhere else for his mind to go besides that cabin in the woods in Massachusetts. Sometimes he even found himself laughing: the English were so afraid of Acadian spies that now they had created one.

At sunset on the second day he came to a tavern and went inside. All they had to eat was bread and cheese and onions, but they had very good beer. André explained to the barmaid that he was a Quaker born in Italy, going to visit his stricken sister further up the Mohawk Valley.

After his second quart of beer, André began to feel pleasant. He leaned back in his chair, humming to himself and pretending not to be listening to the men at the tables around him talking of the British general who would lead the expedition and how soon they might be called upon to march. When the barmaid refilled his tankard, André gave her a shilling note and waved away the notion of bringing back change.

The voices around him grew softer and more distant, making for a soothing, low murmuring like a mossy brook. When André finished his third quart measure, the barmaid didn't come to take his empty cup. A man in shirtsleeves and an apron did. The man said: "*Une autre, monsieur?*"

"*S'il vous plait.*"

The man jumped back and roared: "He is!" Instantly all the other men were on their feet and charging at André. André flung his table at their legs and stood up with his back against the wall. It felt wonderful to throw his fists into men's faces and see them go down, and to pick up a man by his neck and his belt and throw him.

But there were too many of them. In not too long André was staring numbly at the floorplank next to his nose, and someone was tying his hands behind his back.

There was an argument going on above him:

"Henry's got a rope—let's get 'er done!"

"No! It ain't right to hang a man without a trial!"

"He's a French spy, dammit! Spies get hung!"

"Not without a trial they don't! I swear to God I'll shoot the man what puts a rope around his neck!"

"Like hell you will!"

Another voice shouted: "Take him to the General!"

"I ain't haulin' him all the bloody way to Albany!"

"Not the bloodyback General—*our* General!"

Other voices shouted in agreement. André was dragged outside and flung into the back of a wagon. As the wagon set off, André struggled to sit up and blinked the blood out of his eyes. The moonlight showed several other men in the back of the wagon holding guns on him. Another wagon full of men were following behind. Some of them were holding torches and they were all yelling like New Year's.

The wagons halted in front of a high, stone wall with a fortress gate in it. A voice above the gate called down: "Who goes there?"

"We caught us a French spy and brung him to the General."

There was a pause and then the gate opened and a British officer stepped out. He said: "You say you caught a spy?"

"Yep, we did, and we brung him to the General for a trial afore we hang him."

"I see. Two of you, bring him inside. The rest, stay here."

"But, Ensign—!"

"*Two* of you only. Hurry along."

There was an argument as to who the two should be, and then André was dragged out of the wagon. With one man holding each of his bound arms, and the Ensign leading the way, they walked him through the gate and across a courtyard that seemed more like a lawn and garden than a parade square. On the far side of the courtyard stood a tall, stone building with lights showing in the upper windows but none from the ground floor. From inside it came a muffled chorus of male and female voices singing a song that wasn't a hymn.

The Ensign opened the building's door, and André's escorts hustled him along behind the Ensign. There was a tall hallway with a wide, open doorway to the left, where the music was coming from. The Ensign turned into that doorway and stamped to a halt.

The music trailed off. André squinted against the blaze of candles and saw why there'd been no light from the ground floor: the windows were bricked in.

The room was furnished like André imagined a governor's palace, except that there were painted warclubs and feathered headdresses hung up between the pictures on the walls. There was a harpsichord in one corner and other musical instruments here and there. The people in the room all turned their heads toward the doorway, and then most of them looked toward two people sitting on a brocaded settee.

The two people on the settee kept their eyes on the doorway, instead of looking to anyone else to tell them what to think. One of them was an immense, brown-wigged, middle-aged man with one leg propped on a footstool. The other was a very young, Indian woman decked in silk and silver, sitting with her feet tucked up under one hip and one hand resting on the immense man's immense shoulder.

The man growled in a voice like distant thunder: "Good evenin', Ensign. Ye'd better have a demmed good reason for interruptin' Lillibullero."

"These gentlemen, Sir William, say they've caught a French spy."

Sir William's eyes shifted to André like a hawk eyeing a squirrel. André tried to look him square in the eye, but it wasn't possible—the pupils in Sir William's eyes didn't quite align, so they seemed to be looking in two places at once. The eyes shifted to the man holding André's left arm, and Sir William said: "That so, Ephraim?"

"Sure enough is, Sir William."

"What gives ye to think he's a French spy?"

"Well, he sure to blazes ain't English, he speaks French, no one knows where to blazes he come from, and he was sitting all to hisself listening awful hard to us talking about the expydition."

The hawklike eyes shifted back to André. "D'ye speak English, boyo?"

André mumbled: "Some."

"Well now's the time to use it. Tell me who the divil ye are and why I shouldn't hang ye."

"I... I am Acadian. I have be in Albany these past years, have work there, but I thought to get away—back to Acadia. But, I find there is no Acadia anymore."

"Hm. I do have some sympathy for ye Acadians—I'm bound to have some sympathy for anyone who gets caught up in the schemes of that starch-assed wigstand Shirley." The only Shirley André could think of was Governor Shirley of Massachusetts, but he couldn't think of what he had to do with him. "But, sympathy still don't explain what the divil ye were doin' sneakin' up the Mohawk Valley in the direction of Oswego."

André groped for an answer. The young Indian woman took a sip from her wineglass and murmured something to Sir William in an Indian language that wasn't Mi'kmaq. Sir William threw back his head, bellowing laughter, slapped his propped-up leg and cut off his laughter with a gasp of pain. He caught his breath and said to André: "Where ye were workin' in Albany, can ye go back there?"

"Yes, sir."

"Good. Ensign, put the lad up in the barracks for the night and write him up a pass to go from here to Albany—but only to Albany."

Ephraim protested: "But, Sir William—"

"Now, Ephraim," Sir William waved him quiet, heaving himself to his feet and coming forward leaning on a cane. "Ye've been good and watchful, and when ye get back to the tavern serve out a tot of rum to everyone on me for bein' good and watchful. Ye may have caught a fish, maybe not—but if ye *have* it's only a small one that can do us no harm now, so we'll throw 'im back. D'ye happen to have a knife about yer person? Of course ye do. Cut the lad loose."

As the rope popped off his wrists, and Sir William herded the intruders to the door, André said: "Sir William, sir...? If I might to ask...? What is it the lady did say, to make you not to hang me?"

"Oh. Ahem. Well, translatin' from the Mohawk's never perfect... But, um, what Molly said, more or less, so to speak, was somethin' like: 'If *he's* a spy, God help the French.'"

L

ime was kind to Cully in Massachusetts. First, time persuaded Eulalie to start seeing him as her husband again, instead of as the man who'd taken a hammer to André Melanson's head. And then time delivered a beautiful baby daughter, Félicité. Félicité and Eulalie had more mid-wives in attendance than they knew what to do with. Old women from several neighbouring townships used the impending birth as an excuse to get a pass and come visit their cousins in the charity house.

As Félicité grew from a wrinkled, red, skinned rabbit into a baby, Cully tried to keep himself from looking for any signs of a resemblance to him. But it was hard not to do. It wouldn't have troubled him much if there was a chance Félicité might be the child of a husband or lover Eulalie had had before him, but that wasn't the case.

He would forget about it for days or weeks, and then chance to see the Reverend Mister Buckthorn or his hulking, oldest son on the village green. He would start thinking again about the fact that over three years on the Petitcodiac with Eulalie, he'd never got her pregnant. And none of the regimental whores in Halifax or any of his other postings had ever tried to dun him for being the father of one of the pack of ragged children who followed the women who followed the troops. The odds seemed to be heavy that Félicité was the daughter of the man who'd raped her mother.

But then time delivered the best gift of all. When Félicité was a year old, Cully caught her mother red-handed. Maybe it was an old wives' tale that the palms of some women's hands turned red when they were pregnant, but it had happened the last time. As Eulalie grew heavy with her second child, Cully ceased to worry himself about who Félicité's physical father was. He'd never asked for absolute proof, just even odds.

Time was kind to the British Empire as well. The Commonwealth of Massachusetts declared days of public thanksgiving for the capture of Quebec and Niagara.

The next year they celebrated the fall of Montreal, which meant there were no French flags left flying in North America except far-off Louisiana. Some of *les Bostonais* seemed a bit apologetic about their celebrations when Cully and Eulalie wandered by. They didn't understand that most Acadians didn't deeply care which side won the war, just as long as they did it soon.

News came from Nova Scotia that finally gave Acadians something to celebrate. During a grand ball in Halifax to honour the victors of Montreal, Governor Lawrence had stepped out to take the air and caught a chill. The word of mouth the news-sheets didn't mention was that he'd been piss-drunk and passed out in the bushes on a frosty night. Although only fifty years old, and a huge and hearty military man, Governor Lawrence was dead of pneumonia. Every Acadian who'd ever cursed Charles Lawrence's name—and every Acadian had—liked to think that their curse had had some small hand in his untimely death.

With Lawrence gone, and the war in North America finished, most of the Acadians in town thought they'd soon be allowed to go home. Cully didn't have the heart to tell them that with French and British forces still fighting over other parts of the world, the Lords of Trade weren't likely to turn their attention to small matters like ten thousand uprooted Acadians.

But the Commonwealth of Massachusetts was so confident there was no more French threat that they offered free land to Acadians—in a part of the province that had been settled long ago and then abandoned because of Indian raids. Cully wasn't sure whether the Commonwealth's theory was that Acadians got along with Indians well enough to allay any danger, or that a few scalped Acadians wouldn't mar the landscape.

Cully was inclined to take the offer. Free land was free land, and it didn't matter to him whether he lived out the rest of his days in Massachusetts or Acadia or the Outer Hebrides, as long as Eulalie and the children were with him. But he could see that Eulalie felt the same as all the other Acadians in Massachusetts: to accept free land here would be to accept that her exile was permanent, and that her children and grandchildren would either have to grow up to be *Bostonais* or be forever *les étrangers* living in the corners.

So Cully let it lie, and continued to think of their home in Massachusetts as no more permanent than the wickerwork cottage on the Petitcodiac. He walked into town one day, as he usually did at least once a week to see if the storekeeper had overheard anyone muttering about a leaky pot or sprung doorhinge. The weekly news-sheets from Boston were in. Cully bought one, along with a few odds and ends that Eulalie wanted, then headed back home, glancing at the news-sheet as he ambled along in the summer sunshine. His eyes caught an item on the bottom corner of the page that stopped him dead and chilled him to the bone.

After a moment, he realized he was making himself conspicuous standing frozen on the roadside staring at the paper in his hand. So he ordered his feet to start marching again, while his eyes re-read the words that refused to change. He'd broken out in a sweat, his hands were shaking, and he kept glancing around to see if anyone was watching him.

The item was obviously an old announcement that had been printed to fill up space: ONE HUNDRED POUNDS REWARD!

Deserted from His British Majesty's Land Forces, Sergeant Gilbert "Cully" Robin, sometimes calling himself Gilbert Brossard, who did on 12th October 1758 most foully MURDER Captain Namon of the aforesaid Land Forces nearabout Fort Cumberland in His Majesty's province of Nova Scotia. The aforesaid ROBIN is of medium slender build and lank hair and when last seen wore a beard with a smattering of grey. Whomsoever will apprehend the said ROBIN and convey him to the nearest of His Majesty's gaols or military establishment shall be entitled to the above reward.

Even once Cully was safely on the path from the road to the cabin, he couldn't stop his head from jerking around to look over his shoulder. A hundred pounds was an immense amount of money for the British Army to post for a deserter, even one who'd supposedly murdered an officer. Cully guessed that most of the money must have been put up by Captain Namon's family, whoever they were. Regardless where it came from, there it was in black and white.

Eulalie—spraddle-legged from the weight of Félicité's baby brother or sister in her belly—was hoeing in the garden while Josette pulled weeds. Eulalie looked up at him and grinned: "Did you remember this time to buy the—*What's wrong?*"

He had to moisten his throat before he could say: "I'll tell you inside." Eulalie didn't question, just turned and started toward the cabin, using her hoe as a staff.

Cully looked at Josette, weighing whether she should know. She was almost as tall as Eulalie now, and starting to bud breasts. Maybe she wasn't old enough yet to be trusted with such a secret, but she was more than old enough to talk, and carelessly sputter out the wrong name in the wrong company if she didn't have a damn good reason not to. He waved his arm toward Eulalie disappearing into the cabin and said: "You, too, Josette."

When he followed Josette inside, Eulalie was just straightening her back from making sure that Félicité was still asleep in the cradle he'd made. Eulalie sat down at the table and Josette stood close beside her. Eulalie looked up at Cully with anxious eyes and said: "What is it?"

Cully read it to them, translating the more tortuous anglicisms into French. When he finished, there was a silence. Both Eulalie and Josette had their right hands over their mouths. Eulalie lowered her hand and breathed out: "Did you?"

"Did I what?"

"Did you kill him?"

"No! Why would I? I might've wanted to at times, but not after he let me go. And if it wasn't for his nasty little scheme I'd never have met you. But I think the date is the same as the last day I saw him, as far as I can remember. I told you I heard a gunshot that I thought was someone coming after me. Maybe it was a Mi'kmaq, or someone come down from the Petitcodiac to get revenge."

"But... you said he didn't tell anyone at Fort Cumberland who you were."

"I thought not. Maybe he mentioned it to one of the other officers. Or bloody wrote it down somewhere—he loved to have things written down on his bloody lists and stacks of paper. Or maybe one of the garrison thought back and recognized me, once it became something worth thinking about. However the hell it happened, they sure to Christ know Gilbert Brossard was Cully Robin."

He turned to Josette and said fervently: "So you must never, never let it slip to anyone—not even to Félicité or the new one or the ones that might come after— that my real name is Robin."

"But," Josette protested, "you didn't do it."

Cully looked to Eulalie. Eulalie said: "Josette, *you* know he didn't, and I know he didn't, but the English judges would never believe him. Or even if they did, once they had him in their hands they would hang him for a deserter."

He saw that Eulalie was trembling. He leaned across to put his hand on hers and said: "There's little danger of that here, so long as everyone thinks my name's La Tour. It's an old notice, and who would think that a deserter who murdered an English officer would choose to run to an English colony?"

Nevertheless, he shaved his beard off again—he'd grown it back because Eulalie liked it and he didn't like having to face a razor every morning. After a month or two he stopped jumping every time somebody tapped him on the shoulder. But he still wished to hell he'd never let himself get known around the area as "*Cully* the Tinker."

LI

⚜

No one in Albany was afraid of French armies or French spies anymore, so André had given up the porous fiction that he was a Quaker born in Italy. Since his job at the Hendersons' meant the county didn't have to be responsible for him, and he had no plans of trying to sneak away from Albany again, there was no reason he couldn't be openly who he was and spend his Sundays with his own kind. He would wait out the tail-end of the war like every other Acadian, just better-fed than most.

One Tuesday after supper he felt restless instead of tired, and going to knock on the Hendersons' door to spend the evening playing whist didn't seem like the solution. He sat fidgeting in his room in the stables for a while, then put some money in his coat pocket and went out.

He figured he would walk across town to the charity house; if he was feeling less restless by the time he got there, he'd just turn around and come back. When he got about three-quarters of the way, it was clear he wasn't going to be sleepy. He didn't like to go into the charity house without bringing a little food or something, but all the shops were closed. There was an inn not far out of his way. He bought two loaves of bread from the inn's kitchen, for a good deal more money than they would've cost him from a bakery. But what was the good of money if it couldn't put a bit of a smile on a weary face?

There was still light showing in the charity house's parchment window. André knocked softly anyway, in case some of the people inside were already asleep. The door was opened by bald and bearded Sylvain d'Entremont—Sylvain à Gregoire à Anselme—who led the White Mass every Sunday. André said: "Good evening, Uncle, I hope I didn't wake you."

"No, no, André. Come in, come sit."

They moved toward the table and the lone candle, both of them keeping their voices low for the sake of the blanket-covered clumps ranged around the floor. André handed Sylvain the loaves of bread. Sylvain smiled and said: *"Maybe* I'll save them till tomorrow when everyone else is awake." But the smile seemed a little forced, as though something had happened that gave Sylvain even more reason than usual to feel glum. "Well, have you come for another lesson?"

Sylvain was trying to teach André how to read English, with the stack of old news-sheets Sylvain had collected from garbage piles and roadsides, painstakingly smoothing out the wrinkles and scraping off the mud. André didn't feel like he was all that good at learning, and he wasn't all that interested, but it was something to do and it allowed them both to say that André's loaves of bread and such weren't charity.

André said: "I think not tonight, Uncle."

"Just as well. I'm not feeling very cheerful. We heard today from a cousin traveling with a pass from down-river..." Sylvain sighed. "Beausoleil surrendered."

André blinked at him. "That was three years ago, or more."

"Who told you that?"

"An old man in Massachusetts. The winter after Louisbourg fell, Beausoleil's people were starving, so he took them in to Fort Cumberland and surrendered."

Sylvain rubbed a hand across his bald head, puttered his lips and said: "Why didn't you tell me that then, and I could've told you—well, but then you were still pretending you weren't Acadian. You see, André, the English news-sheets always get things *half* right. Yes, the winter after Louisbourg Beausoleil brought several hundred starving people in to Fort Cumberland under a white flag. But all Beausoleil was there to do was negotiate the terms of their surrender. Once that was done, Beausoleil slipped away again.

"Beausoleil and his brother and their families and a few others have been living in the woods along the Miramichi for the past three years, still making raids against the English. The English could conquer Louisbourg, and Quebec, and Montreal, but they couldn't conquer a little band of Acadians on the Miramichi. But now, finally, even Beausoleil has surrendered."

André felt sick. He got up, fumbled out: "I'm sorry, I have to go," and left Sylvain with no further explanation. Once outside, he let his boots decide which direction to walk in, while his mind was busy whacking itself against a stone wall for being such a fool. Three years. Three years he'd been living like a whipped dog in an English town when he could've been running with the wolves along the Miramichi. Three years he'd been building wagons for the people who'd burned Piziquid and sent the tinker to Ardoise valley, when he could've been helping Beausoleil fight them. All because it would never cross his gullible mind to question what an old man said to him on the side of a road.

The worst of it was that he should've known. As soon as Sylvain told him that Beausoleil hadn't surrendered when the others did, he'd realized he should've known.

Everything that he'd ever heard about Joseph Brossard *dit* Beausoleil said that Beausoleil was a different kind of man from André Melanson. Beausoleil wouldn't give up just because rumours said he should, or because he'd got his nose a little bloodied. Beausoleil would keep on fighting beyond the end of hope.

André heard laughing. He stopped and looked around. His boots had carried him down to the waterfront. Mr. Henderson had told him stories of what the Albany waterfront had been like before the war, with fur traders and boatmen coming down the Mohawk River and the Hudson. From the sounds of the laughter and shouting and drunken singing, the fur traders had decided the war was over.

There was a tavern with light streaming out the windows. André went inside. The place was filled with smoke, rough-looking men and even rougher-looking women. Some of the women were Indian, probably Mohawk.

The tavern wasn't quite so full that André couldn't find an empty, corner table with no one nearby. When the barmaid came around he asked for rum and water. He'd gotten better at getting drunk since that night in the Mohawk Valley. Not that he did it that often, but at least now he knew that it wasn't the world that was getting soft around the edges.

The barmaid came back and thumped his cup and pitcher down on the table—not surly, just bored. He peeled a shilling note off the folded roll he'd tucked into his coat pocket. She smiled at him and said: "You're not from around here."

"I have be in Albany now four year and more. Acadian, me. I work at Henderson wagonyard."

"Oh, I heared of you. They say you can carry a anvil in each hand."

"Well, not *each*."

She laughed as though he'd said something clever. Maybe it was, by accident. He watched her sashay over to the bar, swinging her hips, and watched her talking to the man behind the counter—a tall man with a blonde beard. She had brown hair with red highlights, and she wore it tied loosely with a purple ribbon.

When the barmaid came back with his change, instead of setting it down on the table she leaned forward to put it in his hand. Her blouse was very low and thin, more like an undershift, and when she leaned down he could see her breasts as far as the rims of two rose-pink circles. He guessed she was a few years younger than he was, despite the sharp lines around her eyes. When she released the coins into his hand, her fingertips nudged back and forth across his palm before lifting away, like scratching an itch.

He handed her a penny tip and she gave him a smiling, little curtsey. When she smiled the hard lines around her eyes turned into twinkle-rays. She said: "What's your name, sir?"

"Melanson. André Melanson."

"Well, André, I'm Addy. If you want anything, just holler out 'Addy' and I'll come."

André sat drinking his watered rum and pondering the difference between men like Beausoleil and men like André Melanson—men who stood up to life and got something back from it, and men who just endured. André also watched Addy working her way around the room—snatching off a man's tricorn hat and putting it back on him backwards, laughing when one man slapped her rump, pulling the nose of another man who tried it... There was another barmaid patrolling the tables as well, but André didn't notice her much. It seemed to him at times that Addy was sneaking glances back at him, watching him watching her. Probably he was just imagining it.

Addy came back to André's table with another clay jar of Jamaica rum. She said: "Figured you'd be 'bout ready for another." He wasn't quite, but he didn't mind. As he peeled off another shilling note, she stood holding the jar instead of setting it down. She said: "Mind if I takes a sip?"

"No, do."

She took a healthy swallow of straight rum, licked her lips and sighed, "Thank you. A girl gets awful thirsty runnin' tankards around, but if I bought from the bar every time my throat got dry, I'd finish up the night owin' *them* money."

André said: "I could buy for you drink, if you like."

Her smile was broader than before. "I sure *would* like. And another one for you, long as I'm goin'?"

André had barely poured from the jar she'd just brought, but he said: "Why not?" That made her laugh again. She winked at him and went back to the bar. It seemed to André that she took more time talking to the man behind the counter than was necessary to get two jars of rum. Probably the barman was giving her trouble for pausing to take a drink for herself.

Addy came back and set two fresh jars on the table, plunked down on the chair cornered to André's, arched her back to stretch stiff muscles—incidentally pushing her breasts out so that André could see her nipples through the blouse—and fanned her face with her hand. André was feeling a little warm himself.

They talked for a while about the weather, and the cost of rum finally coming down from war-prices, and about André. Addy thought it was a crying shame what had been done to the Acadians. André shrugged that that was life. Addy went to get two more jars. This time the barman didn't argue with her.

Halfway through her second jar, Addy leaned across the table on one elbow to talk closely to André. He could feel her breasts pressing softly against his arm. Under the table, her hand settled onto his thigh. She said: "What I earn in wages and tips here wouldn't keep a cat alive. So, sometimes, when a nice man comes in here—they don't come in here often... I took a shine to you, André. Five shillings."

André thought about it. He was twenty-six years old and if a wagon fell on him tomorrow he would die without ever knowing what it was to be with a woman. Oh, he'd had dreams some nights that he remembered in the morning, but he had no way of knowing whether that was what it really felt like. Who was he being faithful to— Eulalie?

André separated a five-shilling note from the sheaf in his pocket, tore it in half and held out one half to Addy. She winked at him and laughed low in her throat. "I knew you was no fool, André. I wouldn't try to cheat you—I'd be cheating me, too— but some tarts would. There's a shed out back—you'll see the light. Wait a minute afore you follow me."

Her hand crept further up his thigh and gave him a pat. Then she rose up off her chair like a cat stretching. She moved through the room and out the door. André took another couple of swallows of rum and then followed her. It wasn't just the rum that made walking a little difficult.

He found the shed—the light of a candle through an open doorway. There were barrels and crates stacked against the walls, and in one corner a straw-tic mattress with a couple of blankets. Addy was lounged back on the mattress with her skirt pulled up to her waist. Her hip bones pointed down and in toward a triangle of red-brown curls.

André closed the door behind him. As he moved toward Addy, she put one hand down to the triangle and moved one finger up and down, licking her lips. He saw a trace of bright pink on either side of her finger. He stopped at the edge of the mattress, reached his hands up to unbutton the flap of his breeches, then suddenly was too embarrassed at the thought of standing in front of her standing in front of her. So he knelt down between her legs and leaned his head over to blow out the candle.

She put her hand up to his cheek and said: "No, I want to see you," then unbuttoned his breeches herself. His whole body jolted him when she wrapped her hand around him. She said huskily: "Oh my, André, I don't know if I'm that big," and pulled him toward her.

The shed door crashed open and a voice roared: "What the hell are you doing with my wife?"

André rolled away from Addy, fumbling to button up his breeches. It was the tall, blonde-bearded man from behind the bar, looming in the doorway with a belaying pin in his hand. He stomped toward the mattress, shouting: "Damn your eyes, Addy, I told you I'd kill you if you ever did it again!"

André looked at Addy. She had pulled her skirt back down and covered her face with her hands. She sobbed through her fingers: "Don't hurt him, Eli..."

André stood up slowly, with his arms hanging slack by his sides. He said to the barman: "She did not tell me she was marry..."

Eli snorted back: "That what you gonna tell *your* wife—'I didn't know that woman they caught me fucking was a married woman'?"

"I have no wife."

"Then is that what you gonna tell the people you work for, or the people at your church?"

André looked from the barman to Addy and back again. He said bitterly: "Maybe if I give to you some money you will forget this did happen...?"

"Well..." Eli rubbed the back of the hand holding the belaying pin across his mouth, as though thinking about it. "It's hard to put a price on a man's pride."

"I already did give her money."

"You callin' my wife a whore?"

"No, sir. Not I. But I will give you what you ask for." André's right arm shot up from his side and smacked his fist into Eli's chest. It was too abrupt for André to get much of his shoulder into it, but Eli dropped the belaying pin and staggered back gasping, pressing his hands to his chest.

André stepped toward him, holding up both fists and saying: "Is that enough I pay you? I have more..."

Eli's backward stumbling reached the doorway. André pushed him outside, saw him trip over his feet and fall, then yanked the shed door shut and pulled the latchstring inside. There was a bent nail on the doorframe at just the right place to wrap the latchstring around.

André turned back to Addy. She seemed to be looking at him differently than she had before. The smile that crept across her face was soft and evil—but not an unpleasant kind of evil. She reached her hands down to the hem of her skirt and said: "Well, André—looks like you're gonna make a honest whore of me after all."

LII

⚜

ulalie was whiling away a rainy day inside when Celina's oldest son yanked open the door and shouted: "*Maman* says come to the house! The *Grand Dérangement* is over!"

Eulalie said: "What...?" But already he was gone, leaving the door hanging open. She stood there numbly for an instant, asking herself if he'd really said what she thought he'd said. Then she scooped up Félicité, told Josette to grab baby Gilbert out of his cradle, and charged out into the pelting rain without even a shawl. Cully was away in a town down the road, putting new rivets in someone's old horsecollar, but he would know where they would be if they weren't home.

The charity house was giddy with laughter and jumping and singing. A bottle of cider hoarded away for medicinal thimblefuls was being poured out freely. Celina put her hands on Eulalie's shoulders and said: "It's true, Eulalie. The selectman came to tell me. The King of France and the King of England signed a peace treaty. All Acadia belongs to England now, but Acadians are free to go back there if we want."

Eulalie laughed, tears cascading out of her eyes, "If we *want*?" Celina laughed, too, and hugged her, almost smothering Félicité between them.

A few Acadians from neighbouring towns wafted in, now that there was no more reason for *les Bostonais* to order where Acadians could wander. People were making plans and talking about the future for the first time in eight years, gabbling away at each other like they'd just been given the gift of speech.

Eulalie was sitting feeding Gilbert when Cully appeared in the doorway, looking cheerfully bemused at the capering lunatics inside. Eulalie cupped her free hand around the back of the downy little head and hurried to Cully with his son's mouth still clasped around her nipple. Cully opened his mouth to ask if everyone had lost their minds, but before he could say a syllable she burst out with the explanation.

Instead of throwing his arms around her and crowing, he hunched his shoulders, crossed his arms and stared grimly at the floor. She wanted to shake him and ask him why he couldn't at least be happy for her happiness, even if going back to Acadia meant nothing to him. Then she realized that going back meant a lot more than nothing to him.

Eulalie turned away from Cully and went and sat dumbly in a corner, no longer part of the jubilation. As she abstractedly shifted Gilbert from her breast to her shoulder and stroked his back, she wondered what the odds were on his father living very long in the valley of Ardoise. If Cully were just another deserter who'd disappeared years ago, no one would be looking very hard for him. But this deserter had a price on his head for the murder of a British officer.

In Massachusetts, the killing of Captain Namon was only an old news-sheet item about a minor happenstance in a distant province. But Eulalie had no doubt that when the reward notice first came out it had been nailed to every gatepost in Nova Scotia. It might even have been posted anew, now that Acadians who might have information would be coming home. A hundred pounds was a lot of money. Not only would it make everyone who'd known Cully as a soldier very eager to recognize him again, it might even tempt some of the people who'd known l'Anglais along the Petitcodiac.

The deliriously shifting and swaying bodies crowded into the cabin occasionally parted enough for Eulalie to catch glimpses of Cully slumped in a far corner with his elbows on his knees. She thought of going and telling him that he should stay in Massachusetts and she would take the children back to Acadia—maybe after five years or so the reward notices would be far enough in the past that he'd be safe to come and join them.

She thought about a lot of things. She thought of Cully going in to Fort Cumberland to give himself up, and then making his lone way through hundreds of miles of wilderness to find her. She thought of him throwing off his uniform at Fort Edward and riding through the night to warn her and Beau-père. She thought of the night last week when once again she'd woken up in the dark and started crying when she realized that walking through the wildflowers in the valley of Ardoise had only been a dream.

Eulalie stood up, settled Gilbert into the crook of her arm, and went to where Josette was happily chair-dancing with Félicité on her lap. She said: "Come along, Josette. We're going home."

"I know!" Josette beamed up at her. "And when we get there we'll dig up the money Papa buried and buy Félicité a pony and—"

"No. We're not... We're not going back to Acadia."

"What? Why—?"

"I'll explain it to you when we're back in the cabin. Come along."

"But—!"

"Please, Josette. I'll tell you when we're alone, and you'll understand."

As Josette stood up reluctantly, Eulalie made her way over to Cully. He looked up at her the same way Josette had when she'd got her foot caught in the snare and the English soldiers were upon them. Eulalie said: "We'll stay in Massachusetts."

"No." He shook his head and tried to bluster it out. "I'm a good liar, and if I don't poke my nose in places where there's garrisons—"

"It's too much of a risk, and you know it is. What would I tell Félicité and Gilbert—that I would rather see their father hang than see them grow up in Massachusetts?"

"Well..." he elevated his scanty eyebrows, "they might agree with you."

Eulalie realized that the music and jovial noises had stopped and everyone was looking at her and Cully. She would have to give them some kind of explanation. She said: "We won't be going with you. You see... when Cully was with Beausoleil he did such a good job of fighting the English there's a reward for him in Nova Scotia. When Josette is old enough to take care of herself, she can go back and claim her father's farm—and any Acadian young man she wants, once they see how much land she owns. Now... we have to go." She turned and went out the door quickly before anyone could say anything else.

Within a month, she and Cully and the children were the only Acadians left in town. In some of the neighbouring townships there was still a smattering of Acadians, who'd grown so used to living among les Bostonais they saw no call to go back to Acadia and start over. Eulalie told herself that if that was good enough for them, it should be good enough for her. Herself didn't listen very well.

Cully tried to seem enthusiastic about getting some of the free land Massachusetts had offered Acadians, and kept nagging the selectman to ask in Boston whether the offer still stood now that Acadians were free to leave Massachusetts. Eulalie knew that the reason Cully could only try to be enthusiastic was that she wasn't doing a very good job of pretending she was. She tried shaming herself into pretending harder—after all, Cully had given up his entire past and future for her, and had never let her glimpse a twinge of regret. But then, he hadn't seen his as much of a future, or much of a past.

LIII

ndré and Mr. Henderson were fitting an iron rim onto a wagonwheel—Mr. Henderson sitting wedged on a high-legged stool with arms—when Sylvain d'Entremont burst into the courtyard yelling: "André! André! France and England have signed a treaty! The English declare that now as they've won the war we can go home!"

André dropped his tools and he and Sylvain à Gregoire à Anselme threw their arms around each other. Then Sylvain stepped back and added bitterly: "Well, they say we *can* go home, but they don't say *how*. They found it easy enough to muster a fleet of ships to carry us away, but now they say it's up to us to find our own way back. We none of us have enough money to pay sea passage."

André did, but he didn't like the idea of throwing away his savings on a leisurely sail down the Hudson River to New York City and from there to Piziquid. Once he got home, he'd need every shilling he could lay his hands on to start rebuilding from the ashes.

"So," Sylvain said, "what some of us have decided is we're going to walk—up through Massachusetts and all the way around the bay to Piziquid and Grand-Pré and Annapolis Royal. If we start soon, we should be home before winter."

André said: "That's what I was going to do when it was still against the law. If it made sense then, it makes even more sense now."

When André explained to Mr. Henderson what all the noise in French had been about, Mr. Henderson said: "Well, André, I'm happy for you, but I don't know where I'll ever find another pair of shoulders like yours."

There was an old wagon in a corner of the work yard that André and Mr. Henderson had been refitting when they had nothing else to do. André decided to buy it for the journey, to carry provisions and camp gear and the old people. He figured he should be able to resell it when they came to the northernmost New England settlements and had to take to the trails through the woods. But Mrs. Henderson flatly declared the wagon wasn't for sale, and gave it to him instead.

The Acadians set off from Albany like a holiday parade. When they stopped at night, the conversation around the campfires was joyful and wistful at the same time:

"In a corner of my place, by my wife's garden, there's an old willow tree whose roots keep getting caught in the plough. But I could never bring myself to chop it down, because so many songbirds nest in it every year..."

"From my back window you can see Cape Blomidon, even though it's more than a day's ride..."

"The *aboiteau* in front of my place will need some mending, after eight years and more..."

André found it awkward to suddenly have a future again. He'd gotten into the habit of only having a present and a past. He tried to confine his picturing of the future to rebuilding the farm and reuniting with his family. He had no doubt that in whatever colony they'd been exiled to, his mother and father were already making plans to get back to Piziquid—perhaps would even be there before him. He wondered how many of his brothers and sisters had managed to live through the *Grand Dérangement*.

There was no good to be had from letting his imagination roam to any other possible aspects of his future. Thinking of Eulalie, or of marrying any woman other than her, was like swallowing broken glass.

But despite his best efforts to keep his mind close-reined, when the road came out of the Berkshire Hills and into Massachusetts he couldn't fend off memories that made him want to pull his hat down over his face. The only blessing was that Sylvain and the other older people making decisions thought it best to stick to the high road, instead of passing through back-country towns like the one where Eulalie lived with the tinker.

In the towns they did pass through, some of the Massachusetts Acadians quickly threw their few possessions in a sack and joined the walking caravan. One of them was one of the boys André used to hunt frogs with along the banks of the Piziquid River. His jaw dropped when he saw André, and he sputtered: "How did you get back from England?"

"I never been to England."

"But... From the deck of the ship I got loaded onto at Piziquid, I saw all you Melansons getting loaded onto the ship that ended up going to Virginia. The Governor of Virginia said Governor Lawrence and his plan could go to the devil, so the ship sailed to England and dumped the people there."

"No," André said wearily. "No, you didn't see *all* us Melansons loaded onto that ship." But if he knew his mother and father, they would find their way home even from England. It would just take a little longer. And he would have a new house and barn waiting for them.

The Massachusetts Acadians told the Albany Acadians that the high road ran east almost to Boston before branching north. As they drew nearer to Boston, André found himself wrestling with something he'd wrestled with many times since he'd crawled away from Eulalie's cabin. He knew of a simple way to rid his life and hers of the tinker. All he had to do was walk into the garrison in Boston and tell them that in such-and-such a town in Massachusetts lived a man pretending to be Acadian who was really a deserter from the British Army.

LIV

⁂

Eulalie heard a horse galloping up the path from the road. She knew it couldn't be Cully—his old nag hadn't been acquainted with a gallop in ten years, if ever. She stuck her head out the door to look.

It *was* Cully—with the poor, brokendown relic straining and panting beneath him, its white-rimmed eyes infected with the mad gleam in its rider's. Cully reined in and jumped down, panting as hard as the horse and grinning like a fool. He gasped out: "Beausoleil!" and herded Eulalie into the house where he could flop down on a chair.

Eulalie waited until he looked to be catching his breath again, then said: "Beausoleil...?"

"He's gone and got himself into trouble again." That didn't seem like much to grin about. "He and all the others imprisoned at Halifax got set free after the war. But it seems a while ago Beausoleil got arrested in Piziquid on suspicion of something-or-other, and he happened to have on him a letter from the French ambassador in London—saying all Acadians were still beloved subjects of the King of France regardless who ruled Nova Scotia.

"Well, that was the last straw. The new governor gave Beausoleil permission to charter a ship to take himself and his family, and whatever other Acadians wanted to go with them, wherever the hell out of British territory they wanted to go.

"Beausoleil made an Acadian Ark of the ship. A few hundred Nova Scotia Acadians chose to go with him, and they sailed down to the French islands in the Caribbean to load on the Acadians who ended up there in the *Grand Dérangement*—however many of them survived the tropic fevers. Then Beausoleil means to take them all to French Louisiana and build a New Acadia."

He reached across the table to take her hand. "You see, Eulalie, we can go there. British law can't touch me in Louisiana. And you and the children will be surrounded by Brossards and Thibodeaus and Beliveaus and Perrins and second cousins of your second cousins, and so many people we spent three years with on the Petitcodiac. And Josette will have young men come calling on Tuesday and Thursday evenings and Sunday afternoons. And there'll be White Masses and *fais-do-dos*, and *corvés* and…"

She just said: "Oh, Cully," and squeezed his hand like a rinse rag. It meant saying good-bye to her old home forever, but it would mean the children would have a place where they belonged. She murmured: "*Merci au bon Dieu.*"

"Well, *merci à* Beausoleil, as usual—no blasphemy intended. I don't know if he was dropped on his head as a baby or why it is, but the man doesn't seem to grasp the notion of giving in. Even when they finally got him cornered, he's always looking for a seam between the walls."

Eulalie smiled. She knew of another man like that, even though he wasn't the kind to rally other people around him.

"Once we get settled there permanent," Cully said, "we'll find a good, Acadian carpenter to build you a loom."

"Oh good, more work for me to do." They both laughed like giddy children. Then Eulalie said: "Thank you for thinking of that, Cully. But we're not there yet."

"Well, we don't have the money to take a ship to Louisiana, but one of the things Celina's husband made to try to sell to *les Bostonais* was a cart—only none of them wanted it, so it's still sitting rotting behind the charity house. We can head south on the cart till we get near the Mississippi River, then sell the cart and whatever else we have to to buy an old boat or the makings for a raft, then just float down the Mississippi to New Orleans. And I can make a little money along the road mending farmwives' stewpots—a lot more than I can make around here anymore, since like a cully I went and mended so many things so good they don't need mending again. I don't know how long it'll take us to get there, but how hard can it be to find the Mississippi River? I worked it all out on the way home."

It turned out they couldn't start immediately, as one of the wheels on the cart needed a little mending. While Eulalie was packing their things together she caught glimpses through the doorway of Cully tinkering with the cartwheel. It put her in mind of the pair of cartwheels André Melanson had been labouring on so doggedly for her ten years ago. She wondered if André was still alive, and whether he'd found his way home to Piziquid. She prayed he wasn't one of the ones who'd gone to Louisiana.

They set off on a misty morning, planning to camp by the side of the road each night instead of wasting money on inns. They spent the second night camped on the edge of a town. As Eulalie was packing up camp gear and children to get on the move again, Cully rummaged in the cart and said: "Oh damn."

"What's wrong?"

"Captain Namon's pistol. I left it behind."

"No, I wrapped it up in the spare blanket."

"I know you did. But you can look for it, it won't be there. I took it out again to make sure it wasn't loaded, and I must've set it down on the table or on the ground. There's a livery stable in this town. The pistol's worth ten times the cost of hiring a saddlehorse for the day. You can keep on going and I'll catch up with you. Once I've brought the horse back to the livery stable, I can still *walk* twice as fast as this poor old sack of bones can drag the cart. If I haven't caught up with you by nightfall, just stop and camp and I'm bound to find you even if your campfire goes out—I'll be able to hear Josette snoring from a mile down the road."

Josette said: "Cully!"

Cully affected to ignore Josette, and shrugged at Eulalie: "I'm sorry to throw a stick in the works just by being forgetful, but you knew you were marrying a cully." But he didn't seem sorry, he seemed almost giddy, like a dog let off its chain. Eulalie thought maybe he'd just got caught up in being silly after having to admit he'd been silly enough to forget the pistol.

Before heading off to the livery stable, he slung his rifle over his shoulder, saying: "If I get lucky enough to stumble across a slow-witted deer along the road, I'll keep the horse till I catch up with you. A whole deer's-worth of meat would be worth a lot more to us than an extra day's horse-hire."

When he was gone, she hitched the cart up and started ambling south again. When the sunlight started slanting from the west, she started worrying and looking back over her shoulder. But before the sun set she heard him shouting: "Eulalie!" behind her.

She reined in the horse and looked back. Cully was coming on at more of a lope than a walk, swinging his rifle like a balance pole. His lope turned into a sprint when he saw she'd stopped the cart. He scrambled up beside her, panted: "Still another hour before we have to make camp," and prodded the old nag's bony rump with his rifle. His eyes were glittering and his mouth drawn as thin as a razor cut.

Eulalie said: "Did you find it?"

"Find what?"

"The pistol!"

"Oh. Yes." He patted his coat pocket.

"Where?"

"In the grass beside the house. Fool that I am."

He didn't make much more conversation, and he seemed intent on squeezing every last ounce of sunlight out of the day before they camped. He also seemed to find many interesting things to look at on the side of the road away from her. She got the distinct feeling that although his head was pointed toward the side of the road, his eyes were angling back over his shoulder.

When they finally stopped for the night, he said blandly: "Josette, could you start making camp, and watch the children? Eulalie and I have to take a short walk in the woods."

Eulalie looked at him for some hint why, but he just put his arm through hers and started into the woods. When they'd gone a little ways, he stopped, let go of her arm and stepped away from her. He didn't look particularly giddy anymore. His face had that trace of scoured iron that she'd seen when the tinker first doffed his hat in the valley of Ardoise.

He said: "I may have broken a promise I made you."

"'May have'?"

"Well, I made the promise because we were trapped in that town. We're not now. But there's one thing to be said for being a tinker who has to get back to the same town every night—you learn all there is to know about the backroads and byways thereabouts. There's a woodlot behind the Reverend Mister Buckthorn's house. I waited there until Nathan Buckthorn was in the yard alone, then whistled to turn him toward me."

He took a rifleball out of his pocket and rolled it between his thumb and forefinger. "Two ounces of lead in a man's heart or head will kill him like swatting a fly. Shot in the guts, it takes a long time to die. But die he will, no matter how long his loving father weeps and prays over him."

Eulalie thought of the Beatitudes that Beau-père used to read aloud on Sundays. She thought of the fact that someone else's suffering couldn't erase what she'd suffered in the Buckthorns' barn that night. She thought of the fact that vengeance belonged to the good God and Him alone. She thought of the fact that if any human soul had the right to make the decision Cully had made, it was her, not him. She thought of the fact that if he'd told her what he was going to do, she would've said no.

She put her hand on Cully's arm and said: "Good."

LV

hen André caught sight of Cape Blomidon looming in the distance he started walking faster. He stopped paying attention to the barrow he was wheeling and it started to tip. Its cargo squawked at him and flailed at his arms with her cane. He shifted the wheelbarrow onto an even keel again and said: "I'm sorry, Madame Thibodeau."

"Sorry? One more fall is all these old bones have left in them. Your arms must be getting tired. Let someone else take a turn."

André's arms weren't really all that tired, but he was more than willing to let one of the other young men push the wheelbarrow for a while. They'd been taking it in turns all the way around the Bay of Fundy. Madame Thibodeau's legs had given out on the woods trails north of New England, so they'd carried her on their backs until they'd got to the settlements along La Rivière St. Jean where they could buy a wheelbarrow. Madame Thibodeau's husband and her ten children all lay in Protestant cemeteries in Massachusetts, victims of smallpox or the other diseases that preyed on the malnourished and ill-housed. She was determined to be buried in the sanctified ground at Grand-Pré beside her grandmothers.

The road curved inland to the ford across the St. Croix River. Through the yellowing treetops ahead, the spearhead tower of Fort Edward poked up out of the hill between the rivermouths. Some of André's *confrères* from Piziquid muttered curses at it, but André preferred to think of what lay just a few minutes in front of him rather than what that tower made him remember. He found it hard to rein in his legs to the pace of the straggling line stretching back along the road.

The road forked, one branch going down to the beach where fishermen might be persuaded to ferry returning Acadians across the Piziquid, the other branch running up-river along the north shore. André and the others whose land was on this side of the river made a quick job of shaking hands with everybody else. Although they'd been brothers and sisters of the road for half a year, all of them had the smell of home in their nostrils now, and the ones from Annapolis Royal still had a long way to go.

André finished his good-byes before anyone else and half-ran down to the riverbank and the old path along the top of the dike. His eyes were trying to carry him a mile ahead of his feet, and his heart felt too big for his chest. He'd been away from home for half as long as he'd lived there.

The dike path was grown over and wasn't level like it should be, as though the base had been washed away in places or had been tunnelled by muskrats and not shorn up before it caved in. There were pools of water in the fields, as though some of the *aboiteau*s were clogged with silt or had collapsed with rot. The fields were stubbled as though someone had taken off a crop this year, but it couldn't have been much of a crop on ground where saltwater seeped in and didn't seep out again.

Up ahead, where the house he was born in used to stand, he could see a new house and barn and sheds. André laughed and shook his head—leave it to his father to not only get back from across the ocean faster than he could get back from New York, but to have rebuilt the farm in the bargain.

But as André got closer, he saw that it wasn't the kind of house his father would build: clapboard instead of squared logs, shingles instead of thatch, and the roof was pitched too steep to leave much room for a sleeping loft. And, when he thought about it, it wasn't like his father to build a new house before putting-right the *aboiteau*s.

André jumped down off the dike and headed across the field toward the house. In the barnyard, three men were unloading sheaves of oats from a wagon. One of them wore a straw hat and seemed to be doing more overseeing than unloading. He saw André coming into the yard and called out in English: "Good afternoon. What can I do for you?"

"You can tell to me what you think you are doing on my land—my family land!"

"Bloody Christ, another damned Acadian." The straw-hatted man gestured at the other two, "Remove him from my land."

The other two men put down their sheaves and started toward André. There was a pile of tree branches beside André, waiting to be sawn up for firewood. He picked up a good-sized one and cocked it over his shoulder. The two fieldhands hesitated.

André shouted at the man in the straw hat: "How can this be *your* land? My grandfathers and uncles built that dike to make land from the sea! My father clear the forest from where this house stand!"

"The 'how' is very simple: this land was granted to me by the Governor of Nova Scotia, upon authority of the Lords of Trade and His British Majesty. I have the deed to prove it."

"*I* have deed—in the parish record before this governor was borned!"

"Perhaps you once had a deed, perhaps you hadn't. It can't be proved one way or t'other. A few years back there was an accidental fire in the building where the old records were kept. The whole place went up like Guy Fawkes Day. It makes for an unholy mess, I grant you—with no one knowing who owned what—but the governor is sensitive to the problem. He's granting free land to returning Acadians, along the Fundy shore south of Annapolis Royal."

"Land? There is no *land* there—only rock and sand!"

"If you want to argue about it, you can go to Halifax and argue with the governor."

André's arms were trembling, even though the tree branch wasn't much of a weight for them. His eyes were stinging and blurry. When he looked around for what to do, he saw nothing but walls. He lowered the branch to the ground and turned away.

"Wait a moment," the straw-hatted man called after him. André stopped and turned back. "You say your family built this dike...? I'm not taking that as any proof, mind, of any claim of prior ownership, but your saying that would seem to suggest you know something about maintaining dikes and the... the wooden troughs that—"

"The *aboiteaus*. Oh yes, I do know them."

"This salt-marsh farming is new to me. A bloody mystery to me, in fact. If you would undertake to repair and maintain the dike, and show my indentured men how to go about it, I will give you your board and a bed in the barn and half-a-shilling a day."

André's mouth tasted like he was bridled with a brass bit. He wanted to say that he would rather let the tides wear down the dikes, the salt eat away the Englishman's crops and the sea eventually take back the land. But he had nowhere else to go. He swallowed the brassy taste and what was left of his pride and said flatly: "Where I did work in Albany, the last years they did pay me *two* shilling a day. And room and board."

"That was New York, this is Nova Scotia. *One* shilling a day."

"Yassuh."

LVI

❦

Eulalie lay on her back with her blouse unbuttoned, on the planked part of their raft floating down the Mississippi River. Or at least she guessed the river must be the Mississippi. There couldn't be two rivers this wide in North America. The fur traders they'd bartered their horse and cart to along the Tennessee River had assured them that the Tennessee flowed into the Mississippi, and all they'd have to do to reach New Orleans was ride the currents and keep clear of snags and sandbars.

Cully was hunkered at the front of the raft with a long pole, making sure they did just that. Eulalie thought of picking up one of the other poles and sitting beside him, to feel like she was doing something useful. But the air was so thick and hot, she thought she'd just lie where she was a little longer. It was supposedly springtime, but she'd detected no trace of spring freshness—at least no trace resembling the freshness of every other springtime in her life. When the raft passed near wooded islands, or came close enough to either shore to see it as more than a green blur, even the trees seemed to be drooping with sweat—trees with multicolored bark peeling like burned skin, trees with trunks that looked like cracked shards of granite sticking up out of the water.

Eulalie didn't know exactly how long they'd been on the raft, but it was long enough for Félicité and little Gilbert to have grown used to always wearing a cord under their armpits pegged to the middle of the raft. They hardly ever got their cords tangled together anymore. At the moment, Gilbert was asleep under the awning they rigged for a sail when the wind was right. There was no wind of any kind today. Josette was entertaining Félicité with cat's-cradle, sitting on the rim of the raft with their legs in the water.

Cully stood up, balancing his bare feet on the roped-together logs, and shaded his eyes with his hand. He called over his shoulder: "Do you see?"

Eulalie very slowly rose to her feet and squinted in the direction he was pointing. Far ahead on the western shore there were several thin columns of smoke rising over the trees. Eulalie said: "Indians, maybe...?"

"Maybe. Or maybe we're close enough to New Orleans to find some settlement. If it turns out to be Indians, we can just wave to them from the raft and keep on going."

Eulalie nodded. If this had been Acadia, she wouldn't have thought twice about hoving-in to a camp of Mi'kmaqs or Maliseets, but she knew nothing of the tribes along the Mississippi.

Eulalie picked up one of their crude, hand-hewn paddles, knelt down on the larboard edge of the raft and beckoned Josette to do the same. The paddles could never propel something as unwieldy as the raft, but they could help to steer it a little. Cully went to the back of the raft to angle the plank they used for a rudder and lash it into place, then picked up the third paddle and joined her and Josette.

As the western shore grew closer, Eulalie could see a stubby wooden wharf with a spit-polished skiff moored beside it. But she could also see that the current was going to carry the raft past it before they angled in close enough to make a landing. She knew Cully wasn't much of a swimmer, so she stripped off her blouse and skirt, picked up the end of the rope coiled at the front of the raft and jumped into the muddy water in her shift.

When her head came back up above the surface, she felt cool for the first time all day. But she had no time to enjoy it; she was too busy kicking against the current and trying to breathe with the end of the rope clutched in her teeth. She just managed to snag an arm around one of the end pilings before she was swept past the wharf. She tied the rope to the piling and climbed onto the dock as Cully and Josette went to work hauling the raft in.

Eulalie stood on the wharf and looked inland. There was a forest of tall, strange trees with bearded branches, and gnarled roots thrusting out of their trunks like spiders' legs. In the gloom below the trees was a wide, low, porched log building with the *fleurs de lis* floating above it. Two white-uniformed soldiers were coming down from it toward the wharf. The two soldiers looked curious but not unpleased to see her standing there with her wet shift sticking to her like a thin coat of paint.

Eulalie could feel herself blushing, but she pointed matter-of-factly at the raft and said: "We are Acadian."

One of the soldiers said to the other: "You'd best go tell the lieutenant we have more Acadians."

"Why should I go? *You* go tell the lieutenant."

"*You* go—I'll stay here and keep an eye on things."

The raft bumped against the wharf. Eulalie jumped down onto it and hastily buttoned her blouse and skirt over her sopping shift. By the time she was dressed again, one of the soldiers had fetched the lieutenant. The lieutenant said: "*Bonjour*. Where do you come from?"

Eulalie was taken aback, and it took her a moment to figure out why. It was the first time in her life that someone representing government authority had spoken to her in French as though it were the language he spoke to everyone else.

Cully said: "From Massachusetts. We'd heard a lot of Acadians were coming to make new homes in Louisiana."

"Yes," the lieutenant nodded, "that's true." But he didn't sound necessarily happy about it. "Best you come up to the fort."

As the family and the soldiers made their way up to the 'fort', the lieutenant added: "Well, you were lucky at least you came today. Another day and we'd be gone back to New Orleans and you'd have to wait to make arrangements until the next time we came up-river. Years back there was a proper establishment here, until *les sauvages* burnt it down."

The inside of the log building was something like what Eulalie imagined when Cully told stories about barracks life—cots, tables and benches spread around one wide, open room. There were a few other soldiers lounging around the tables, and men who looked like labourers or boatmen, and in one corner an immaculately cassocked priest studying a book at a desk. As the lieutenant called a clerk over to an empty table, Eulalie called brightly to the priest: "Good morning, Father."

The priest looked up at her as though she should know better than to intrude on his meditations. But he said with Christian forbearance: "And to you, daughter. Where have you come from?"

"From Massachusetts. And before that, Acadia."

The priest said: "Ah," as though that explained everything. "When did you last make confession?"

Eulalie tried to count back to when Father La Brosse left the Petitcodiac for Quebec. "Seven years...? Eight years...?" She shrugged. "Things happened."

"Seven years without confession is nothing to be made light of. I have to say mass today and then we go back to New Orleans tomorrow, so I will not have time to hear such a lengthy confession until I pass this way again. But that will give you time to think back over those seven years, or eight."

Eulalie could see that the lieutenant and the clerk now had several sheets of paper spread out in front of them and were ready to get down to business, so she just said obediently: "Yes, Father," and headed toward their table. But she did wonder what she had to confess outside of doing her best to stay alive.

The lieutenant asked their names and the clerk wrote them down. Félicité was disoriented to suddenly hear she was a Robin, not a La Tour. Eulalie promised to explain later.

Eulalie was disoriented herself, suddenly faced with new people after so long on the raft where the world consisted of her little family. What was even more disorienting was the impossible notion that ten years of being hunted and caged was over, just like that.

The lieutenant unfurled a map and said: "His Most Christian Majesty has allowed that every Acadian fled to Louisiana shall have fifty acres. Just above New Orleans is already a settlement of Germans, so we are settling you Acadians between here and there. The nearest allotment still unoccupied is... here." He pointed to a blank square on the map and the clerk dipped his pen to write in 'Robin'.

Eulalie said excitedly: "So there's other Acadians around here, too?"

The lieutenant nodded. "Two hundred at last count. You'll be seeing them soon, when they come in to hear mass."

Cully said: "Beausoleil?"

The lieutenant said: "Beausoleil?"

"Joseph Brossard *dit* Beausoleil."

"Yes, I've met him." The lieutenant didn't sound like it had been an entirely happy experience. Eulalie assumed that it was for the same reason that most people in authority were never entirely happy with Beausoleil—he wouldn't do what he was told. "He *is* in Louisiana, but not here. He and his people were settled on the Attakapas prairie, some fifty miles west."

Cully said: "Then Akata... Appata..."

"Attakapas."

"Then that's where we want to settle."

"You Acadians have to get it through your heads that we can't give you everything you want. It's been decided there are more than enough Acadians at Attakapas already."

Eulalie said: "But if it's only fifty miles—"

"Fifty miles *as the crow flies*. And that crow would be flying over Bayou Lafourche and the Atchafalaya Basin—a trackless hellhole filled with alligators and water snakes. Anyone foolish enough to venture into there will never venture out again. The only safe way from here to Attakapas is to sail south to New Orleans, west along the Gulf of Mexico and then march inland north.

"Here at St. Jacques de Cabannocé we can easily send you occasional supplies upriver from New Orleans. The ones who went to Attakapas, we had to send them off with six months' provisions and all the tools they'd need to establish themselves. His

Majesty's warehouses in New Orleans are almost empty, and now that there'll be no more shipments from France—"

"Why no more?" Cully interjected.

"*Soon*—I meant no more *soon*."

It didn't sound to Eulalie like that was what the lieutenant had meant, but maybe it was just her ears. Regardless, it was clear that once again they couldn't go where they wanted to go, and there was nothing they could do about it. But she and Cully had fifty acres in this part of Louisiana, and that was fifty acres more than they had yesterday.

Acadians began to drift in, either walking through the woods or paddling home-made boats. Some of them were Eulalie's cousins, or people she remembered from market days at Piziquid. She grew dizzy with all the handclaspings and tears of surprise. The big room filled up quickly. Eulalie hadn't been among so many of her own kind since the Petitcodiac.

Before she'd been handed around to more than a quarter of the people in the room, the priest appeared in his vestments and the gathering grew silent. Before launching into the mass, the priest delivered a short sermon about showing the proper respect to Holy Mother Church and the representatives of God on earth. It seemed that last night several Acadians who'd come to speak with him had walked in actually *smoking pipes and telling jokes.* The priest generously acknowledged that ten years wandering in the wilderness would naturally make the Acadians forget how to behave, but they were no longer in the wilderness. Eulalie wondered what he would say if she told him that the priests she'd known in Acadia would've been hurt if their parishioners kept their jokes and tobacco to themselves.

After mass, the tables and benches were cleared back against the walls, and people began to bring in pots and platters steaming with the home-smells of Acadian food, mingled with some odours Eulalie didn't know. She glimpsed a stooped old man with two canes being helped toward one of the benches, and felt a stab of recognition. She went over and crouched in front of him. "Uncle Benoni? It's me—Eulalie."

"Who? Eulalie...? Eulalie! Bless me, bless me—Eulalie! Look at you, a full-growed woman now! Did André à Thomas à Mathieu find you?"

"Yes... Yes, he did, but... I was already married. This is my son, Gilbert."

"Ah, and what a hearty-looking young man he is." Benoni's watery eyes blinked, and seemed to blink him back to where he'd been a moment ago. "I always thought that you would marry André."

"So did I. Things changed. The world turned over."

"Yes, yes," Benoni sighed. "Ten years ago I tried to warn everyone, but would anyone listen to that old woman Benoni?" He squinted darkly at the room around him, then suddenly wheezed a laugh and patted the bench beside him. "Come sit, Eulalie, and you will see your first Hummers' Dance. Yes, yes—a Louisiana Hummers' Dance."

A man Eulalie didn't know stood up and began to lustily la-la an old Acadian dance tune, clattering time with his wooden shoes. Two women stood up beside him and joined in. Soon the floor was filled with dancers, some of them humming along to help keep the tune afloat. Eulalie said to Benoni: "Did everyone lose their fiddles in the *Grand Dérangement?*"

Benoni laughed. "No, no—most would likelier lose their wives than their fiddles. But you can see the priest ain't happy—well, *you* can see, I can't see that far, but I know."

Eulalie picked out the priest glowering mutely from a distant corner. Benoni cackled: "He don't like this, but there's nothing he can say against it, because he made the rule and we are obeying it. You see, he told us that he would allow no more playing of musical instruments on the day he said mass or he would come to say mass no more. He didn't like it that we figured as long as we were all gathered together to say mass, we might as well have a dance after. He thought it disrespectful to mix mass and dancing. So, as you can hear, we are all obedient children of the church, and there are no fiddles or flutes or even jew's harps playing."

Uncle Benoni stopped in mid-cackle and shifted abruptly to another mood. He sighed: "So many gone... so many gone... I heard about your Beau-père Joseph à Jacques à Thomas and all his children..."

"Not *all* his children. There is Josette, dancing in the pink dress." It had once been red.

"Where?"

"There, with her gold hair and blue eyes shining."

"Little Josette? No, it can't be."

"It is." But Eulalie had no trouble understanding how Uncle Benoni found it hard to believe. She found it hard to believe herself. The last time she'd seen Josette dancing, back in the charity house in Massachusetts when they learned the *Grand Dérangement* was over, Eulalie had been watching a gawky girl. Now, with only the turning of a card, she was watching a lithe young woman. The Acadian young men and French soldiers obviously saw Josette as a woman, too.

Benoni suddenly switched back to a thread Eulalie had thought he'd let go a few minutes ago. It seemed that the shuttle of his mind now skipped from warp to woof indiscriminately, weaving halfway up, halfway across and then down again. He said: "These priests from France here, they put me in mind of what my old grandfather told me of why his old grandfather left France for Acadia. An honest farmer in France was expected to take off his hat and look at the ground if a carriage went by. It seems things haven't changed much there. Or here. If you ever go into New Orleans, and you pass by people on the street speaking French, don't say *Bonjour*. They may be Creoles, who will shit on your shoes for speaking to them.

"Creoles, you see, are what they call the old families whose grandfathers came here from France. They ain't all the same—no more than any other tribe—but many of them seem to think that because they were born here they can walk on the Mississippi water, and we Acadians are just new mud in the river.

"Ah well, perhaps in time we could educate the priests here like we did in Acadia, but I'm afraid we won't have time before the Spaniards get here."

"The Spaniards?"

"Oh yes," Uncle Benoni nodded and chewed his gums. "Spaniards. The lieutenant and the men above him think it's still a secret, but Beausoleil found out somehow, and once one Acadian knows a secret we all do. Some while ago there was another treaty made in Europe. A secret part of it was that the King of France gave Louisiana to the King of Spain in trade for some island-or-other. Someday soon the lieutenant and the soldiers and the governor and the priests and all will go back to France, and men from Spain come to take their place. I don't speak any Spanish. Do you?"

Fortunately for Eulalie's peace of mind over the next few months, and hence Cully's and the children's, she didn't get much time to dwell on the ways Louisiana hadn't quite turned out to be the New Acadia she'd been led to expect. They were too busy clearing a corner of their fifty acres and putting up a house more permanent than their poplar cottage on the Petitcodiac. Eulalie did wonder, though, how permanent the new cabin would prove to be: within a month the corner posts were already showing signs of damp-rot and termites.

For the first time in all their years together, Cully finally had no excuses not to put his hand to gardening. Eulalie found the depths of his ignorance astounding. She even had to explain to him that a good reason to get a pair of piglets as soon as possible was that their rooting would automatically clear more land to make a bigger garden. But at least he was willing to admit he knew nothing, so he learned quickly.

Eulalie had a lot to learn herself. The government supplied them with seed corn and rice. She knew something about growing corn, but had to be hand-led through each step of raising rice. And one of the neighbours introduced her to the mysteries of a strange, pink-flowered, root vegetable called a sweet potato.

But seeds put in the ground take a while to turn into food, and in the meanwhile the rations the government parcelled out to new settlers were pretty lean. Eulalie was fetching water from the stream one day when she noticed something whitish scuttling in the shadows. When she looked closer, she saw that they were crayfish—bigger than the gray ones back home, but still unmistakably crayfish.

She'd never heard of anybody eating crayfish—except maybe someone lost in the woods and starving—but crayfish were just little lobsters, after all. She got her soup ladle from the house and managed to scoop a dozen of the slower-moving ones into her pail. Once she had a pot of water boiling on the hearth, she dropped the crayfish in until they turned red.

When Eulalie set the platter of crayfish on the table beside the flatbread she'd baked in the skillet, Félicité gagged and squealed: "Bugs! Beetles!"

"Beetles!" Gilbert echoed his big sister, as usual. Even Cully and Josette were looking a little queasy.

Eulalie wanted to slap them all—they couldn't live on nothing but flatbread and mushrooms until the garden ripened. She said: "They aren't bugs, Félicité, they're lobsters. You remember one New Year's when you were little and your Aunt Celina's cousin got a pass to come and visit and he brought a sack of lobsters with him? You sure liked the taste of them then."

"*Those* aren't lobsters. Lobsters are *big*. Those are *bugs!*"

"They *are* lobsters, dear. You see... back in Acadia, lobsters and us Acadians were good friends. So, when the English made us leave, the lobsters were lonely and followed us all the way here to Louisiana. Only, well, lobsters aren't very good swimmers, so they had to walk over land, with nothing to eat along the way. So by the time they got here they'd shrunk down to just this size—but they're still lobsters."

Félicité looked like maybe she believed that, maybe not. Cully looked like he was working very hard not to laugh. Eulalie picked up one of the crayfish, wondering how she was going to go about eating it. It *did* look like an oversized mosquito— dead eyes staring it her across its long, bony nose. She broke the head off so it couldn't stare at her anymore, put the body to her mouth and sucked out the meat.

Eulalie chewed and swallowed, then put the empty shell back down and pulled the platter to her. "You're right, Félicité, they're just bugs—you don't want to eat any of these." As Eulalie picked up another crayfish, Cully reached for the platter. She batted at his hand, but he managed to snag one anyway.

Pretty soon they were all chewing on Louisiana lobster, and Cully was making plans to build a scoop-net so they could catch crayfish by the potful. And pretty soon everybody in St. Jacques de Cabannocé was telling their children about how the lobsters had followed them here from Acadia.

Eulalie began to feel steadily less alien as elements of Acadia came back to life along the Mississippi. There was a genuine, old *corvé* to work on the levee that was hoped to keep the river's floods from washing them away. And a young neighbour named Valentin Chenier started visiting Josette on Tuesday and Thursday evenings and Sunday afternoons.

It turned out, too, that the Acadians on the Mississippi weren't entirely cut off from their cousins at Attakapas. There were more young men than young women at Attakapas, and under those circumstances fifty or sixty miles didn't mean much. The Acadians on the Attakapas prairie had decided that their part of the country was best suited for raising cattle, and consequently raising horses to herd them. Every now and then a gaggle of young horsemen would ride east across the prairie and leave their horses at a farm on the west edge of the swamp.

As for the "trackless hellhole" of swamp country, *les sauvages* had been fishing in it and crossing it since the dawn of time. Some remnants of tribes who'd picked the wrong side in recent wars now lived on islands in the bayou. Acadians and Indians had been trading secrets since the days of Charles La Tour.

The best piece of news the young men from the west carried with them was that Beausoleil was working to convince New Orleans that the Acadians on the Mississippi should be allowed to sell the land they'd cleared and move to Attakapas. All the Acadians in Louisiana wanted to believe that Beausoleil would find a way to make that happen. Eulalie and her neighbours encouraged each other to believe it by retelling the story of how Beausoleil had fooled the Governor of Louisiana. Beausoleil had solemnly promised the governor that the Acadians he'd brought on his ship would build their homes in clustered-together villages that would be convenient to govern. But as soon as Beausoleil and his people got to the prairie, they spread out and built scattered farms like in Acadia, and there wasn't a damn thing the governor could do about it after it was done. Beausoleil would always find a way.

In the meanwhile, there were enough Acadians on the Mississippi to make something resembling a community. Eulalie saw the proof of that on a rainy day in midsummer. The priest was up from New Orleans again, and it seemed he'd decided that enough time had passed since his edict against playing music on mass days that he could add on a ban against dancing on mass days without sounding like he couldn't make up his mind.

After mass, everyone sat or stood uncomfortably around the hall, uncertain of what to do. Then the woman sitting on the bench next to Eulalie began to sing in time to the drumming of the rain on the roof, and move her feet in a step-dance pattern. Eulalie joined in. Everyone who was standing quickly found a place to sit— and sat humming, singing, swaying, clapping their hands in rhythm and moving their feet on the floor.

The priest could only glower mutely again. They weren't playing musical instruments, and he could hardly call what people did when they were sitting down "dancing". To Eulalie, the humming and clapping and bench-dancing meant more than just a happy joke. It meant the heart of Acadia was still beating. A thousand miles from Acadia, the

people around her hadn't lost the instinct that had kept Acadians free through generations of revolving masters: the art of being obedient without obeying.

But in spite of all the good reasons Eulalie could point to to prove she'd found a
home out of the wreckage of the *Grand Dérangement*, there were still nights when she
woke from walking in the wildflowers in the valley of Ardoise.

In the fall—or what passed for fall in Louisiana—Cully came home from mending a neighbour's stewpot looking like a cold hand had hold of his heart. He said:
"There's a young fellow come from Attakapas with news. The people Beausoleil
brought from San Domingo—the ones that survived the tropic fevers there—they
brought the fever with them. The young fellow couldn't count all the dead and dying
at Attakapas. But he knew for certain that among the dead is Alexandre Brossard
and his wife. And among the dying is Beausoleil."

Eulalie put her hands up to her eyes to hold the tears in, but what Cully said next
jolted her into a different emotion entirely. He said: "I have to go say good-bye."

"What? *Why?* If he lives through it, your going to say good-bye is ridiculous! If he
doesn't, nothing you can say will change it!"

"You don't understand. For three years he and I ducked the same bullets, drank to
the same little victories, buried the same friends... The last words he said to me was
that he'd be very annoyed if we didn't meet again in this life. I won't be gone more
than two weeks, three at the most. You and Josette can manage just as well without
me—"

"Not forever! *You* don't understand! People are *dying* there!"

He said: "Oh!" and then laughed. Before her hands could leap up to choke the
laugh out of his throat, he said: "I'm sorry—I never told you, did I? But then, why
would it come up? And I suppose I feel a bit of guilt about it...

"You see, I'm immune to fevers. I don't have the least notion why, but I've seen it
proved time after time. Ten times as many soldiers die of disease than bullets and
bayonets. But in fourteen years of soldiering—living in bivouacs and troopships and
barracks where sometimes every man around me was out of his head with Walchern
fever, or ship's fever, or tropic fever, or any kind of fever you could name—I never felt
a tremor. The same that first winter on the Petitcodiac, when so many grew sick and
died and the worst I suffered was going a little hungry.

"No, the only thing to worry about about me going to Attakapas is getting lost
along the way. And there ain't much danger of that, since I'll be going with the young
fellow that brought the news, and he's been back and forth a few times. I'll leave you
my rifle—in case one of those fat egrets wanders too close to shore—and take Captain Namon's pistol, in case a wild rabbit attacks me on the road."

LVII

❧

lmost there, Cully!" the young fellow in the bow called over his shoulder.

Cully grunted: "How can you tell?" and kept concentrating on trying to keep his balance standing in the stern and poling the dugout canoe through a forest of swampgrass taller than he was. In the last four days they'd carried the canoe over every kind of terrain from sandbars to rocky outcrops, and poled and paddled it through every kind of water from clear-flowing rivers to woodrot sludge. Cully had grown almost used to wearing a coating of mud on his neck and hands to keep the gnats from eating him, and always having his smouldering pipe clenched in his teeth to keep them out of his eyes.

For once, Cully's *How can you tell?* had been rhetorical. If they were almost at the place where he would start back from, he wouldn't have to take out his pencil and add it to his list of landmarks. The young fellow, Isidor, found it amusing that Cully had to write such things down. Cully was willing to admit Isidor might be right that learning to read and write atrophied a man's ability to remember; or maybe it was just that everyone had less faith in their memory once they got past forty. Either way, Cully had no intention of dying lost and starving in a swamp.

The canoe stopped abruptly and Cully thumped down onto his knees rather than toppling overboard and soaking the list in his pocket. Isidor climbed out and said: "We're at land."

"I noticed."

There were a few other dugout canoes stowed under the brush on the shoreline. They stowed theirs alongside of them and Isidor led Cully down a path through Louisiana's version of elephant grass. After awhile they came out onto a meadow where the grass had been grazed down. Ahead there was a thatched house and barn. Isidor pointed and said: "That's where I left my horse. Maybe Anselme à Victor à

Jean Baptiste will borrow you one of his."

As they neared the house, a gray-bearded man came out of the barn. Cully squinted at him, painting the gray out in his mind's eye, then called: "So, Anselme à Victor à Jean Baptiste, do you still limp from that musketball outside Fort Cumberland?"

Anselme's eyes slitted at him, then flared wide. "L'Anglais...?" They pumped each others' hands and expressed their mutual amazement that the other was still alive.

Cully noticed that Isidor was gawking at him. Isidor said: "Cully, you're l'Anglais?"

"Well, that's what some people called me in the old days."

"You saved my father's life. When the English burned the Petitcodiac. He says there was two redcoat soldiers coming at him with bayonets, and l'Anglais bursted out of the woods with a cutlass like the Wrath of God."

"I, um, don't remember. Maybe your father exaggerated a little."

"He's not one to exaggerate."

Anselme saved Cully further embarrassment by asking where he'd sprung from after seven years. When Cully said he was on his way to see Beausoleil, Anselme turned sombre. "He was still alive yesterday, last I heard, but who knows today? Or maybe he will wrestle down the fever just like he wrestled down that big, Mi'kmaq bully on the Miramichi. I'll loan you one of my horses, but I only got a homemade saddle so you'll have to hold on tight."

Beausoleil's home didn't look any different from the other knocked-together cattle farms Cully passed along the way. Cully bade his guide adieu, climbed down off his borrowed horse and knocked on the door. It was opened by Beausoleil's wife. Anne looked like she'd been carrying around a tombstone for the last seven years. But her hair, in the deceptive way of blondes, didn't look like there was any white in it, only that she'd gone a lighter shade of gold.

The instant Anne's eyes touched on him, she gaped: "Mon Dieu!" and flung her arms around him. When she stepped back, she said: "He will be so glad to see you, but you shouldn't have come, so many people here are—"

"No fear," he shook his head. He explained to her about his immunity to fevers, although it made him feel a bit like a man with a full belly in the midst of a famine.

Anne said: "He may still be asleep," put one finger to her lips, took hold of Cully's hand and led him into the house. One corner of the house had been partitioned off to make a bedroom. Anne moved the curtain in the doorway aside and beckoned Cully to enter.

A man who might once have been Beausoleil was lying in a feather bed with his eyes closed. His heavy bones had almost no meat left on them, and his gray thatch of hair was sweat-curled at the edges. His skin looked like paraffin left in the sun. He was breathing in shuddery gasps.

Cully was about to nod at Anne to let Beausoleil sleep, when Beausoleil's eyelids cracked open. The fever-bright eyes wandered around the room, touched on Cully and held. Beausoleil's stubbled cheeks twitched several times and then he rasped out: "Son-of-a-whore. Annie, I'm seeing things again." His bony hand came up off the bed and clasped Cully's with surprising strength. "How come the stupid English didn't hang you when they had the chance?"

Cully sat on the edge of the bed and proceeded to tell him. Beausoleil chuckled weakly at times, and at other times slapped Cully on the knee. But before the story was half done, Beausoleil's eyes glazed over and he began to tremble, shaking spittle out of the corners of his mouth. Anne put a damp cloth on his forehead and Cully held it there while she ran to get a cup of some sort of medicine-tea she had steeping on the hearth.

Cully stayed and helped Anne nurse her husband. His nursing duties didn't extend to helping her clean Beausoleil when he soiled his sheets. He could've brought himself to do it, but he knew Beausoleil would've found it embarrassing if he became conscious at a moment when *l'Anglais* was washing his ass.

During one of Beausoleil's lucid moments, he said: "You know, *l'Anglais*, we Acadians will always be—no matter how they try to stamp us out. Because we are like the little mice that can live in the woods or in the meadows or in your roof-thatch or under the snow; like the water that shapes itself to any bowl you pour it in. When our great-grandfathers and grandmothers came from France and found not much good farmland in Acadia, we learned to make land from the sea. When our farms weren't enough to feed our families, we learned to fish the saltwater and read the Fundy tides. When some of us found ourselves on the Acadian isthmus—where there's nothing but sand that grows nothing but grass—we learned to farm cattle. We will learn to make a life out of these prairies and bayous. But, one thing I hope we learn damn soon is how to make a house that won't turn into an oven when the Louisiana sun shines and rot when it don't."

In another of Beausoleil's lucid moments, Cully asked him: "Why didn't you and Alexandre surrender in the winter of '58 when everybody else did?"

"I will tell you a secret, *Anglais*. Well, it shouldn't be a secret, but from the way a lot of people's lives turn out it seems to be. Often when you see someone get beaten down it's because they *decide* they are beaten—that any fool can see the wind is against them and the sensible thing to do is stop fighting the wind. But, you know, winds have been known to change. Not the wisest man in the world can tell you for certain which way the wind is going to blow tomorrow. So if you keep fighting for another day, or another month, or another year..."

"But you did surrender eventually."

"Well there's no sense being an idiot about it." Beausoleil laughed wheezily, and then his voice grew softer. "But, you know, me and Alexandre and Anne and the other idiots who didn't surrender in '58, we did win something out of it."

"What was that?"

"We were free for three more years."

In one of Beausoleil's not-so-lucid moments, Cully held his hand and told him: "You're a *courier de bois*, Beausoleil—you've beat so many odds in the past, you can beat this. How can a man who's had so many bullets shot at him die in a sickbed? You've already half wrestled it to the ground—everyone else who caught this fever was dead in days, but you're still here. Next year Eulalie and me will be putting up a house next door to you and you'll be fighting with me over whose cattle got mixed in with whose herd."

On the 20th of October, Cully was proved wrong. Joseph Brossard *dit* Beausoleil was buried at Camp Beausoleil, the place where his Acadian flotsam and jetsam had first pitched their tents in their new land.

The day after the funeral Cully started home. He rode his borrowed horse back to Anselme's and then marched down the tall-grass path to where the boats were beached, with a rolled blanket slung over his shoulder and a provision sack swinging from his hand. He was a bit nervous about his list of landmarks, but after the first two turned out to be just where they should be—the fallen cypress pointing east, the forked marsh-stream where he was supposed to take the channel to the left—he began to relax about it. After all, the bloody British Army had trusted him to make a list for them, why shouldn't he trust one he made for himself?

After his first night's camp—on an island with a charred campfire circle where he and Isidor had made their last night's camp—he woke up shivering and found he had to stop and sit down for a while after poling the boat not very far. The weather was miserable for travelling: stifling hot one minute and chilly damp the next. But he still managed to keep up with his list of landmarks and campsites, even though he frequently had to unbutton his breeches and perch on the gunwale of the dugout.

His attention got rivetted by too many passing details that weren't landmarks, and didn't even seem quite real: a speckled water snake with its jaws around a half-swallowed fish three times as wide as Mister Snake; a furry, blue, swimming spider the size of his hand... The next landmark on his list was supposed to be a heron rookery that any fool could see towering above the reeds. It wasn't there.

Cully ran his boat up against an island covered with translucent ferns and stopped to think. He thought of judging his direction by the current flowing south to the Gulf of Mexico, but he was in Bayou Lafourche now, and Isidor had told him that what made a bayou not a river was a bayou flowed in both directions.

He dropped his paddle into the boat, picked up the pole and climbed out. There was an old trick Beausoleil had taught him, one of the tricks that had helped get him from Fort Cumberland to Massachusetts. He planted the pole upright in the muddy loam of the island and then foraged around in the shallows till he had a handful of stones. He set one stone down where the tip of the pole's shadow touched the ground, waited a while and set another stone down where the tip of the shadow had moved. In not very long he had a line of stones pointing more-or-less east—if at was after noon, and he was quite sure he'd been paddling in circles for more than a few hours.

Some while later he was sweating and shivering again, and dragging the canoe across a spit of bayou land that didn't seem to end. He stopped and thought about it. Maybe the reason the spit of land hadn't ended was because the bayou had. He picked up his provision sack out of the boat and left the boat behind.

Eventually he found the Mississippi, but there was no sign that human feet had ever stepped within a hundred miles of this stretch of riverbank. Either he was up-river of home or down-river. He sat down to think about it. It seemed he dozed. When he woke up again he thought he saw a very large egret hovering over the water. It was a sail coming downstream.

Cully stood up shouting and waving his arms. The boat turned in toward him: a barge-like craft with bales of hides piled amidships. As it neared the shore, Cully called out in French: "I am going to St. Jacques de Cabannocé!"

The man at the helm called back in a French dialect that wasn't Acadian: "Then you're a hell of a long way north of where you're going!"

"Are you going past there?"

"Well we seem to be going down-river, and St. Jacques de Cabannocé is down-river, so I guess we'd pretty much have to, wouldn't we?"

"I have no money, but my wife has a little at home. If you'll take me aboard, I can pay you when you put me ashore there."

"Well... Fair enough—but if your wife has no money, we'll tie you back on board and take you all the way down to New Orleans and see how you like walking from there."

Cully climbed into the bow and the boat pushed off again. He scooped a few handfuls of muddy water over his face and settled his head against the gunwale.

The next thing he knew, something hard was poking into his ribs. He opened his eyes. The boat was ashore again and the boatmen were all clumped in the stern, jabbing at him with their long oars. The boatmen shimmered in the heatwaves.

Cully looked over his shoulder and saw no evidence of human settlement, just the Louisiana jungle. He said: "What...?"

The helmsman yelled: "Get out! Get out! You have the fever, you'll kill us all!"

"But... How can you—?" An oarblade jabbed him hard. "All... All right..." He was finding it difficult to make his mouth form words. "But first... I have something..." He reached both hands into his provision sack, cocked Captain Namon's pistol and brought it out. The oars ceased jabbing him.

The helmsman yelled: "You can't kill us all with one bullet!"

"No, but I can sure as hell kill *you*," although that was an open question, given that both the pistol barrel and the helmsman kept weaving mistily from side to side. Cully giggled. "Well, maybe not you, but I'm bound to hit *someone*. Two ounces of lead in the guts."

"What good will it do to take one of us with you? You're going to die anyway."

"I'll tell you..." Cully found it even more difficult to speak, now that the helmsman had voiced what seemed to be the fact. If this fever could kill Beausoleil it could sure as hell kill Cully Robin. "I'll tell you... what good... My wife has to know. I won't shoot... if you swear... on your mother's hope of salvation... you will stop at St. Jacques de Cabannocé and say to someone... any Acadian..." He had to swallow before he could say it himself, "*L'Anglais* is dead."

"Langley?"

"*L'Anglais*! Say it! *L'Anglais* is dead!"

"*L'Anglais* is dead."

"Good. Now cross yourself and swear."

The helmsman said flatly: "I swear, upon my mother's hope of—"

"I don't believe you!" pointing the pistol for punctuation.

"*I swear upon my mother's hope of salvation!*"

"Good. Now I believe you." Cully crawled over the bow and flopped down in the mud. The boat pushed off quickly.

Cully levered his back up against some knock-kneed treeroots. Louisiana had become an icehouse. He unrolled his blanket and draped it around himself. After a while he stopped shivering and the river waves ceased leaping crazily. He wasn't going to die after all. He felt terrible that he'd sent the false message to Eulalie. Maybe if he set off at a quick march he could get to her before the boat did. In a moment or two he would get up and start walking.

A granite island rose up out of the Mississippi River, with a stone castle growing out of the rock. Cully knew the island and the castle well. He used to sit on the shore of Jersey Isle and dream of living in The Hermitage. The Hermitage was an island only when the tide was high; when the tide was low you could walk back and forth across the ocean floor. A boy who lived there would have a moat between him and the rest of the world, but still be able to walk away from hermiting when fancy suited.

Voices started calling to him out of the trees and the river:

"*Corporal Robin!*"

"Yes, Sergeant?"

"*You've made a fine ballocks of it, haven't you?*"

"As usual, Sergeant."

"*Cully Stupid Robin!*"

"Yes, Mother?"

"*Gilbert Roland Robin!*"

"Yes, Father?"

"*What have you ever done with your life?*"

"A fuck of a lot more than either of you ever expected. Bugger off."

"*Cully...?*"

"Eulalie...? Oh hell, now you've gone and made me cry."

LVIII

⁘

André had got into the habit of spending his Sundays with the Acadians who lived in a cluster of shacks and sheds on the edge of the new, English town of Windsor, which nestled in the shadow of Fort Edward. Whether they earned their bread as laundrywomen or deckhands or day labourers, they were all in the same case as he—servants on the farm lands or fishing boats their families had made. The population of the shantytown kept changing, as newly-returned exiles came back to the Piziquid River, and older returnees decided to give up Piziquid forever and take the government's offer of free acres of storm-scoured bayshore a hundred miles south.

But no matter how many Acadians flowed away from Windsor with the tides, there was always someone there to lead a White Mass Sunday morning. And there was usually some news from other parts of the world, now that Acadians were allowed to take to the sea again and trade stories with other sailors. That was how André had learned where his family was—or where he guessed they probably were. After the treaty that ended the war, the Acadians being held in England had all been shipped to France, where the Abbé Le Loutre was shepherding them to corners of his homeland where no one else wanted to live.

This particular Sunday morning was blustery with snow blowing in off the Minas Basin. André angled his head against the wind, clutched his coat tight around his throat and trudged along the trail beaten down by his employer's matched bay geldings and sleigh-runners. If the wind didn't die down, there would be no White Mass today, since none of the buildings in Acadiantown were anywhere near big enough for everyone to gather in.

When André got to Acadiantown, he went first to the cabin of Louis Saulnier—who would likely be the one to lead the White Mass if there was one—and knocked on the door. It was opened by old Louis's big-breasted daughter, Anastasie. She blushed and said: "Oh, André—come in out of the cold." She was always blushing, which nicely set off her blueberry eyes.

As soon as he stepped through the door, André felt an atmosphere of gloom. There was another guest there before him. André had met him once or twice before, when his ship happened to be docked in Windsor. The man was only a common sailor now, but he was famous among Acadians for having been part of the crew on Beausoleil's privateer.

Old Louis said grimly: "André, Beausoleil is dead."

André murmured: "Mercy on his soul," and sat down heavily. He'd never set eyes on Beausoleil but, like all Acadians, felt he knew him. Beausoleil wasn't supposed to be mortal.

Anastasie brought André a cup of blackberry tea. The sailor intoned: "It was a tropic fever the ones from San Domingo brought with them. Beausoleil was only one of many—so many of the tough, old comrades from the Petitcodiac that all the English cannonballs couldn't kill. Alexandre Brossard and his Marguerite, Barthelémy Bergeron, Jean Dugas and his Marie-Charlotte, l'Anglais—"

"L'Anglais...?" André interjected.

"Yes—an English soldier who joined with us, so we called him l'Anglais."

"Was he a tinker?"

"It could be. It seems to me that Beausoleil sometimes called him 'tinker,' like it was a joke."

"And what of l'Anglais's wife?"

"His wife...? His wife... A La Tour, yes?"

"Yes, Eulalie La Tour."

"I don't remember. There were so many names of the dead, I can't remember them all. But the fever was so catching—when Alexandre caught it his wife did, too, and the same with Jean Dugas and Charles Thibodeau and so many others. So since l'Anglais died of the fever, most likely his wife did, too. You knew her?"

"Yes. Yes, I knew her."

Anastasie said: "Would you like another cup of tea, André?"

LIX

Eulalie sat slumped in the house she and Cully had built, clutching the money she'd just got from selling it and the land they'd broken. Along with the money she'd got from selling his rifle and the pigs and anything else someone would buy, there should be enough to pay ship passage for her and Josette and the children from Louisiana to Nova Scotia. With Cully gone, there was no reason not to go home, and a lot of reasons not to stay in a place where she could see his hands on every wall post.

Today was one of her good days, when she felt numb. In the weeks since she'd got the message that some kind boatmen had found him dying on the riverbank and given him a decent burial, there'd been more than a few days when she kept having to go off into the forest so as not to upset the children with weeping. And there'd been other days when she'd raged at him in her mind for having been so stupidly cocksure that he could walk into a fever house and come out untouched.

There was only her and Josette in the house at the moment; Félicité was old enough now to be pretty much trusted to look out for her little brother while they hunted crayfish. Josette leaned across the table toward Eulalie, put her hand on hers and said: "Eulalie... Eulalie...?"

"Hm?"

"I... I have to tell you... Valentin Chenier... His mother says she would be glad to have me in her home as a daughter until I can become her daughter-in-law."

"What...? Daughter-in-law? You never said anything to me about—"

"There was nothing to say yet. And there wouldn't be, but—you going meant we had to decide now. Valentin has a cousin at Attakapas who will give us enough cattle to start our own herd when the day comes. The fever left plenty of empty land there."

"But you already have land, in the valley of Ardoise."

"It's yours, Eulalie. It was always yours more than anyone else's."

"But... Josette, you and I can't—after all these years..."

Josette's whole face screwed into wrinkles, like it used to when she had to have turpentine dabbed onto a scraped knee. She whispered: "All these years? All my life, *petite mère.*"

❊ ❊ ❊

Félicité and Gilbert wailed and screamed at the steadily diminishing picture of their Aunt Josette waving good-bye from the wharf of St. Jacques de Cabannocé. Eulalie just held onto them and turned her eyes front, past the prow of the supply ship carrying them down the Mississippi. In New Orleans she found a ship going to Boston, and in Boston another ship going to Piziquid—or Windsor, rather. After generations of trade between Acadia and Boston, since back in the days of Charles La Tour, it had only taken ten years for *les Bostonais* to forget the name Piziquid had ever existed.

As soon as her feet touched the Windsor dock, Eulalie started walking east, with Gilbert's hand in her right hand, Félicité's in her left and a sack holding all their possessions slung over her shoulder. The sack held three blankets, a folded sheet of canvas, a firebag, some ships' biscuit and salt cod, a very small cooking pot and a very large knife.

There were a lot of new buildings clustered around the hem of Fort Edward, but Eulalie paid them no attention. As far as she was concerned, the English could go ahead and build all the coastal towns they wanted; the valley of Ardoise was still safely tucked away back in the woods.

Eulalie hadn't left the town very far behind before she had to pick up Gilbert and carry him. She didn't mind, since it meant she and Félicité could walk much faster when they didn't have to hold their pace to his stubby legs. But she couldn't carry him all the way, so she put him back on his feet from time to time when his legs grew rested and her arms tired.

The road had grown wider and more deeply rutted since the last time she'd travelled it. She was surprised at how many roadside boulders and old trees and riverviews she recognized—she would've thought the road too long for separate bits of it to carve themselves on her memory.

By the time they reached the red-veined boulder marking the foot of the hidden cart trail branching off to the north, Félicité was overtired and whining. Eulalie let the children rest for a moment in the cool shade of the forest, even though the last thing she wanted to do was pause when she could almost smell the valley of Ardoise. She said: "Along this path we'll cross seven streams where we can drink all the cold, sweet water we want. Do you remember the little song me and your Aunt Josette used to sing? Well, now you'll see where that song came from. Come along, now. *Three hills home, my dears, three hills home...*"

Eulalie was a bit apprehensive that the old path might be impassably grown over, but it wasn't, and it seemed wider than she remembered. That didn't make it any shorter, though. By the time it came down to "One hill home" she was carrying Gilbert in her arms and Félicité piggyback. The sun was going down when she stumbled through the last stream.

She knew she was exhausted to the point of delirium, so when she came out of the poplar grove on the north side of the hollow—Beau-père's old "pole garden"—she thought at first she was seeing things. She'd expected to see the fields overgrown with alders, and the old house and barn either falling in upon themselves or just lumps of charred timbers, if the soldiers who'd followed the tinker's list had put them to the torch. What she saw was fenced, cropped pastures, and an odd-shaped house and barn in different places than the old ones had been.

Eulalie set down Gilbert and Félicité, took hold of their hands and started slowly up the sloping meadow. The wildflowers had all been grazed away. A big dog started barking furiously—a mastiff lunging against its chain. A man came out of the house and shouted down at Eulalie in muddily-accented English: "What the hell do you want?"

"This is... This is my home."

"Not anymore it ain't. I didna come all the way from Ulster just to have some papist frenchwoman come minge-ing around what's mine clear and square and legal. You're just billy-be-damned lucky you came onto my property before I slipped Goliath off his chain for the night. Now clear off."

Félicité and Gilbert had started crying, although they couldn't have had any real understanding why. Eulalie's eyes drifted dazedly around the farm. The big, old elm tree had been cut down, and its stump smoothed for a chopping block. But there were still a few trampled chives growing between its roots.

The farmer said, slightly less roughly, "There's still some of your people living edgewise to Windsor. No doubt they'll take you in and tell you where you ought to go. Now be off with you."

Eulalie turned and stumbled down the hill, still holding her children by the hand. But when she got to the stream in the hollow, she didn't cross it. Instead, she turned right and followed along the streambank. There was just enough light left to find the foot of an old path further downstream running north through the woods. Once she got her feet on the path, she didn't need sunlight to find her way.

After not very long she had to pick up Gilbert and carry him again. Her arms felt like they were falling off. Félicité suddenly sat down on the path and wailed: "I can't walk anymore!"

"You'll have to. I'm too tired to carry you and Gilbert both, and his legs aren't as strong as yours."

"But I can't!"

Eulalie said fiercely: "Then sit here crying until a bear or a wolf hears you! *We're going on!*"

Eulalie started trudging along the path again. She hadn't gone far before she heard: "*Maman!*" and footsteps hurrying to catch up.

A few miles north-west of the valley of Ardoise there was a meandering, little river, where at this time of year there was usually at least one family of Mi'kmaqs camped waiting for the salmon run. Eulalie saw their fire before they heard her. She cast back in her mind for a language she hadn't spoken or heard for almost eight years, since back in Petitcodiac days, and called out: "*Kwa-hee Nichemaw.*"

The Mi'kmaqs made them welcome, gave them birchbark bowls to dip into the pot of fish soup, and cleared a space on the floor of one of their bark wigwams to curl up in. Eulalie slept well into the next day. When she woke up, her children were gone. She wasn't worried. As she expected, they were happily running with the pack of other children hunting frogs along the riverbank.

Running with the pack of children was a pack of dogs. Among the scruffy, little Mi'kmaq dogs were some a little bigger, with a reddish tinge to them—like Rouge of the Rouge and Noir Beau-père had left tied the morning after Cully slipped the British Army's leash.

Eulalie went into the woods to find a certain kind of mushroom, and scrubbed her hands in the river after picking them. She spent the rest of the day trying to make herself useful around the camp. When the sun got low in the west, she begged a piece of meat and set off back down the path, leaving Félicité and Gilbert with their very distant cousins. In the valley of Ardoise, she climbed the slope opposite the farm, found a spot where she could see between the trees and sat down to wait. She waited until the sun went down, waited until the last light in the farmhouse went out, waited until the moon came up. Then she stood up and started down the hill.

When Eulalie came out of the hollow the stream flowed through, she gave a little whistle and stood still. She heard the mastiff before she saw him, roaring and charging down the slope. She hoped he was the kind that would stop at the last minute and warn you to come no further. She had her long knife, but those teeth could still tear her arm to pieces while she was stabbing.

He leaped out of the shadows with the moonlight gleaming on his teeth, and came to a stiff-legged halt, still barking and roaring. Eulalie said: "*Bonsoir*, Goliath," lobbed the meat in front of him and backed away.

When she was back among the poplars, she stopped and listened. Goliath wasn't barking anymore, and through the rustle of the poplar leaves she thought she could hear chewing and snuffling. Maybe she wouldn't have to use her mushrooms after all. It would be a pity to have to poison a poor, dumb, dutiful dog who wouldn't know the *Grand Dérangement* from a hole in the ground.

Eulalie came back with another piece of meat the next night and again the night after, coming a little further onto the property each time. On the fourth night, she held the meat out to him—with the knife poised in her other hand in case he tried to take some of her fingers to flavour his piece of muskrat. He didn't.

The next night she brought a deer leg with a bit of haunch meat on it, and a moosehide shoulder pouch flapping against her hip. While Goliath was happily crunching at the bones, she went to the elm stump and started loosening the soil with her knife so she could scoop it out with her hands.

She'd intended to carry Beau-père's strongbox into the woods before shifting the money into the shoulder pouch. But once she'd lifted the tin box out of the earth, she said to hell with it and just set the box on the stump to pry it open with her knife. Inside it, along with the coins there was a small, canvas bag that felt like it was filled with lumpy grains of rice, but rice that weighted as much as lead. She remembered how every now and then Beau-pére would disappear into the woods for the day to go "hunting" alone, and come back empty-handed from the direction of the played-out, old gold mine on the other side of the valley. She put the sack and the coins in her pouch and left the empty box sitting on the stump beside the open hole.

She gave a few of the coins to the Mi'kmaqs, who were reluctant to take them until she said they were a gift, not payment. Then they had to give her two child-sized pairs of moccasins as a gift for her gift.

In the morning, Eulalie and the children started back along the road to Windsor. She had no idea what she was going to do once they got there, only that the Acadians who'd been back for a while should be able to tell her what possibilities were left for an Acadian in Acadia.

It was a hot and hazy day. By the time they got to Windsor, Eulalie found it hard not to head straight for the beach, strip naked and jump in. It wasn't hard to find where the Windsor Acadians lived: a ramshackle clutch of temporary-looking shelters on the edge of town.

Beside the first shack she came to stood a wide-shouldered man with his back to her, sharpening an axe on a grinding wheel. He looked over his shoulder. André Melanson.

He turned around slowly, as though if he moved too fast he would shatter the air. She saw herself in his eyes: a worn-out, beaten-down woman with another man's children clinging to her skirt. He said: "So, Eulalie, now we can be married? I have made many pairs of cart wheels."

EPILOGUE

On a dusty summer day two hundred years after Eulalie La Tour married André Melanson, a bus pulled into the sugarcane town of Broussard, Louisiana and Private Gilbert "Gib" Melanson limped out leaning on an aluminum cane. He wasn't wearing his uniform; word had it that green berets weren't popular on the streets of the U.S.A. these days. He knew he certainly wasn't the only Nova Scotia boy to volunteer for the American army fighting in Viet Nam, but he suspected he was the only one to get wounded on his first day of active service and invalided back to a stateside military hospital. From what he'd seen and heard in the short time he'd been over there, that made him one of the lucky ones.

He had no good reason to come to the town of Broussard, except that this was his first weekend pass, he had nowhere else to go and his mother's maiden name was Broussard—well, *Brossard*, but everybody knew Americans can't spell. And there was also the old family tale that one of his father's great-great-great grandmothers had been one of the partisans who hid out in the woods along the Petitcodiac with Joseph Brossard *dit* Beausoleil.

Gib wandered around the town feeling more alone and nameless than he ever had in his life. In his Hawaiian shirt and squint-saving shades and his buzz-cut grown out a bit over hospital time, he didn't even have the generic identity of a soldier.

The doctors had told him his leg was at the stage of use-it-or-lose it, so he made a circuit of Beausoleil Square then headed along Main Street. There were huge-spreading shade trees of the kind some southern boy had told him were called Live Oaks. Gib had asked him how Dead Oaks grew, but hadn't got an answer. And there were huge, spit-polished, multiporched, old houses that didn't compute with a phrase a guy in boot camp used to toss around: "Coonass Cajuns."

Gib stopped on the sidewalk for a moment, thinking he heard something. What breeze there was carried him a snatch of jump-beat music. He followed the music to a red brick church with bright white lapels. On the lawn beside the church, a plywood dance floor had been laid down, and a makeshift stage set up with a couple of ancient microphones and tube amps.

The crowd swirling around the dance floor and the picnic tables was dressed in neon tuxedos or pipestem jeans or flowerprint dresses, except one young woman in a long, white gown that looked to've been worn more than a few times before. On the stage, an accordion, electric bass and snare drum were pumping away behind a singer sawing at a fiddle held against his chest, broken bow-hairs flying like a horsetail. The song was in French, but a different brand of French than Gib had learned before he started kindergarten.

Gib leaned against a tree and hung around to watch and listen. He was aware that some of the wedding guests were casting unfriendly glances at this stranger watching them like they were monkeys in a zoo. He didn't move on, though, and he muttered in his mind: "If I can fight your damn war for you, I can listen to your damn music."

The jig-time song ended with a flourish, and a girl with pale blonde hair and dark blue eyes was waved up to the microphone. She began to sing a softer song that jolted Gib before she'd sung three notes. He hadn't thought anyone else in the world knew that song. His grandmother used to sing him to sleep with it, and told him she'd learned it from her great-grandmother:

"Three hills home, my dear,

"Three hills home..."

Gib began to sing along with her, softly at first and then louder to match her miked voice. He knew he didn't have a trained voice, but a hell of a strong one and relatively true. People in the wedding crowd turned to stare at him. He felt himself blushing, but kept on singing anyway. Where he grew up, Saturday nights were a kitchenful of relatives and neighbours with guitars, squeezeboxes, fiddles and clacking spoons, and you got used to bulling through the embarrassment when it came your turn.

By the time he'd sung the last "One hill home" he was surrounded by grinning strangers thrusting bowls of filet gumbo and jars of homemade liquor into his hands, and telling him: "Three hills be damned—you're home."

Author's Note

Unlike earlier historical novels I've written (there might still be a few copies kicking around out there somewhere), I couldn't base this story entirely around historically documented characters. I certainly wanted to, but the more research I did, the clearer it became that they weren't there to be found. The Acadians in exile didn't keep diaries, and when they finally found homes they didn't tell their children many stories about it. Even in old Acadian folksongs—and folksongs are usually one place you can absolutely rely on to find memories of horrible things that have happened to people—there is little or no mention of the *Grand Dérangement*. I guess they just didn't want to talk about it.

There are plenty of records of the Acadian Dispersal: exiles' petitions to the government of Massachusetts, mentions of Acadians making an escape north from South Carolina until their boat gave out near Delaware Bay, British officers' journals... But they all refer to Acadian individuals who are either nameless or whose names only appear once, so there is no connecting thread to build a story around. So the only choice I had, if I was to tell the story at all, was to take all those unconnected bits and pieces and stitch them together into Eulalie La Tour, André Melanson and Cully Robin. Oh, and as for Cully Robin, there are also plenty of records of eighteenth-century British soldiers going over the wall in Nova Scotia. Some of them were caught; some just disappeared.

The one central character who isn't a patchwork creation is Beausoleil. I certainly considered trying to tell the story of the *Grand Dérangement* through Beausoleil's eyes, but although enough is documented to draw a picture of his remarkable life, not enough is known to get inside his skin—at least not for my money. Besides, I'd already written a book about somebody who, though very different from Beausoleil in many ways, inhabited the same kind of territory—Gabriel Dumont.

There is no record that anyone resembling Captain Namon ever existed—but then, there wouldn't be, would there? But there is good reason to suspect that someone, or several someones, in 1750s Nova Scotia performed the behind-the-scenes function that I have Captain Namon performing. And that reason has partly to do with why individual Acadians didn't hand down their stories of the exile. It's illogical but perfectly human for someone who's been mugged to feel ashamed. People who've been herded onto cattle cars imagine the question in their grandchildren's eyes: "Why didn't you fight back?" Most

Acadians didn't fight back because they never got the chance. The progression of subtle steps leading up to September 5, 1755 and beyond was stunningly cunning—the old story of putting a frog in a pot of cold water and very slowly turning up the heat; it doesn't realize it's being boiled alive until it's too late. But no one ever accused Charles Lawrence of having a subtle mind.

Whoever actually put the plan together was operating under the impression that the expulsion of the Acadians had been ordered by the King and Parliament. Everyone in North America was under that impression, except Charles Lawrence and possibly William Shirley of Massachusetts (he didn't stay "of Massachusetts" much longer, recalled to England in disgrace). I don't know whether the planner or planners ever learned about the dispatch from the Lords of Trade.

Some recent research has dug up credible evidence that some high-rollers in London may have backed the Expulsion, but if so it was decidedly under the table. Because that dispatch from the Lords of Trade—the one that arrived in Halifax too late—commanded Lawrence not to proceed with what appeared to be his intentions "until we have laid the whole state of the case before His Majesty and received his instructions upon it." Any way you slice it, the "Orders from the King" read out on September 5, 1755, were a fraud and a forgery, and that was bound to be a bit depressing to anybody who found that out after executing the orders. It would be small consolation at the time that the Crown was still legally responsible for any actions taken by its accredited agents that weren't reversed or repudiated.

I may or may not have been unfair to a character in this story who *is* historically documented—the Abbé Le Loutre. But even the Bishop of Quebec in the early 1750s was trying to tell Le Loutre that inveigling his "beloved" Mi'kmaqs and Acadians into harassing the English was only going to end up hurting the Acadians and Mi'kmaqs.

And when Le Loutre got back to France he took up free lodgings in a place that his Order maintained for members who were in poverty or invalid. The Order tried to remove him, since he had plenty of money and was taking up space needed by people who didn't. Le Loutre launched a lawsuit, saying whether he could afford to live anywhere else was irrevelant, as a member of the Order he had a right to free board and room. Seems to me he was one hell of a nice fella.

It may have been a literary conceit on my part to have Acadian women known by their maternal lineage, as in Eulalie à Marie à Pelagie. The Acadian style recorded in the nineteenth century would have made her Eulalie à Jacques à Charles, or something along those lines. But styles have been known to change in a hundred years. Anyway, I kind of liked the idea. I'm sure that eighteenth-century Acadian husbands were confident enough that they didn't have to be constantly reassured that their wives' daughters were theirs, too.

There is one historical fact, or probable fact, that I consciously fudged. Some contemporary reports have it that the homes at Piziquid weren't immediately put to the torch like the farms at Grand Pré. I thought no one would mind if I combined the experiences of two groups of Acadians thirty miles apart, and there was a reason I had to put André Melanson's home in Piziquid rather than in Grand Pré.

You see, I wouldn't 've had the confidence to write about a historical event where I had to make up the central characters, except that there's one central element of the story I can be sure is real: the little farm in the valley of Ardoise. I live here. It's said to have once been an Acadian farm. The local land records don't go back that far, but the much-mispronounced, archaic French name of Ardoise sure didn't come from some British Loyalist or New England Planter.

Legend has it that there was an ancient, Acadian goldmine somewhere on the south slope of the valley. There is rumoured to be an Acadian family graveyard somewhere on our property, so we have to be careful where we till. The previous owners warned that sometimes we may hear children laughing when there are no children to be seen, and see the empty swings arcing back and forth when there is no wind.

I sincerely hope they approve of the way I've told their story.

❈ ❈ ❈